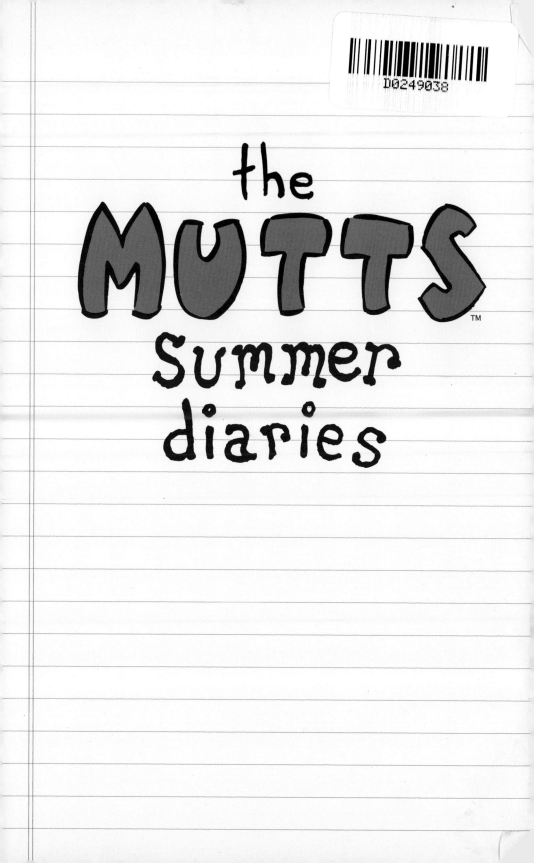

the MUTTS
summer diaries

Other Books by Patrick McDonnell

Mutts
Cats and Dogs: Mutts II
More Shtuff: Mutts III
Yesh!: Mutts IV
Our Mutts: Five
A Little Look-See: Mutts VI
What Now: Mutts VII
I Want to Be the Kitty: Mutts VIII
Dog-Eared: Mutts IX
Who Let the Cat Out: Mutts X
Everyday Mutts
Animal Friendly
Call of the Wild
Stop and Smell the Roses
Earl & Mooch
Our Little Kat King
Bonk!
Cat Crazy
Living the Dream
The Mutts Diaries
Playtime
The Mutts Winter Diaries
Year of Yesh
The Mutts Autumn Diaries
#LoveMUTTS
The Mutts Spring Diaries
You Have Those Wild Eyes Again, Mooch

Mutts Sundays
Sunday Mornings
Sunday Afternoons
Sunday Evenings
Best of Mutts

Shelter Stories
A Shtinky Little Christmas

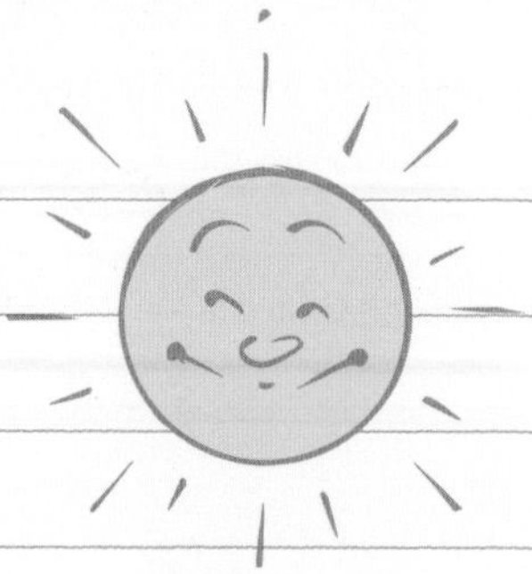

the MUTTS™ Summer diaries

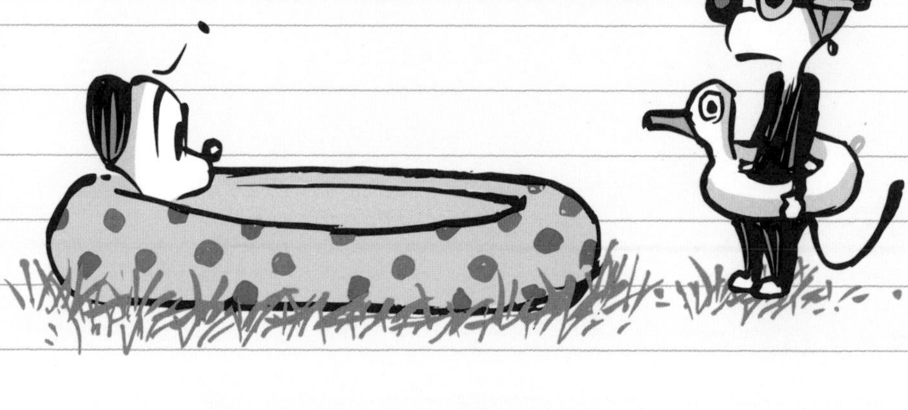

• PATRICK McDONNELL •

Andrews McMeel
PUBLISHING®

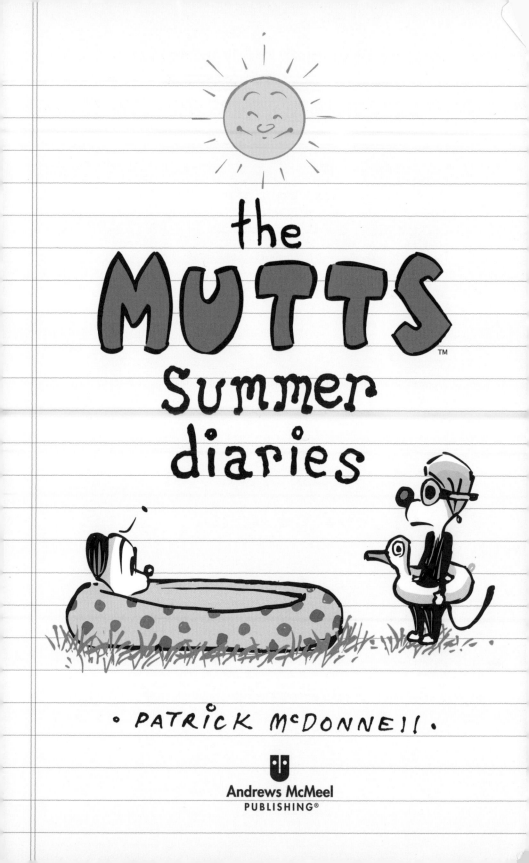

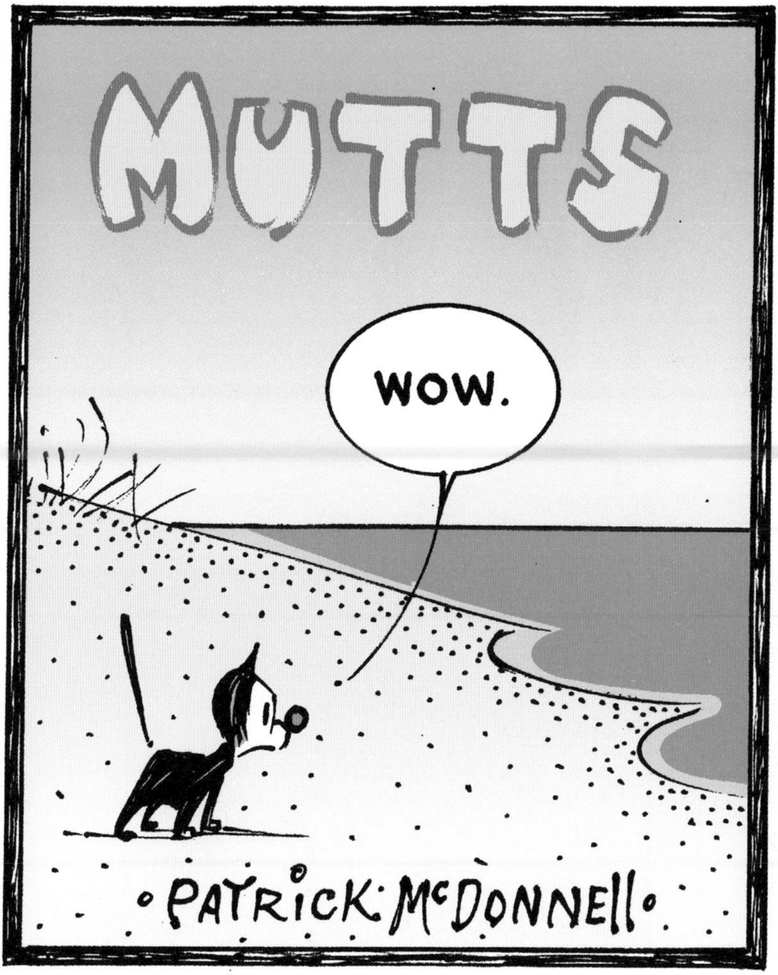
MUTTS
WOW.
PATRICK McDONNELL

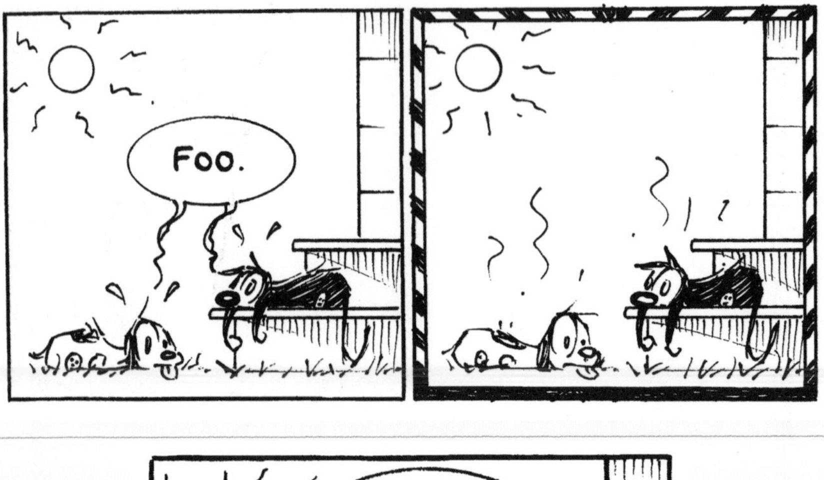
FOO.
IS IT AUTUMN YET?

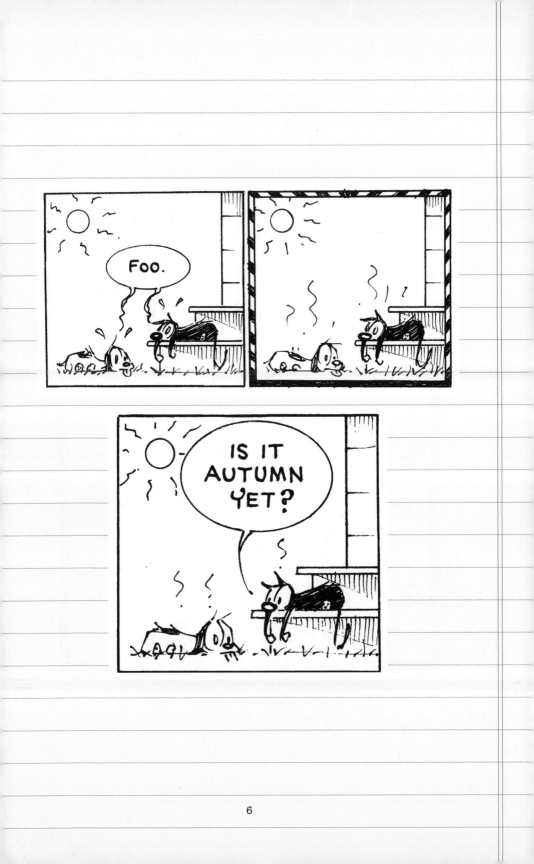

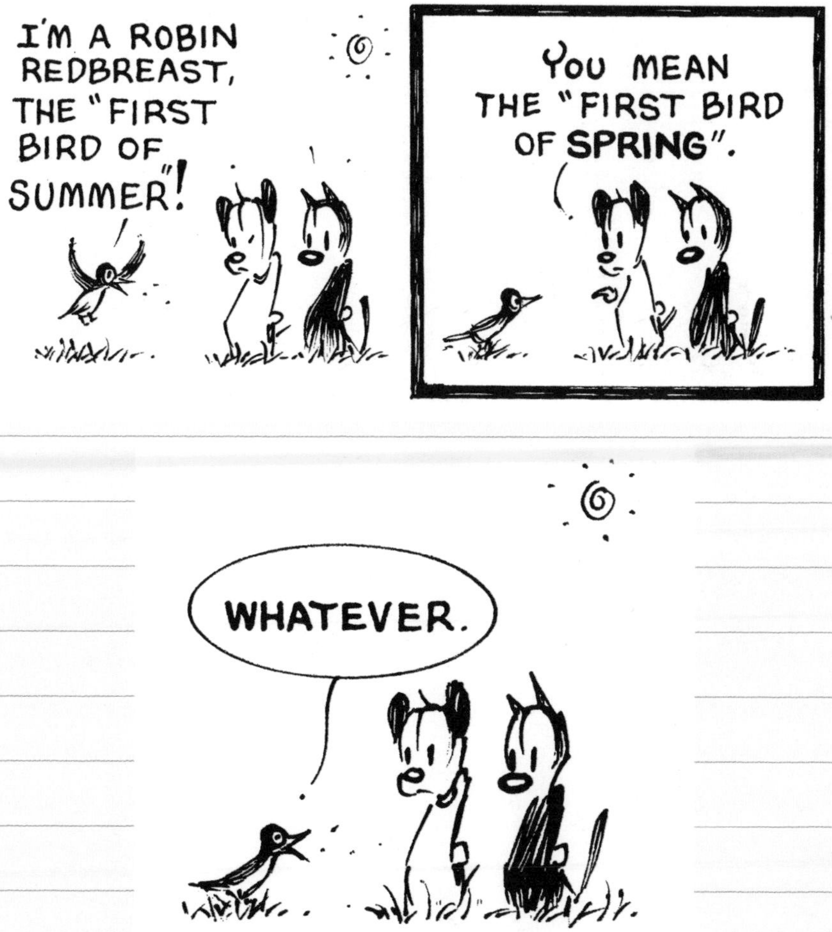
I'M A ROBIN REDBREAST, THE "FIRST BIRD OF SUMMER"!
YOU MEAN THE "FIRST BIRD OF SPRING".
WHATEVER.

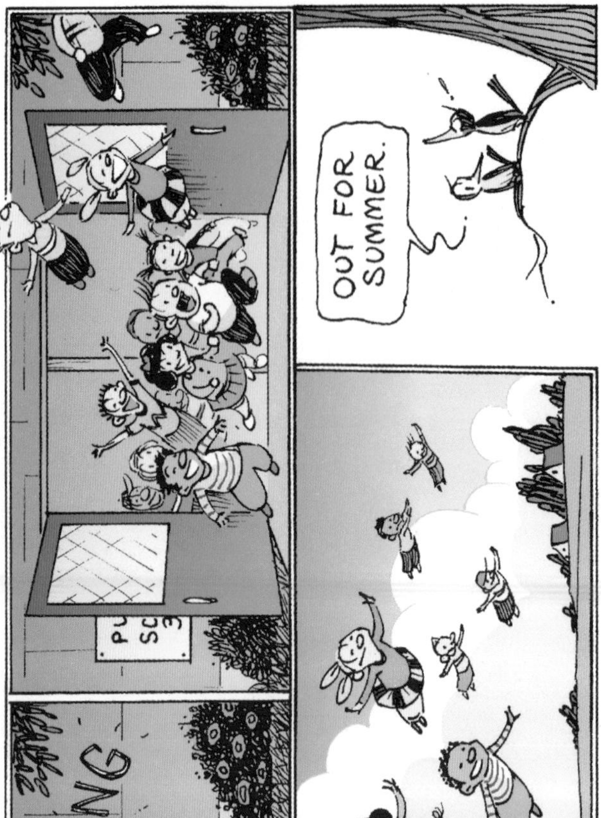
PUBLIC SCHOOL 37
RRRING
OUT FOR SUMMER.
!

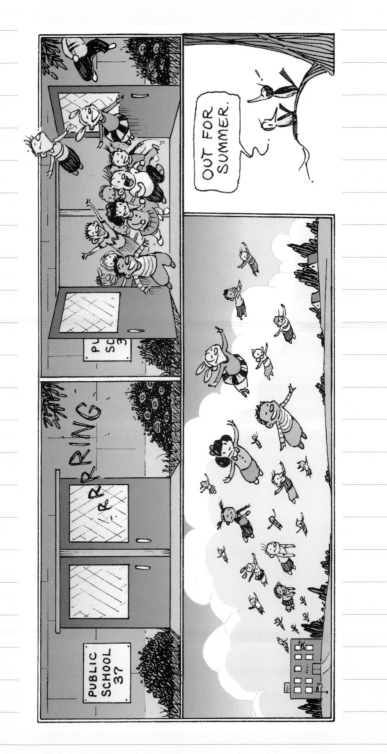

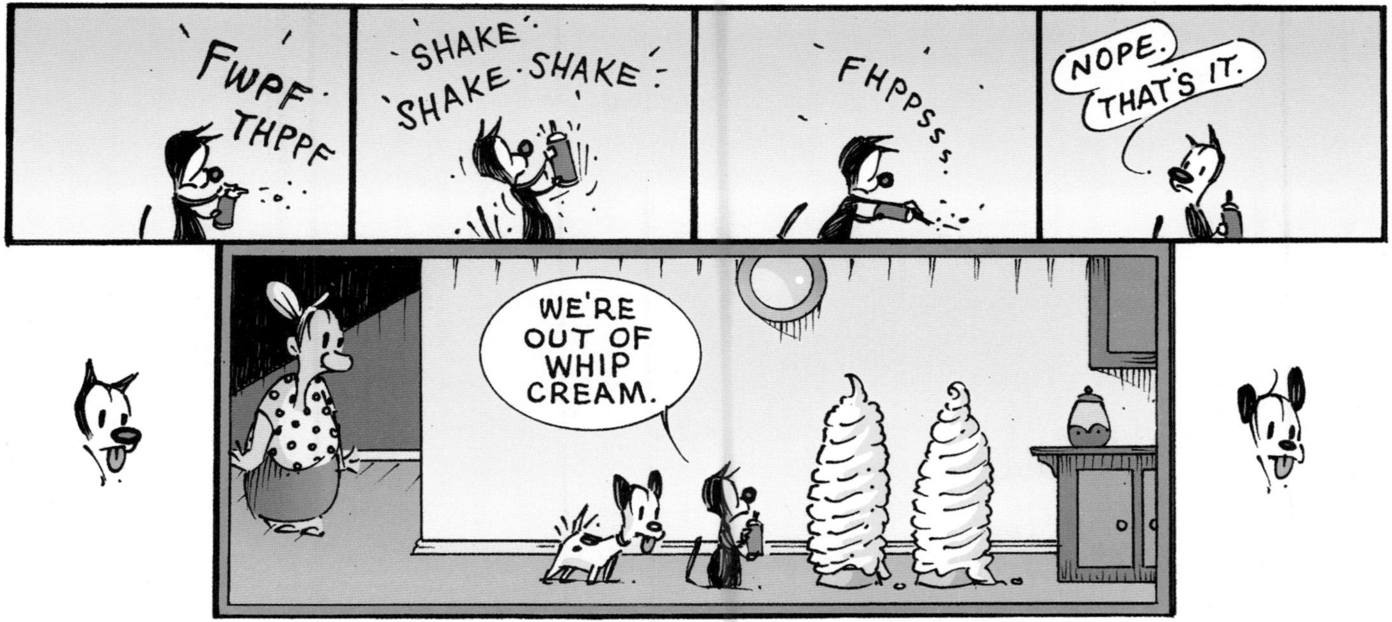
FWPF THPPF
SHAKE SHAKE · SHAKE
FHPPSSS
NOPE.
THAT'S IT.
WE'RE OUT OF WHIP CREAM.

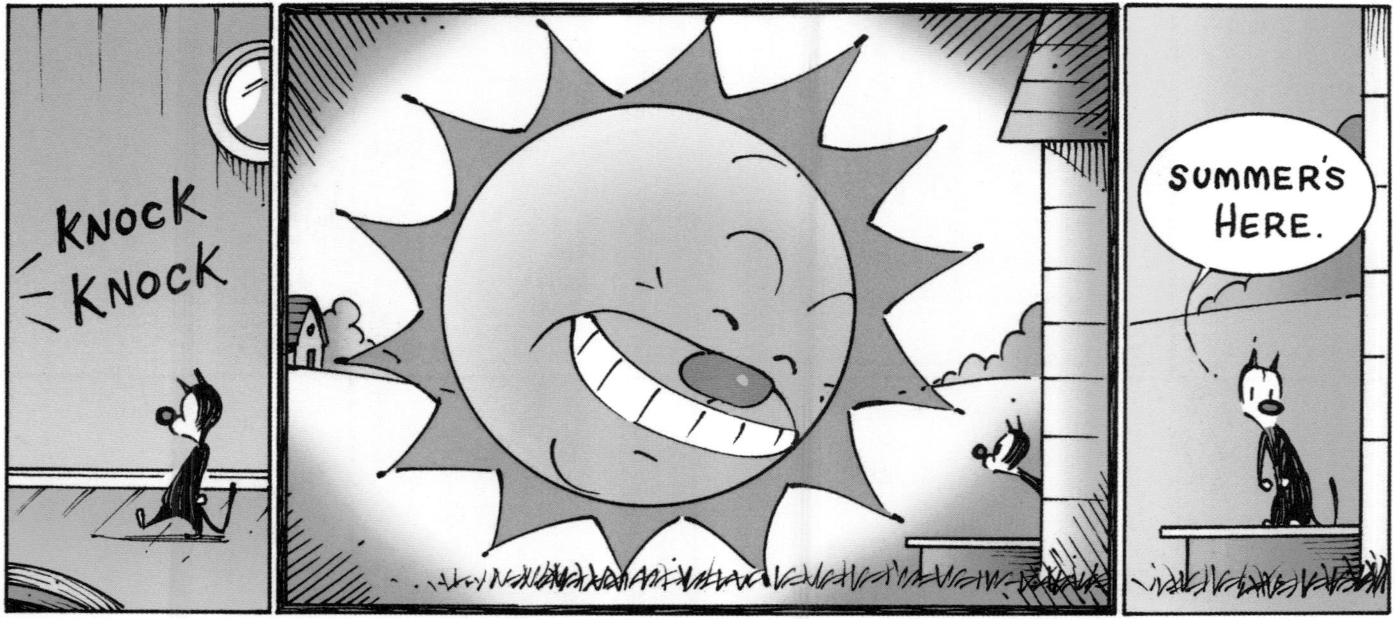
KNOCK KNOCK
SUMMER'S HERE.

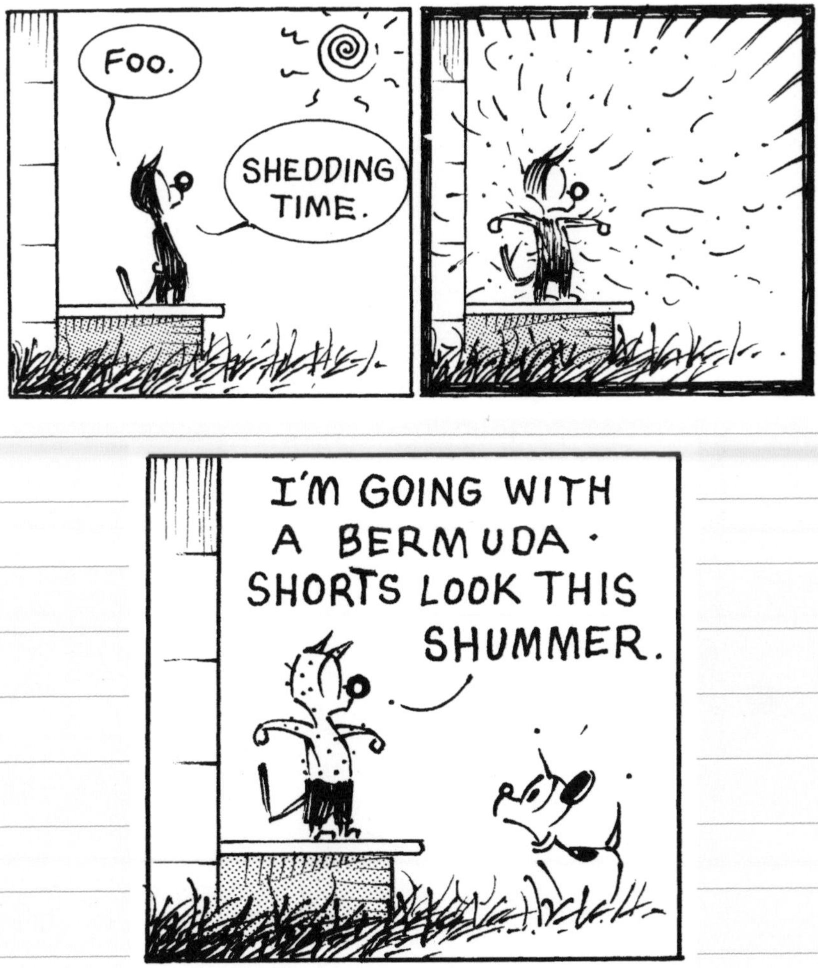
FOO.
SHEDDING TIME.
I'M GOING WITH A BERMUDA-SHORTS LOOK THIS SHUMMER.

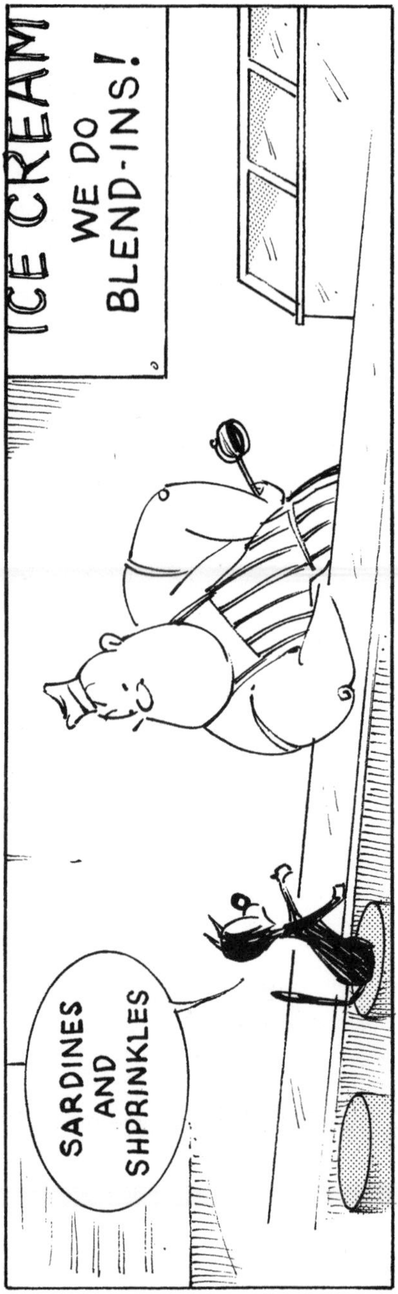
SARDINES AND SHPRINKLES
ICE CREAM
WE DO BLEND-INS!

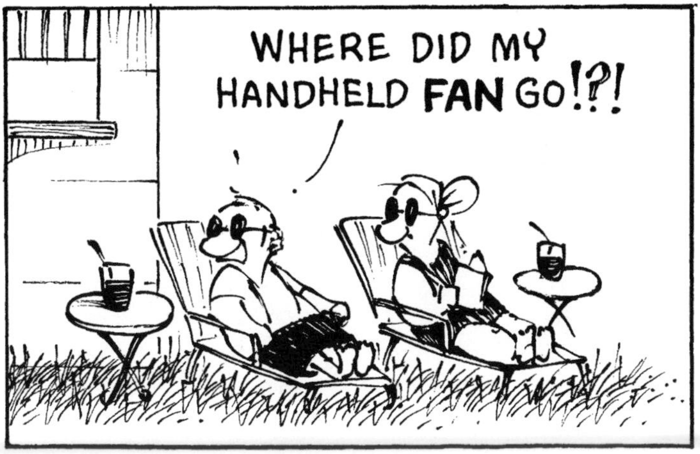
WHERE DID MY HANDHELD FAN GO!?!

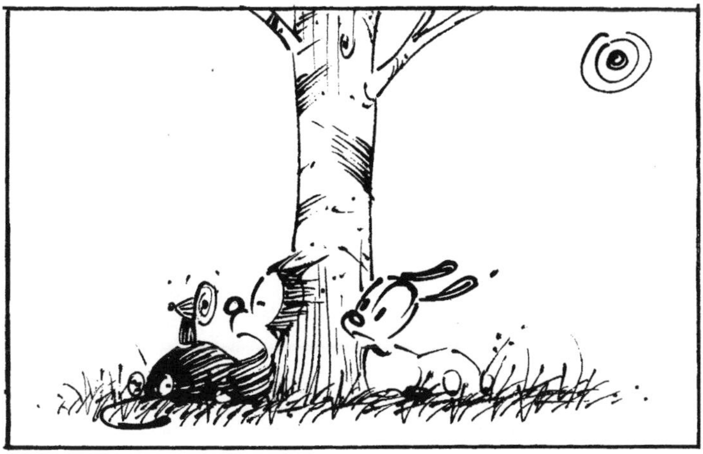

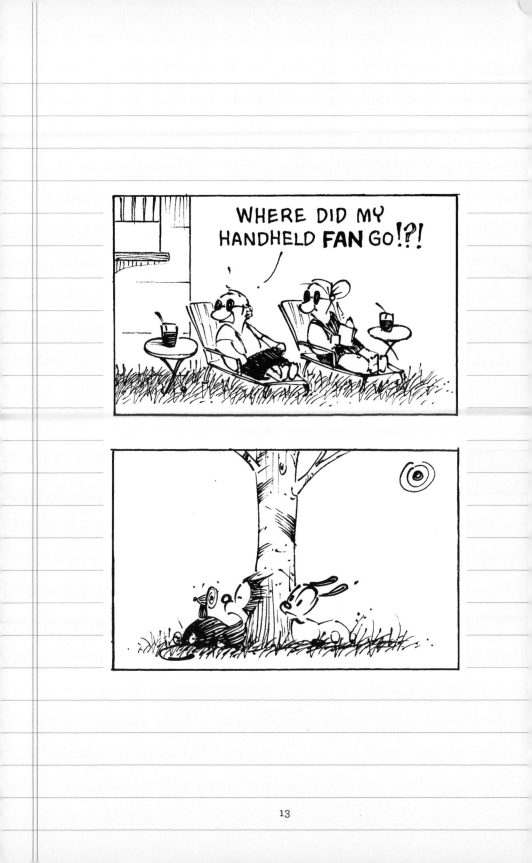

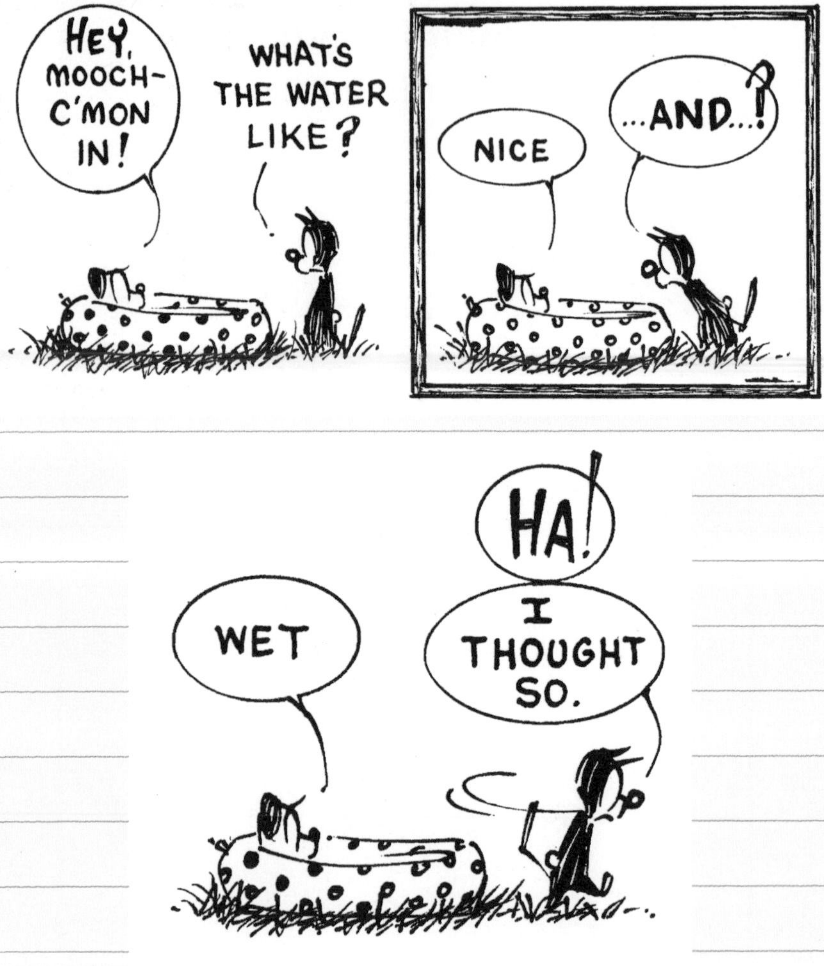
HEY, MOOCH- C'MON IN!
WHAT'S THE WATER LIKE?
NICE
...AND...?!
WET
HA!
I THOUGHT SO.

C'MON, MOOCH-JUST STICK YOUR FOOT IN.
THAT'S NOT YOUR FOOT!-THAT'S YOUR LITTLE PINK SOCK!?!

IT'S A SHTART.

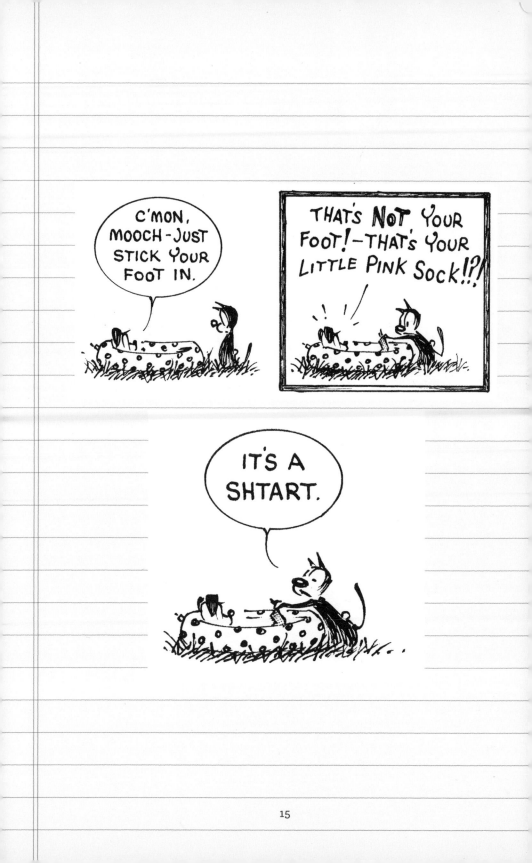

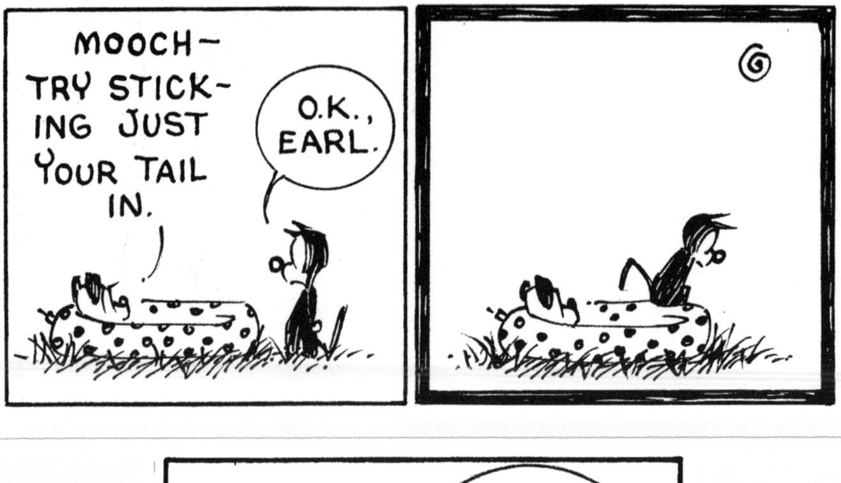
MOOCH—
TRY STICK-
ING JUST
YOUR TAIL
IN.
O.K.,
EARL.
WELL?!
HE'S
A
NO-GO.

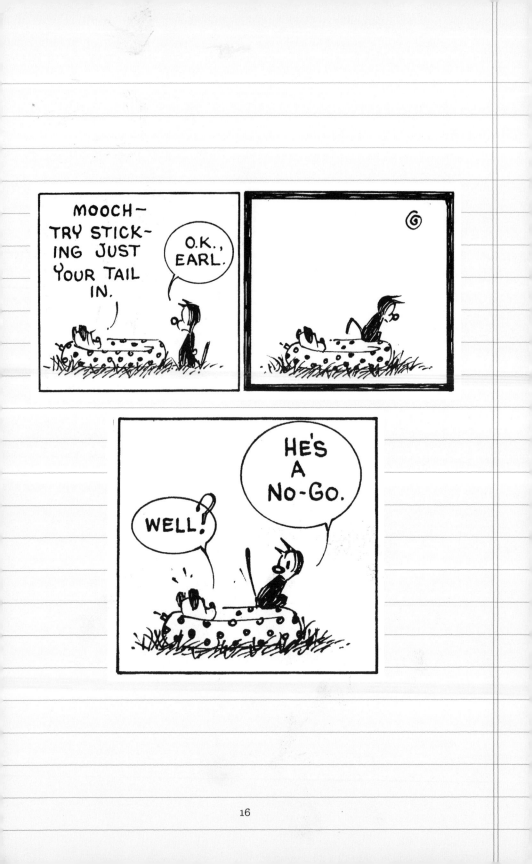

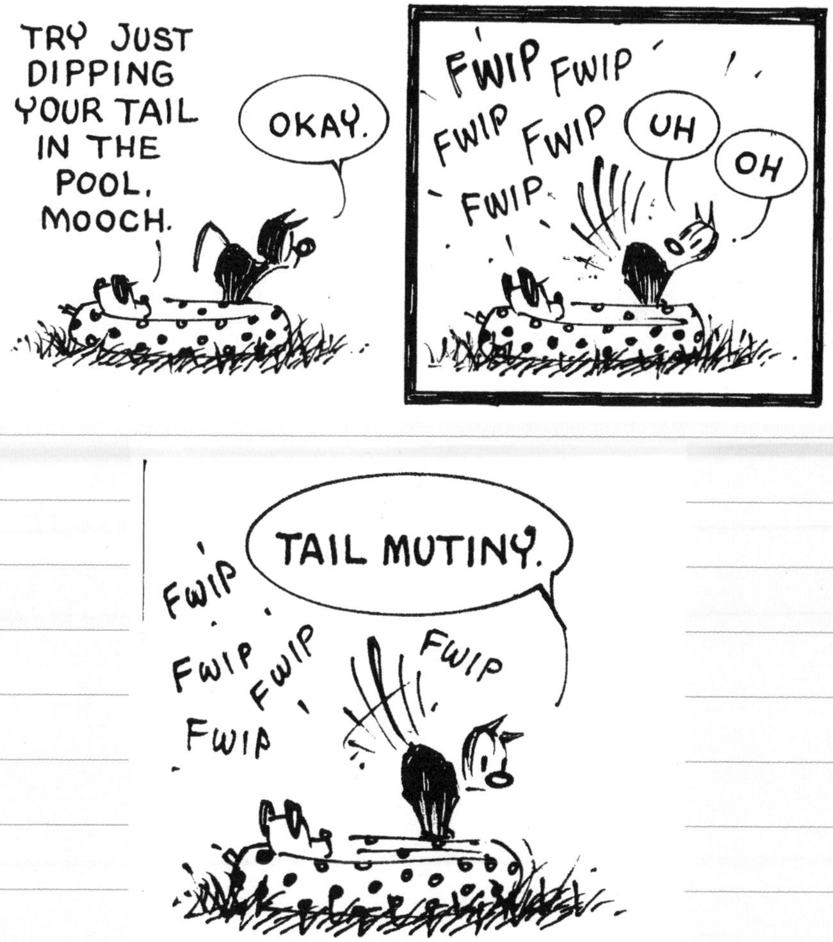
TRY JUST DIPPING YOUR TAIL IN THE POOL, MOOCH.
OKAY.
FWIP FWIP
FWIP FWIP
FWIP
UH
OH
TAIL MUTINY.
FWIP
FWIP FWIP
FWIP
FWIP

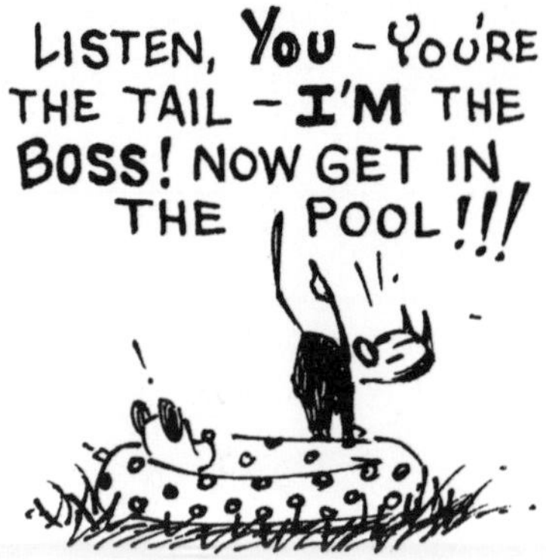
LISTEN, YOU - YOU'RE THE TAIL - I'M THE BOSS! NOW GET IN THE POOL!!!

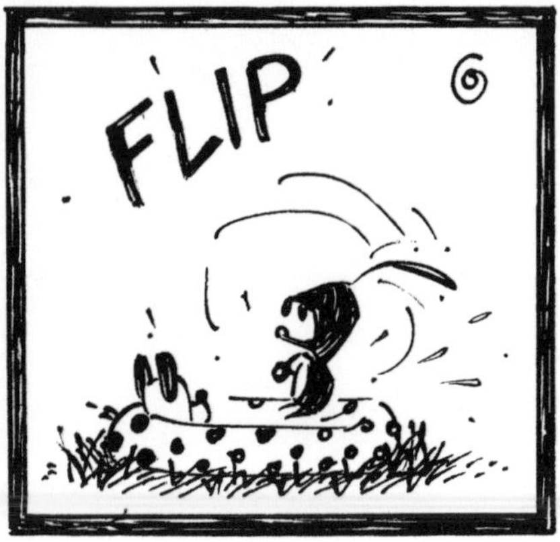
FLIP

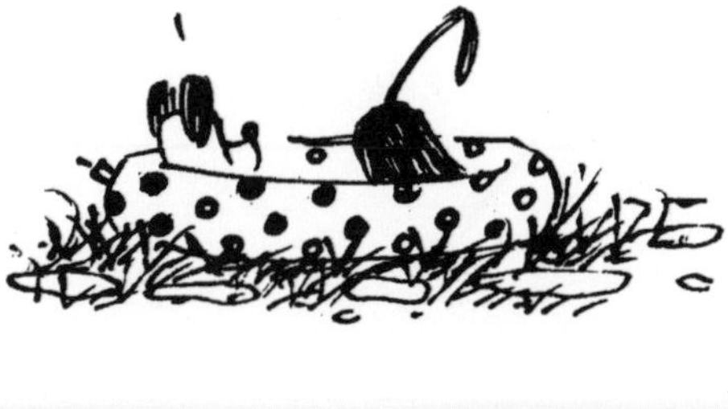

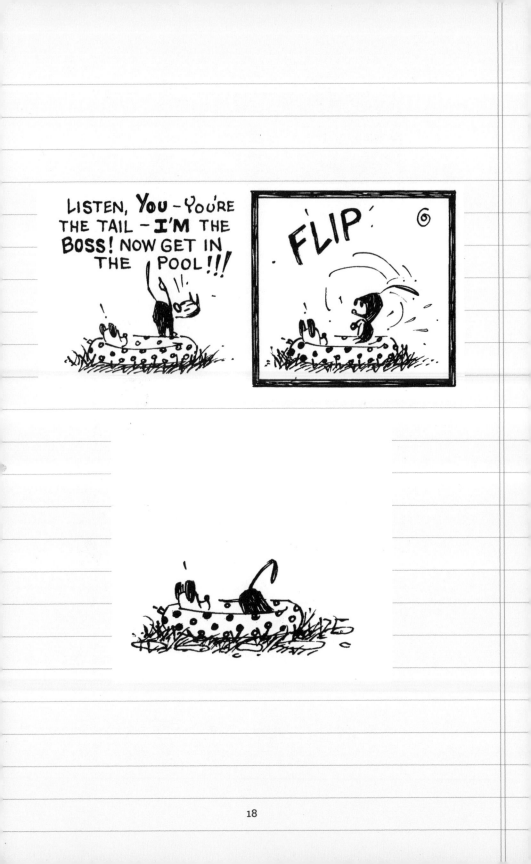

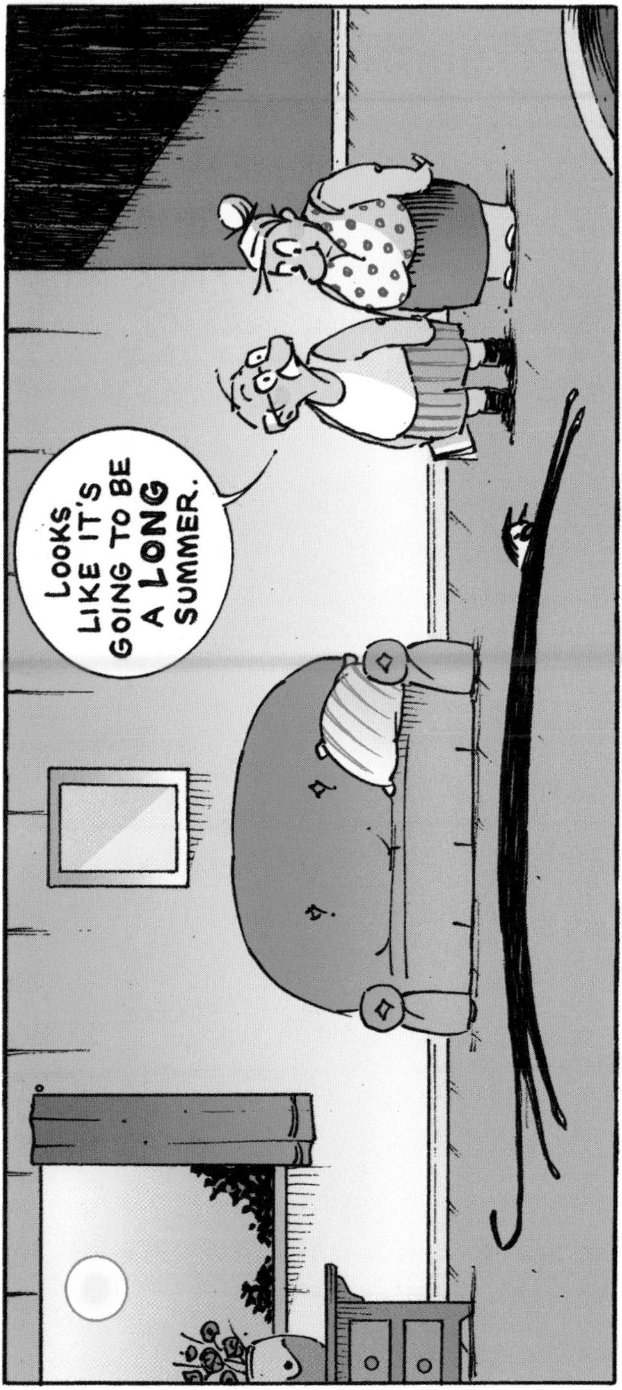
LOOKS LIKE IT'S GOING TO BE A LONG SUMMER.

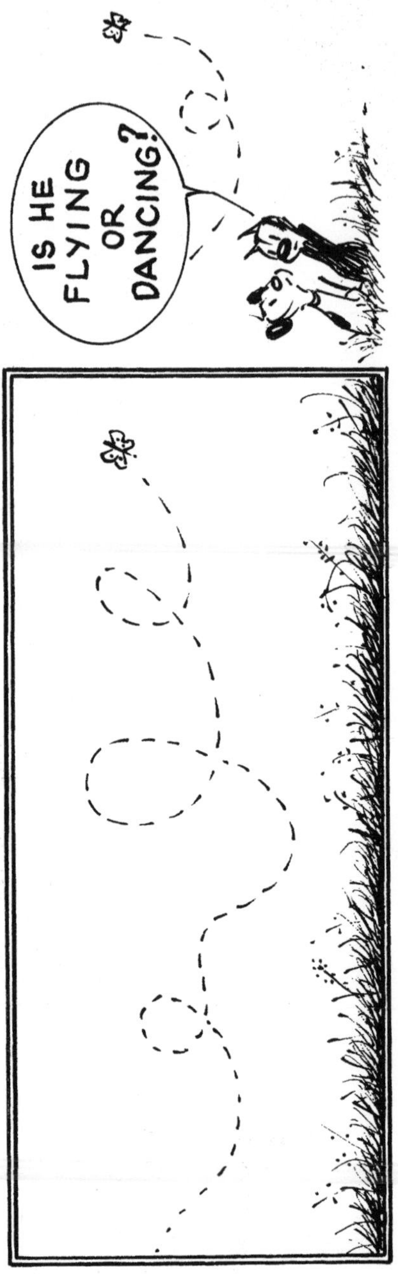
IS HE FLYING OR DANCING?

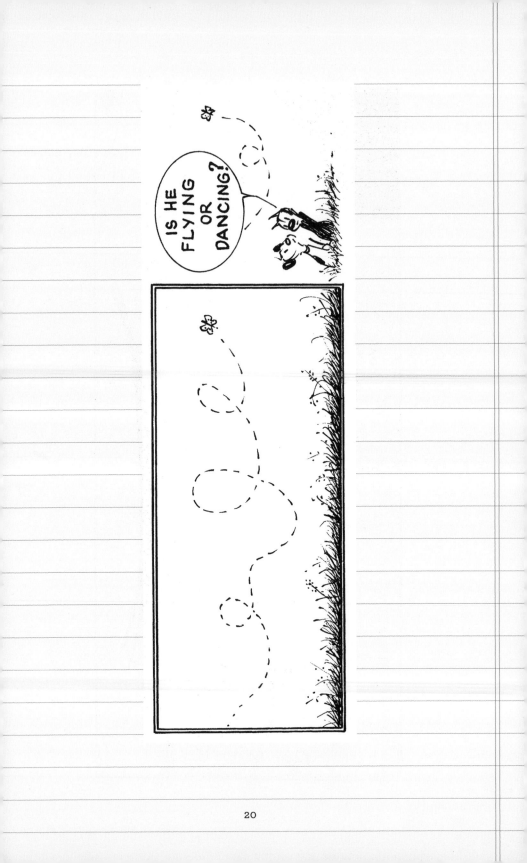

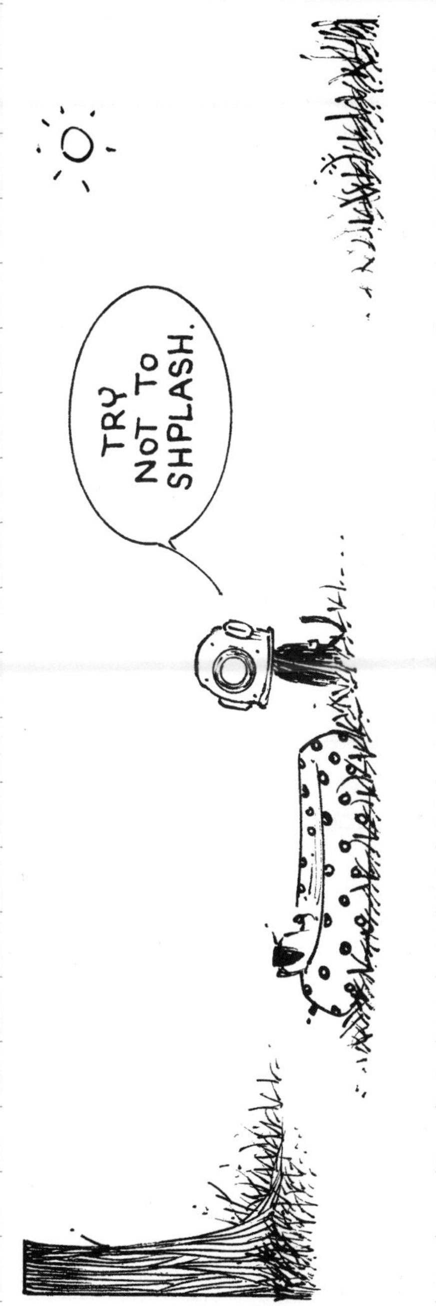
TRY NOT TO SHPLASH.

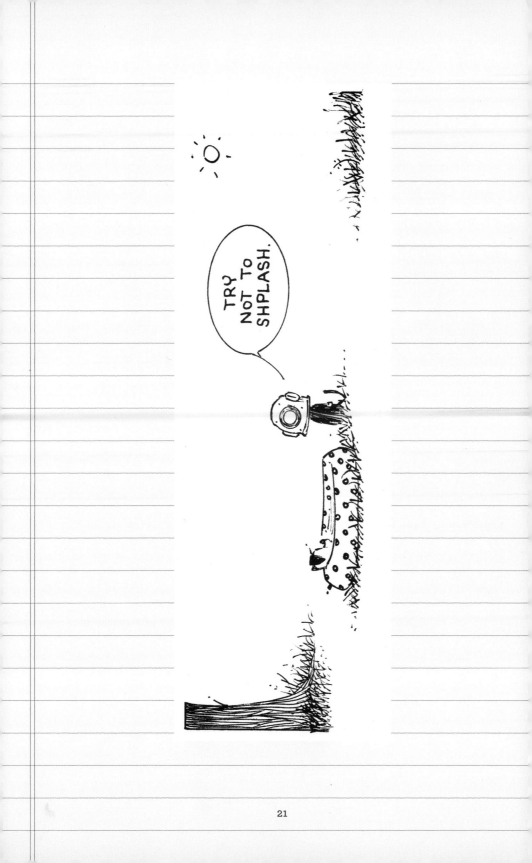

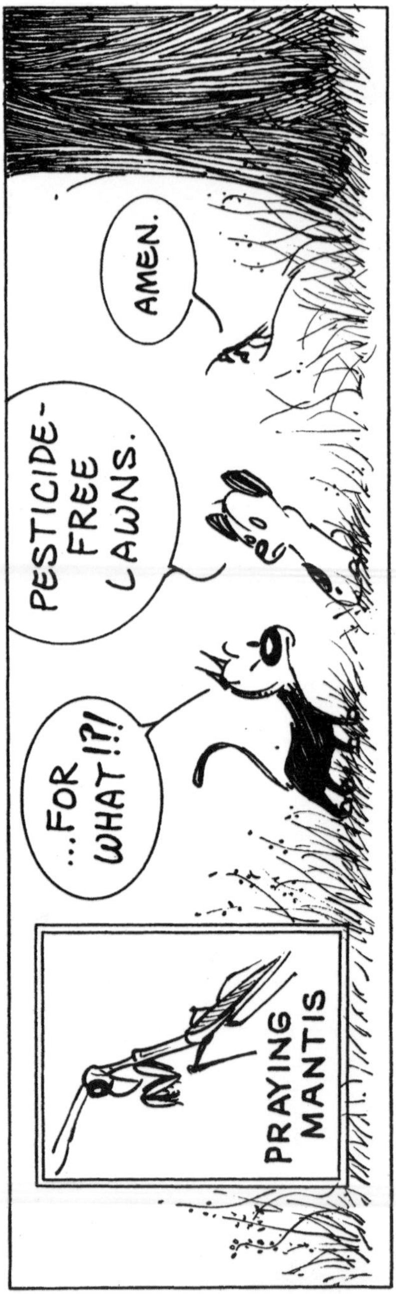
PRAYING MANTIS
...FOR WHAT!?!
PESTICIDE-FREE LAWNS.
AMEN.

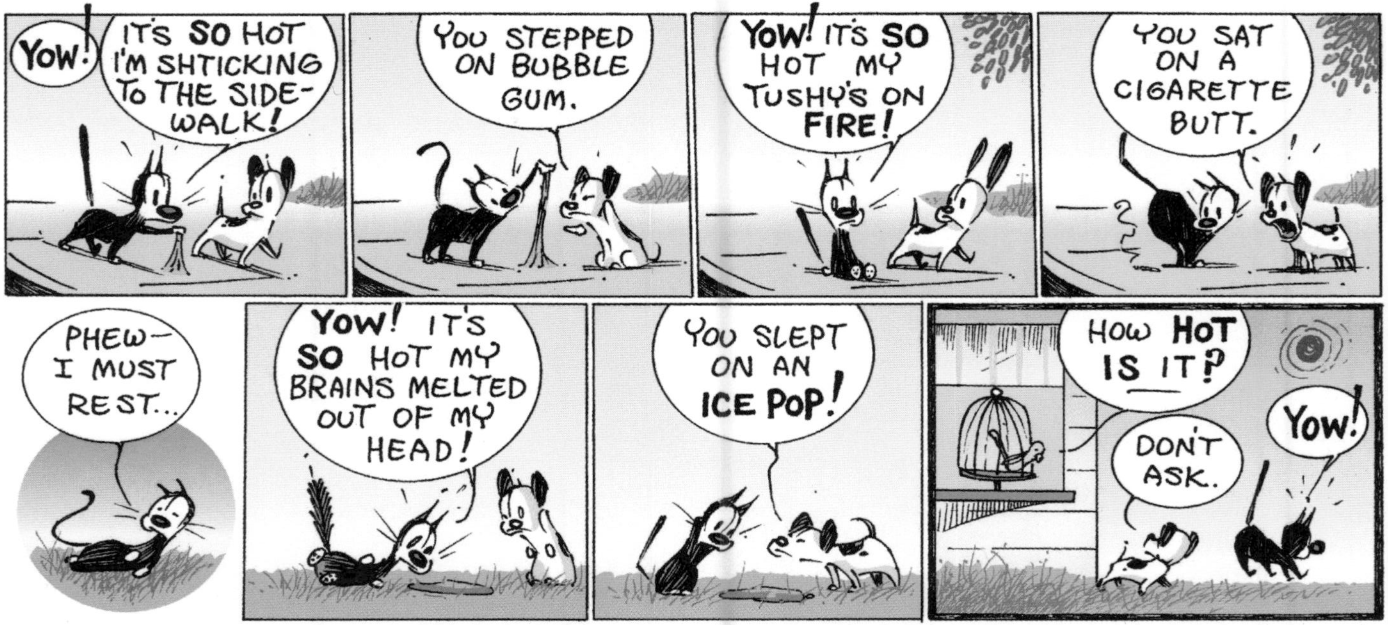

YOW!
IT'S SO HOT I'M SHTICKING TO THE SIDE-WALK!
YOU STEPPED ON BUBBLE GUM.
YOW! IT'S SO HOT MY TUSHY'S ON FIRE!
YOU SAT ON A CIGARETTE BUTT.
PHEW— I MUST REST...
YOW! IT'S SO HOT MY BRAINS MELTED OUT OF MY HEAD!
YOU SLEPT ON AN ICE POP!
HOW HOT IS IT?
DON'T ASK.
YOW!

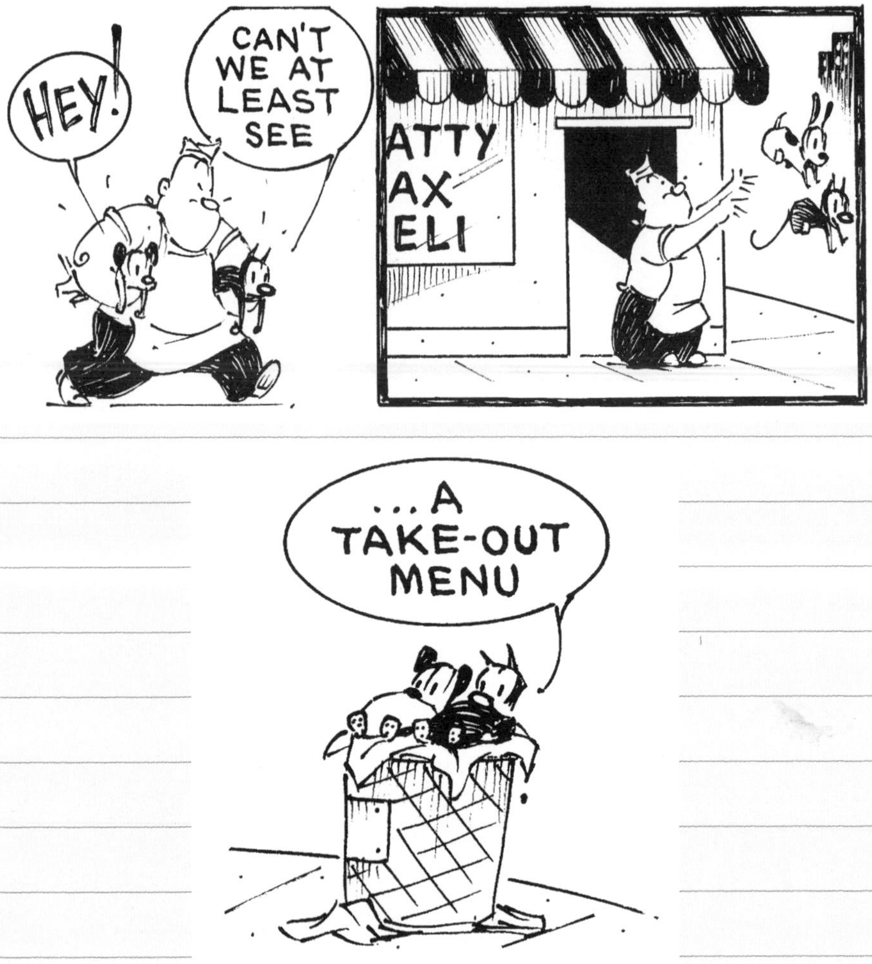
HEY!
CAN'T WE AT LEAST SEE
ATTY AX ELI
...A TAKE-OUT MENU

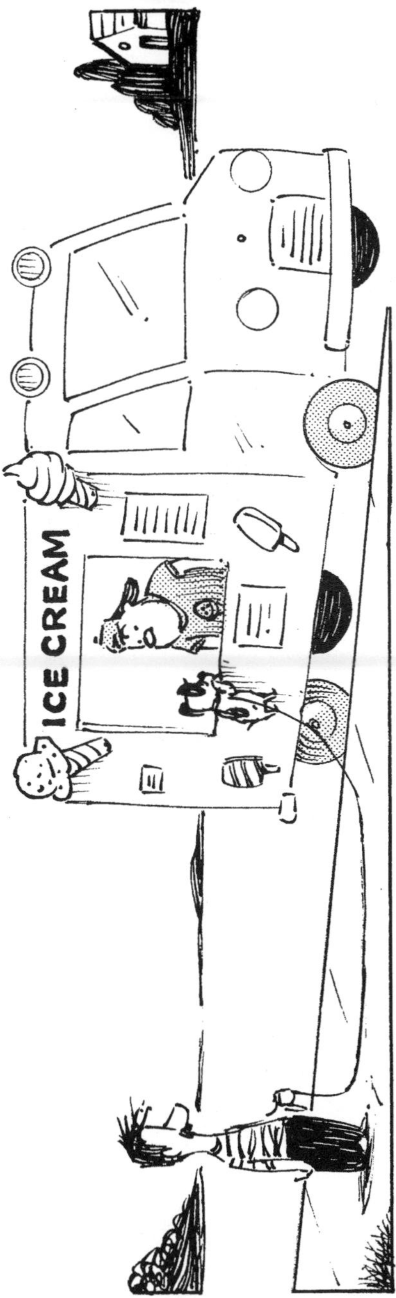
ICE CREAM

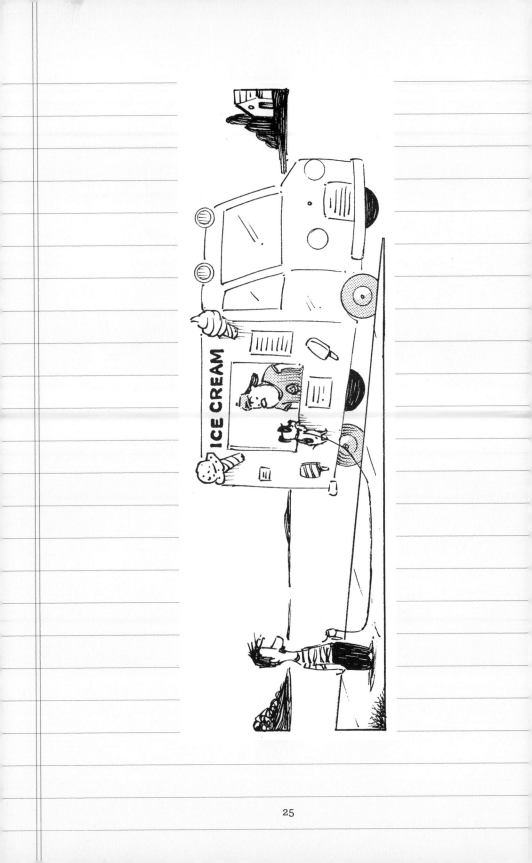

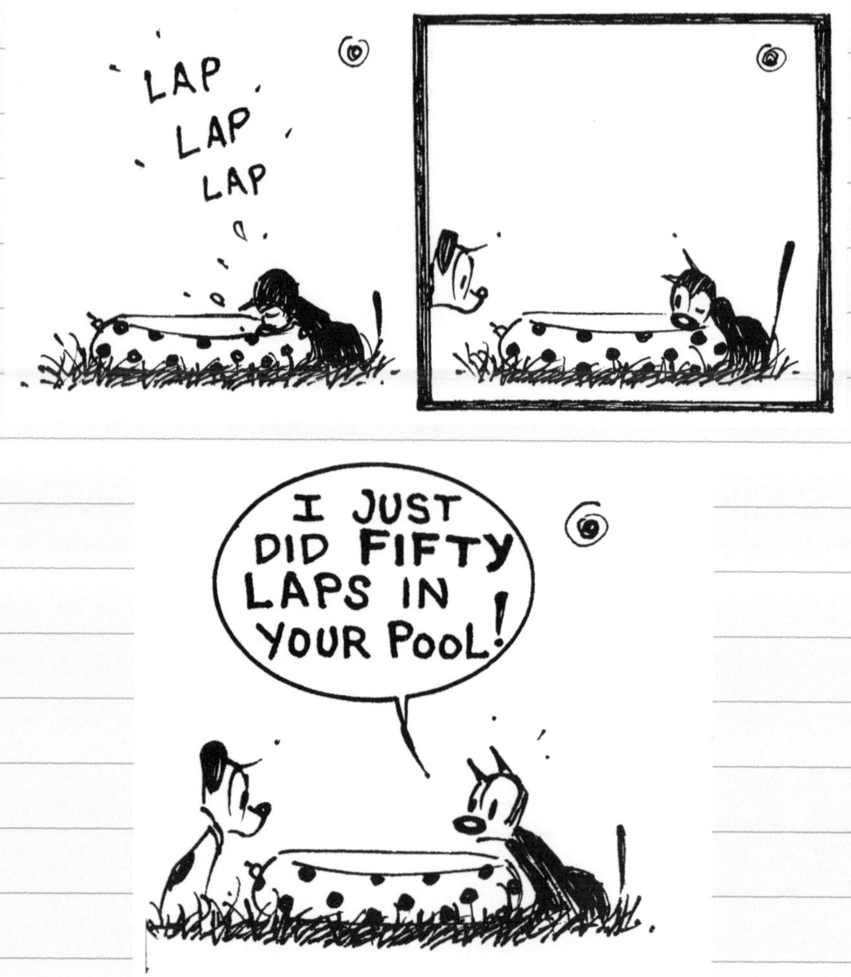
LAP
LAP
LAP
I JUST DID FIFTY LAPS IN YOUR POOL!

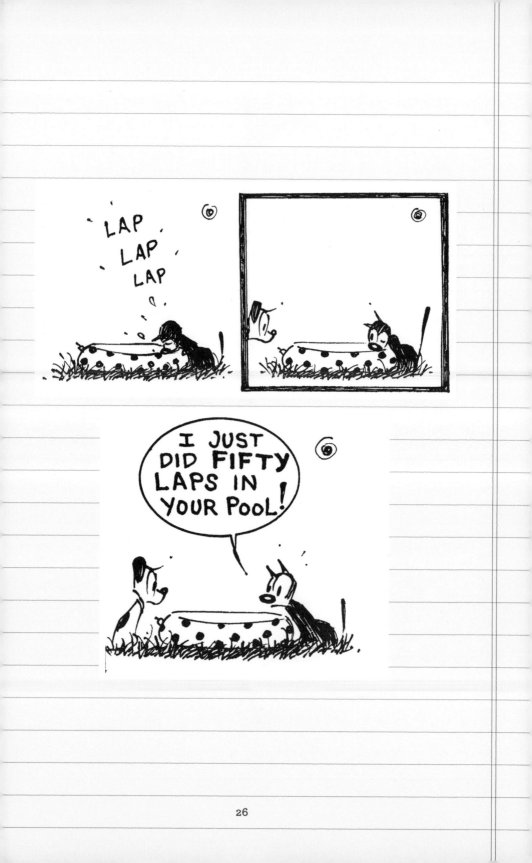

LAP
LICK
LAP
HEY!
THIS IS A
WADING
POOL!!!
OH
I
THOUGHT
IT WAS
"DOG
SOUP".

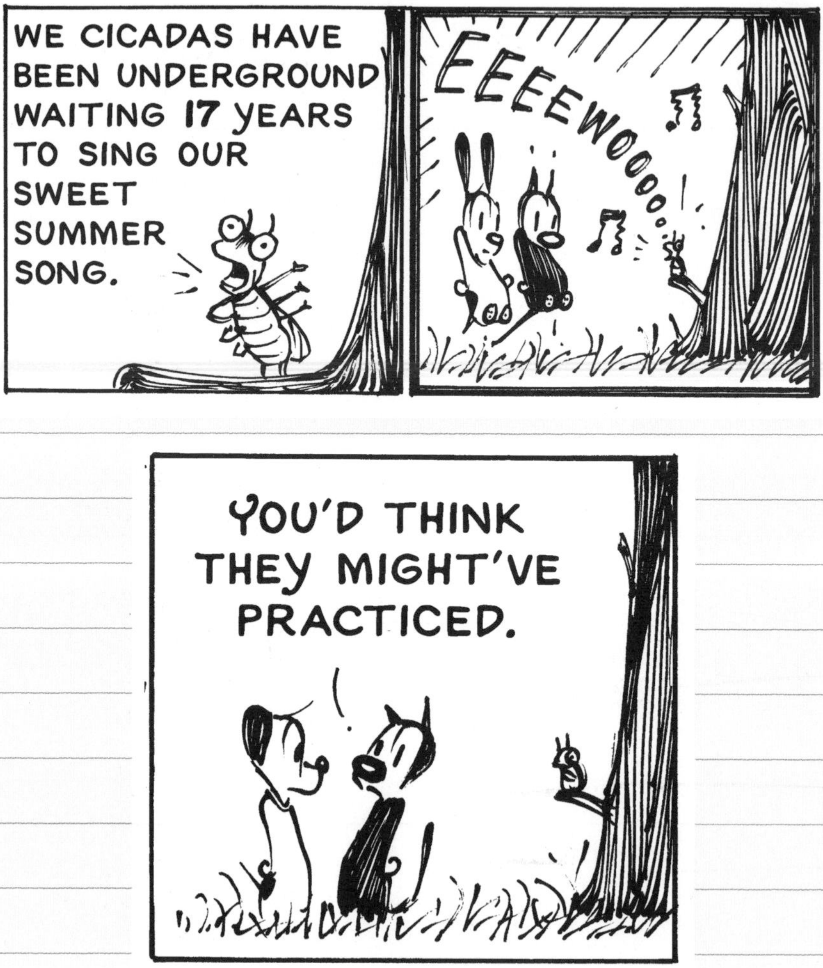
WE CICADAS HAVE BEEN UNDERGROUND WAITING 17 YEARS TO SING OUR SWEET SUMMER SONG.
EEEEEWOOOOO..
YOU'D THINK THEY MIGHT'VE PRACTICED.

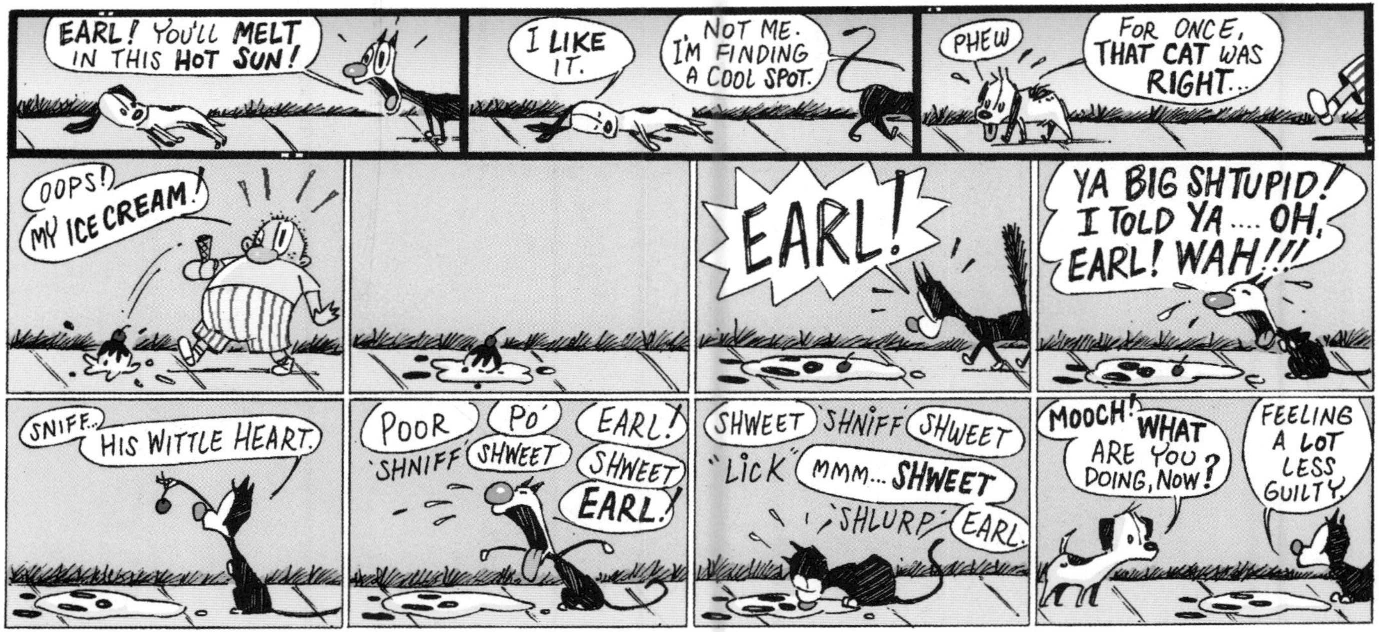

EARL! YOU'LL MELT IN THIS HOT SUN!
I LIKE IT.
NOT ME. I'M FINDING A COOL SPOT.
PHEW
FOR ONCE, THAT CAT WAS RIGHT...
OOPS! MY ICE CREAM!
EARL!
YA BIG SHTUPID! I TOLD YA.... OH, EARL! WAH!!!
SNIFF..
HIS WITTLE HEART.
POOR
PO'
EARL!
SHNIFF
SHWEET
SHWEET
EARL.
SHWEET
SHNIFF
SHWEET
LICK
MMM... SHWEET
SHLURP
EARL.
MOOCH! WHAT ARE YOU DOING, NOW?
FEELING A LOT LESS GUILTY.

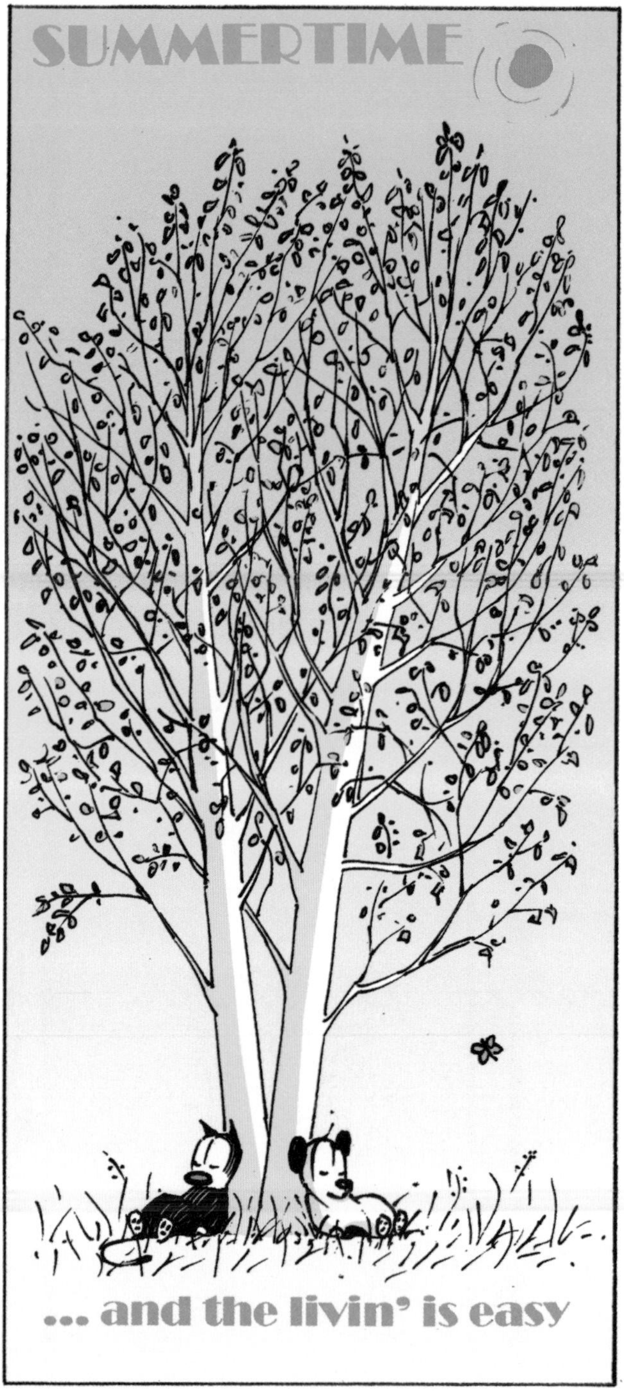
SUMMERTIME
... and the livin' is easy

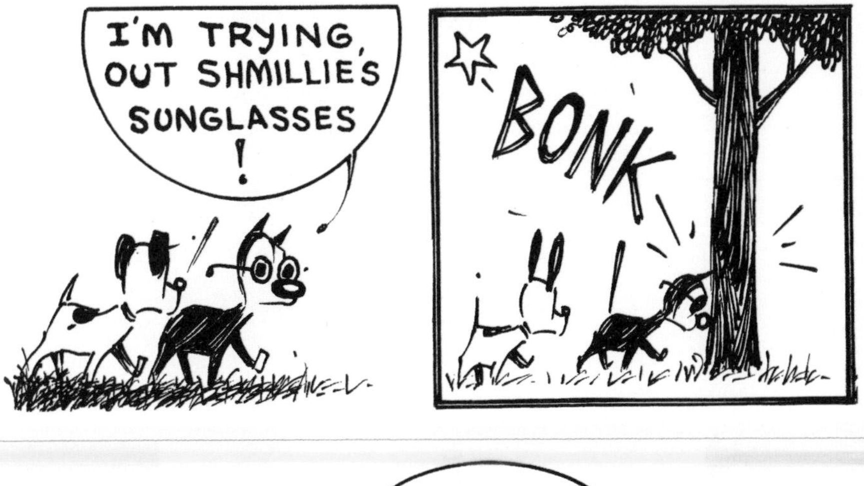
I'M TRYING OUT SHMILLIE'S SUNGLASSES!
BONK
WHAT WAS THAT!?!!

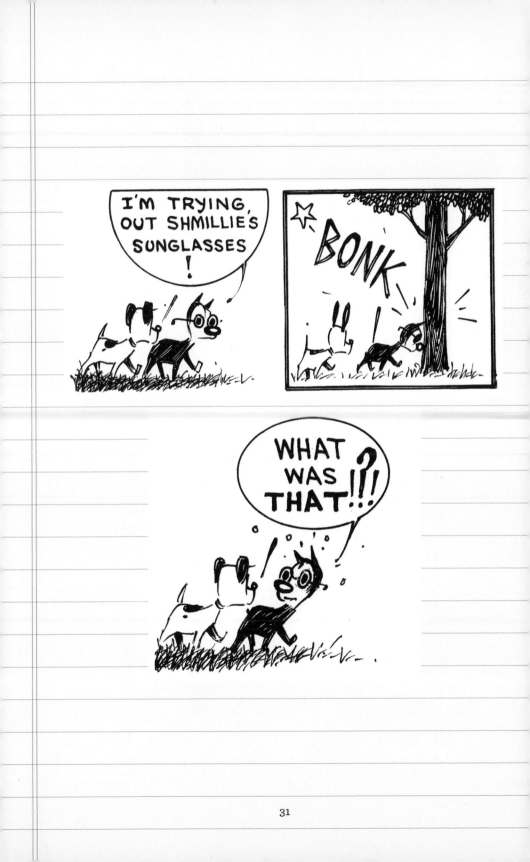

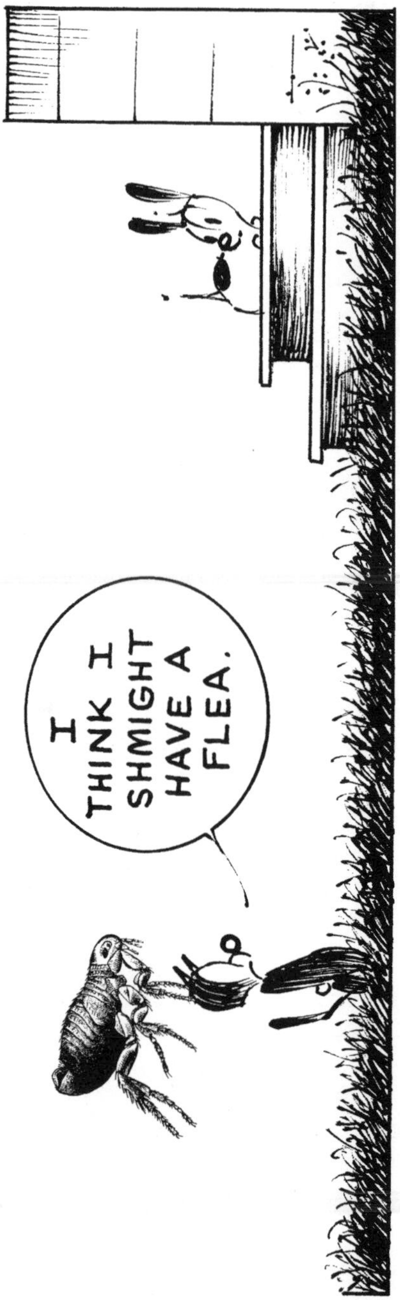
I THINK I SHMIGHT HAVE A FLEA.

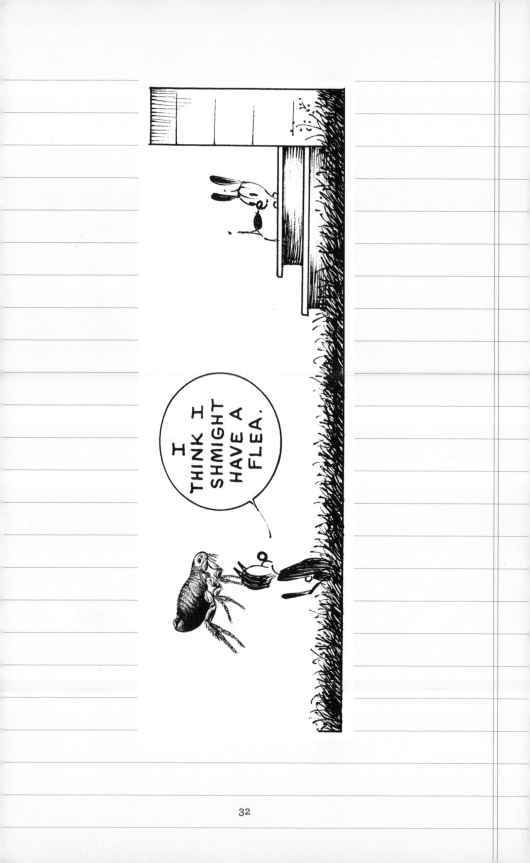

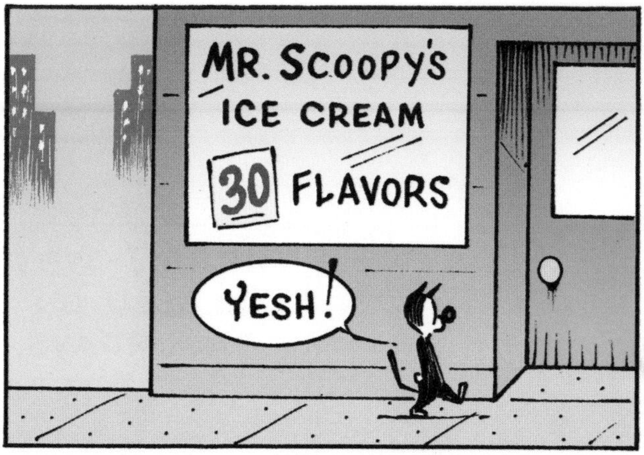
MR. SCOOPY'S
ICE CREAM
30 FLAVORS
YESH!

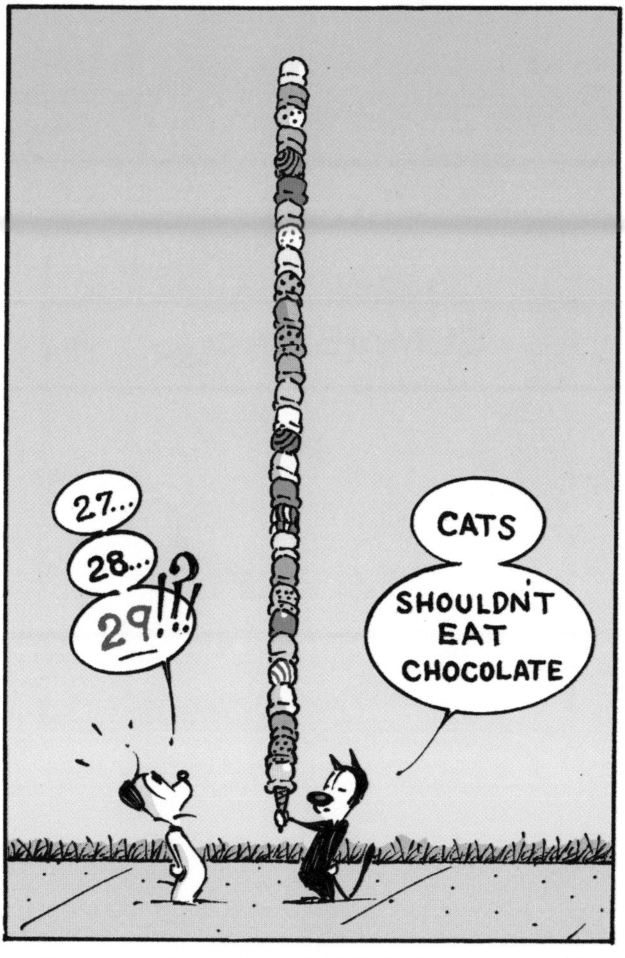
27...
28...
29!!?
CATS
SHOULDN'T EAT CHOCOLATE

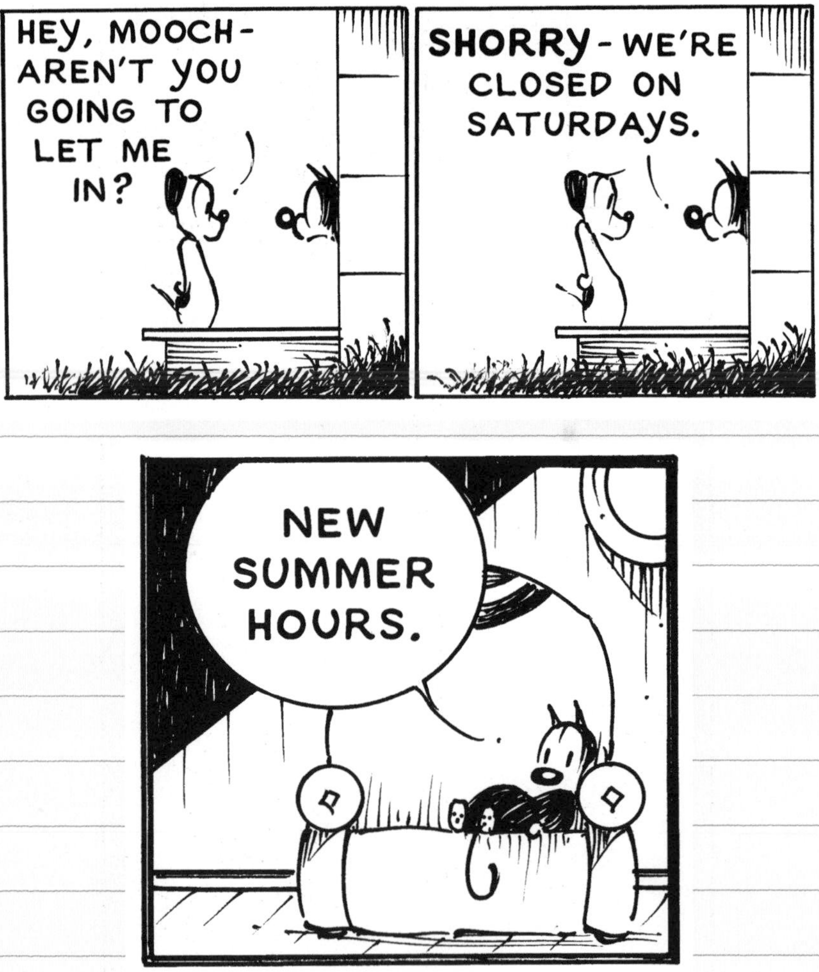
HEY, MOOCH-
AREN'T YOU
GOING TO
LET ME
IN?
SHORRY- WE'RE
CLOSED ON
SATURDAYS.
NEW
SUMMER
HOURS.

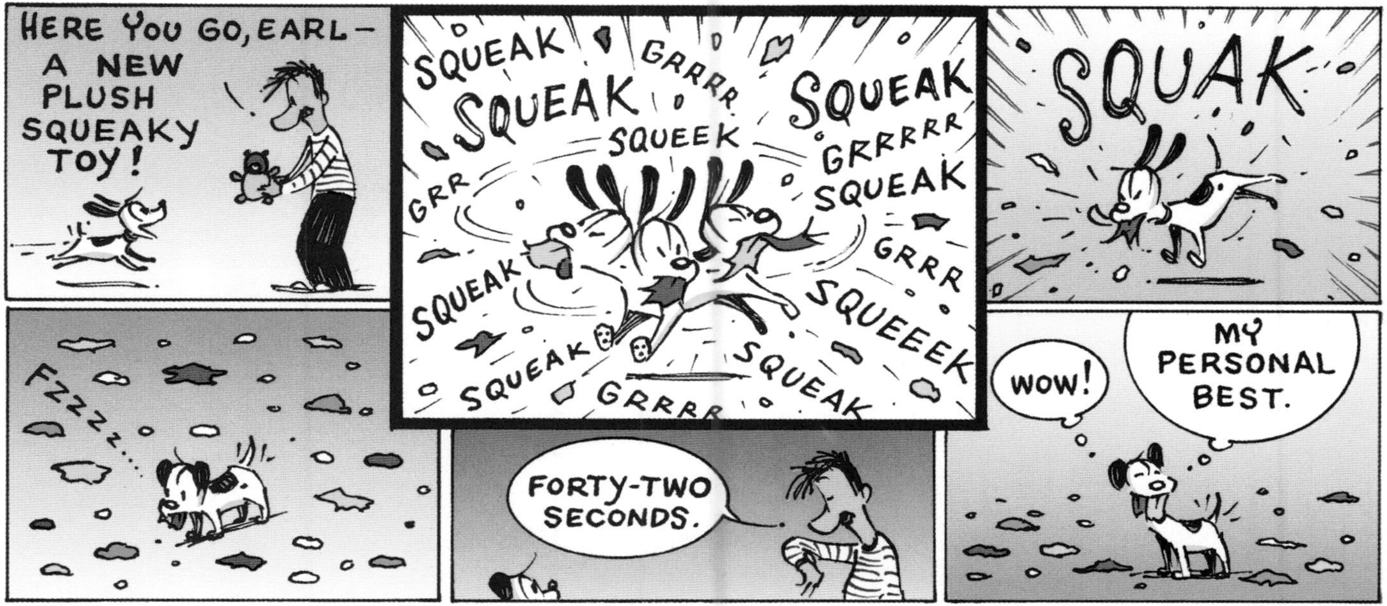
HERE YOU GO, EARL— A NEW PLUSH SQUEAKY TOY!
SQUEAK
SQUEAK
GRRRR
SQUEEK
GRR
SQUEAK
SQUEAK
GRRRR
SQUEAK
GRRRRR
SQUEAK
GRRR
SQUEEEK
SQUEAK
SQUEAK
SQUAK
FZZZZ....
FORTY-TWO SECONDS.
WOW!
MY PERSONAL BEST.

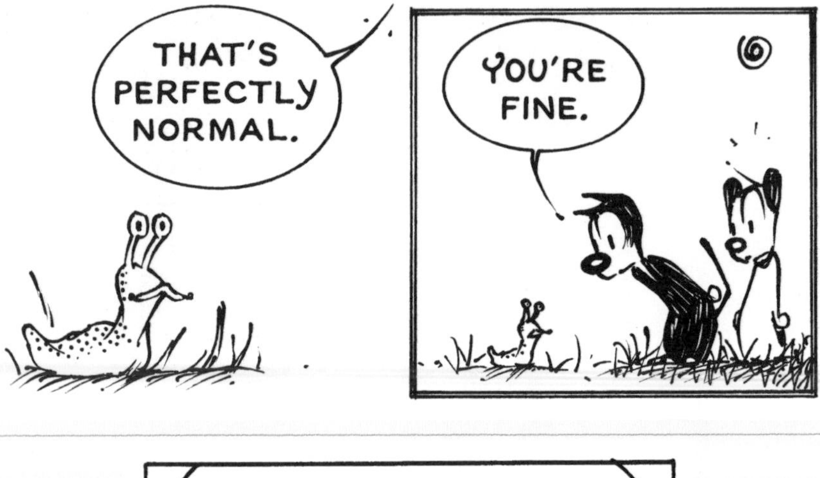
THAT'S PERFECTLY NORMAL.
YOU'RE FINE.
HE WAS FEELING A LITTLE SLUGGISH.

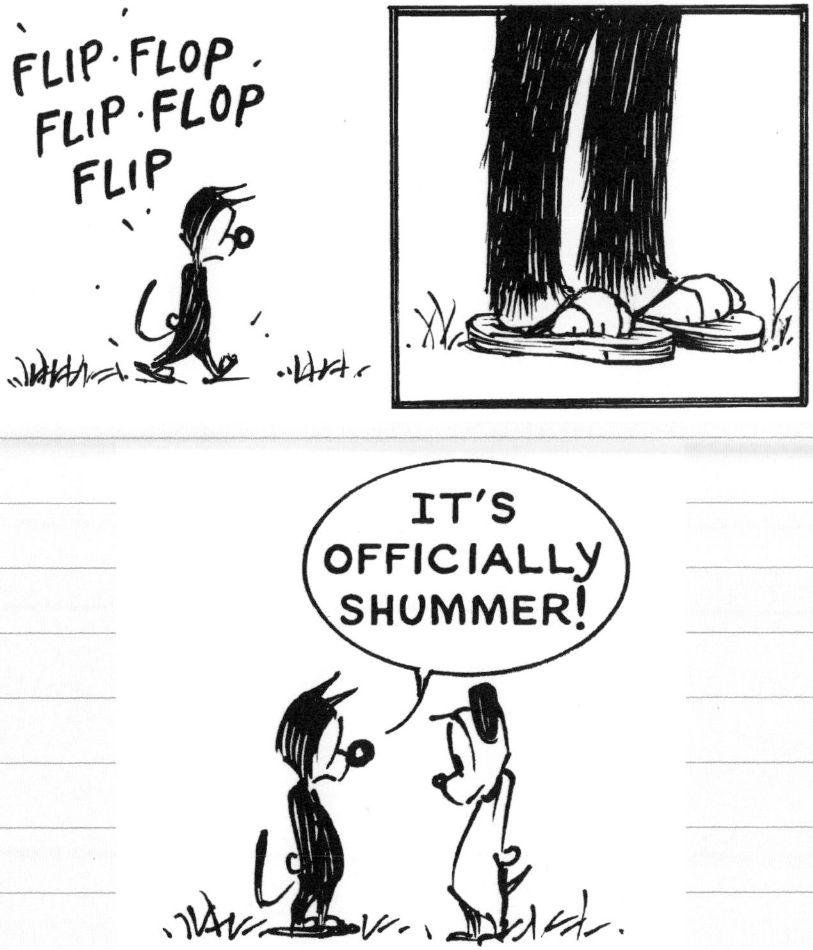
FLIP·FLOP
FLIP·FLOP
FLIP
IT'S OFFICIALLY SHUMMER!

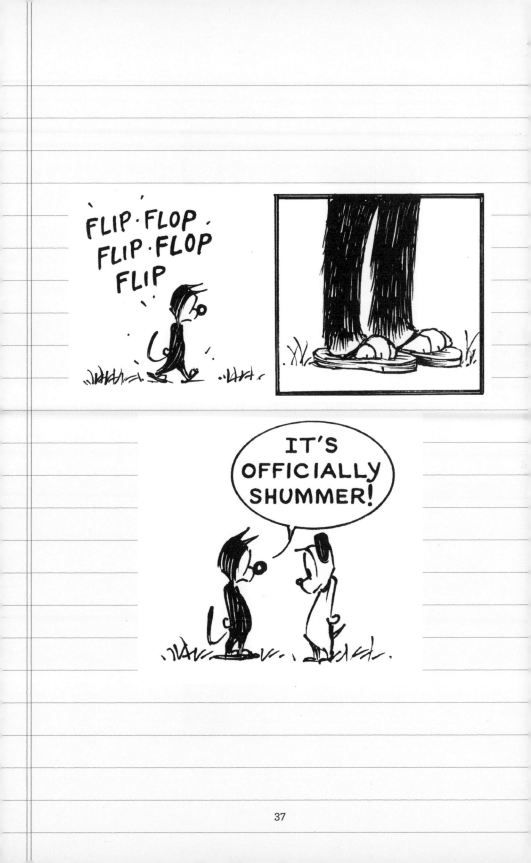

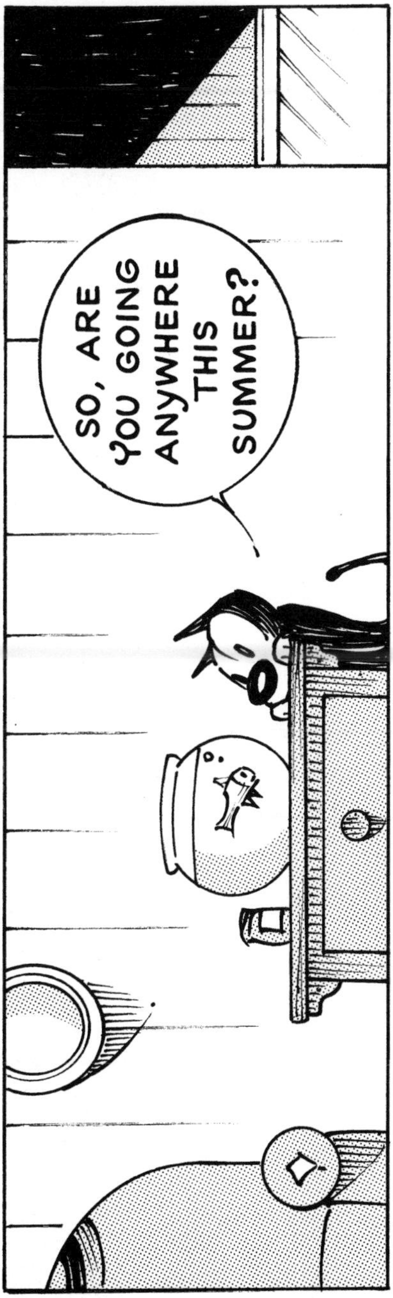
SO, ARE YOU GOING ANYWHERE THIS SUMMER?

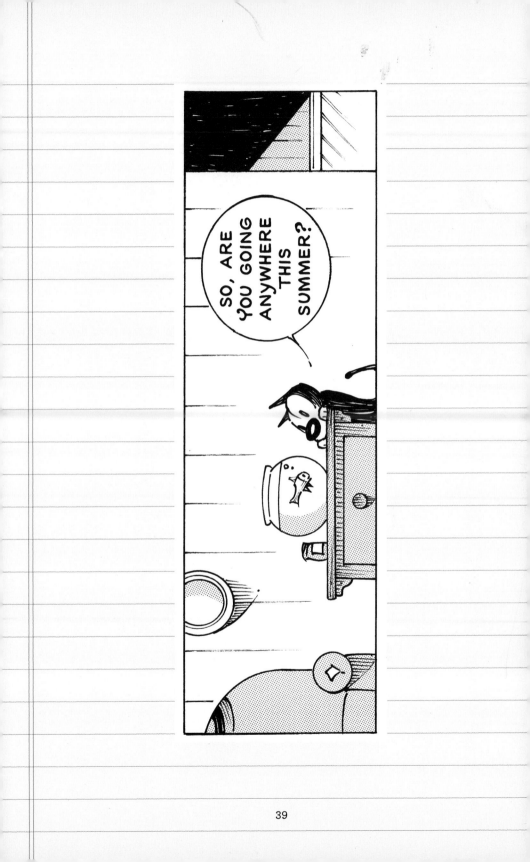

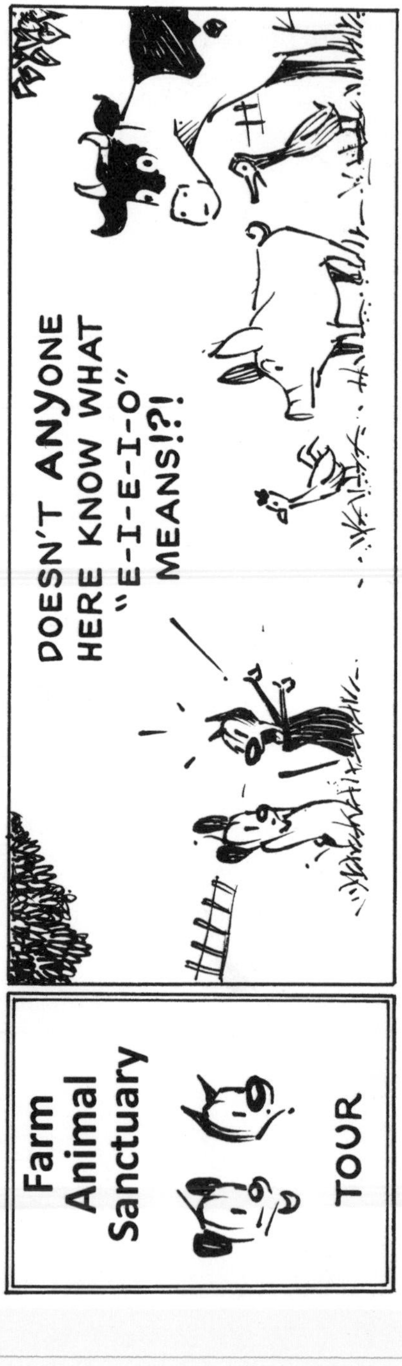
Farm Animal Sanctuary TOUR
DOESN'T ANYONE HERE KNOW WHAT "E-I-E-I-O" MEANS!?!

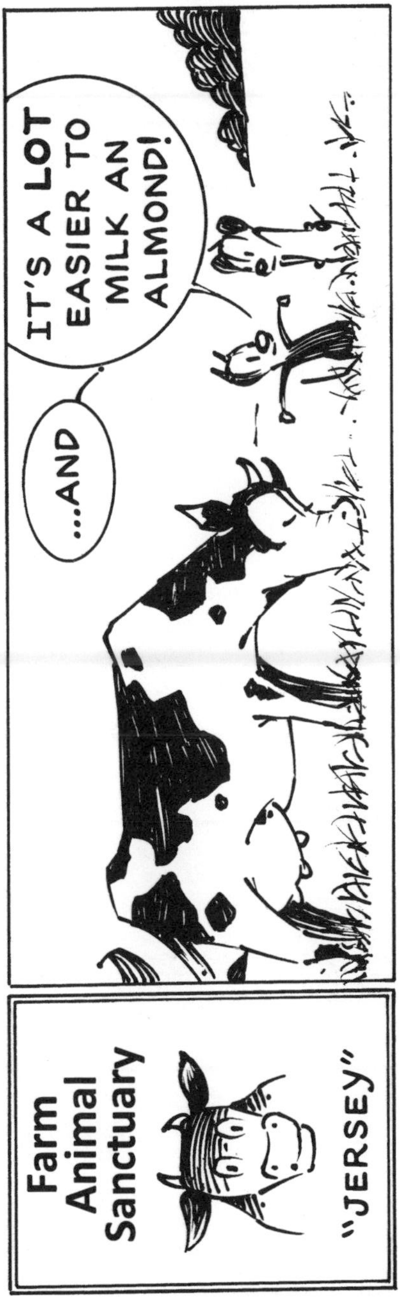
Farm Animal Sanctuary
"JERSEY"
...AND
IT'S A LOT EASIER TO MILK AN ALMOND!

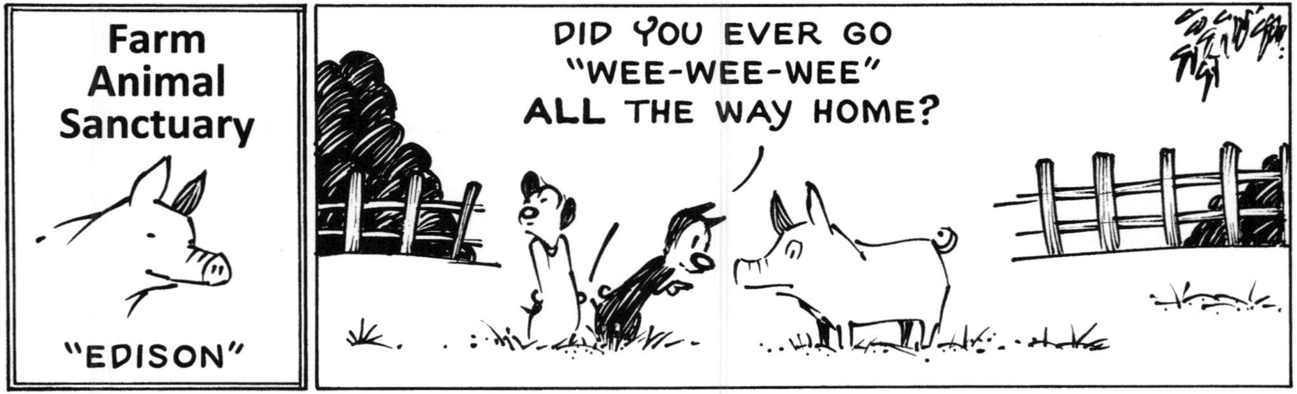
Farm
Animal
Sanctuary
"EDISON"
DID YOU EVER GO "WEE-WEE-WEE" ALL THE WAY HOME?

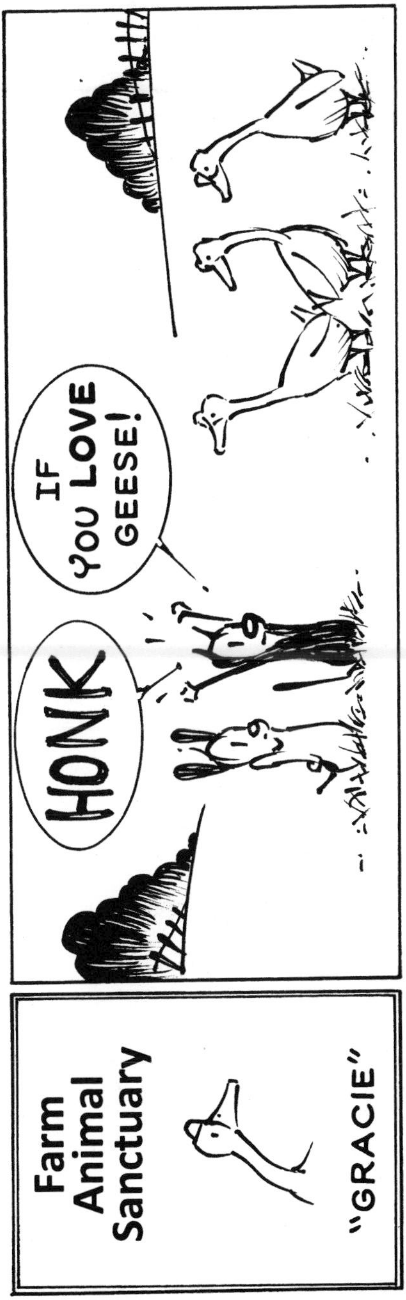
Farm Animal Sanctuary
"GRACIE"
HONK
IF YOU LOVE GEESE!

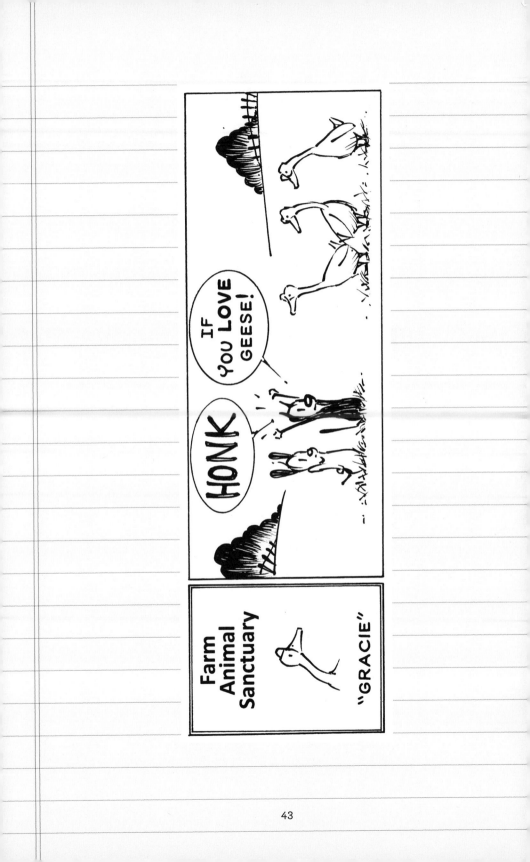

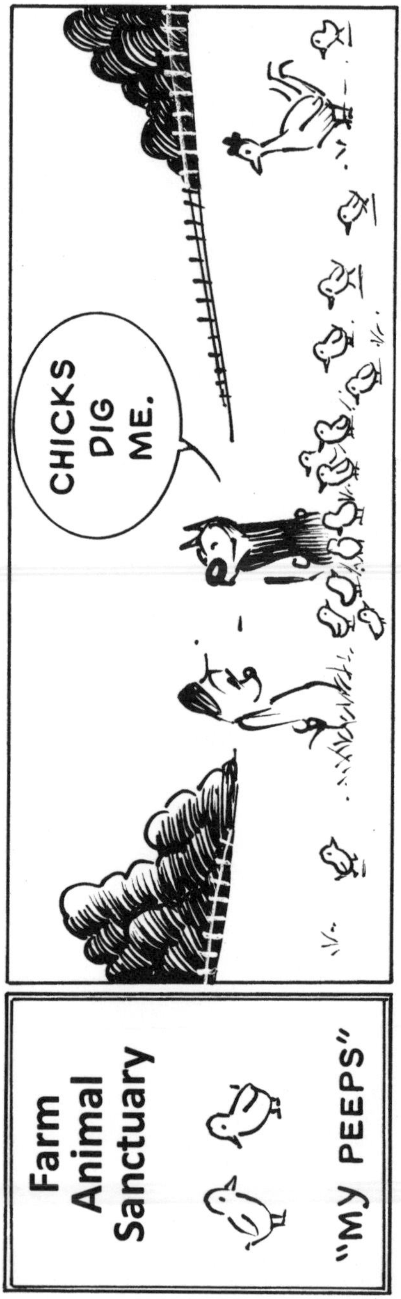
Farm Animal Sanctuary
"MY PEEPS"
CHICKS DIG ME.

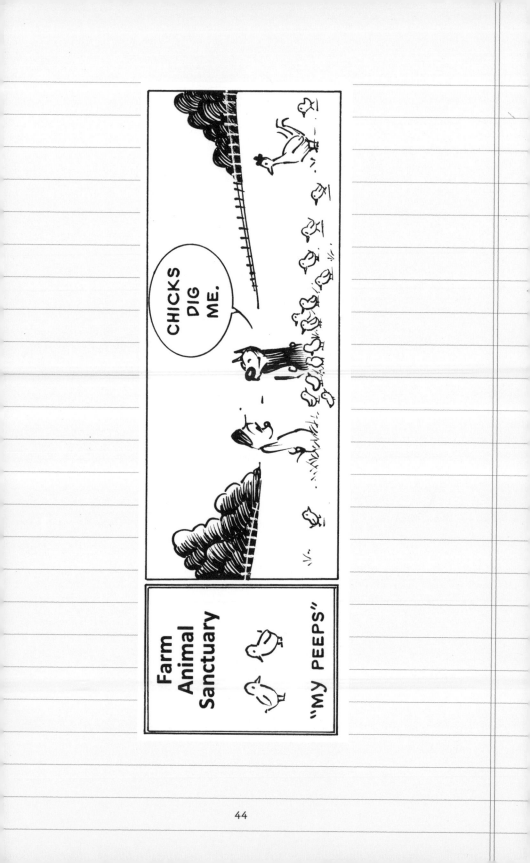

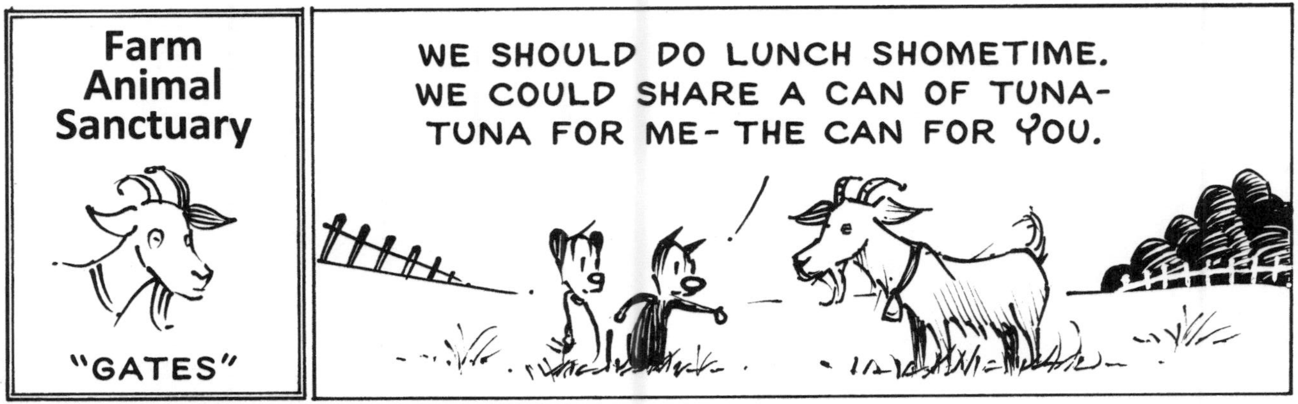
Farm
Animal
Sanctuary
"GATES"
WE SHOULD DO LUNCH SHOMETIME.
WE COULD SHARE A CAN OF TUNA-
TUNA FOR ME- THE CAN FOR YOU.

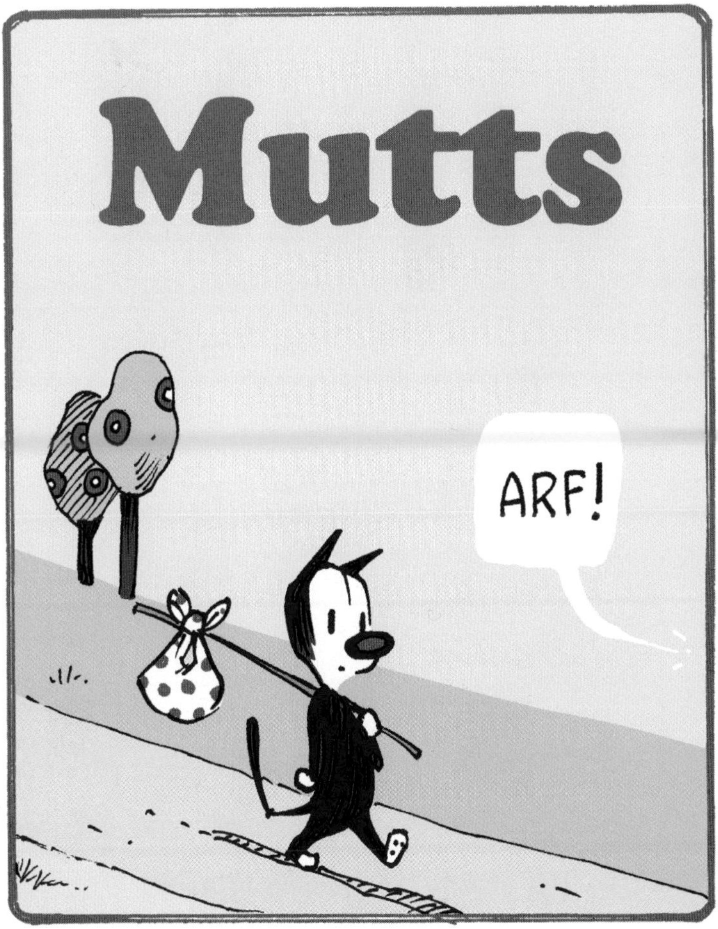
Mutts
ARF!

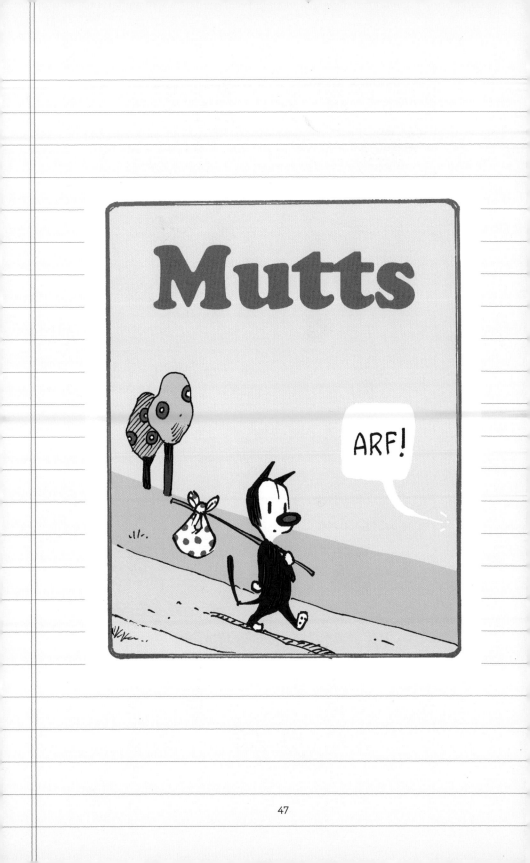

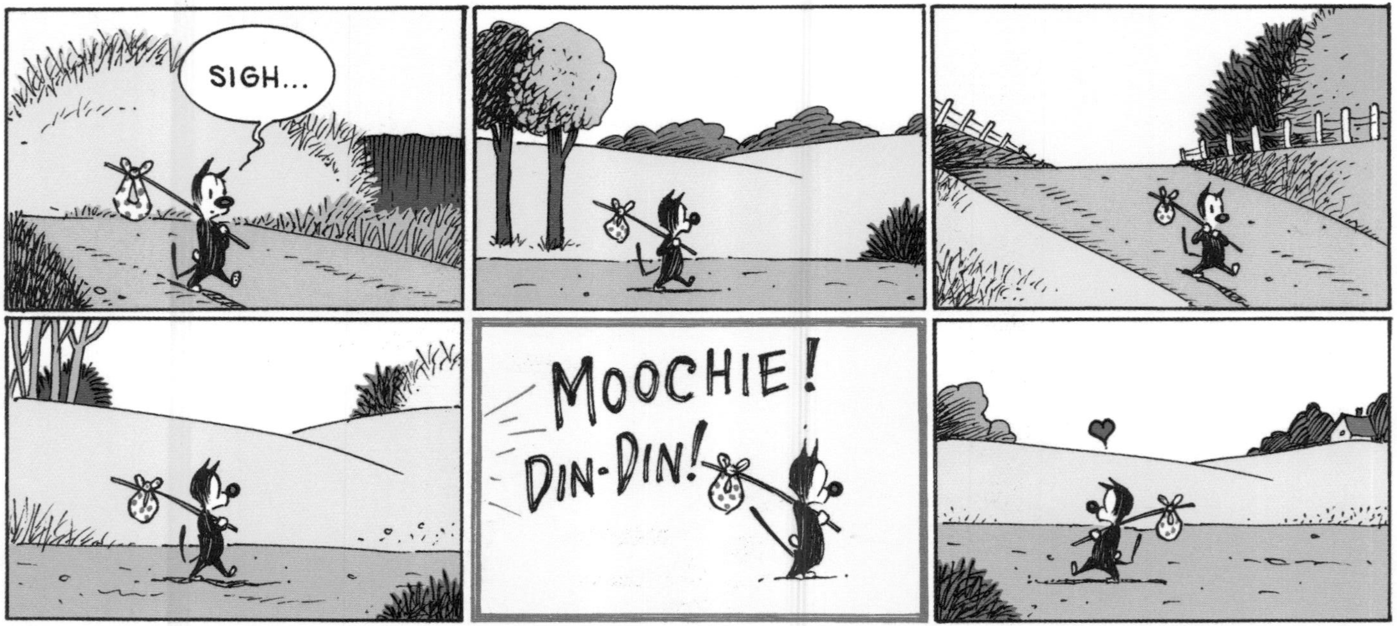
SIGH...
MOOCHIE!
DIN-DIN!

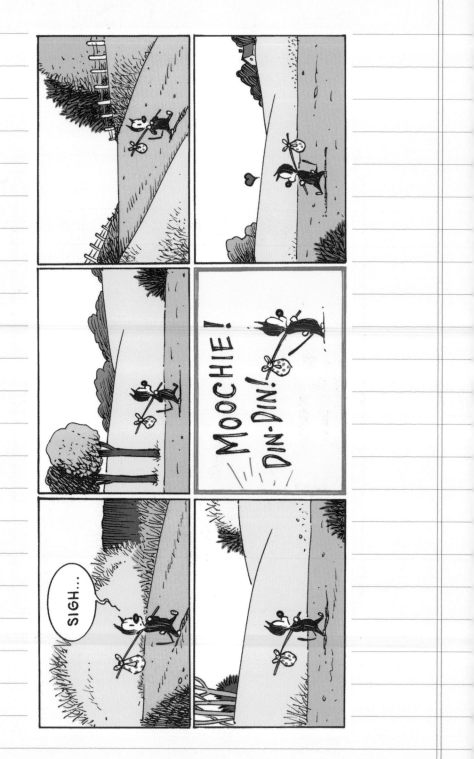

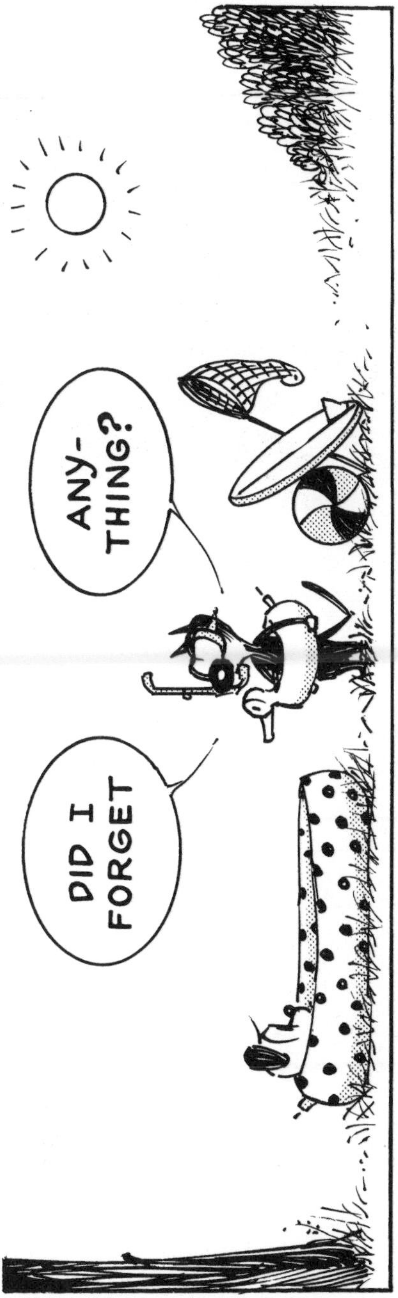
DID I FORGET
ANY-THING?

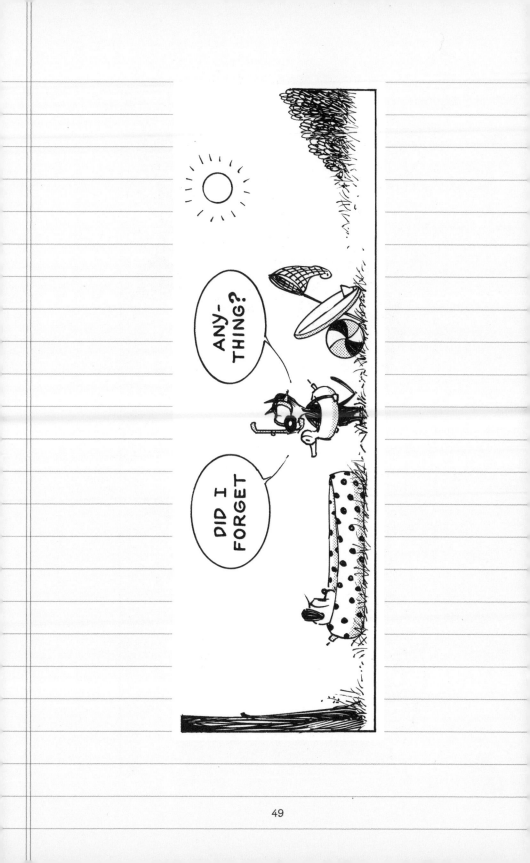

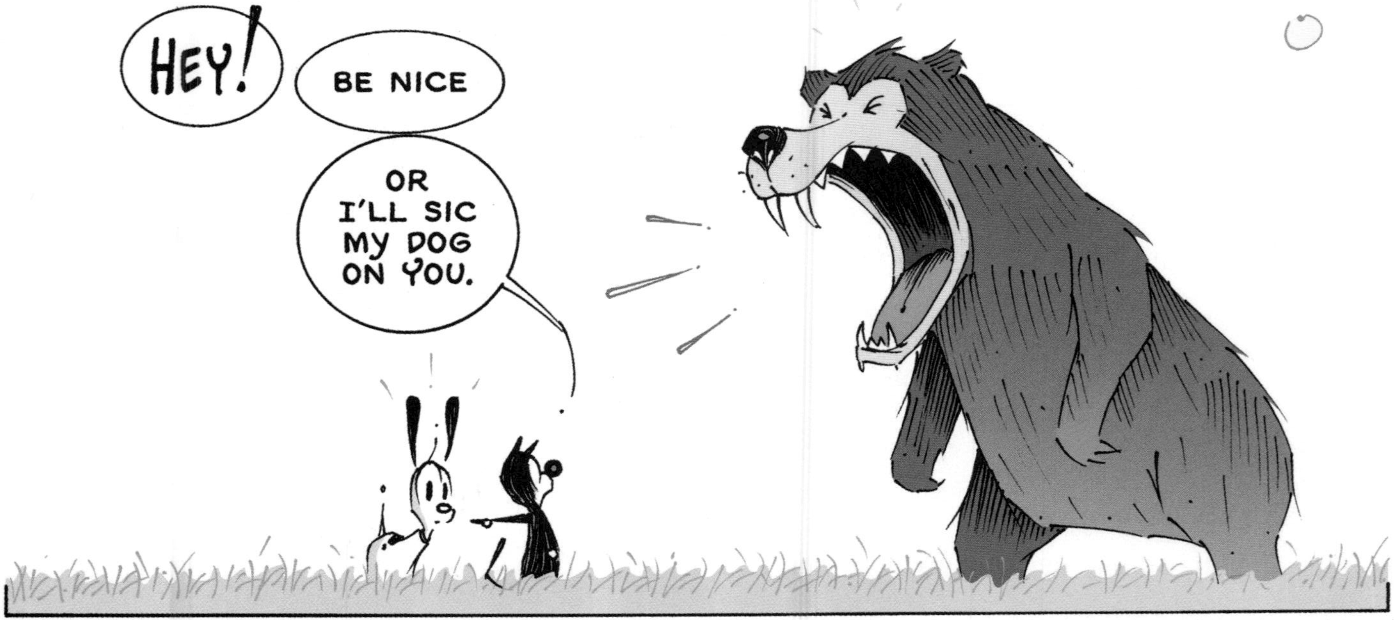
HEY!
BE NICE
OR I'LL SIC MY DOG ON YOU.

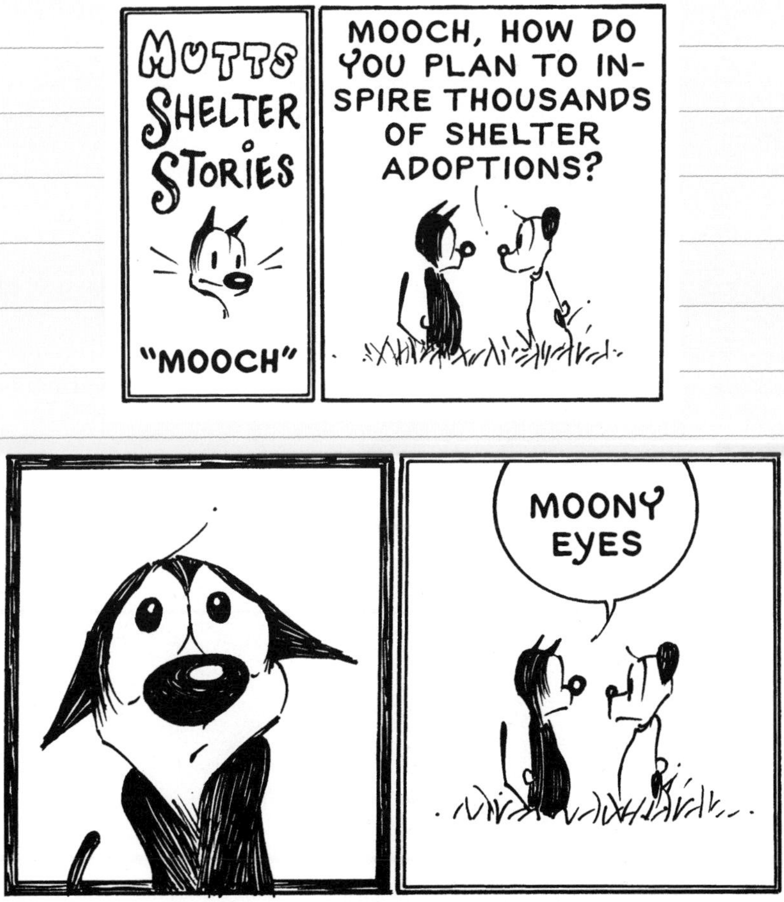
MUTTS
SHELTER
STORIES
"MOOCH"
MOOCH, HOW DO YOU PLAN TO INSPIRE THOUSANDS OF SHELTER ADOPTIONS?
MOONY EYES

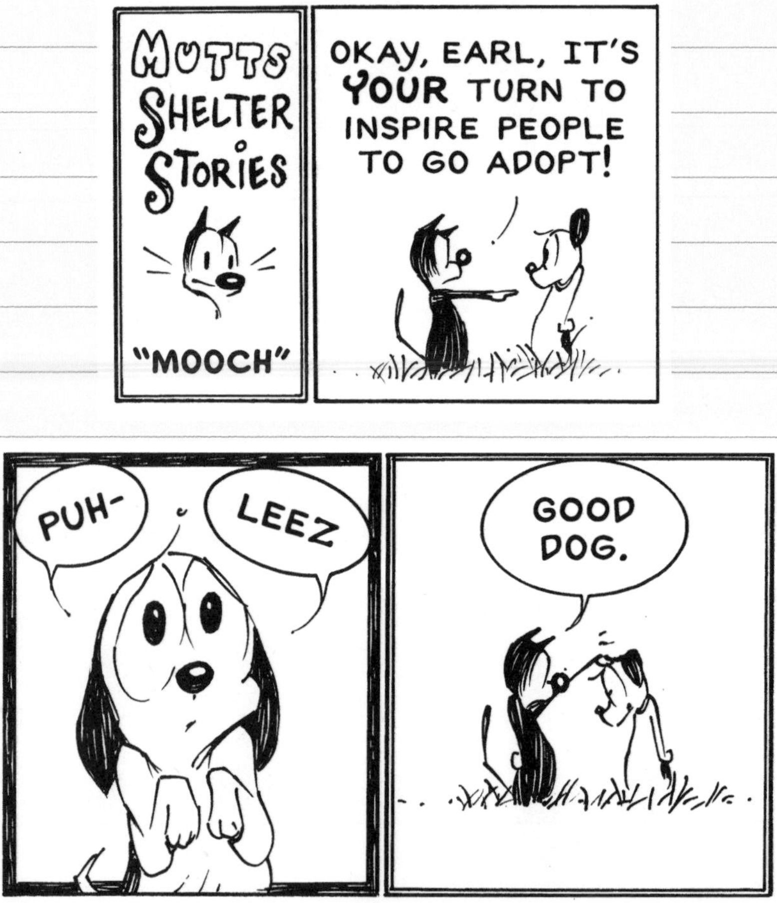
MUTTS
SHELTER
STORIES
"MOOCH"
OKAY, EARL, IT'S YOUR TURN TO INSPIRE PEOPLE TO GO ADOPT!
PUH-
LEEZ
GOOD DOG.

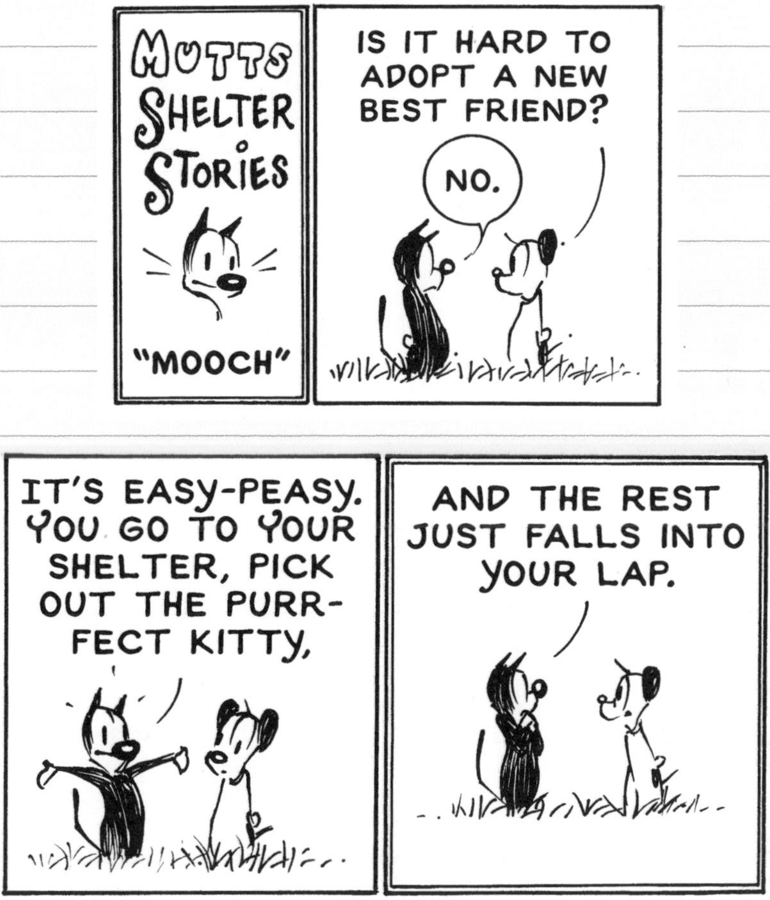
MUTTS SHELTER STORIES
"MOOCH"
IS IT HARD TO ADOPT A NEW BEST FRIEND?
NO.
IT'S EASY-PEASY. YOU GO TO YOUR SHELTER, PICK OUT THE PURR-FECT KITTY,
AND THE REST JUST FALLS INTO YOUR LAP.

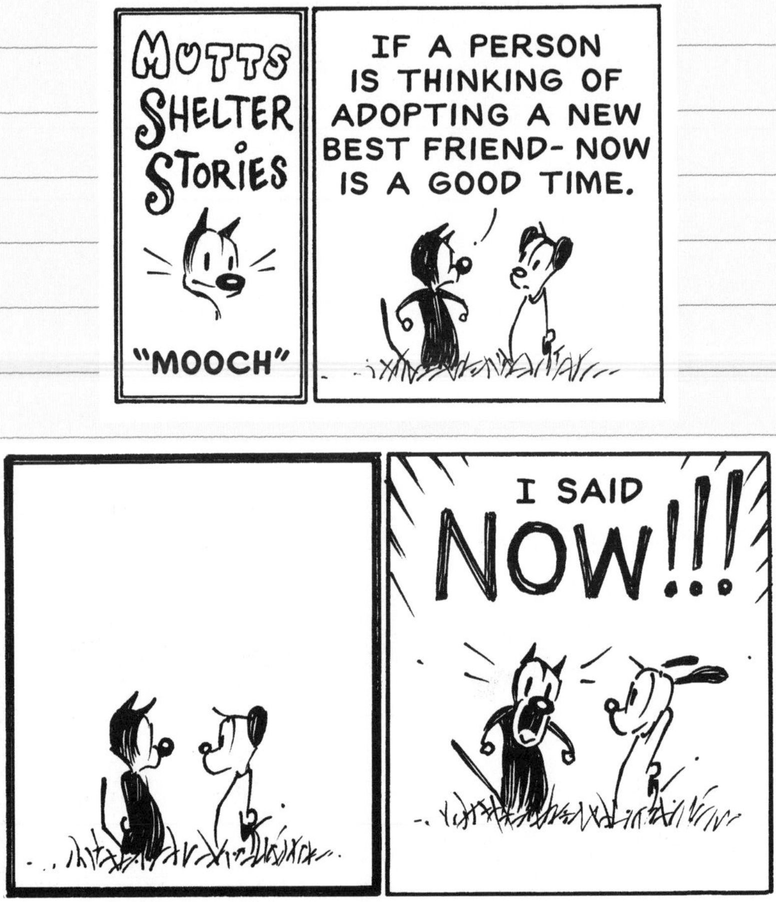
MUTTS
SHELTER STORIES
"MOOCH"
IF A PERSON IS THINKING OF ADOPTING A NEW BEST FRIEND- NOW IS A GOOD TIME.
I SAID NOW!!!

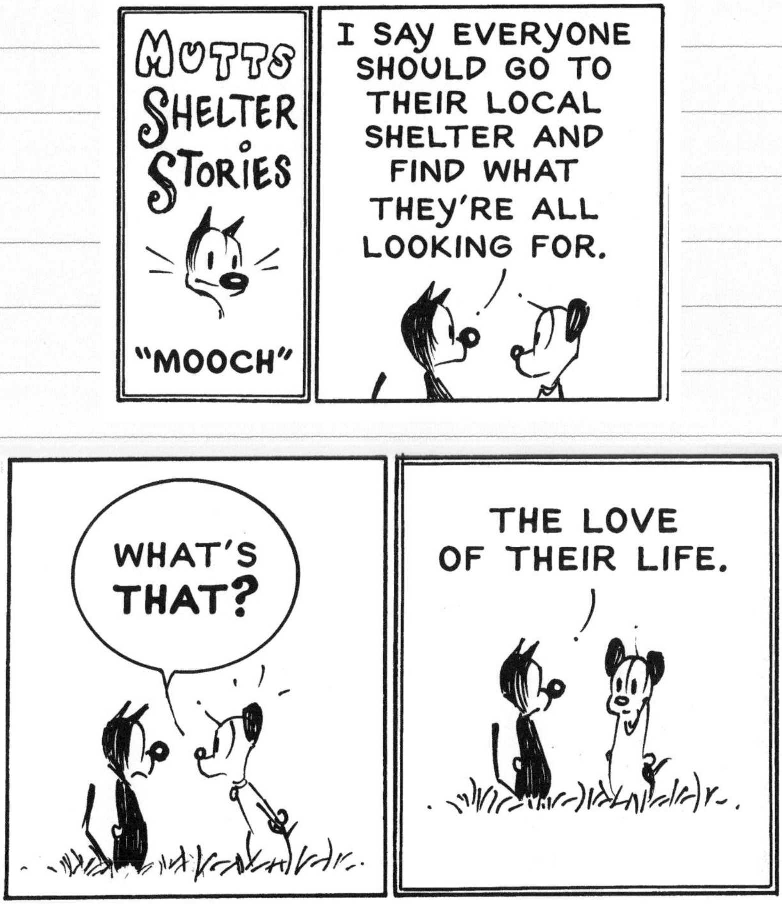
MUTTS
SHELTER STORIES
"MOOCH"
I SAY EVERYONE SHOULD GO TO THEIR LOCAL SHELTER AND FIND WHAT THEY'RE ALL LOOKING FOR.
WHAT'S THAT?
THE LOVE OF THEIR LIFE.

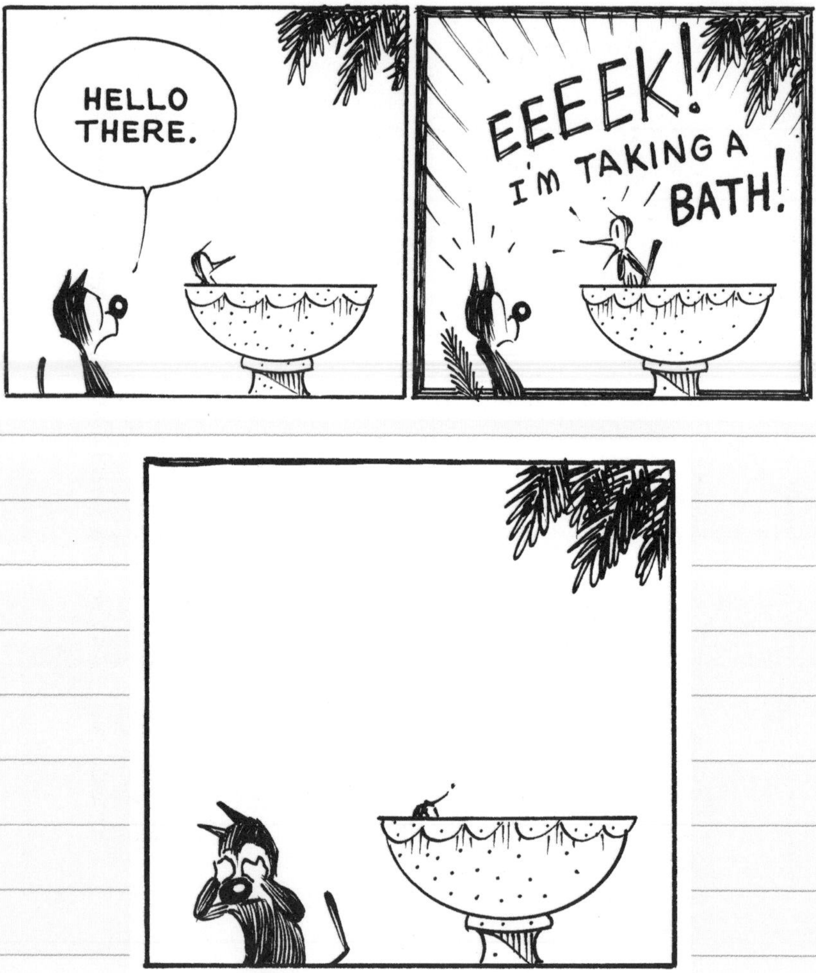
HELLO THERE.
EEEEK! I'M TAKING A BATH!

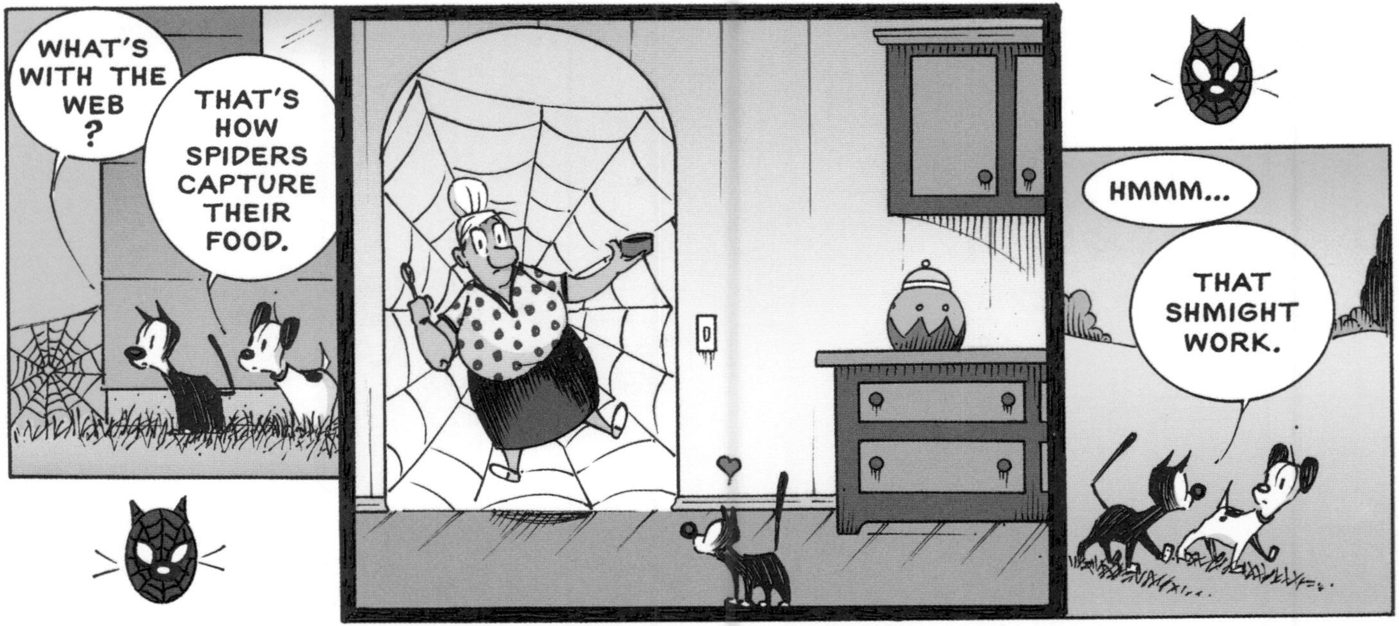
WHAT'S WITH THE WEB ?
THAT'S HOW SPIDERS CAPTURE THEIR FOOD.
HMMM...
THAT SHMIGHT WORK.

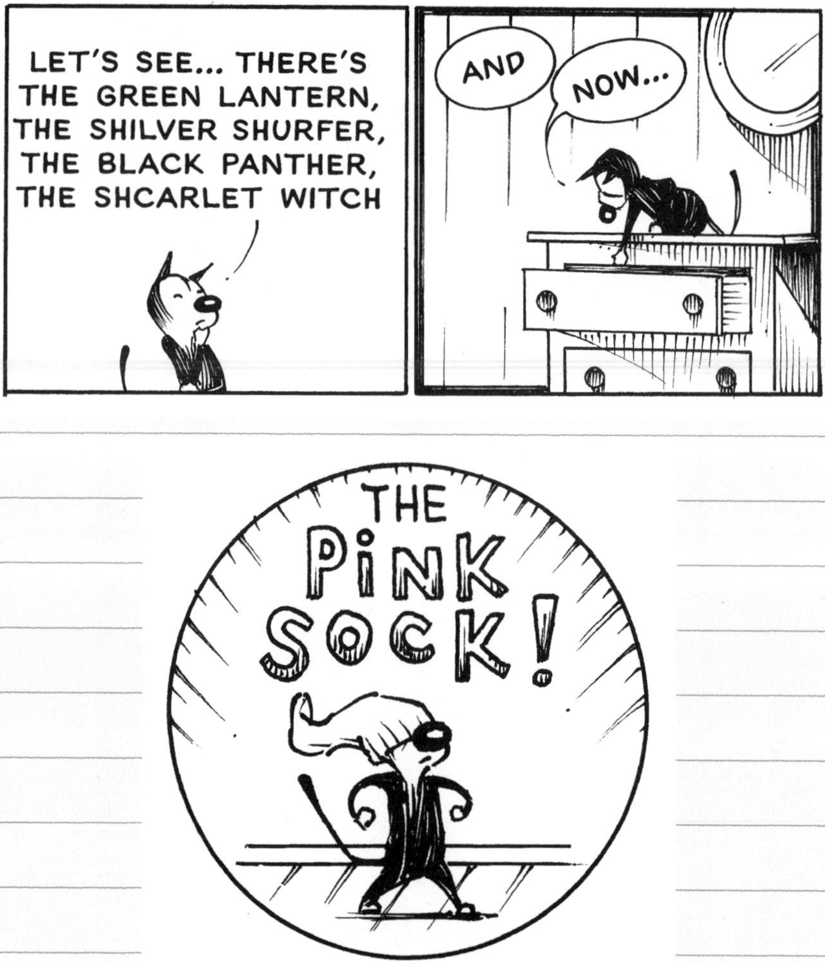
LET'S SEE... THERE'S THE GREEN LANTERN, THE SHILVER SHURFER, THE BLACK PANTHER, THE SHCARLET WITCH
AND
NOW...
THE PINK SOCK!

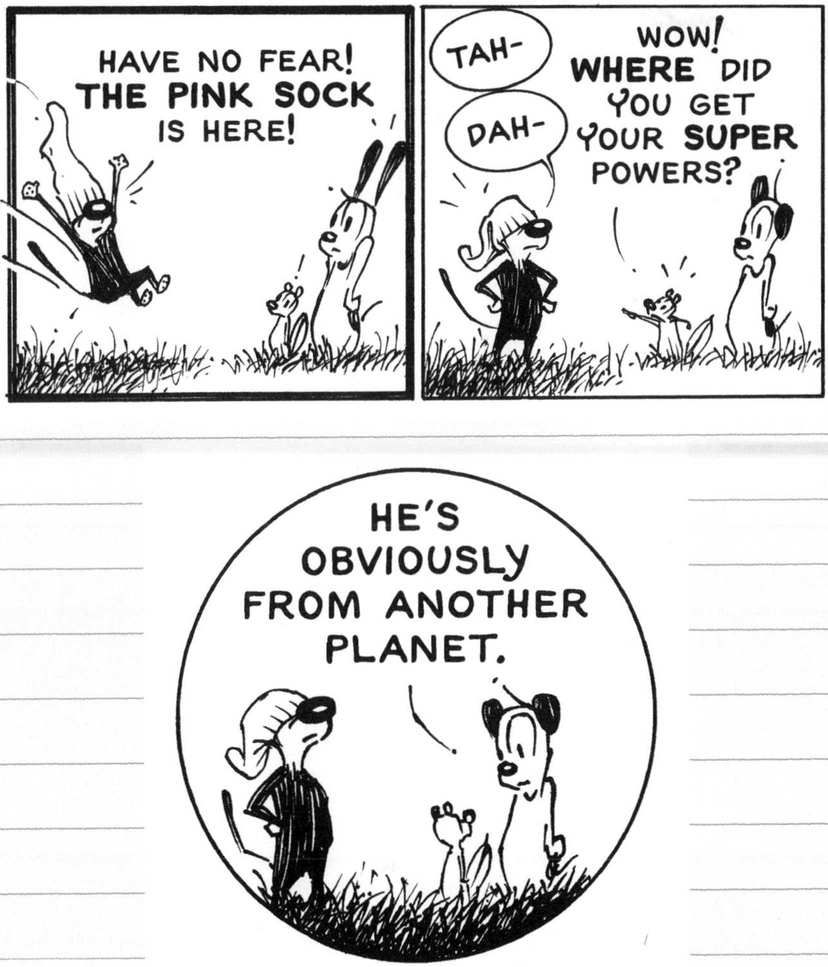
HAVE NO FEAR! THE PINK SOCK IS HERE!
TAH-
DAH-
WOW! WHERE DID YOU GET YOUR SUPER POWERS?
HE'S OBVIOUSLY FROM ANOTHER PLANET.

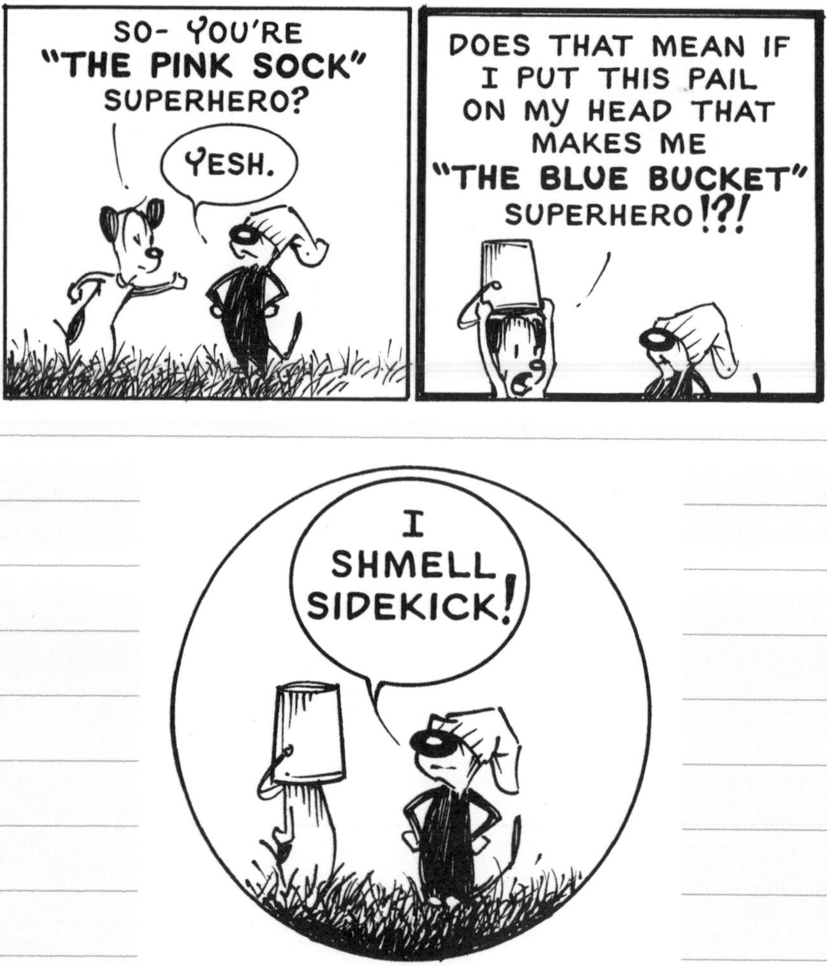
SO- YOU'RE "THE PINK SOCK" SUPERHERO?
YESH.
DOES THAT MEAN IF I PUT THIS PAIL ON MY HEAD THAT MAKES ME "THE BLUE BUCKET" SUPERHERO!?!
I SHMELL SIDEKICK!

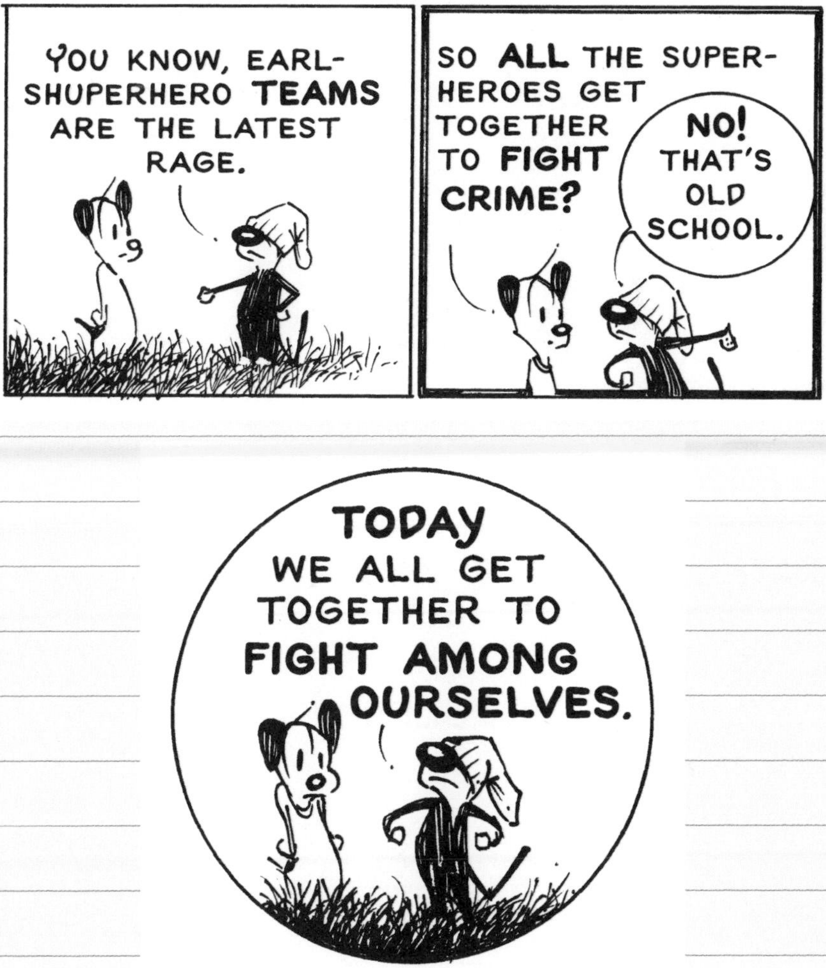
YOU KNOW, EARL-
SHUPERHERO **TEAMS** ARE THE LATEST RAGE.
SO **ALL** THE SUPER-HEROES GET TOGETHER TO **FIGHT CRIME?**
NO! THAT'S OLD SCHOOL.
TODAY WE ALL GET TOGETHER TO **FIGHT AMONG OURSELVES.**

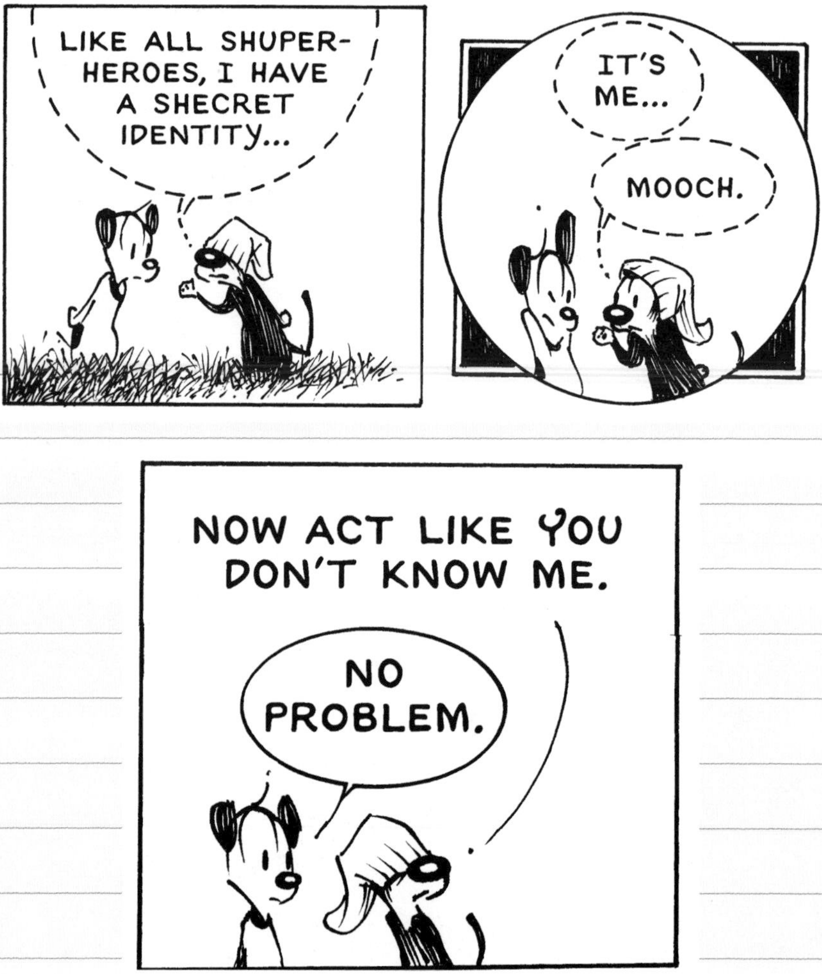
LIKE ALL SHUPER-HEROES, I HAVE A SHECRET IDENTITY...
IT'S ME...
MOOCH.
NOW ACT LIKE YOU DON'T KNOW ME.
NO PROBLEM.

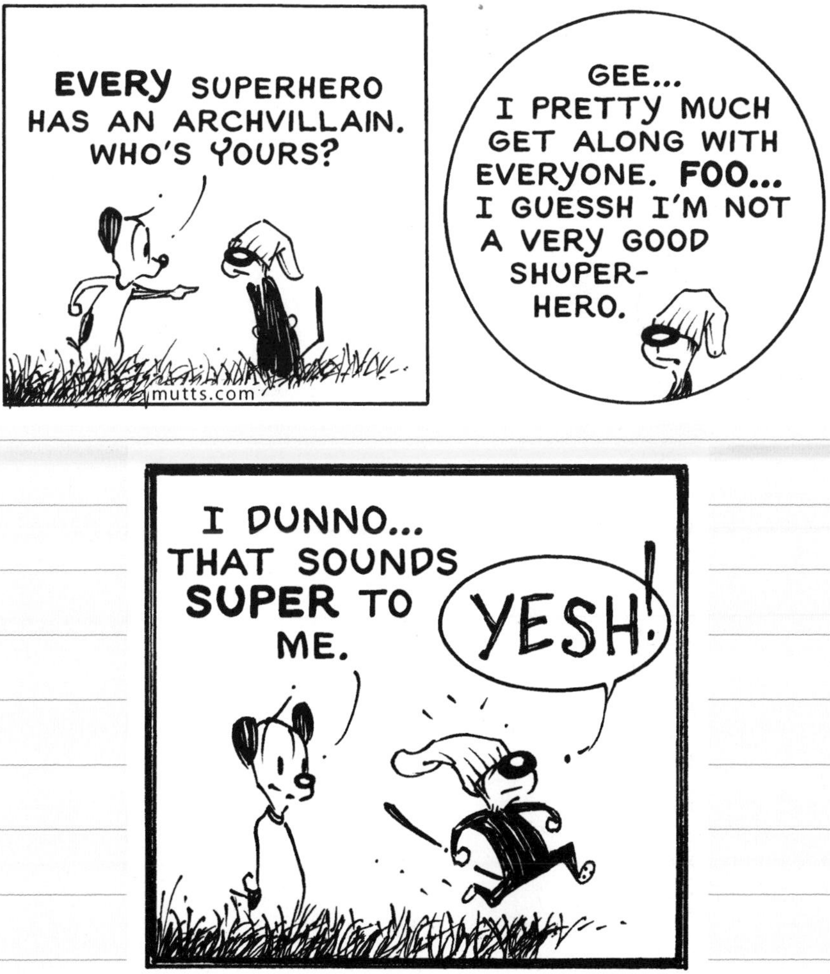
EVERY SUPERHERO HAS AN ARCHVILLAIN. WHO'S YOURS?
mutts.com
GEE... I PRETTY MUCH GET ALONG WITH EVERYONE. FOO... I GUESSH I'M NOT A VERY GOOD SHUPER-HERO.
I DUNNO... THAT SOUNDS SUPER TO ME.
YESH!

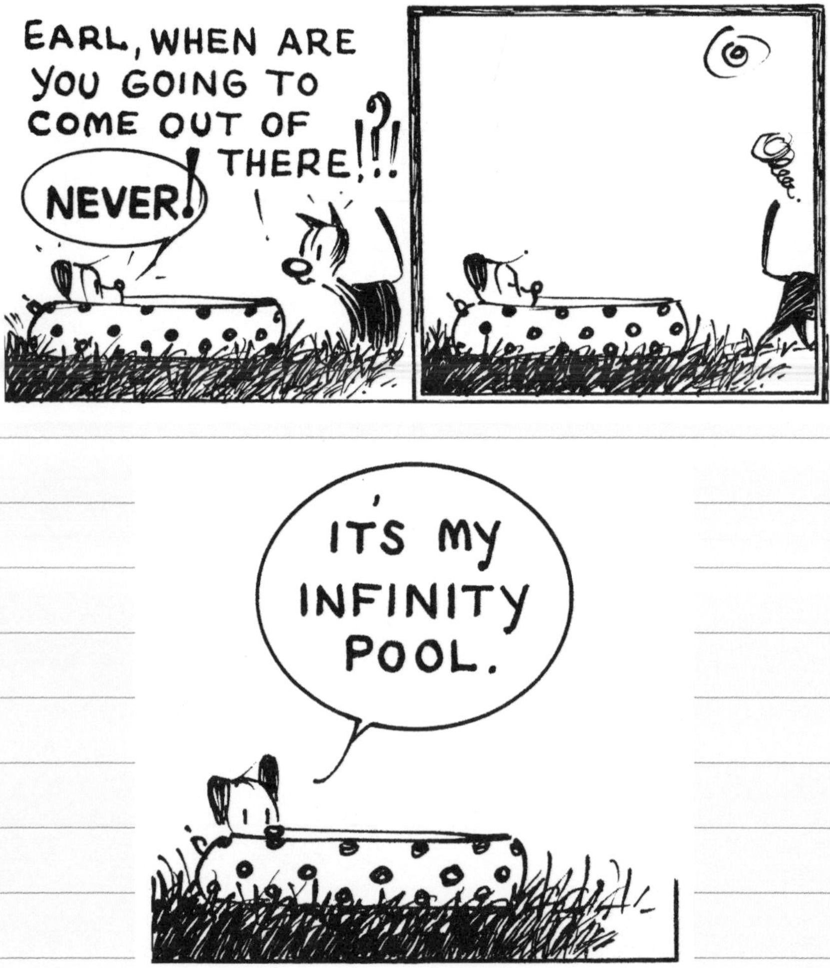
EARL, WHEN ARE YOU GOING TO COME OUT OF THERE!?!
NEVER!
IT'S MY INFINITY POOL.

ARE WE LATE?

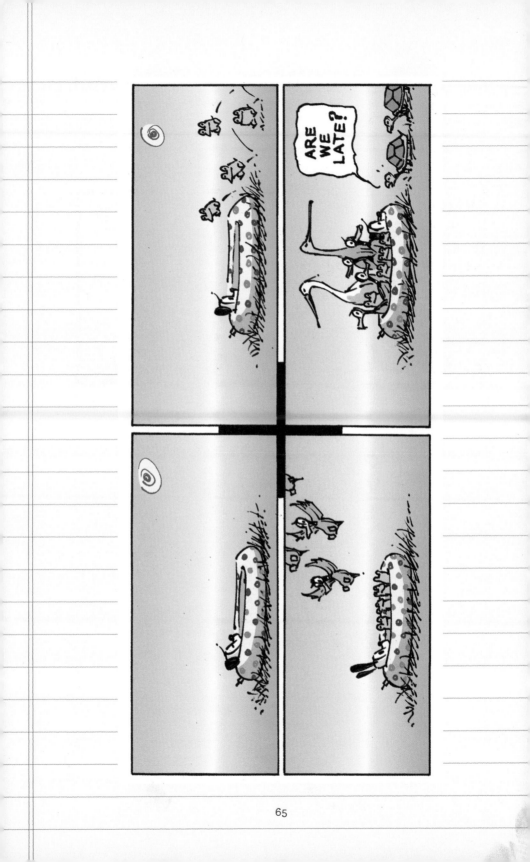

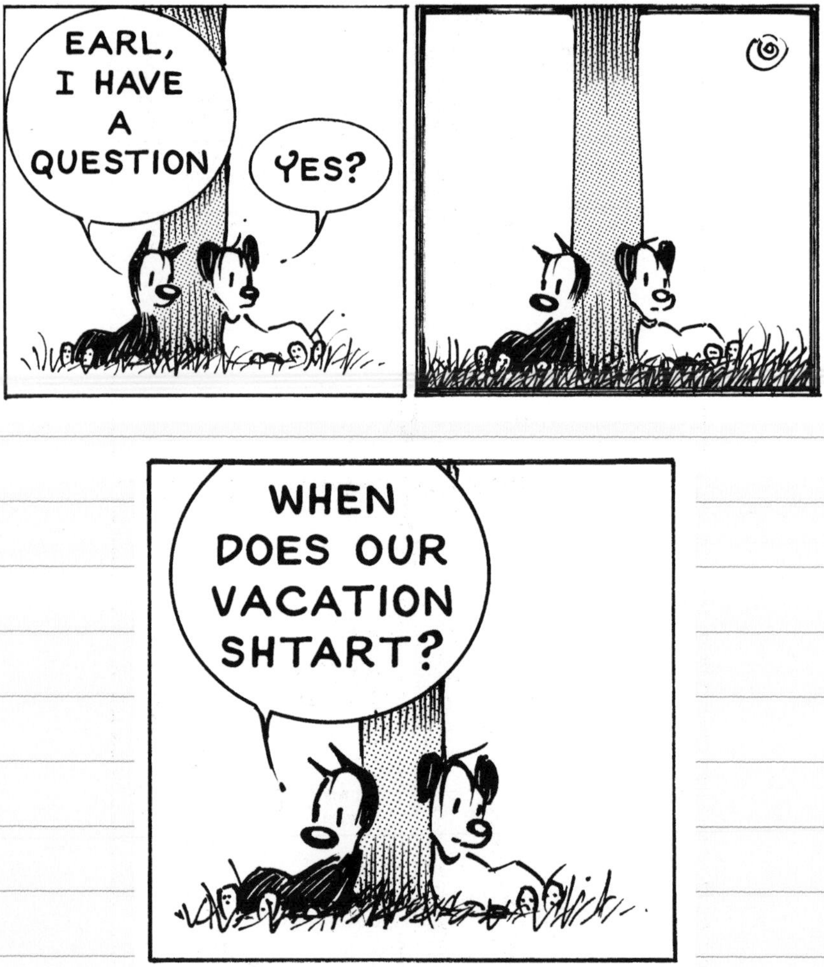
EARL, I HAVE A QUESTION
YES?
WHEN DOES OUR VACATION SHTART?

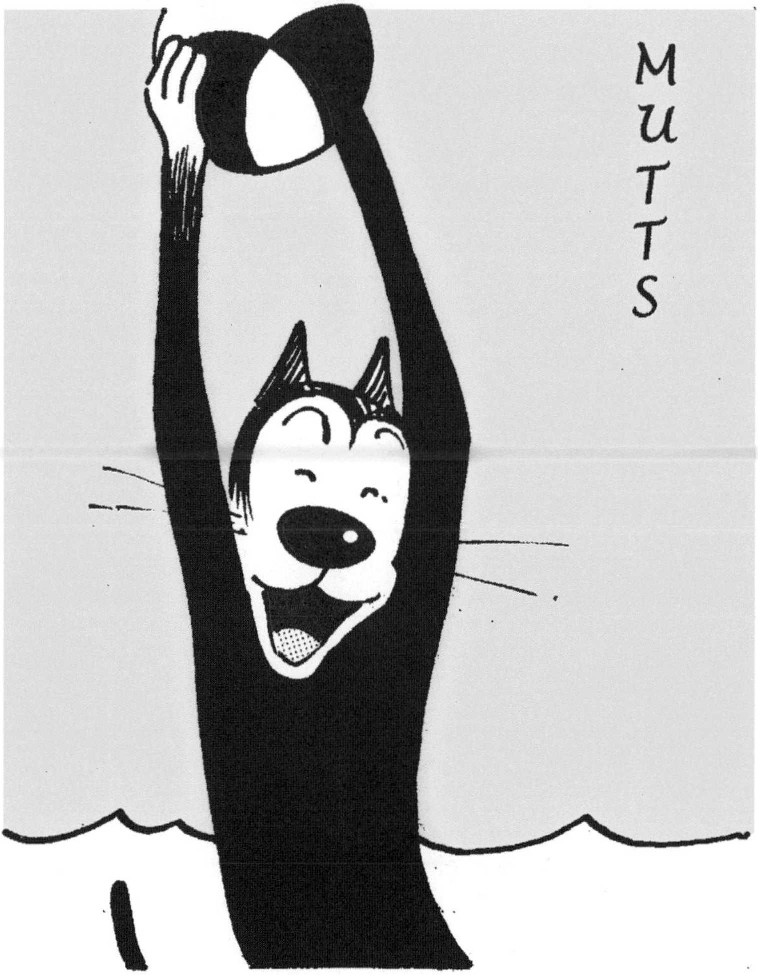
MUTTS

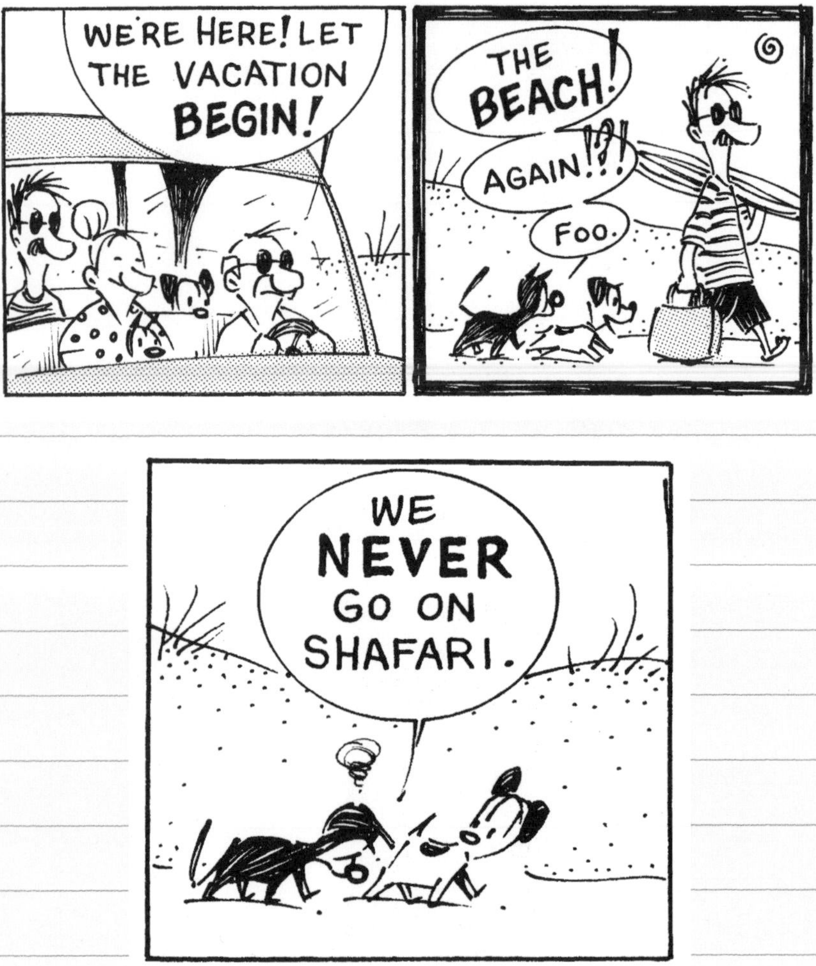
WE'RE HERE! LET THE VACATION BEGIN!
THE BEACH!
AGAIN!?!
Foo.
WE NEVER GO ON SHAFARI.

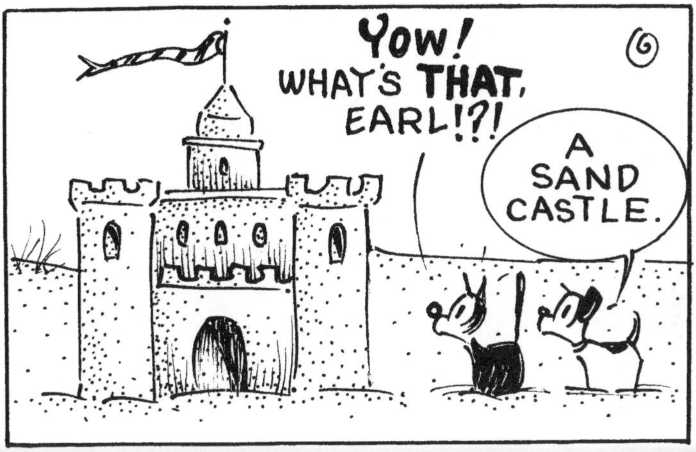
YOW! WHAT'S THAT, EARL!?!
A SAND CASTLE.

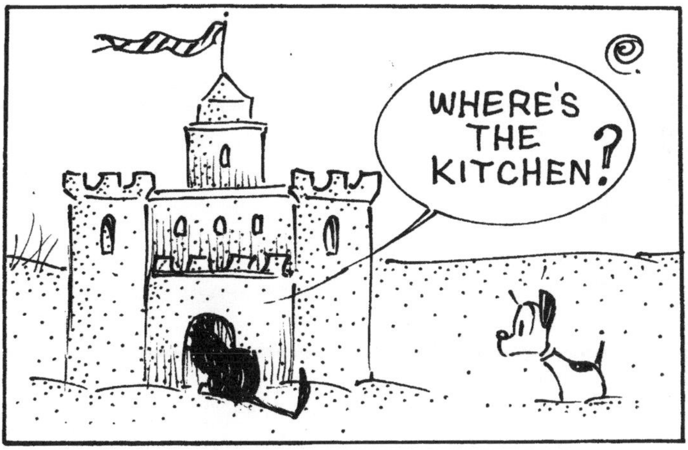
WHERE'S THE KITCHEN?

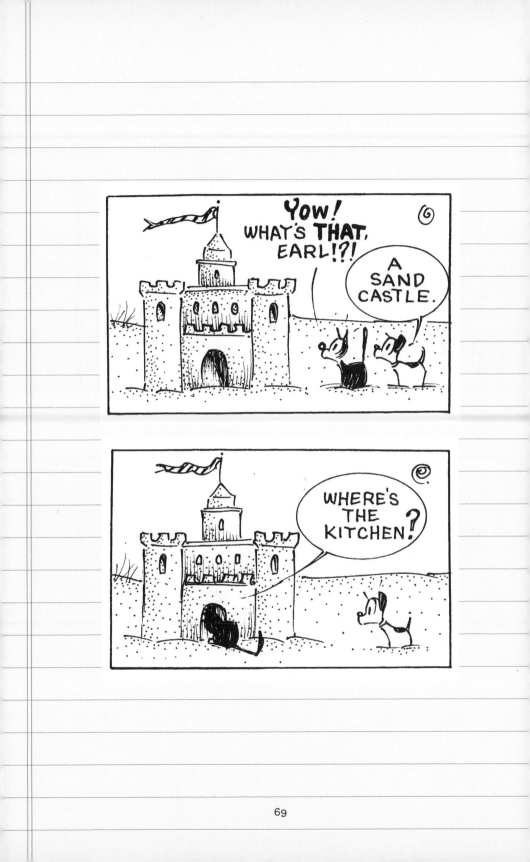

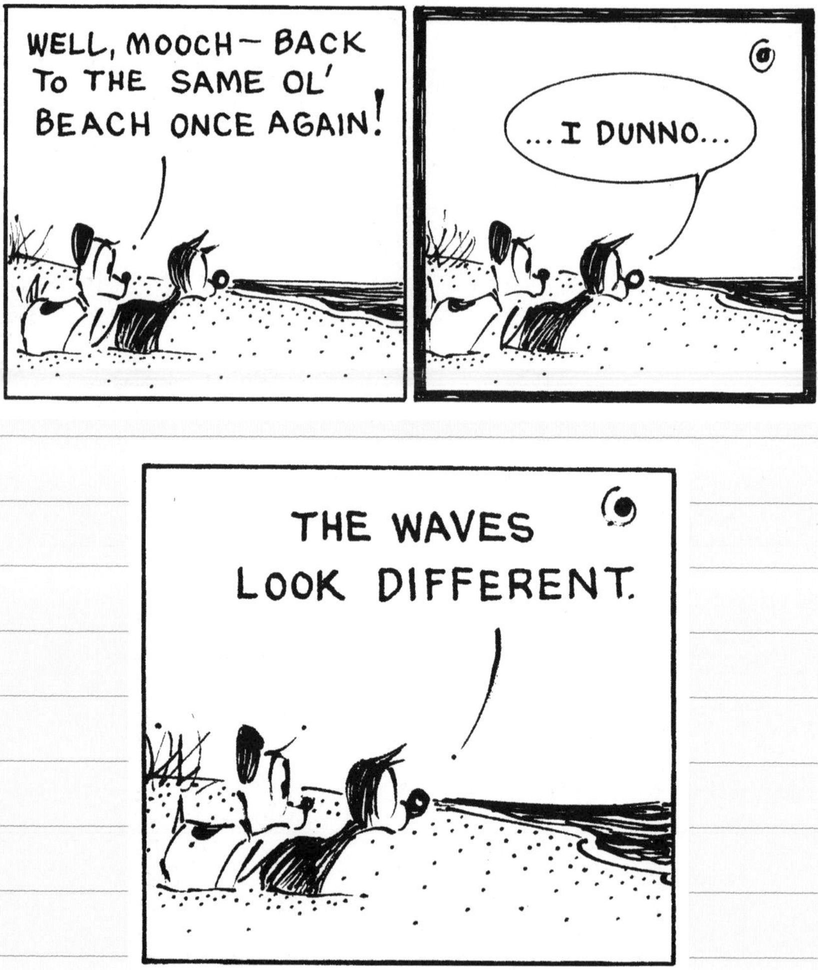
WELL, MOOCH— BACK TO THE SAME OL' BEACH ONCE AGAIN!
... I DUNNO...
THE WAVES LOOK DIFFERENT.

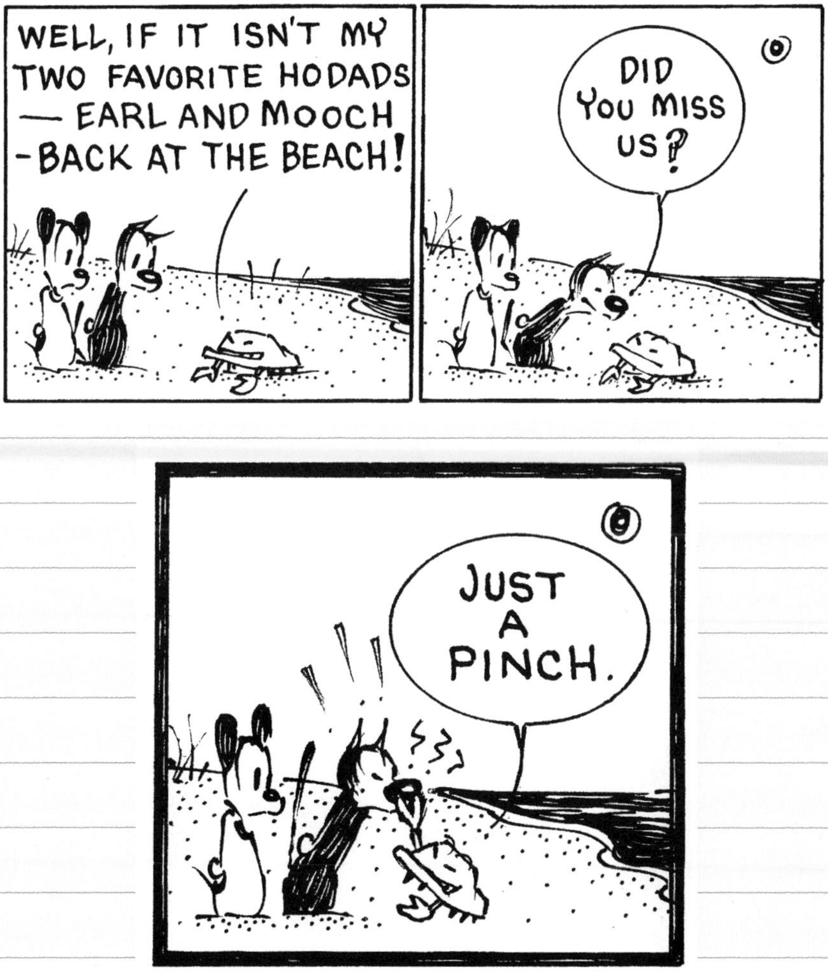
WELL, IF IT ISN'T MY TWO FAVORITE HODADS — EARL AND MOOCH -BACK AT THE BEACH!
DID YOU MISS US?
JUST A PINCH.

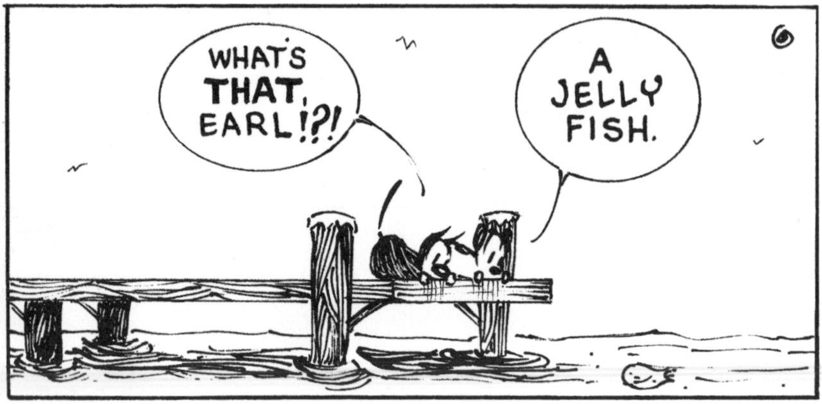
6
WHAT'S THAT, EARL!?!
A JELLY FISH.

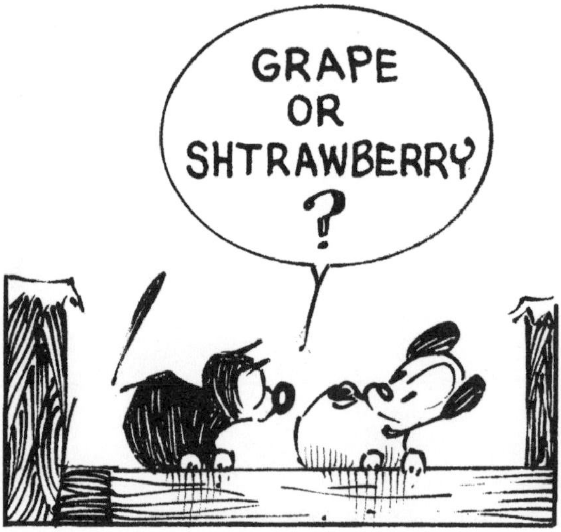
GRAPE OR SHTRAWBERRY ?

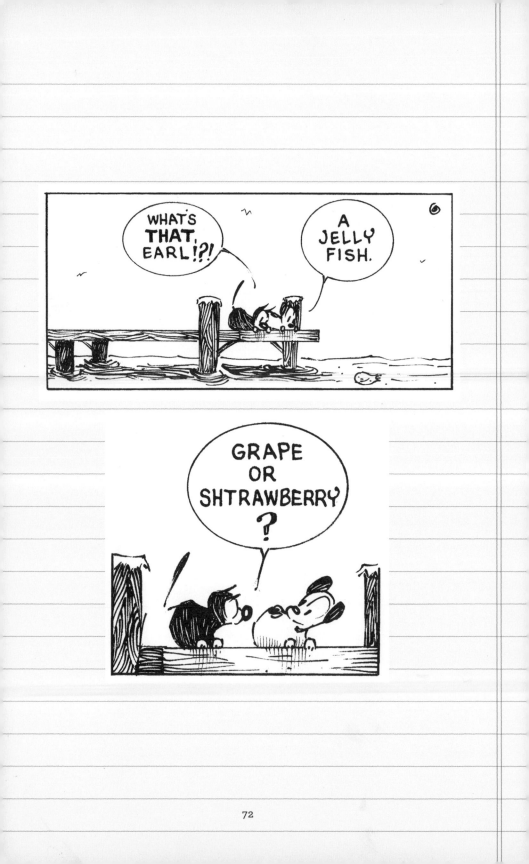

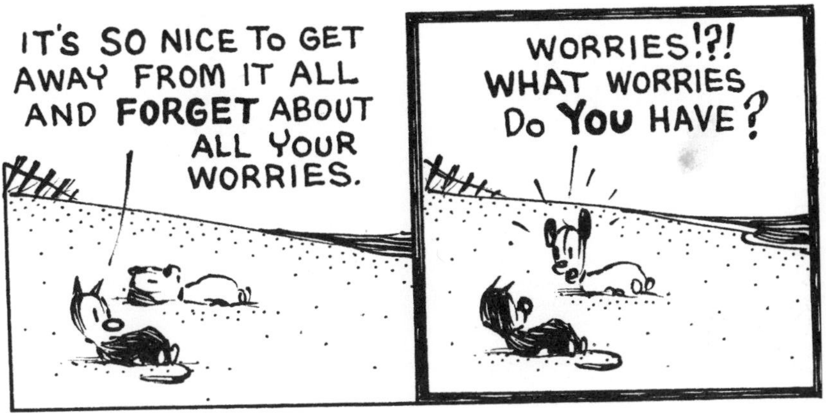
IT'S SO NICE TO GET AWAY FROM IT ALL AND FORGET ABOUT ALL YOUR WORRIES.
WORRIES!?! WHAT WORRIES DO YOU HAVE?

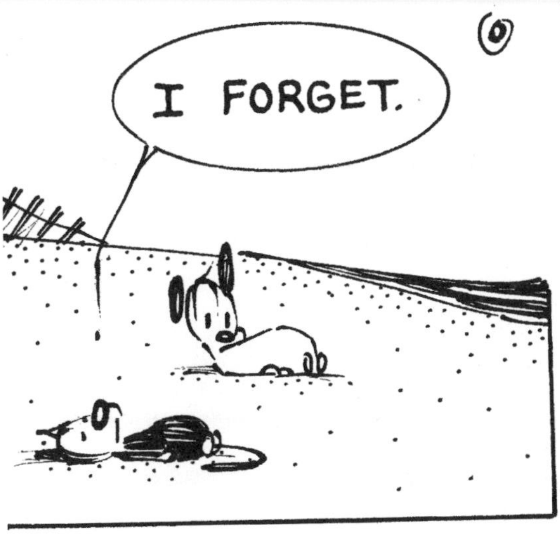
I FORGET.

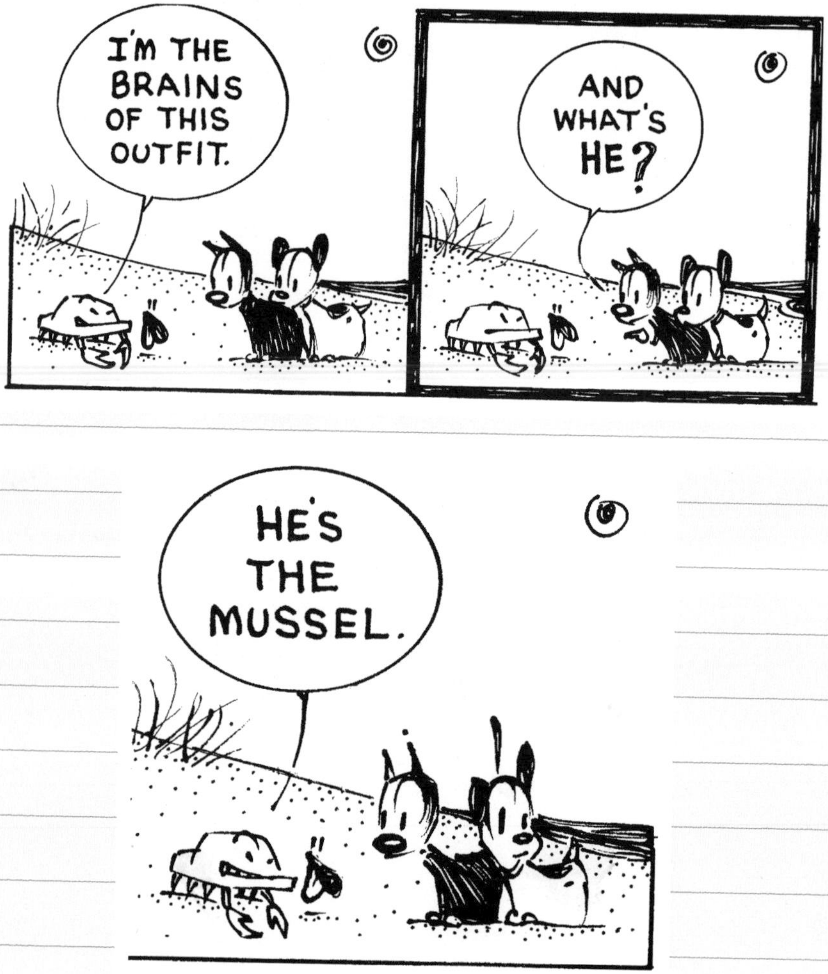
I'M THE BRAINS OF THIS OUTFIT.
AND WHAT'S HE?
HE'S THE MUSSEL.

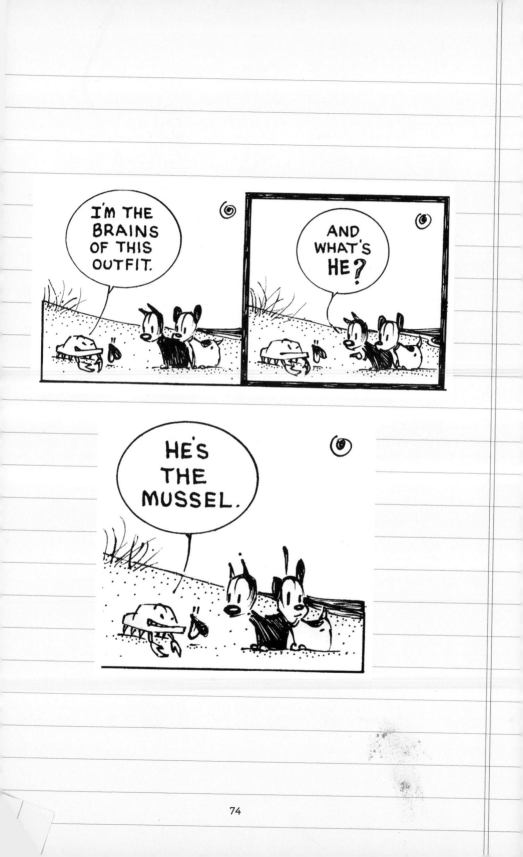

WATCH HIM WHAT?
WHALE WATCH

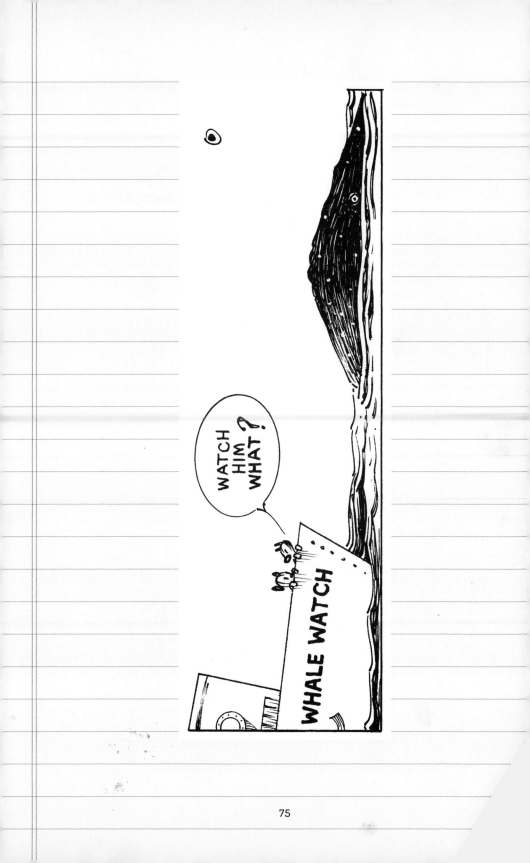

MUSSELS, DID I EVER TELL YOU ABOUT THE TIME I GOT HIT BY A...
...TSUNAMI!
I WAS TOSSED ABOUT FOR DAYS...
UNTIL I LANDED ON A BLUE PLATE SPECIAL OF LINGUINE AT "SAMMY'S HOUSE OF CLAMMIES" IN BELMAR, NEW JERSEY.
@☆✱$!
YIPES, CRABBY! HOW DID YOU ESCAPE THAT?
I LAY LOW IN THE NOODLES, THEN SNUCK OUT ON THE DESSERT TRAY.
GEE... THAT MUST HAVE BEEN SOME-THING!
TELL ME ABOUT IT.— THEIR @☆✱$! CHEESECAKE WAS TO DIE FOR.

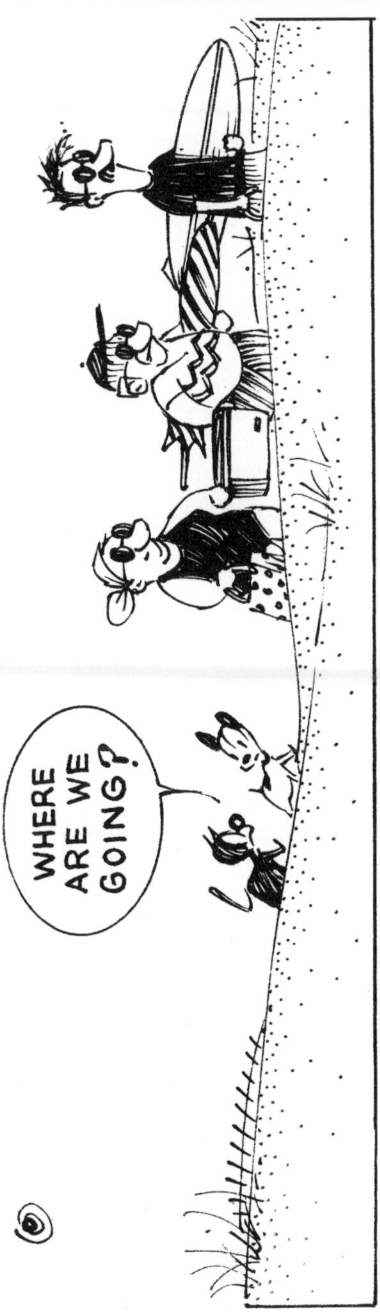
WHERE ARE WE GOING?

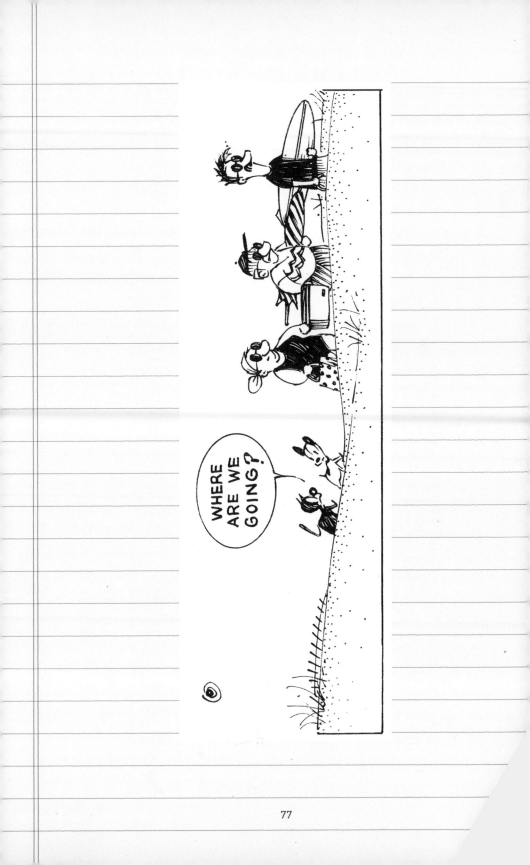

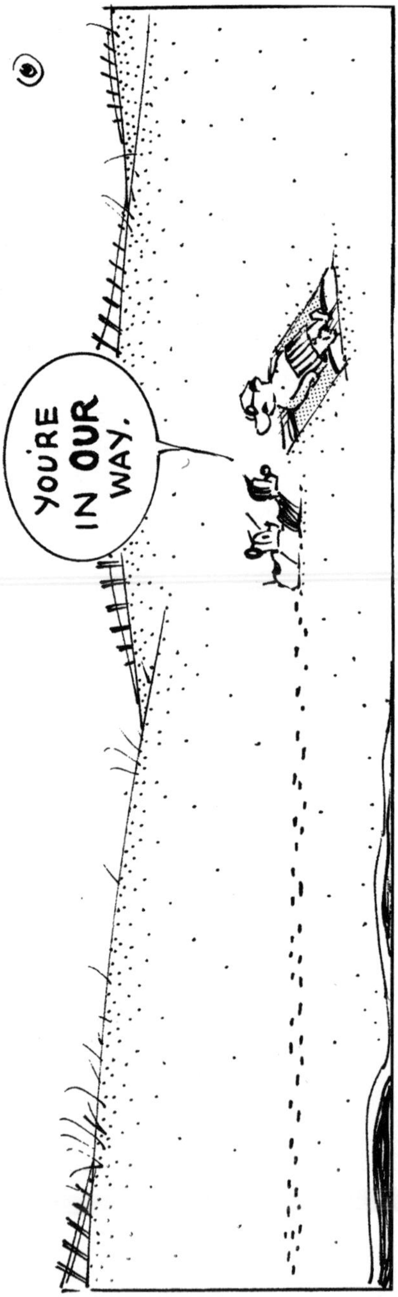
YOU'RE IN OUR WAY.

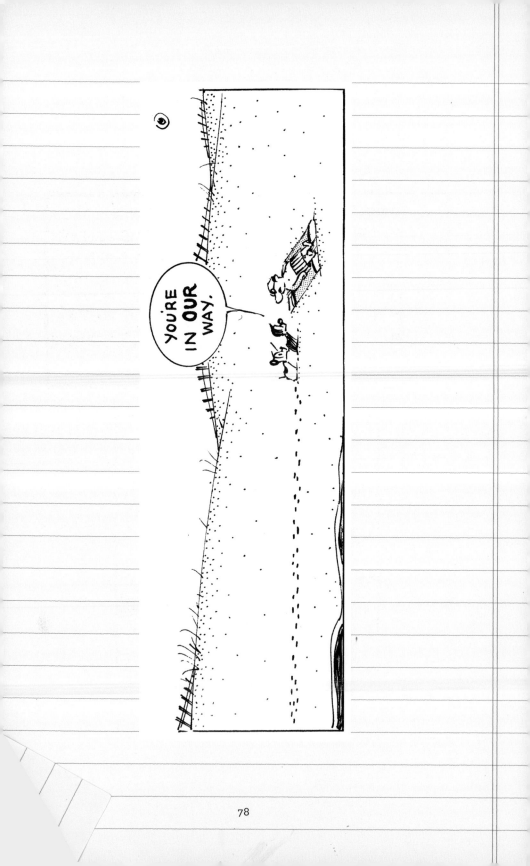

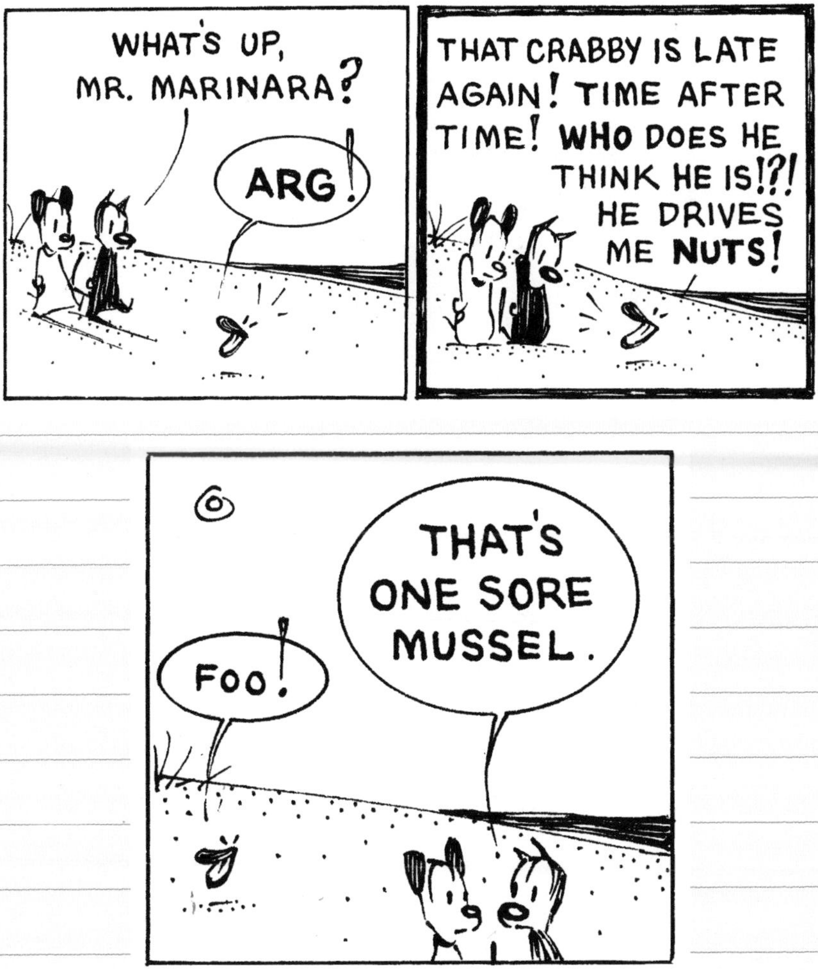
WHAT'S UP, MR. MARINARA?
ARG!
THAT CRABBY IS LATE AGAIN! TIME AFTER TIME! WHO DOES HE THINK HE IS!?! HE DRIVES ME NUTS!
FOO!
THAT'S ONE SORE MUSSEL.

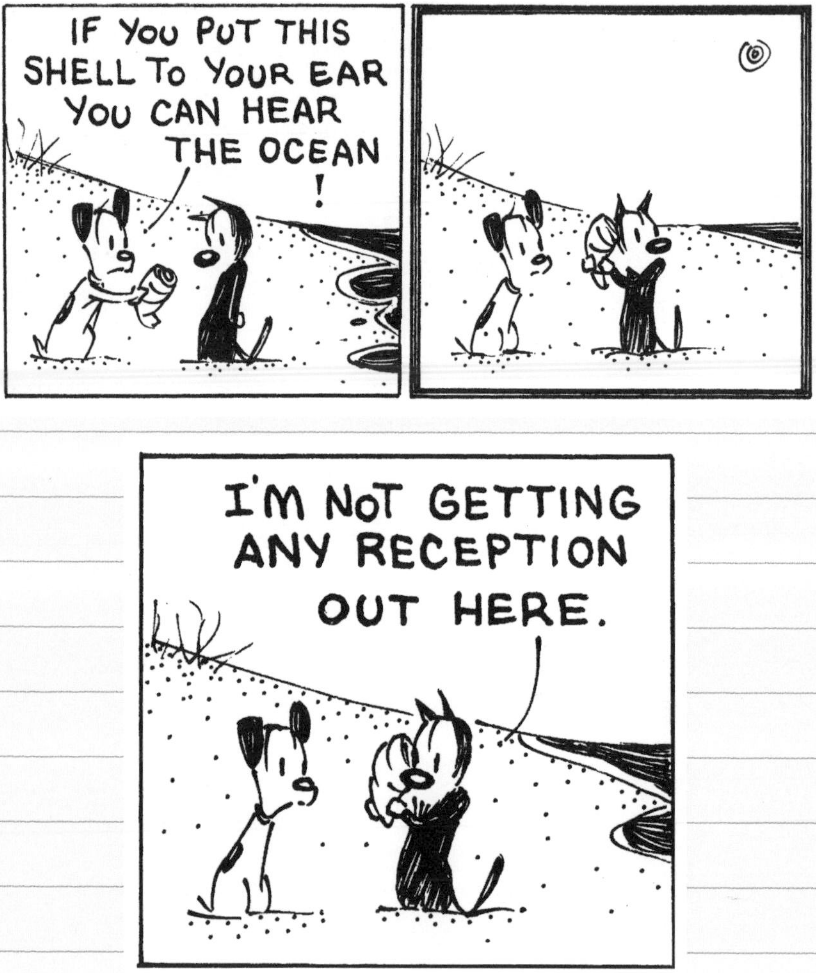
IF YOU PUT THIS SHELL TO YOUR EAR YOU CAN HEAR THE OCEAN
!
I'M NOT GETTING ANY RECEPTION OUT HERE.

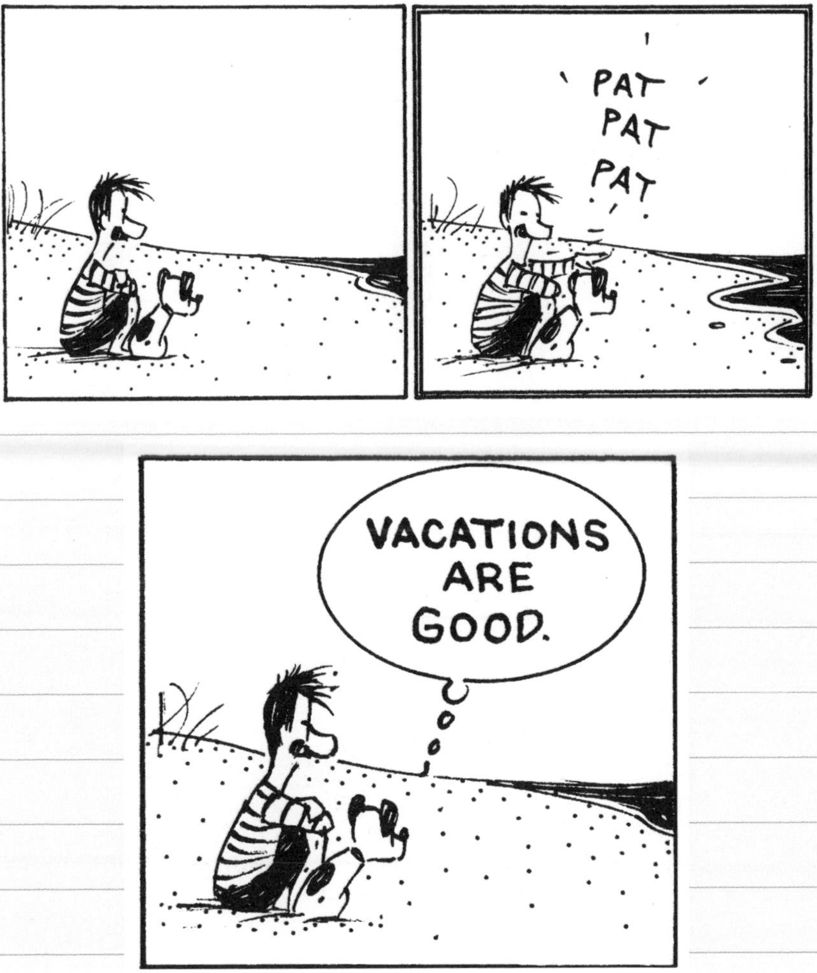
PAT
PAT
PAT
VACATIONS ARE GOOD.

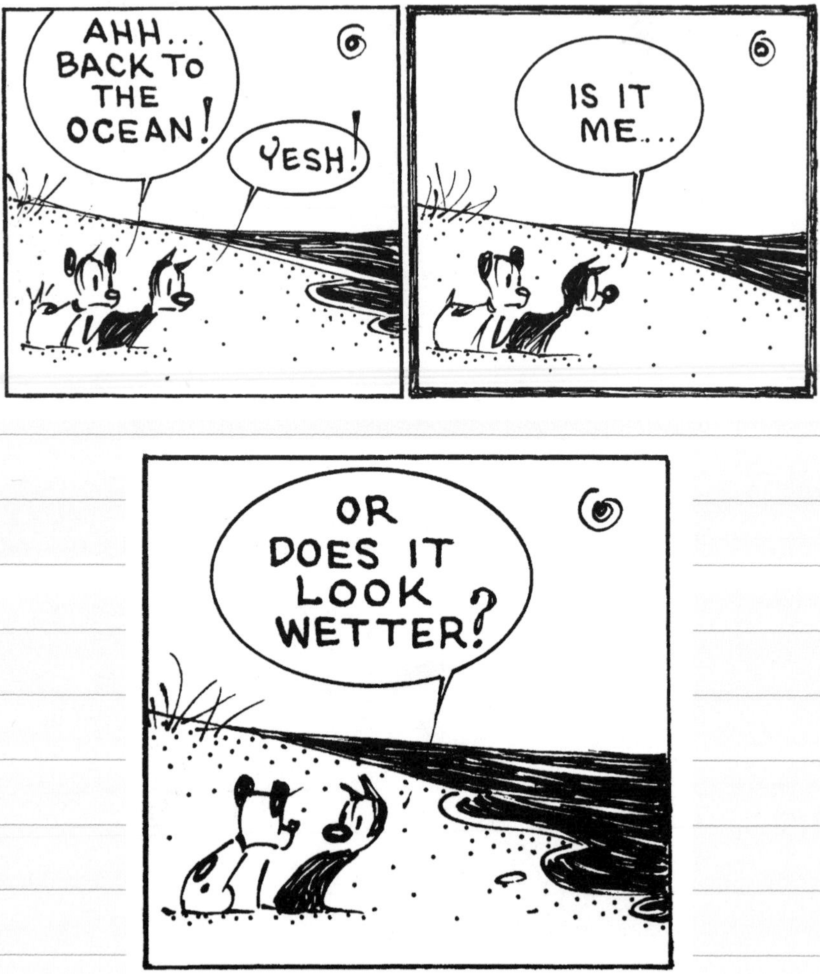
AHH... BACK TO THE OCEAN!
YESH!
IS IT ME...
OR DOES IT LOOK WETTER?

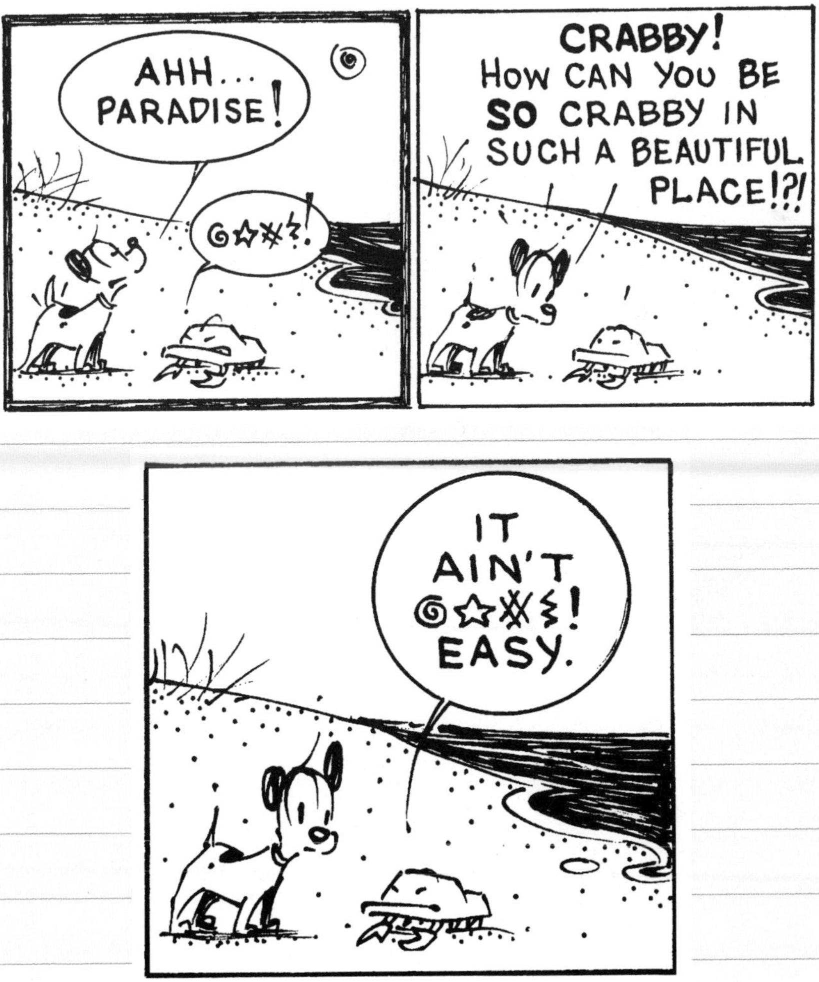
AHH... PARADISE!
@☆#$!
CRABBY! HOW CAN YOU BE SO CRABBY IN SUCH A BEAUTIFUL PLACE!?!
IT AIN'T @☆#$! EASY.

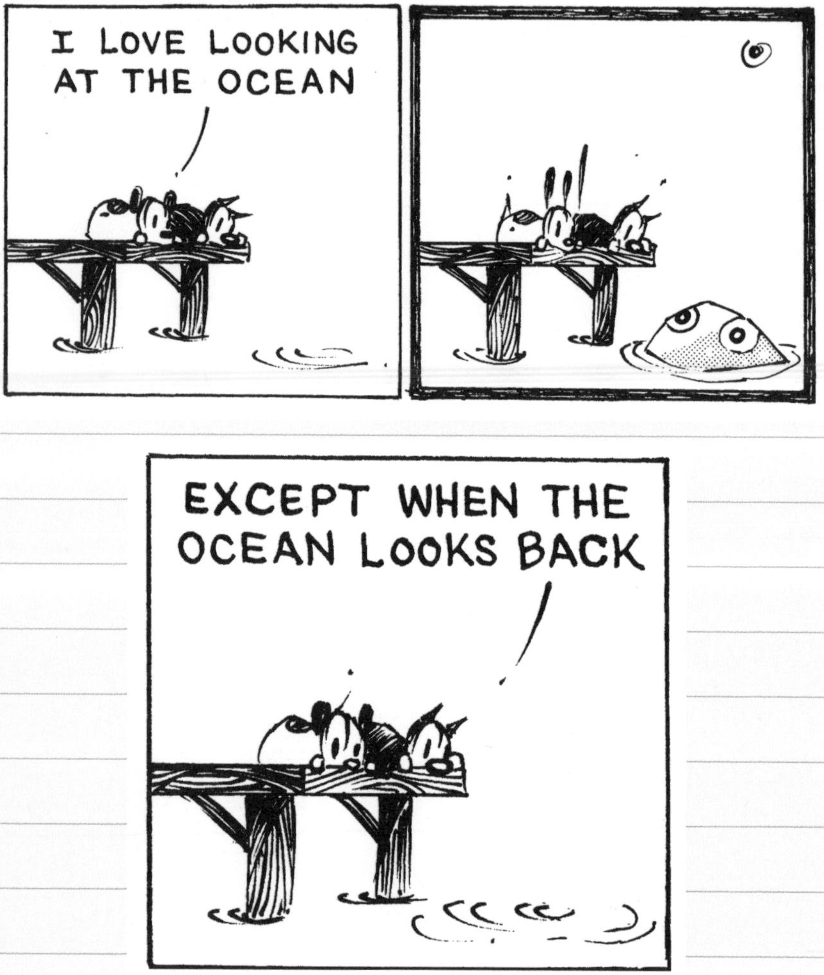
I LOVE LOOKING AT THE OCEAN
EXCEPT WHEN THE OCEAN LOOKS BACK

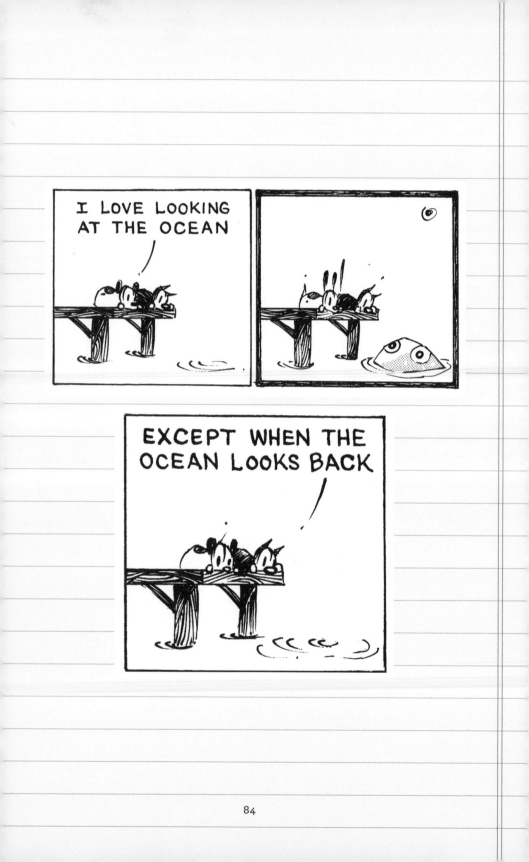

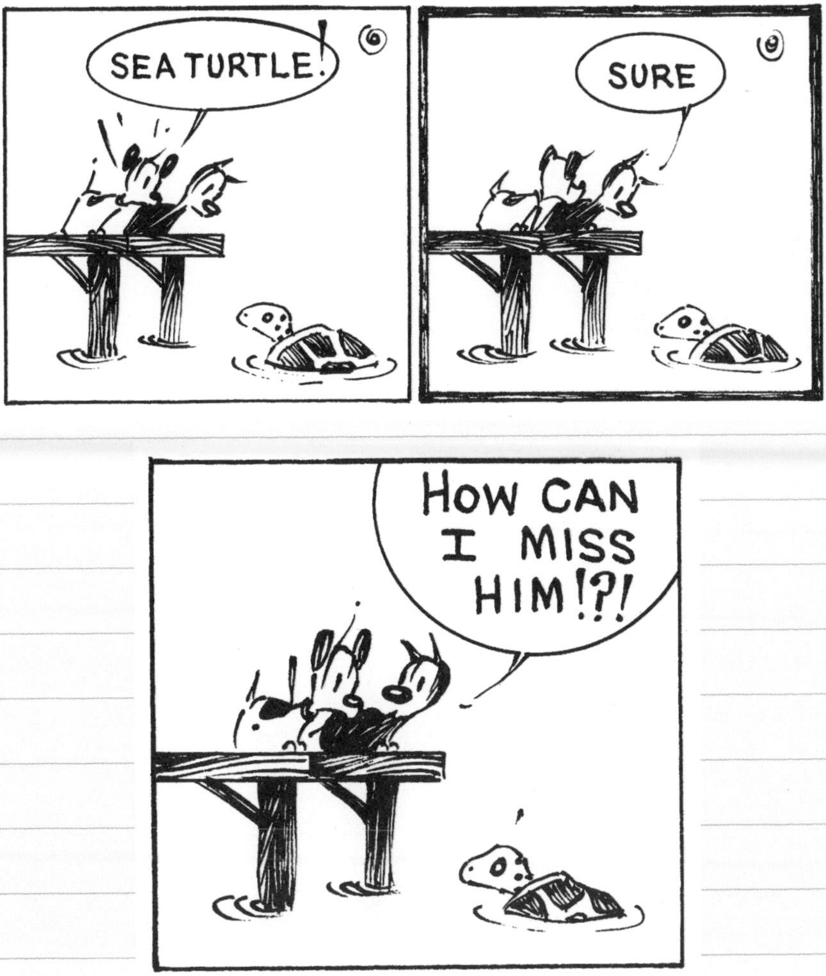
SEA TURTLE!
SURE
HOW CAN I MISS HIM!?!

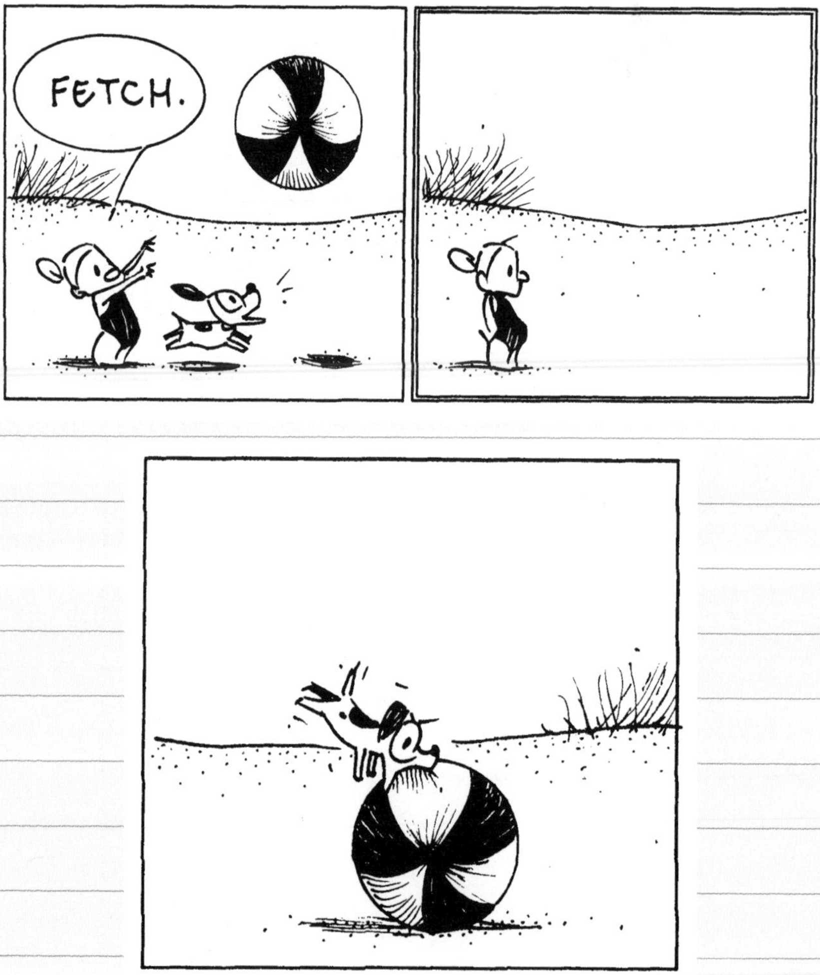
FETCH.

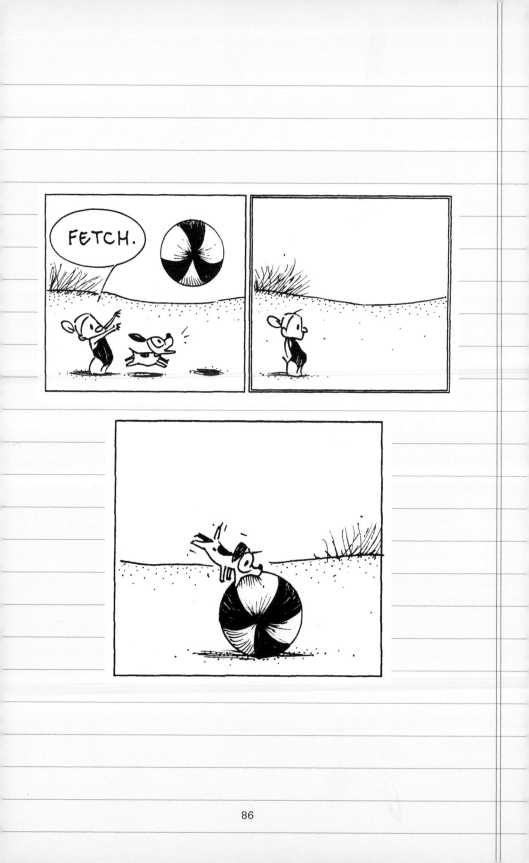

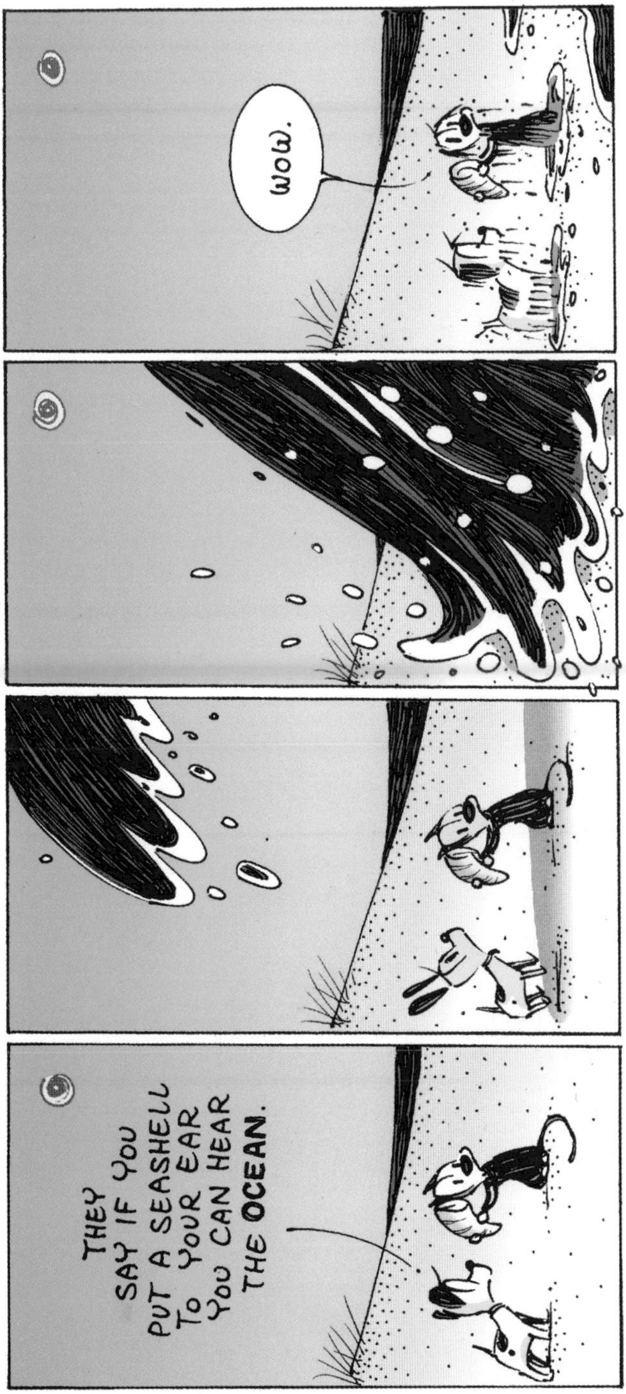

THEY SAY IF YOU PUT A SEASHELL TO YOUR EAR YOU CAN HEAR THE **OCEAN**.
WOW.

Mutts

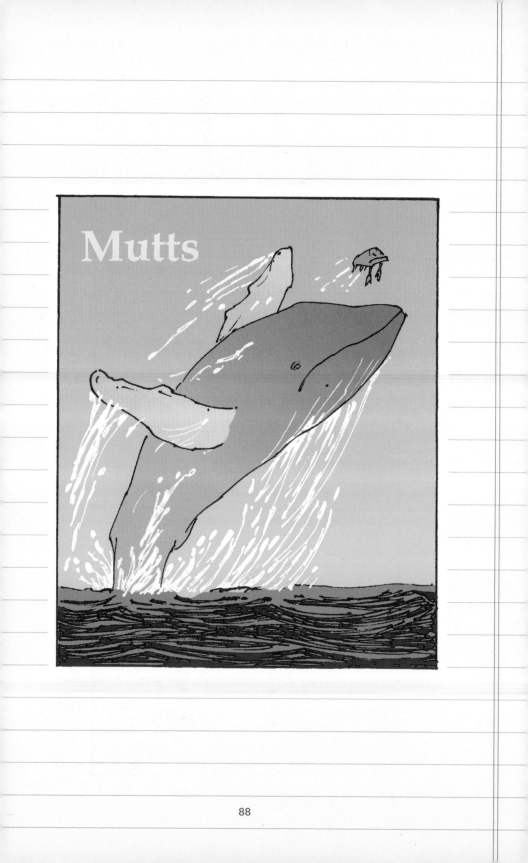

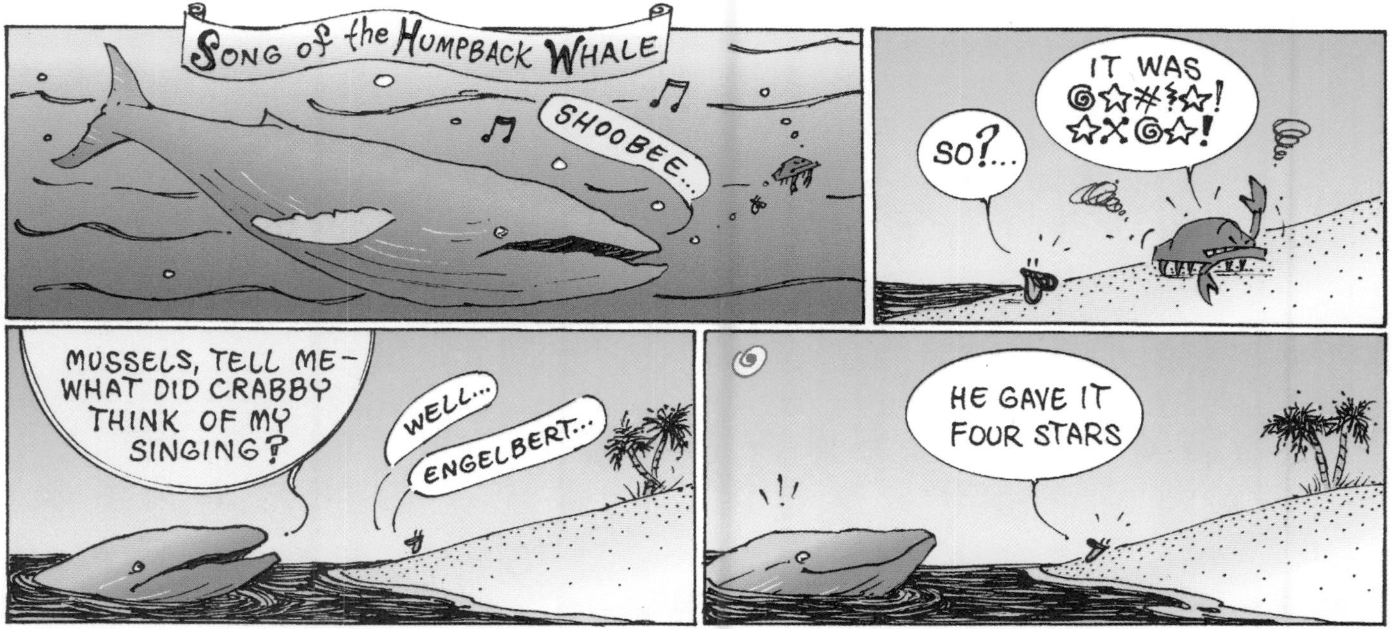
SONG of the HUMPBACK WHALE
SHOOBEE...
SO?...
IT WAS ◎☆#☆! ☆✕◎☆!
MUSSELS, TELL ME– WHAT DID CRABBY THINK OF MY SINGING?
WELL...
ENGELBERT...
HE GAVE IT FOUR STARS

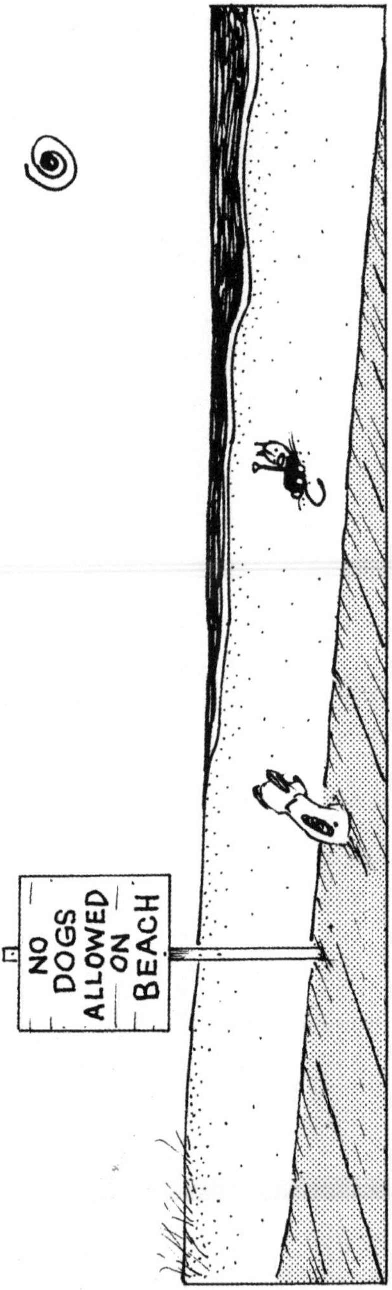
NO
DOGS
ALLOWED
ON
BEACH

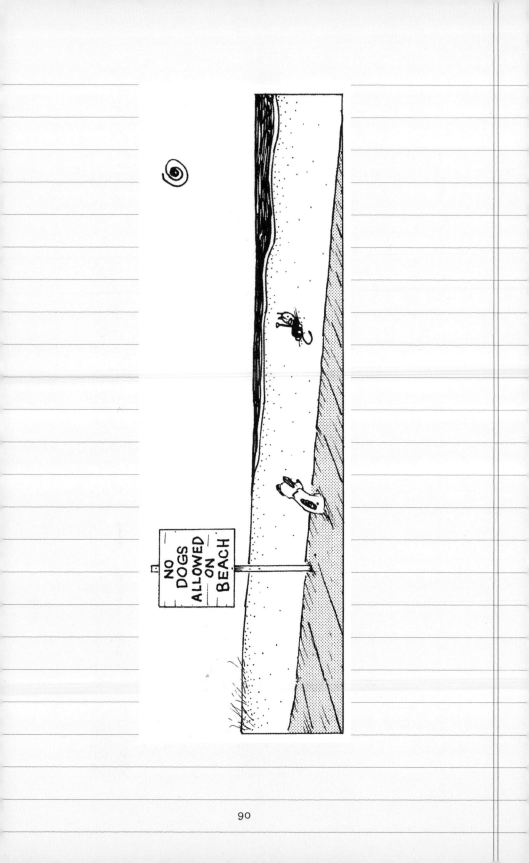

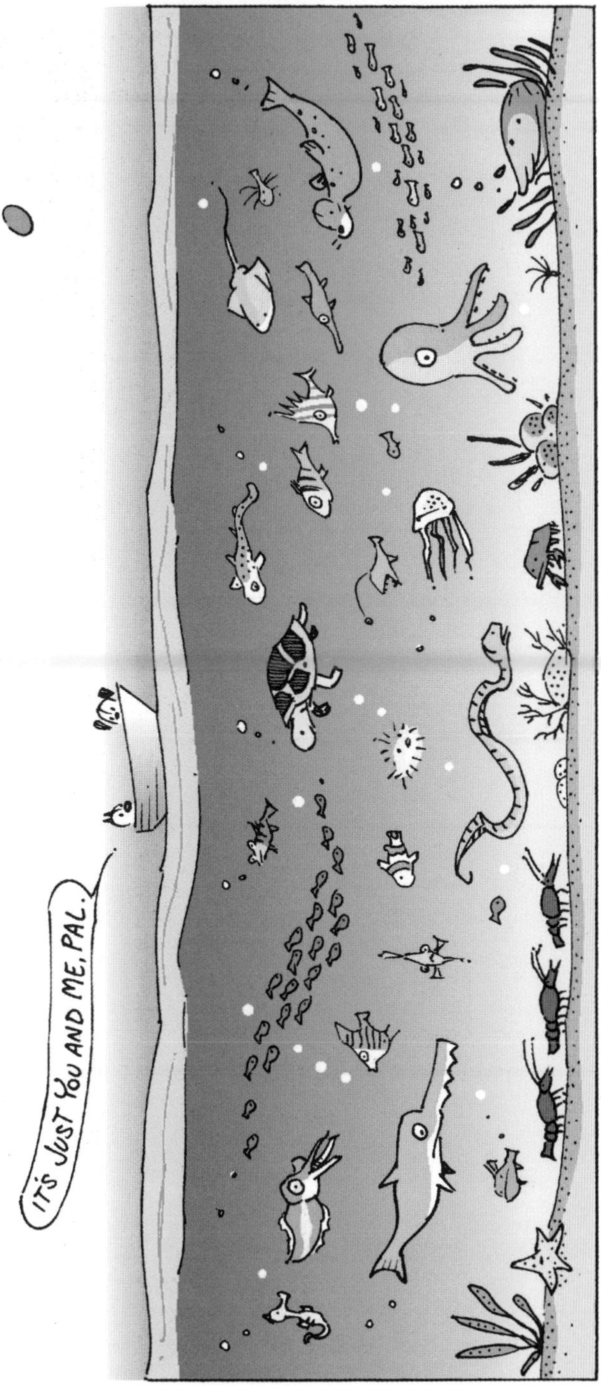
IT'S JUST YOU AND ME, PAL.

HEY! YOU'RE BLOCKING THE VIEW!

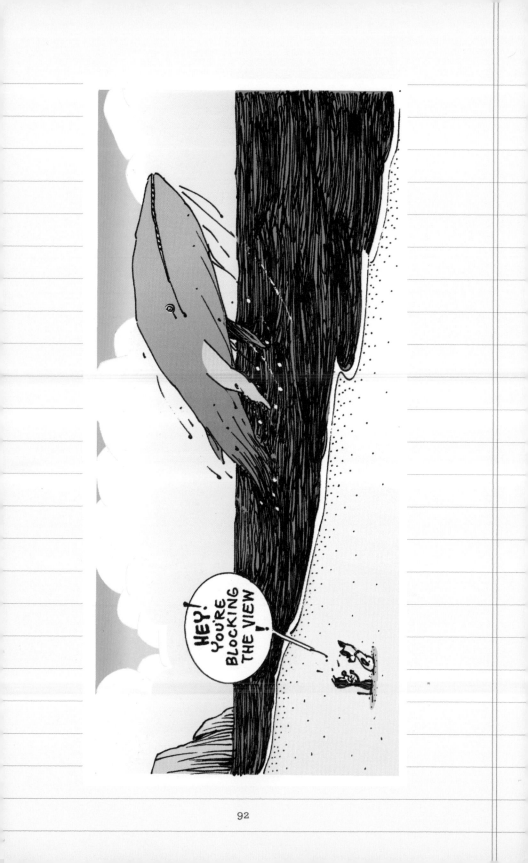

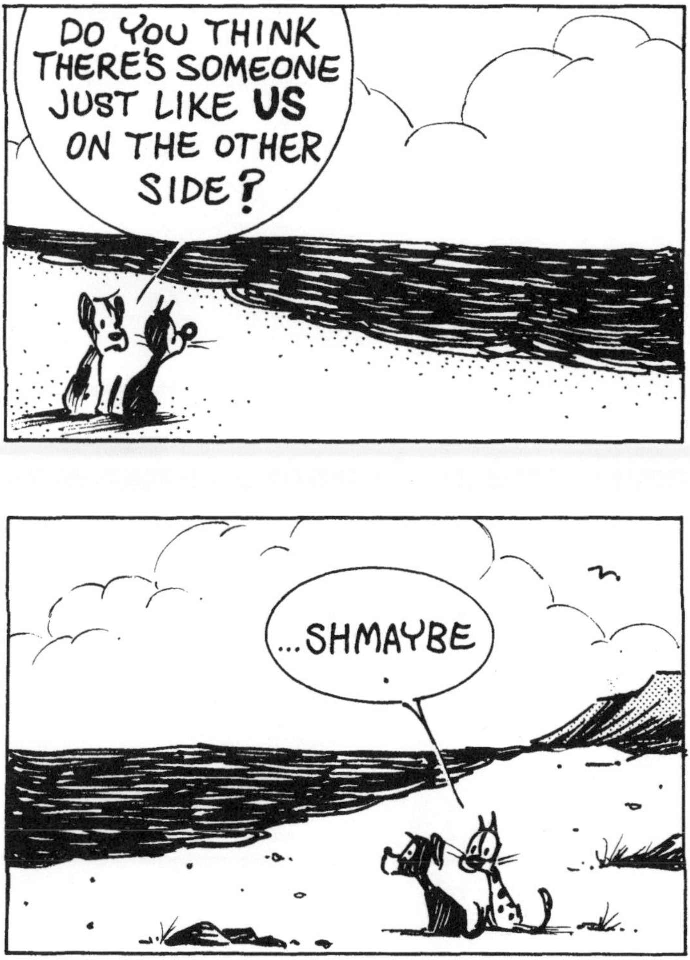
DO YOU THINK THERE'S SOMEONE JUST LIKE **US** ON THE OTHER SIDE?
...SHMAYBE

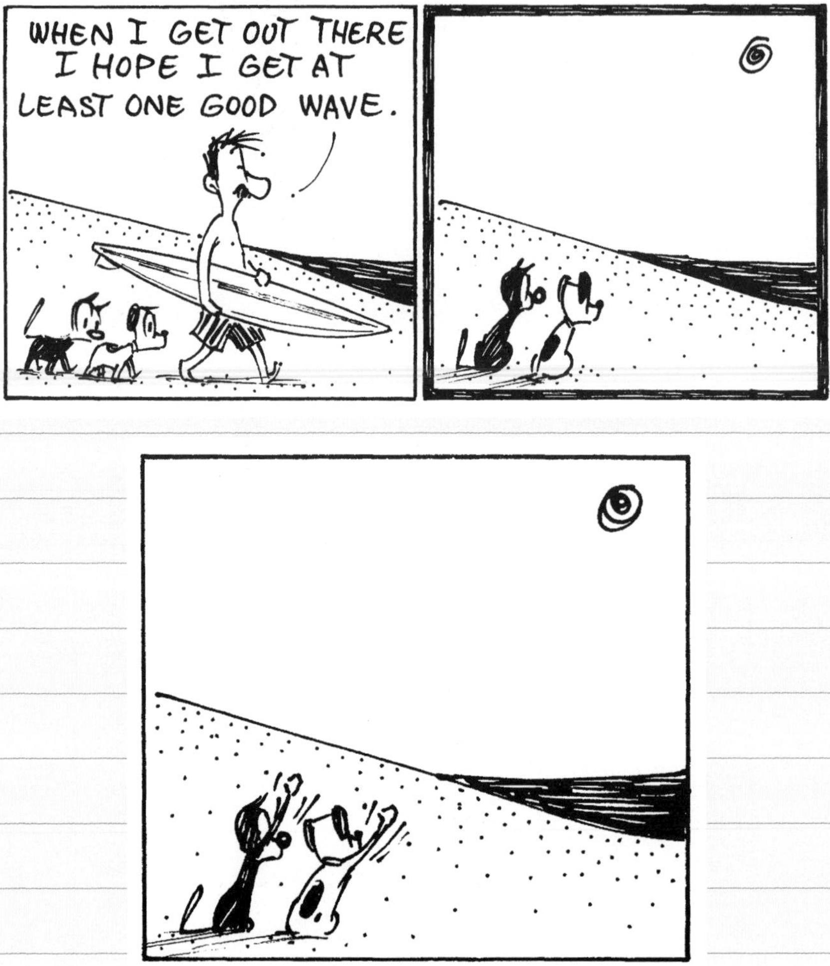
WHEN I GET OUT THERE I HOPE I GET AT LEAST ONE GOOD WAVE.

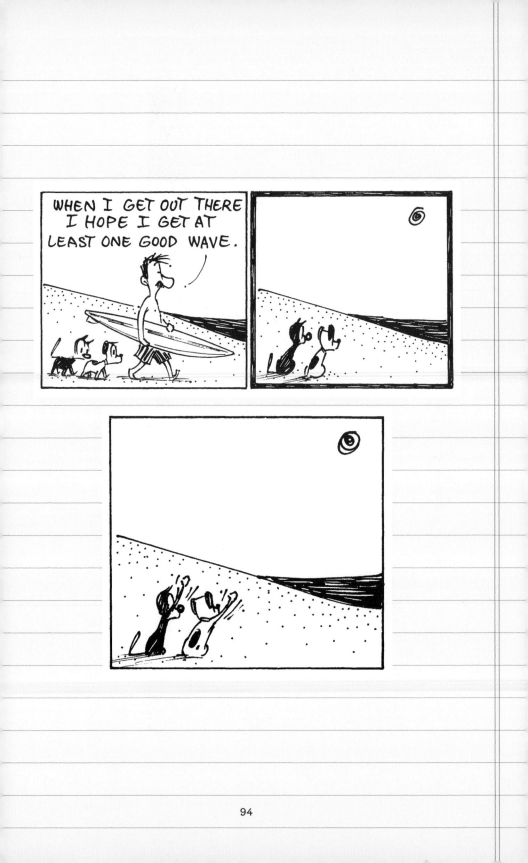

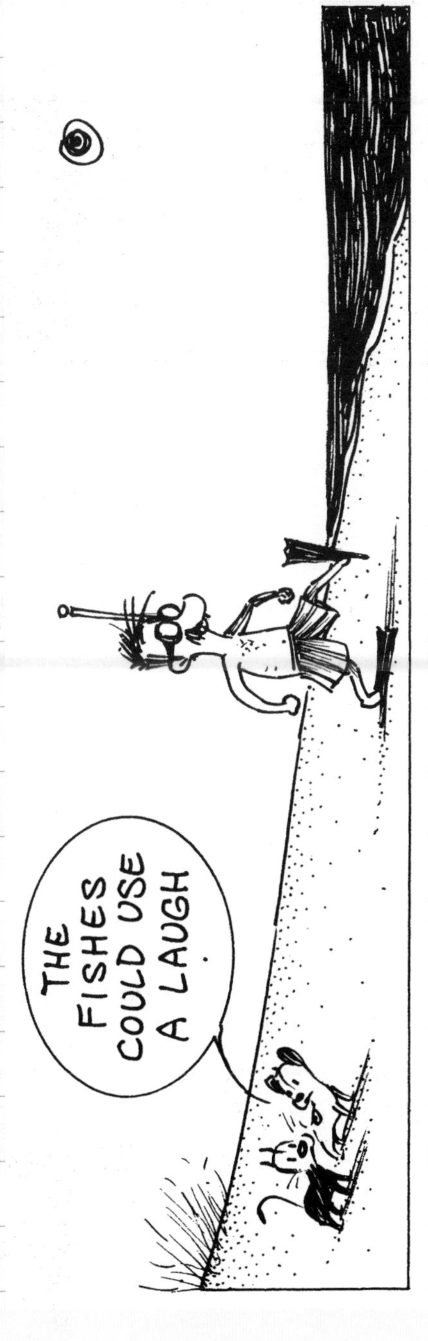
THE FISHES COULD USE A LAUGH.

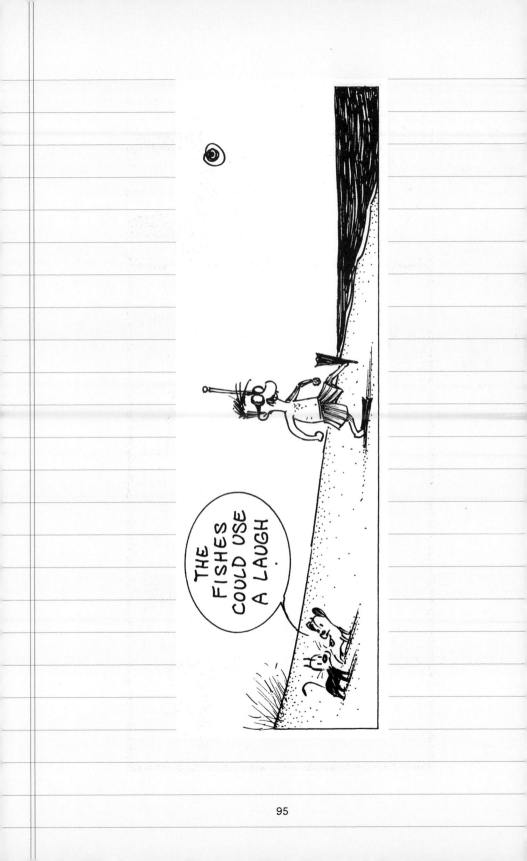

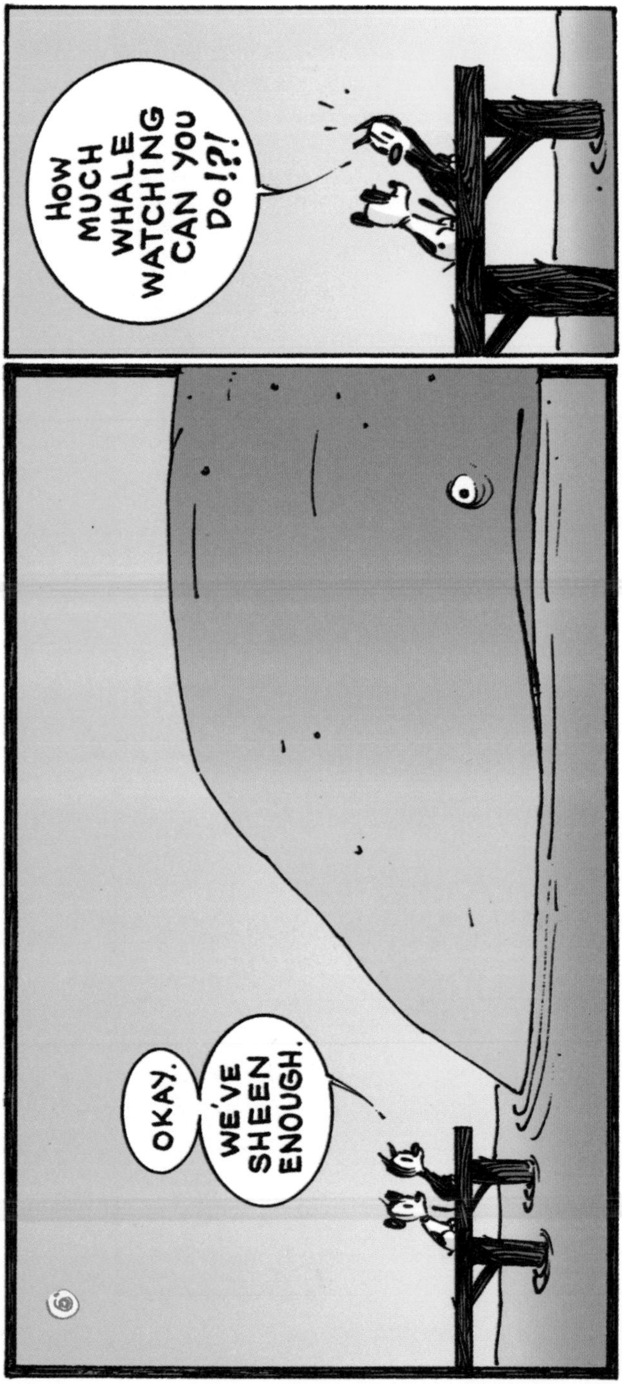
OKAY,
WE'VE SHEEN ENOUGH.
HOW MUCH WHALE WATCHING CAN YOU DO!?!

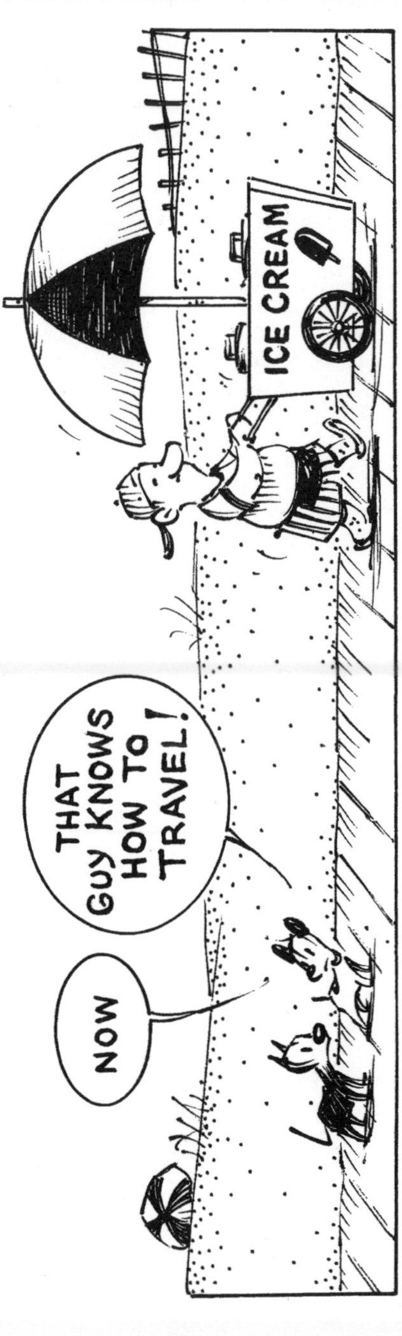
NOW
THAT GUY KNOWS HOW TO TRAVEL!
ICE CREAM

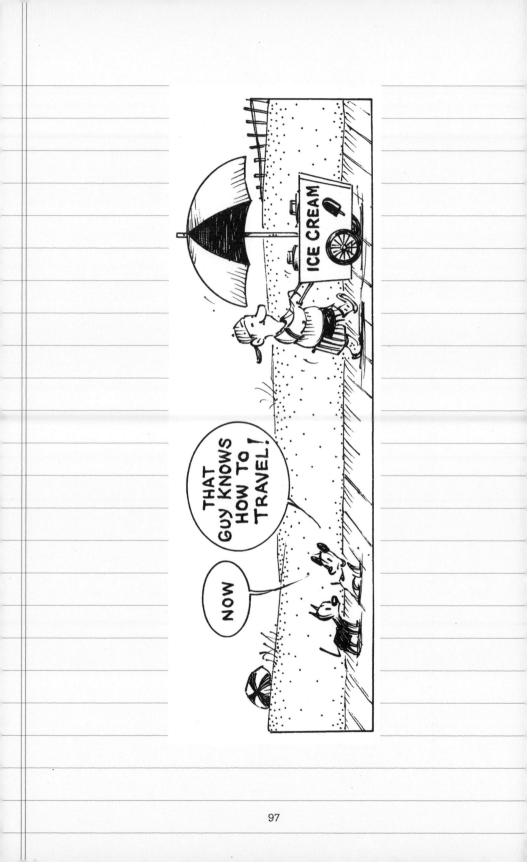

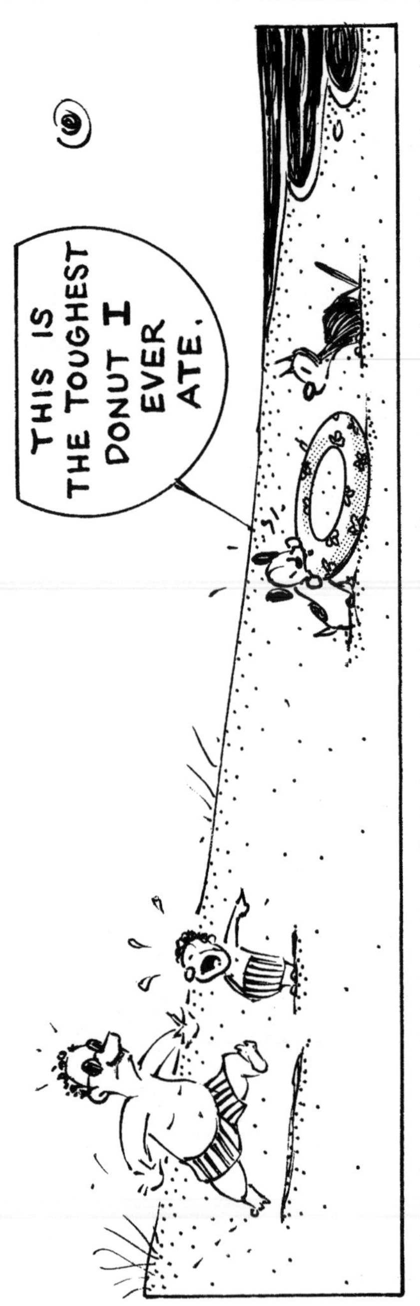
THIS IS THE TOUGHEST DONUT I EVER ATE.

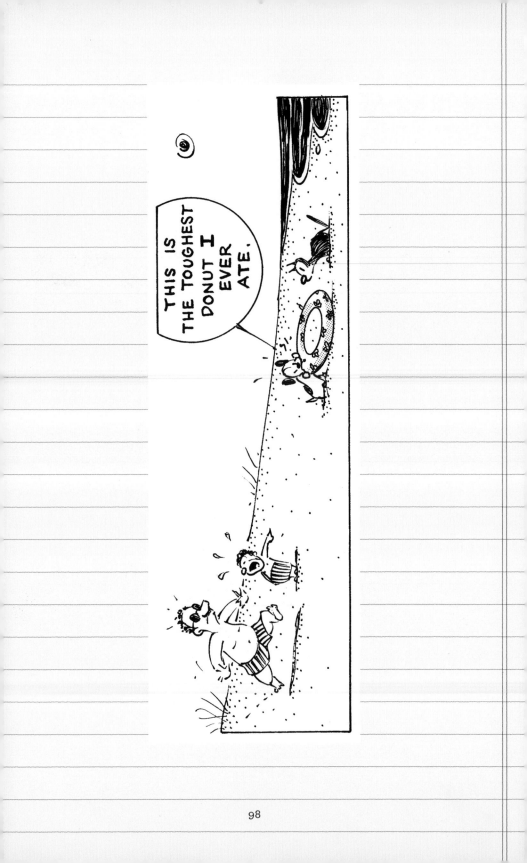

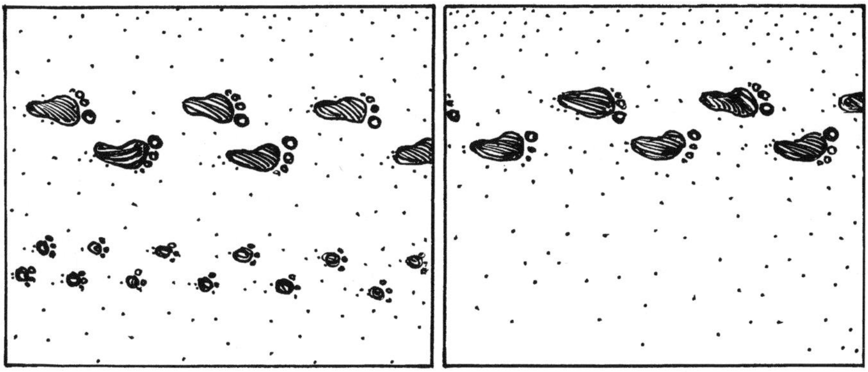

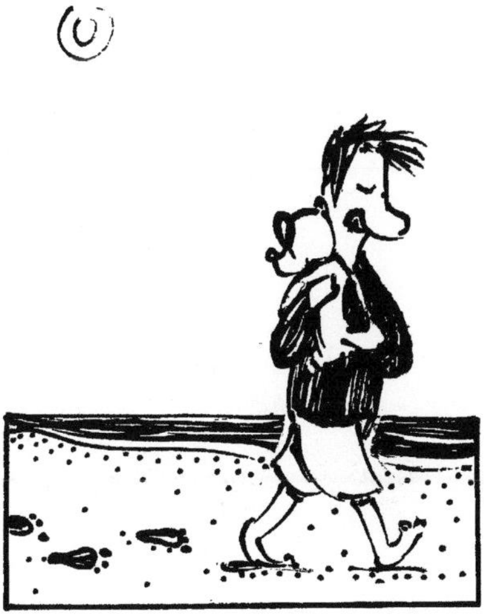

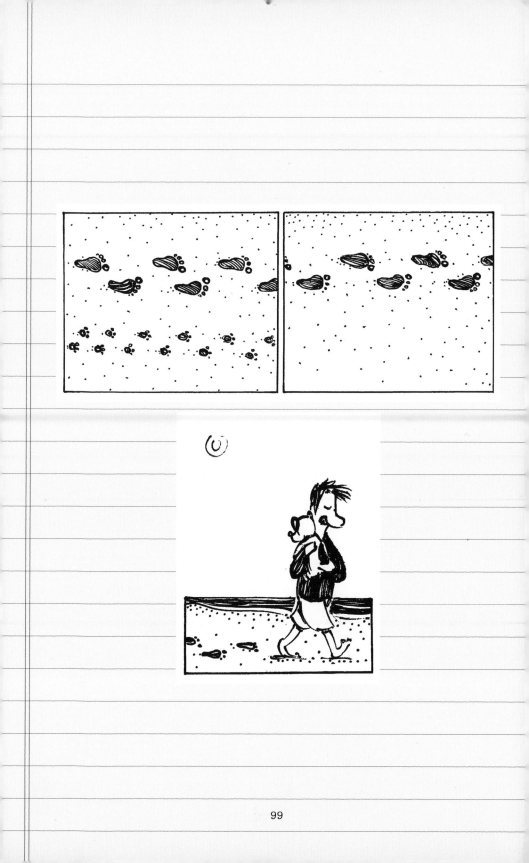

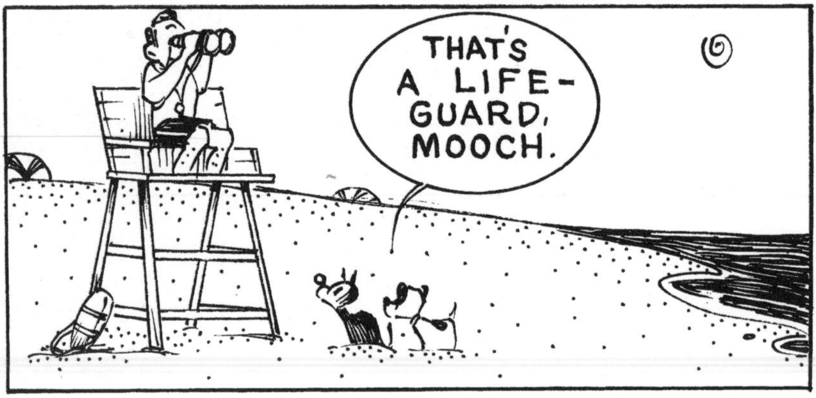
THAT'S A LIFE-GUARD, MOOCH.

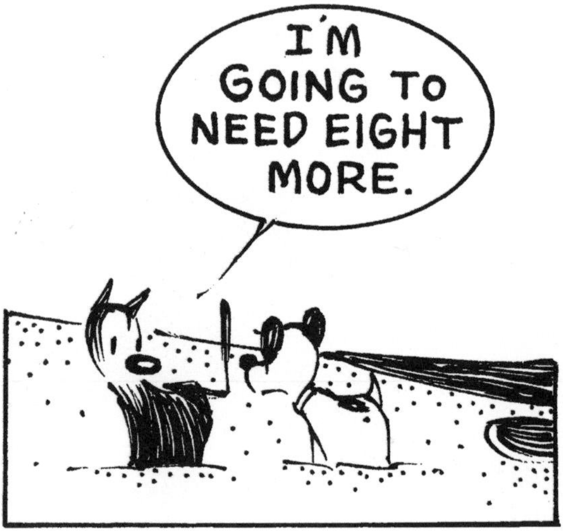
I'M GOING TO NEED EIGHT MORE.

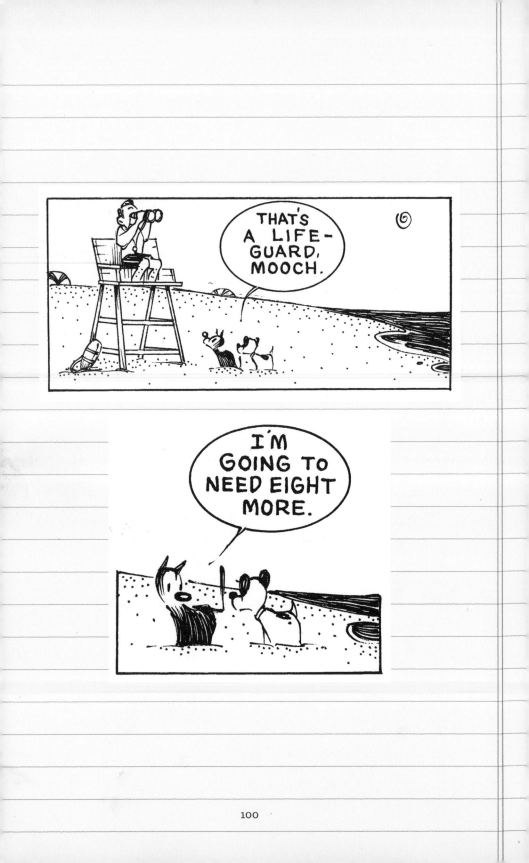

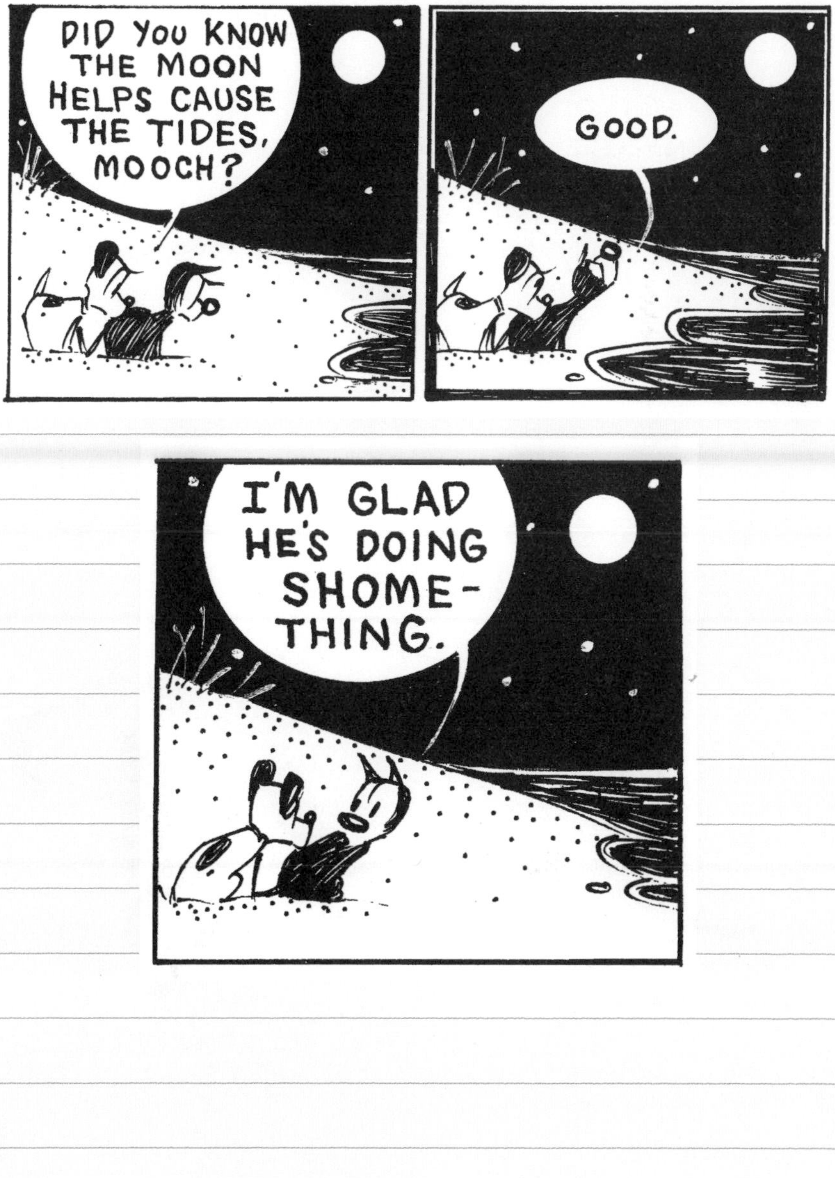
DID YOU KNOW THE MOON HELPS CAUSE THE TIDES, MOOCH?
GOOD.
I'M GLAD HE'S DOING SHOME-THING.

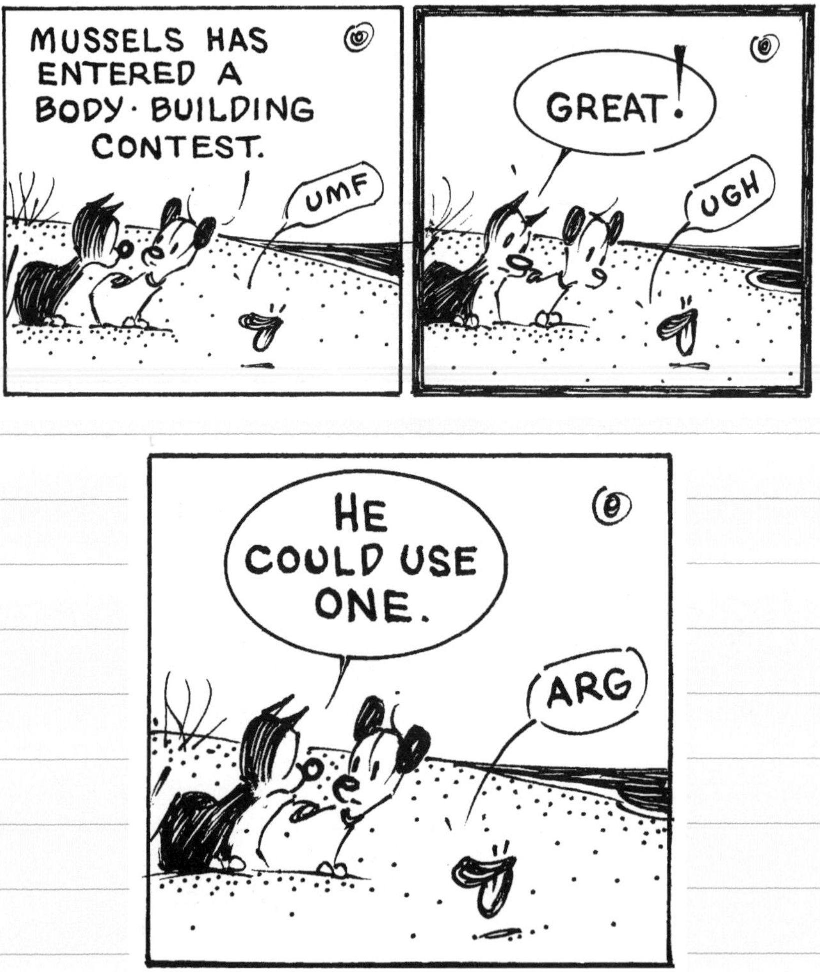
MUSSELS HAS ENTERED A BODY-BUILDING CONTEST.
UMF
GREAT!
UGH
HE COULD USE ONE.
ARG

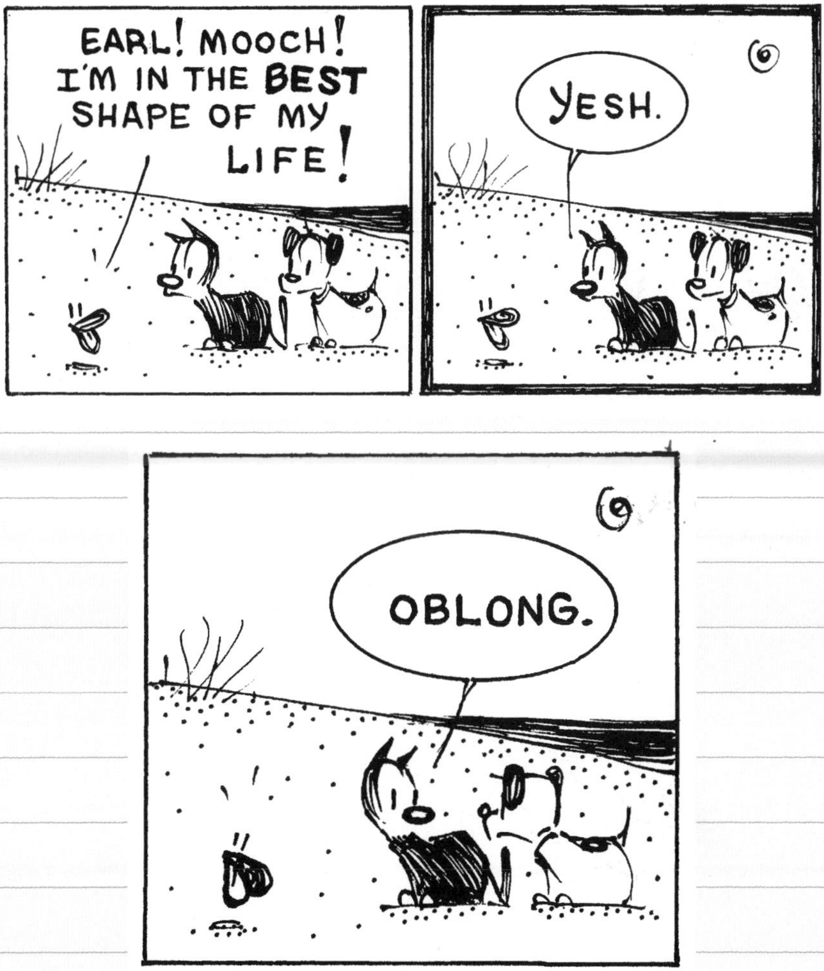
EARL! MOOCH! I'M IN THE BEST SHAPE OF MY LIFE!
YESH.
OBLONG.

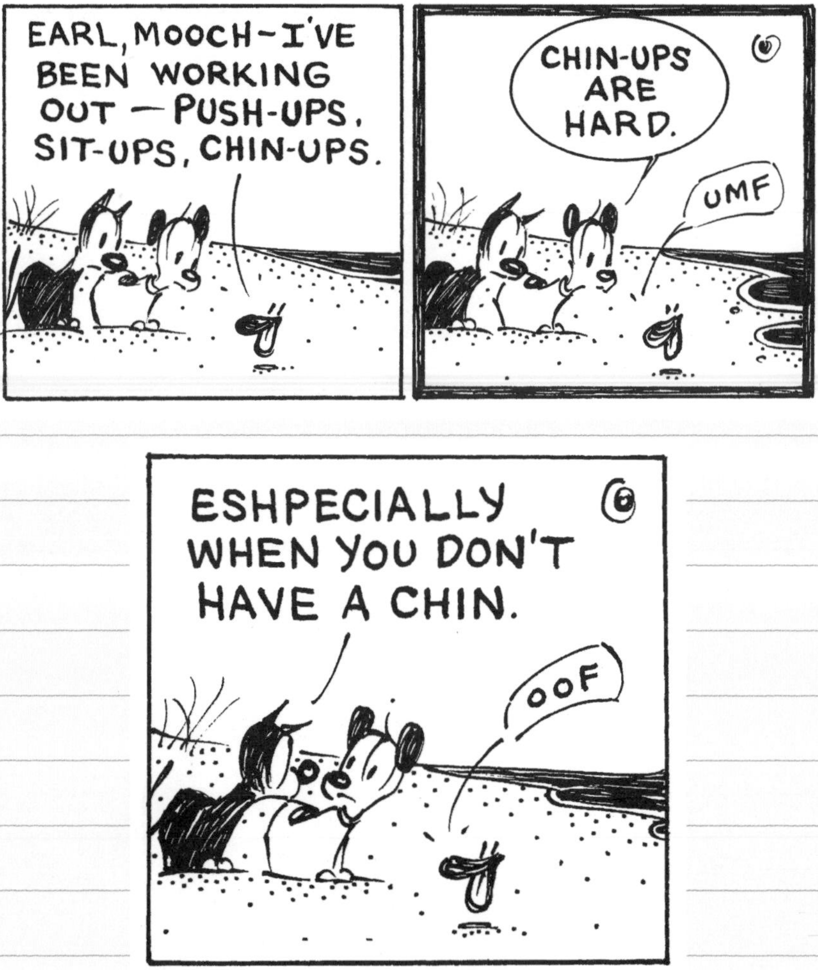
EARL, MOOCH - I'VE BEEN WORKING OUT — PUSH-UPS, SIT-UPS, CHIN-UPS.
CHIN-UPS ARE HARD.
UMF
ESHPECIALLY WHEN YOU DON'T HAVE A CHIN.
OOF

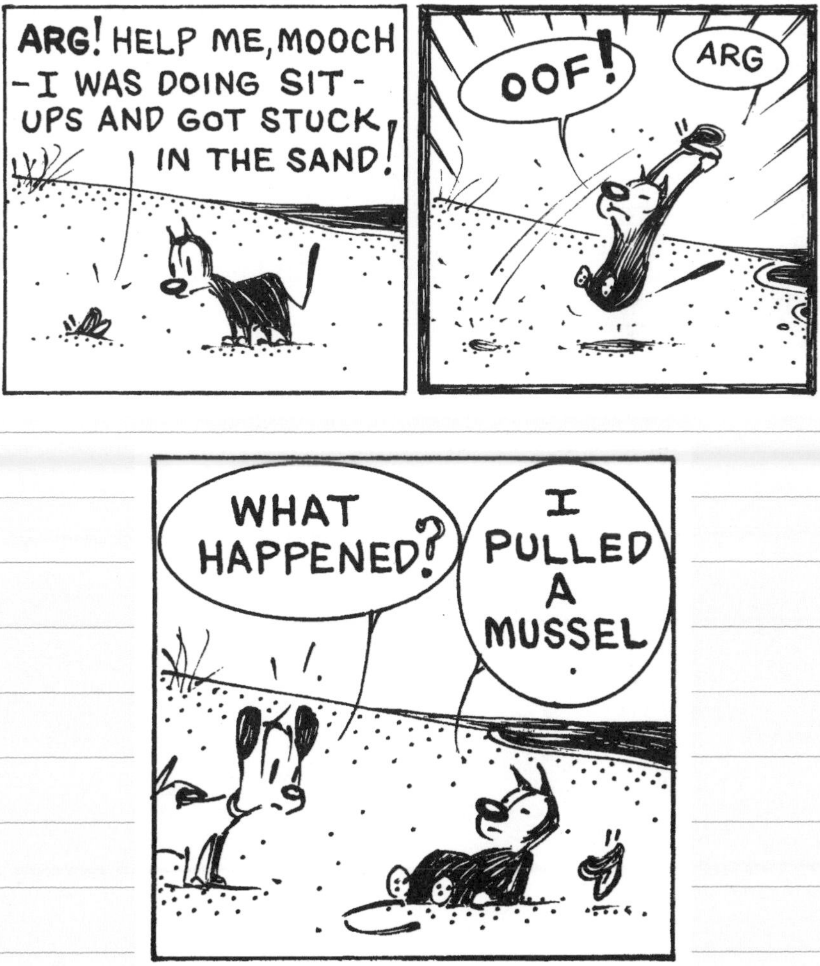
ARG! HELP ME, MOOCH -I WAS DOING SIT-UPS AND GOT STUCK IN THE SAND!
OOF!
ARG
WHAT HAPPENED?
I PULLED A MUSSEL.

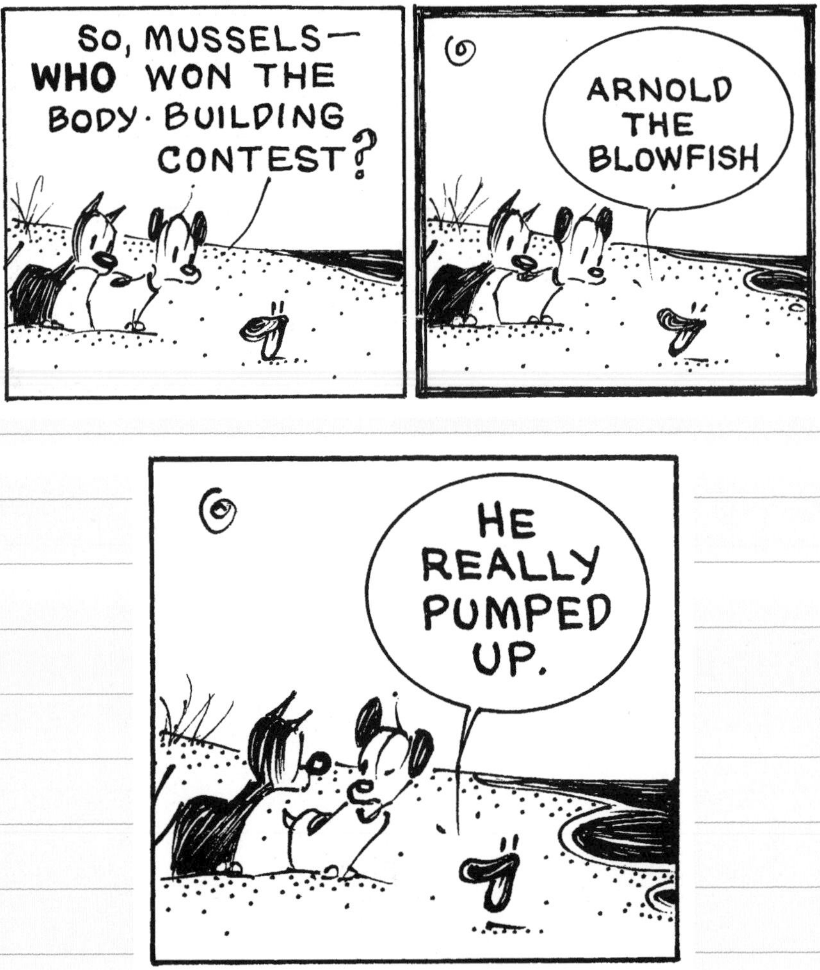
So, MUSSELS— WHO WON THE BODY-BUILDING CONTEST?
ARNOLD THE BLOWFISH
HE REALLY PUMPED UP.

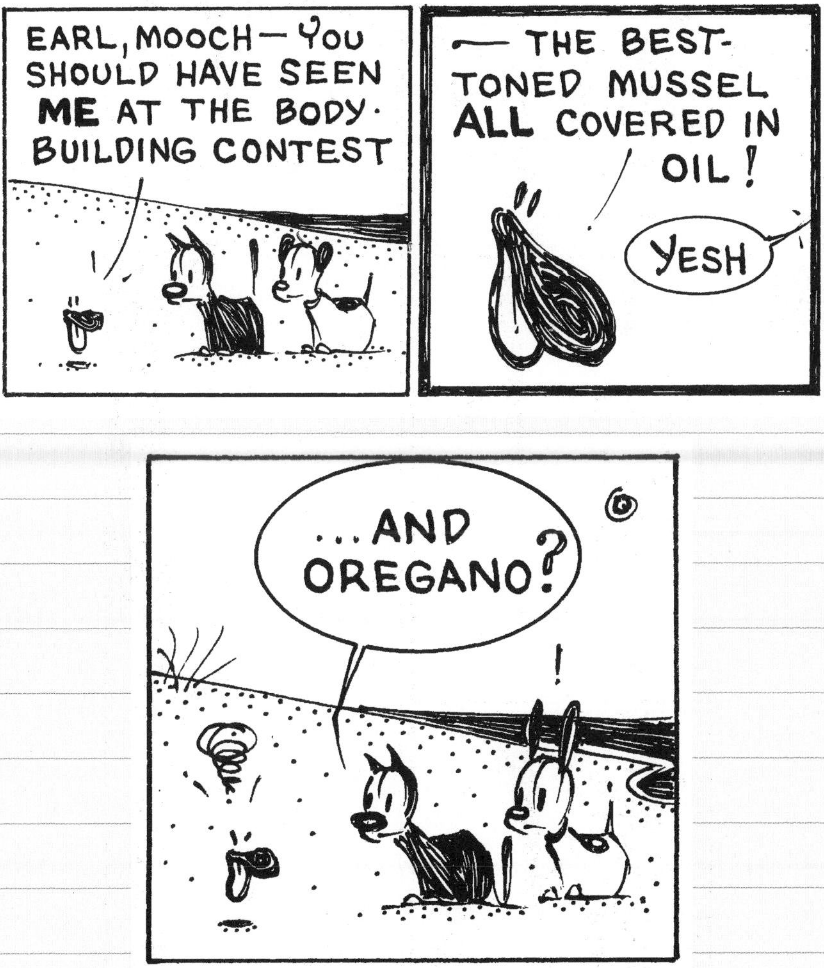
EARL, MOOCH— YOU SHOULD HAVE SEEN **ME** AT THE BODY-BUILDING CONTEST
— THE BEST-TONED MUSSEL **ALL** COVERED IN OIL!
YESH
...AND OREGANO?

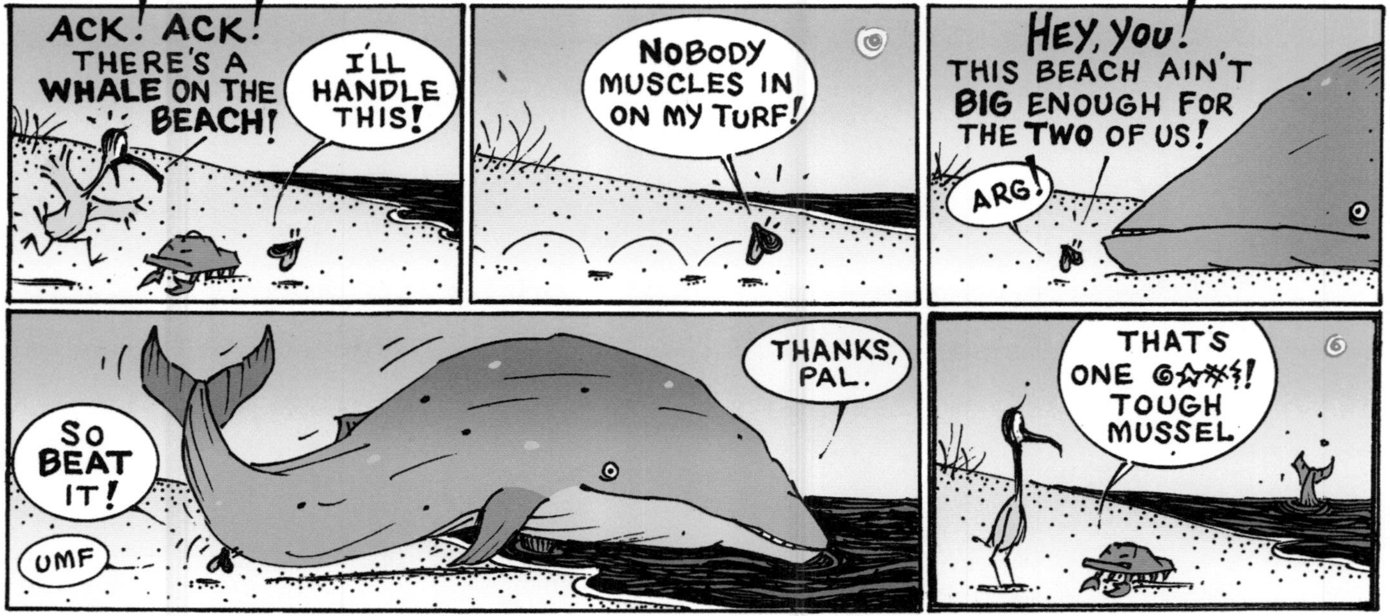
ACK! ACK! THERE'S A WHALE ON THE BEACH!
I'LL HANDLE THIS!
NOBODY MUSCLES IN ON MY TURF!
HEY, YOU! THIS BEACH AIN'T BIG ENOUGH FOR THE TWO OF US!
ARG!
SO BEAT IT!
UMF
THANKS, PAL.
THAT'S ONE @☆#*! TOUGH MUSSEL.

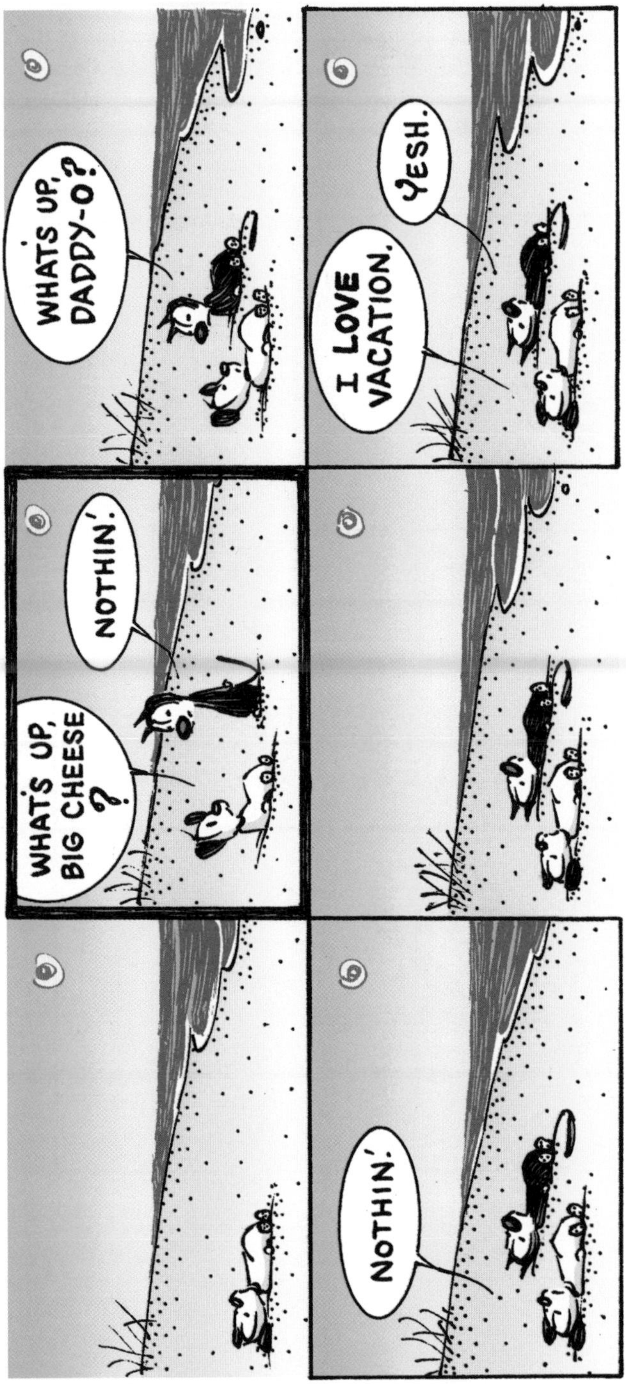

WHAT'S UP, BIG CHEESE?
NOTHIN'.
WHAT'S UP, DADDY-O?
NOTHIN'.
I LOVE VACATION.
YESH.

SQUEEP
WEEEOX
KEE·KAK
I SHPEAK FLUENT DOLPHIN.

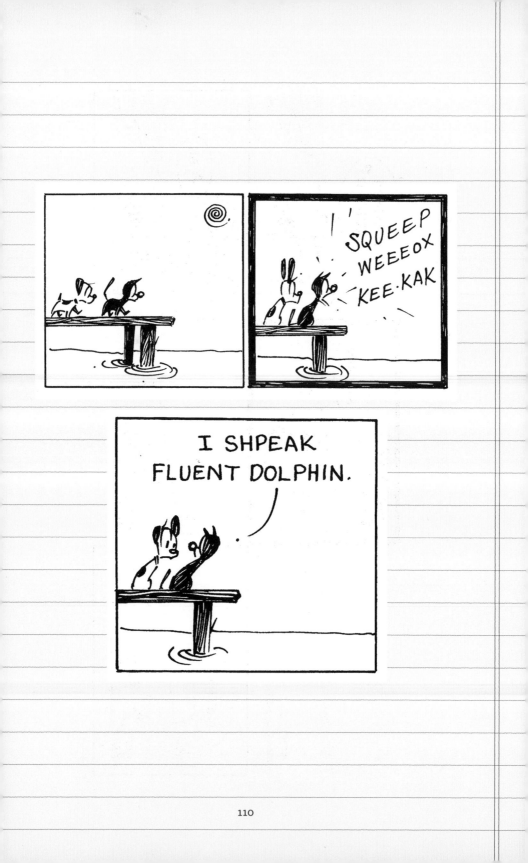

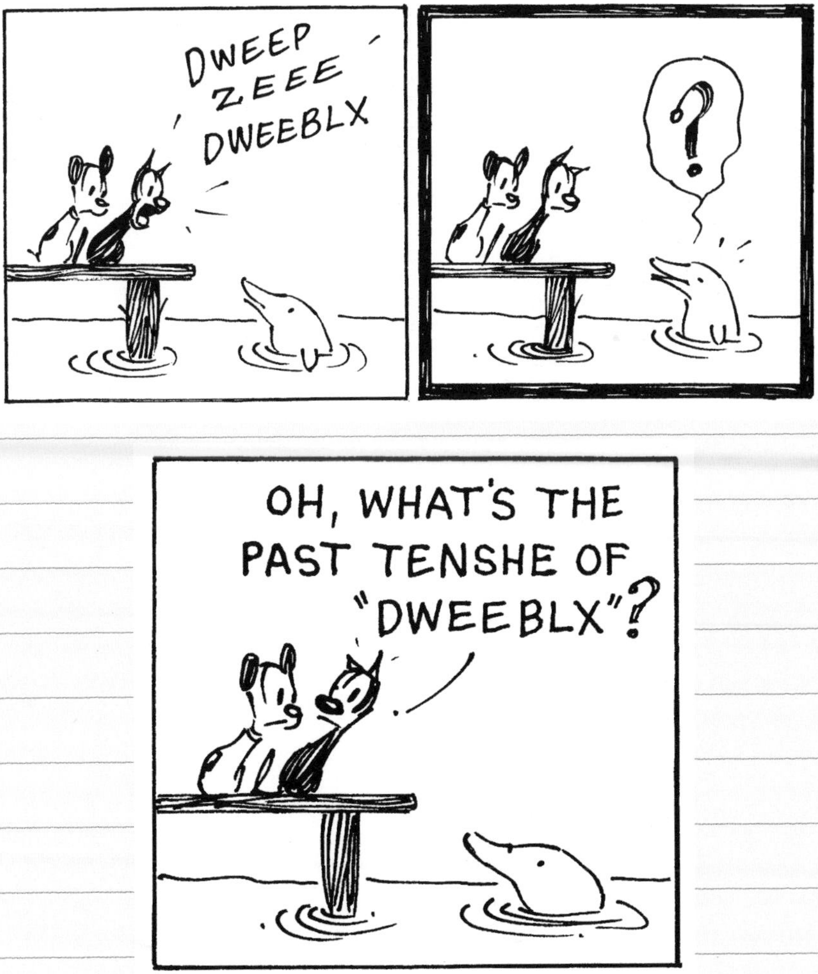
DWEEP
ZEEE
DWEEBLX
?
OH, WHAT'S THE PAST TENSHE OF "DWEEBLX"?

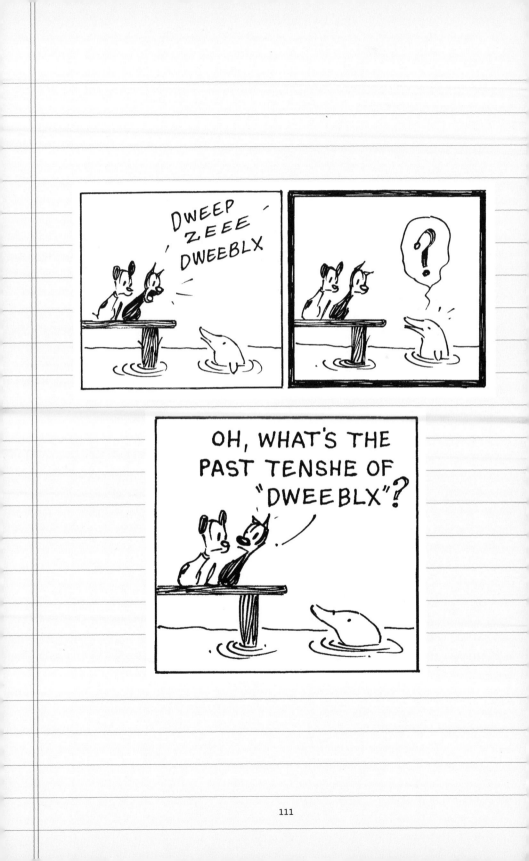

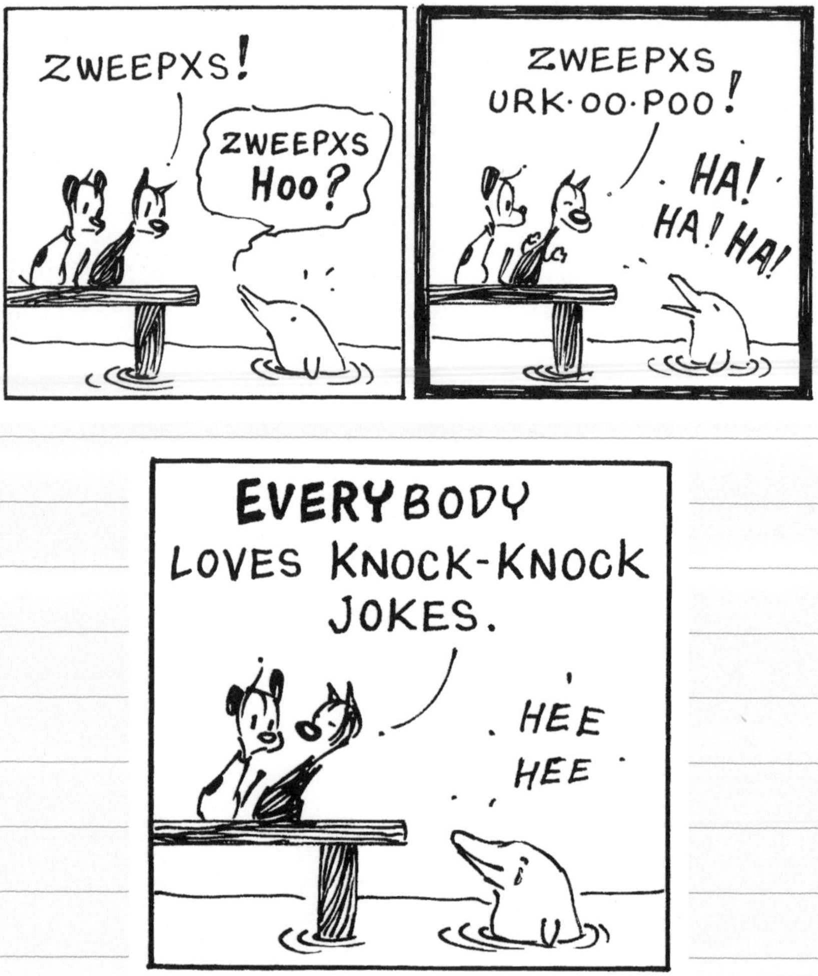
ZWEEPXS!
ZWEEPXS HOO?
ZWEEPXS URK·OO·POO!
HA! HA! HA!
EVERYBODY LOVES KNOCK-KNOCK JOKES.
HEE HEE

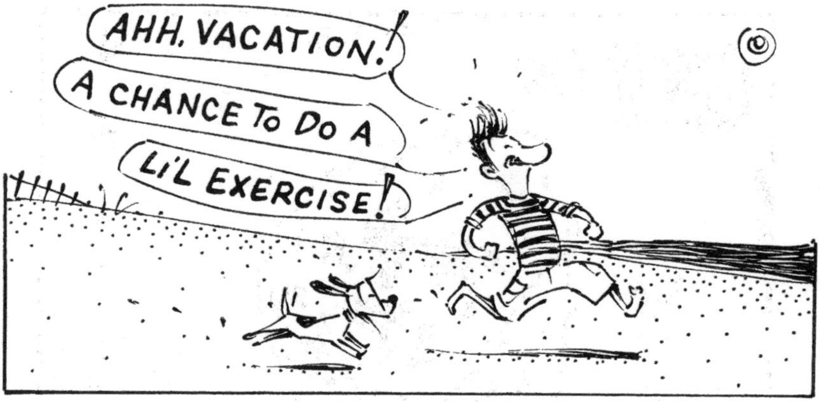
AHH, VACATION!
A CHANCE TO DO A
LI'L EXERCISE!

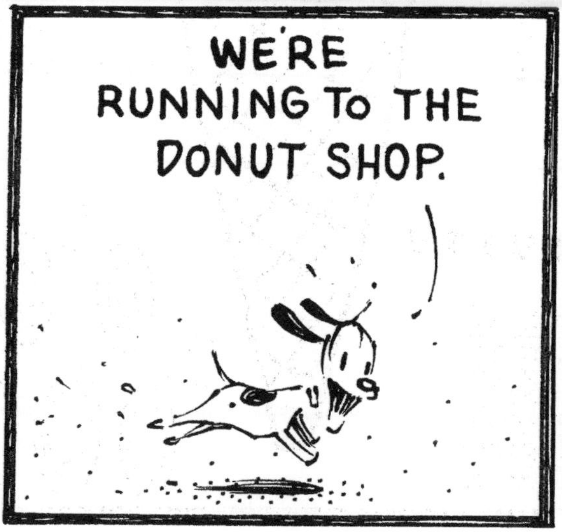
WE'RE
RUNNING TO THE
DONUT SHOP.

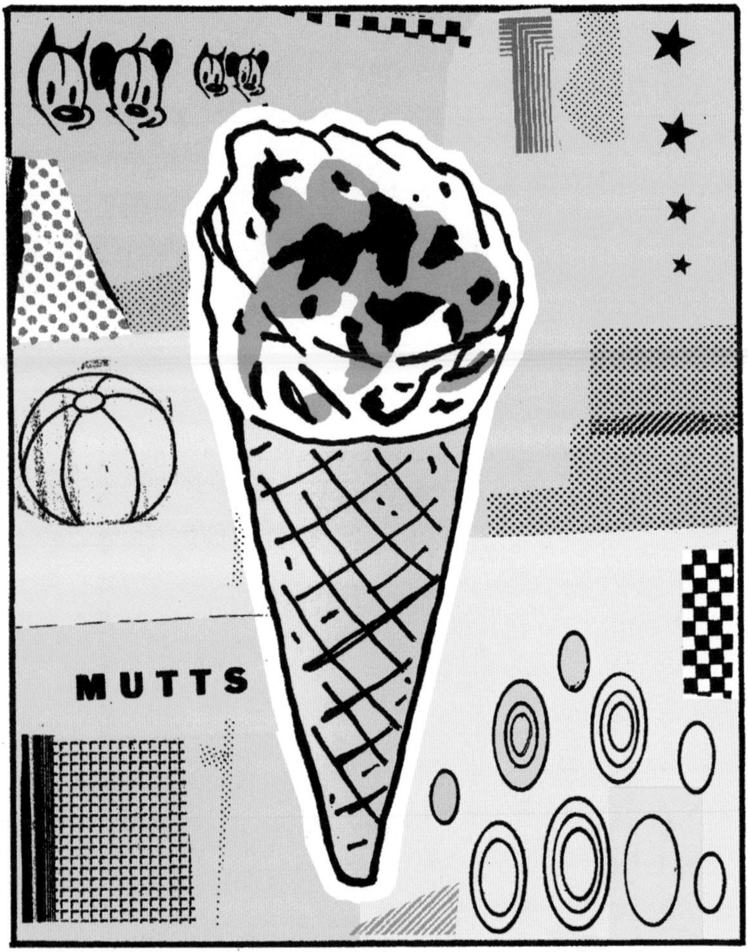
MUTTS

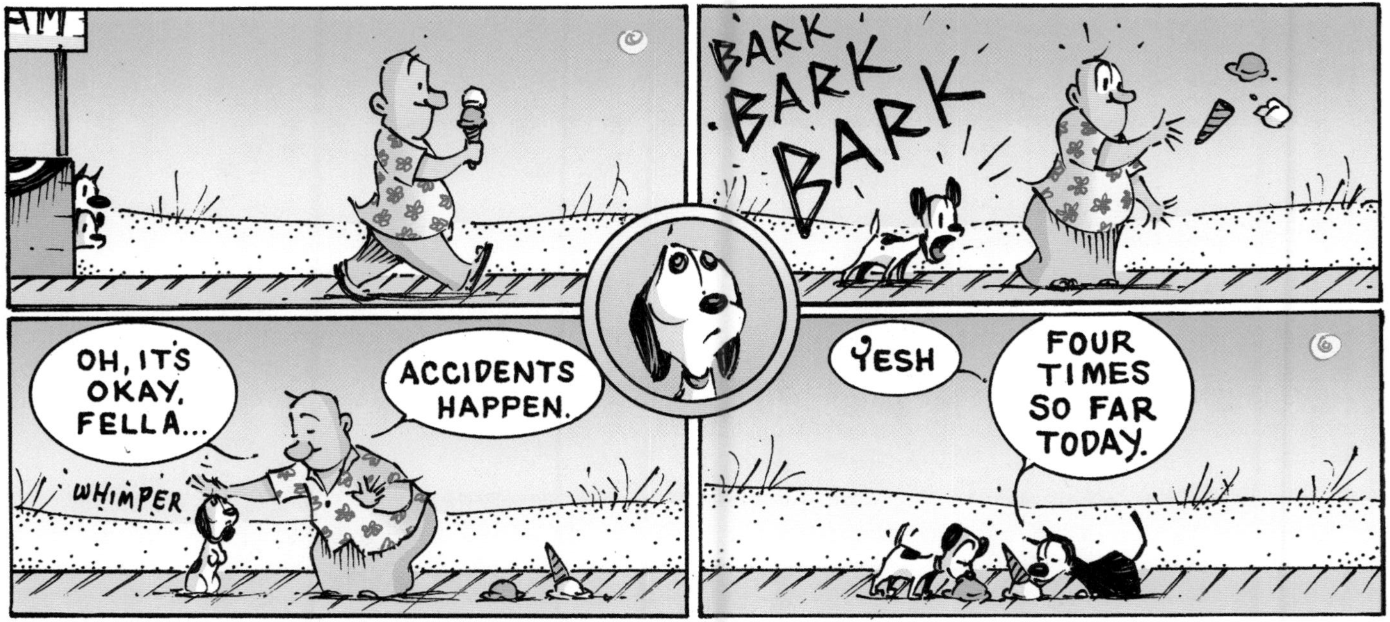
BARK
BARK
BARK
OH, IT'S OKAY, FELLA...
WHIMPER
ACCIDENTS HAPPEN.
YESH
FOUR TIMES SO FAR TODAY.

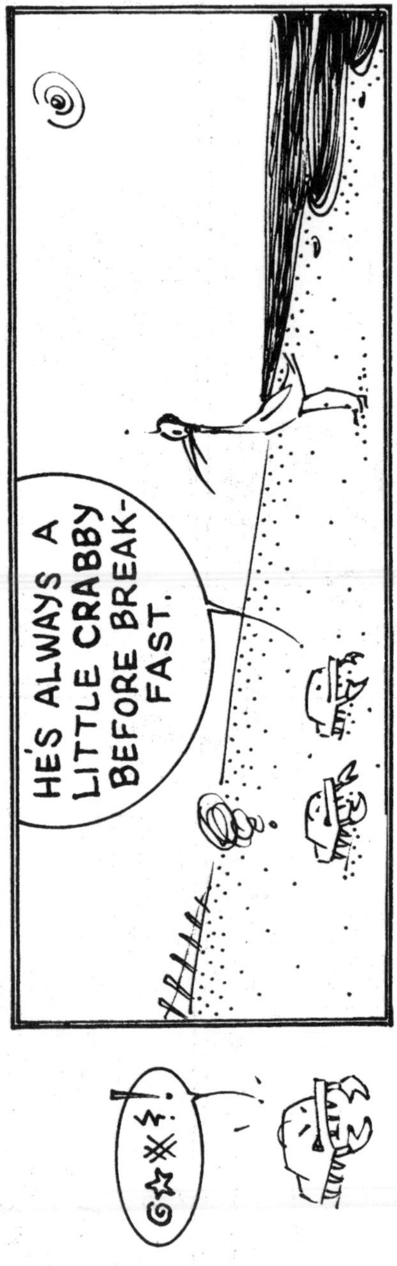
HE'S ALWAYS A LITTLE CRABBY BEFORE BREAK-FAST.

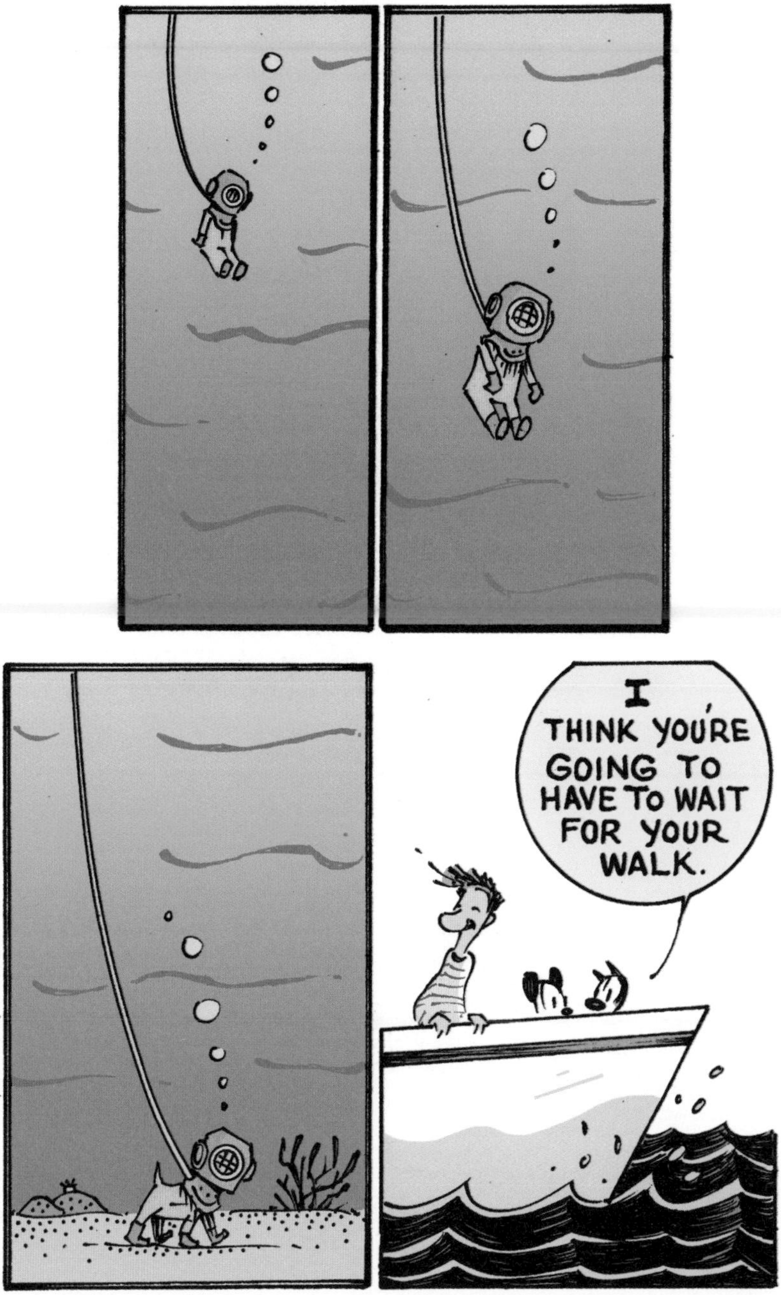
I THINK YOU'RE GOING TO HAVE TO WAIT FOR YOUR WALK.

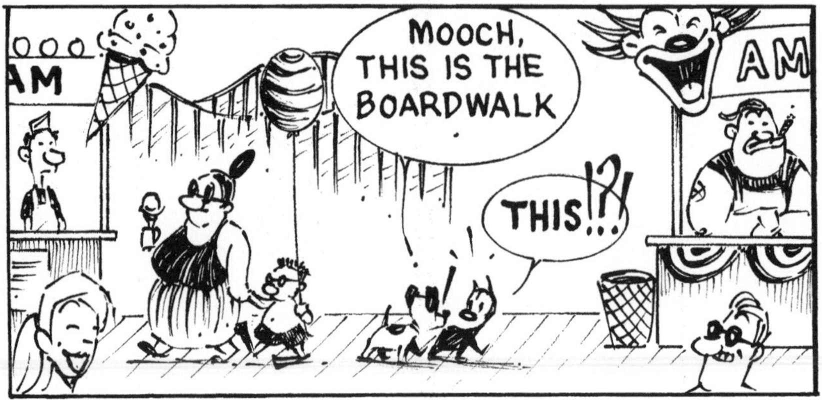
MOOCH, THIS IS THE BOARDWALK
THIS!?!
AM
AM

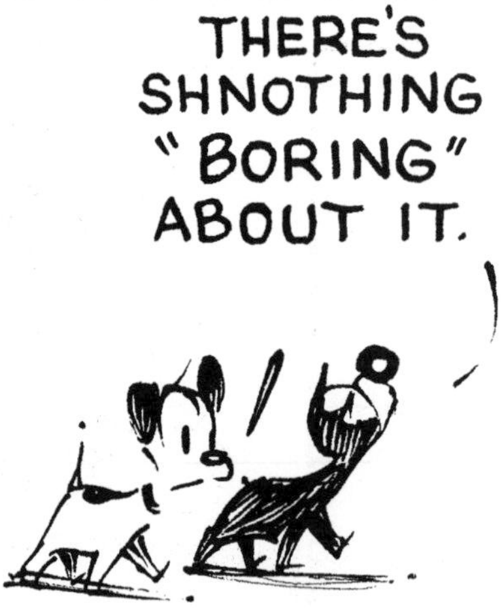
THERE'S SHNOTHING "BORING" ABOUT IT.

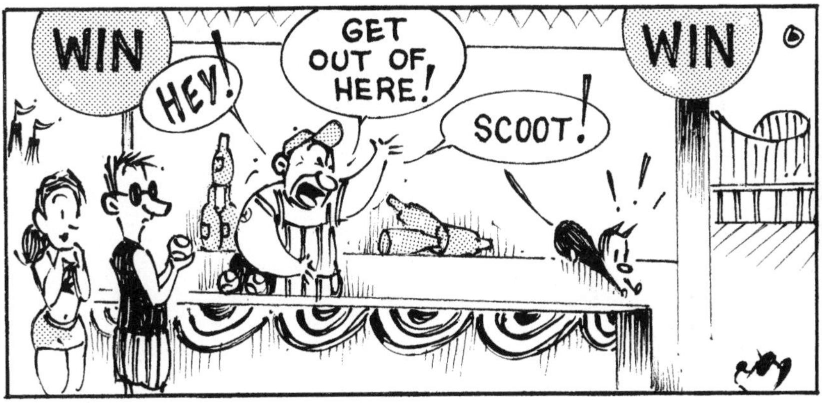
WIN
HEY!
GET OUT OF HERE!
SCOOT!
WIN

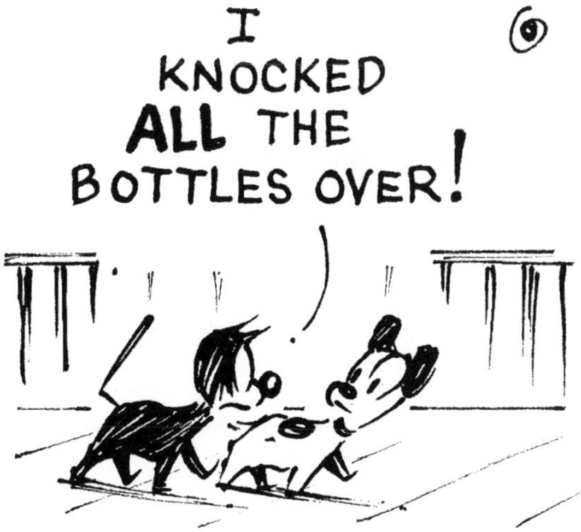
I KNOCKED ALL THE BOTTLES OVER!

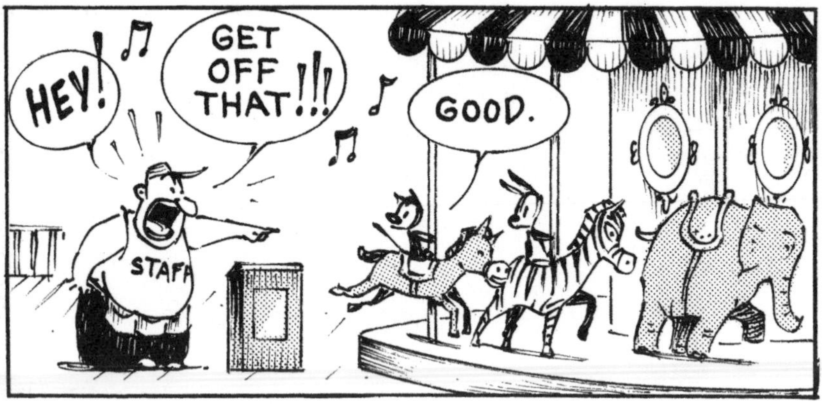
HEY!
GET OFF THAT!!!
GOOD.
STAFF

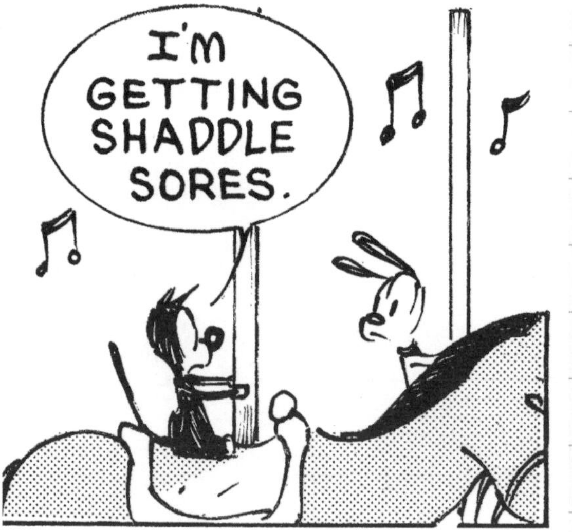
I'M GETTING SHADDLE SORES.

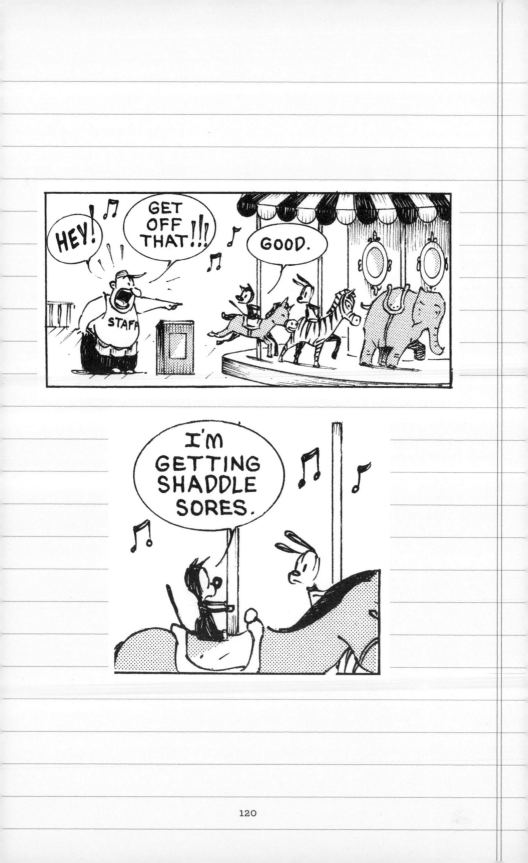

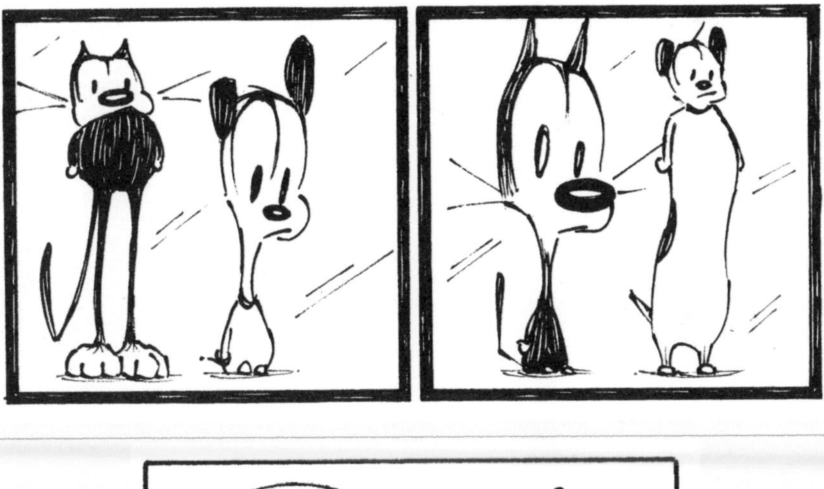
MIRRORS DON'T LIE.

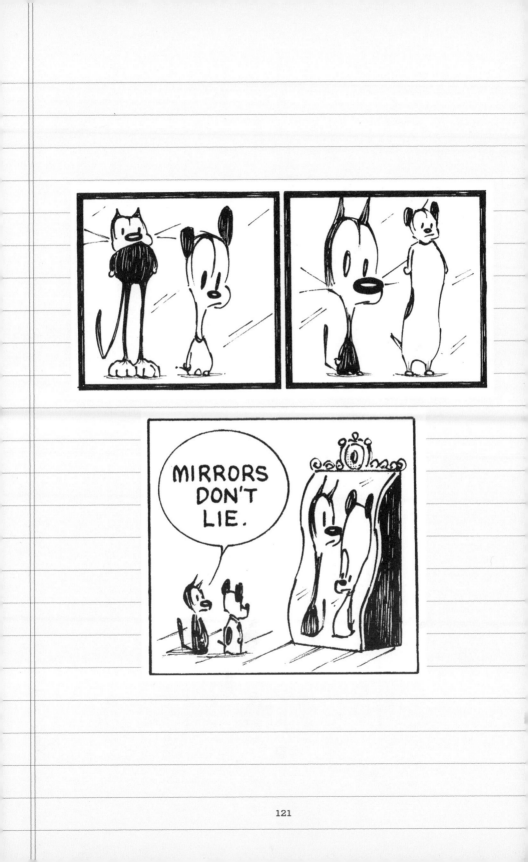

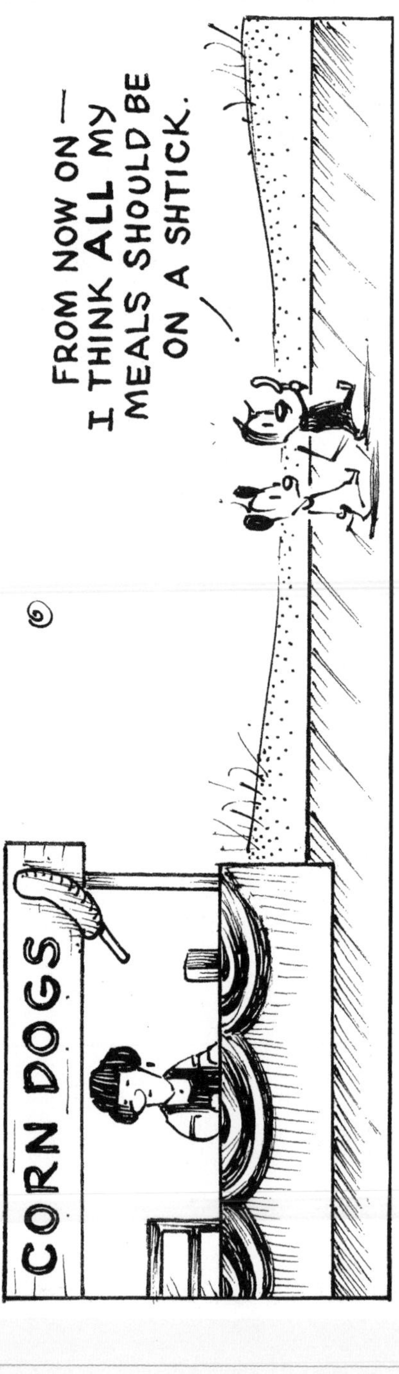
CORN DOGS
FROM NOW ON — I THINK ALL MY MEALS SHOULD BE ON A SHTICK.

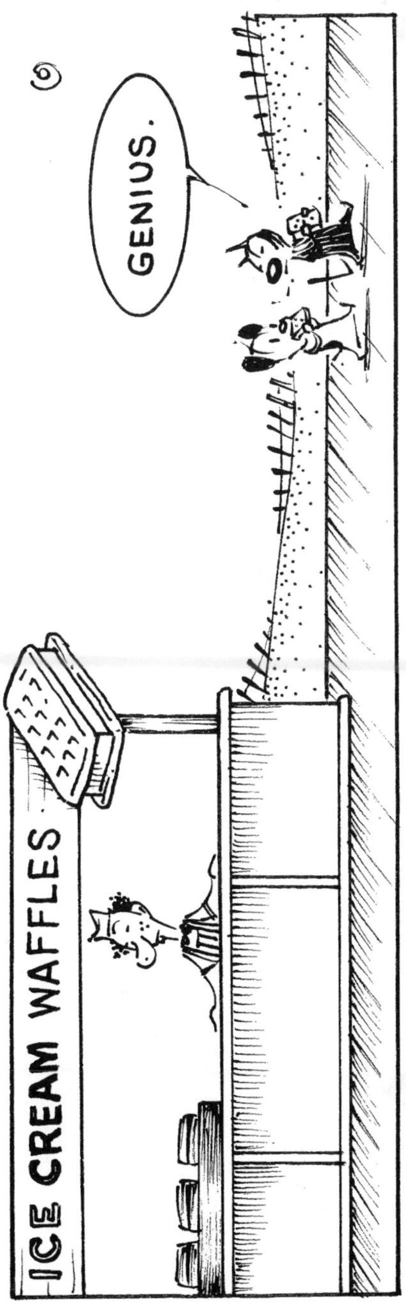
ICE CREAM WAFFLES
GENIUS.

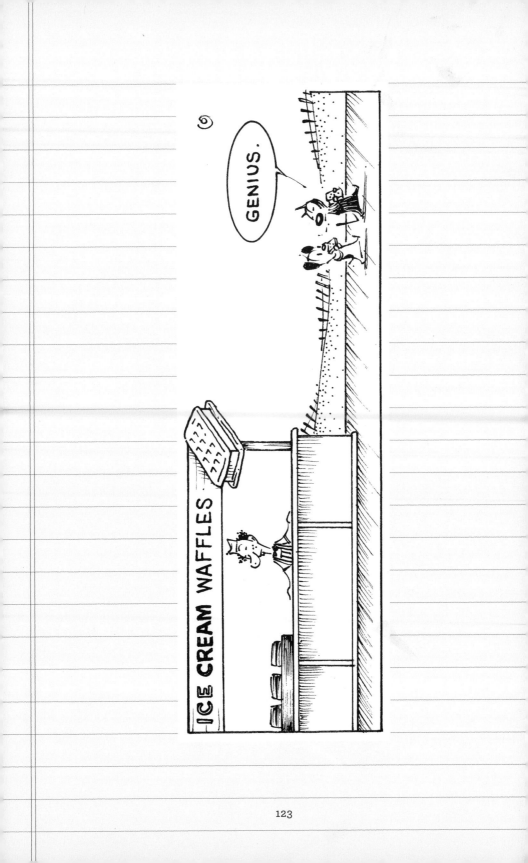

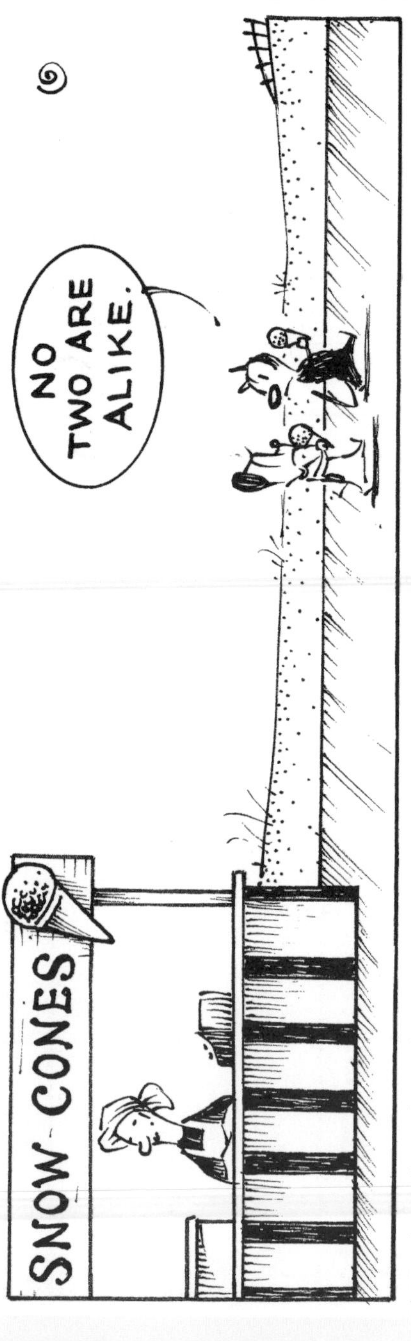
SNOW CONES
NO TWO ARE ALIKE.

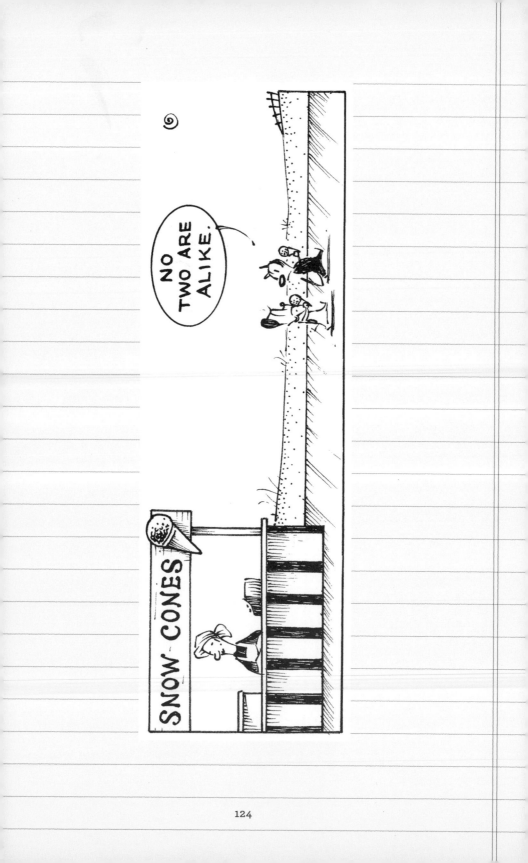

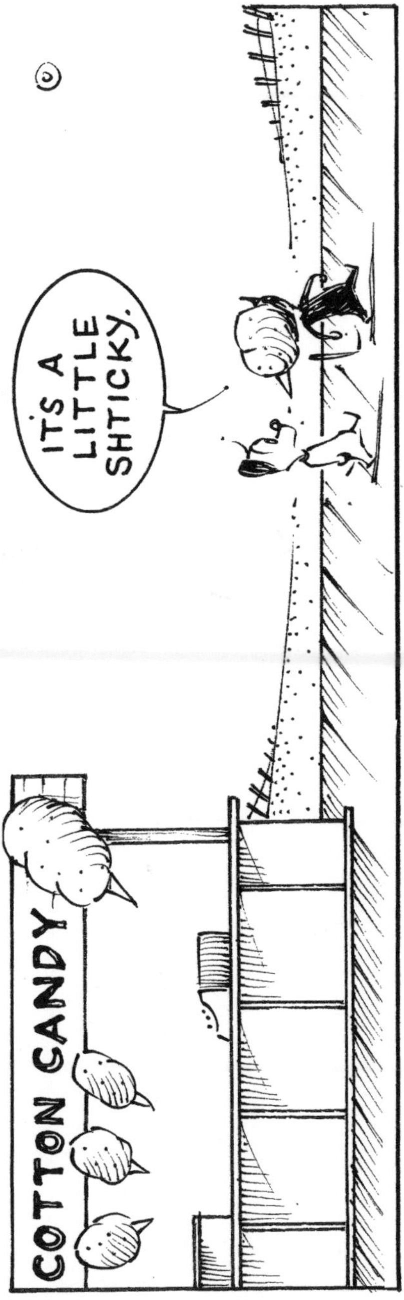
COTTON CANDY
IT'S A LITTLE SHTICKY.

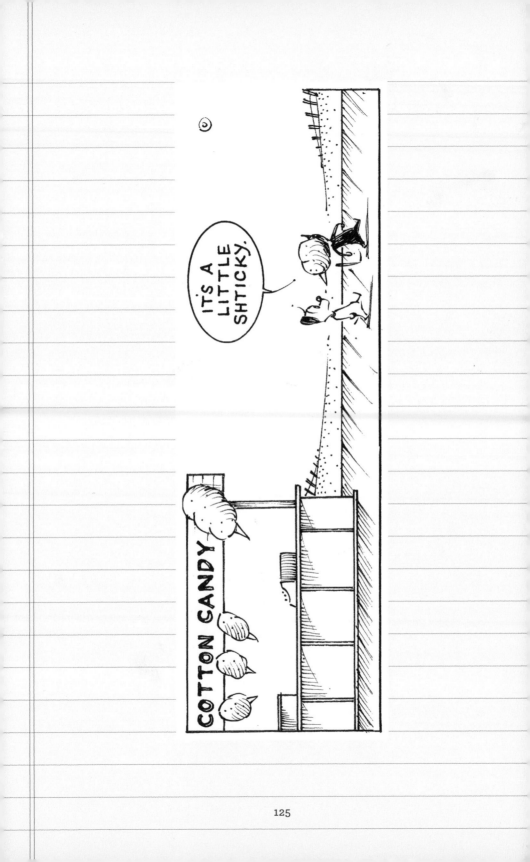

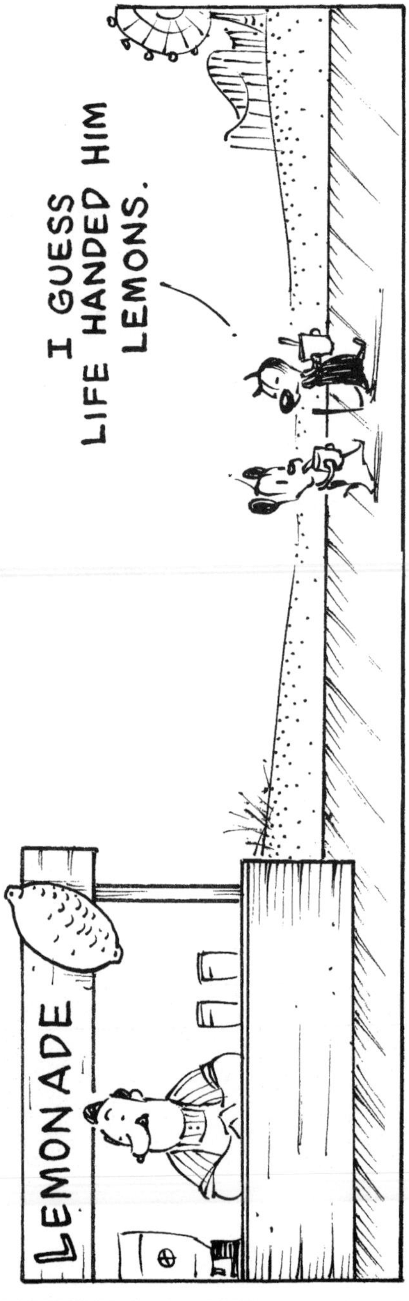
I GUESS LIFE HANDED HIM LEMONS.
LEMONADE

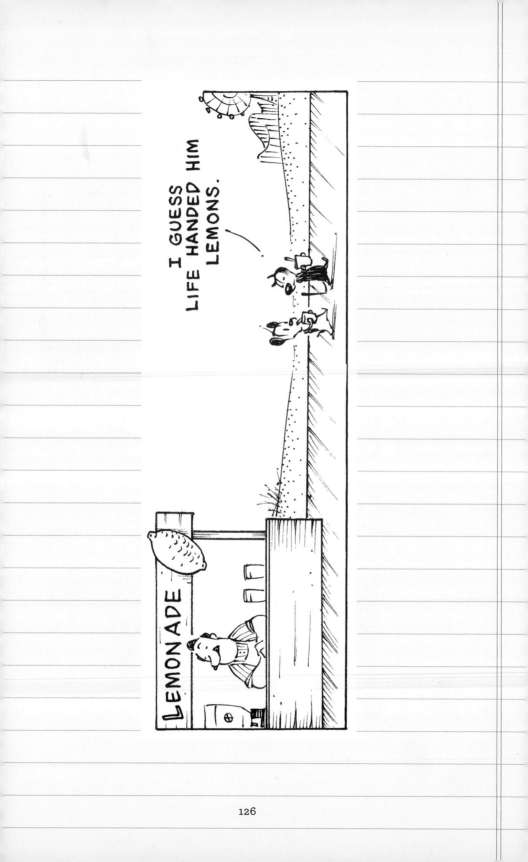

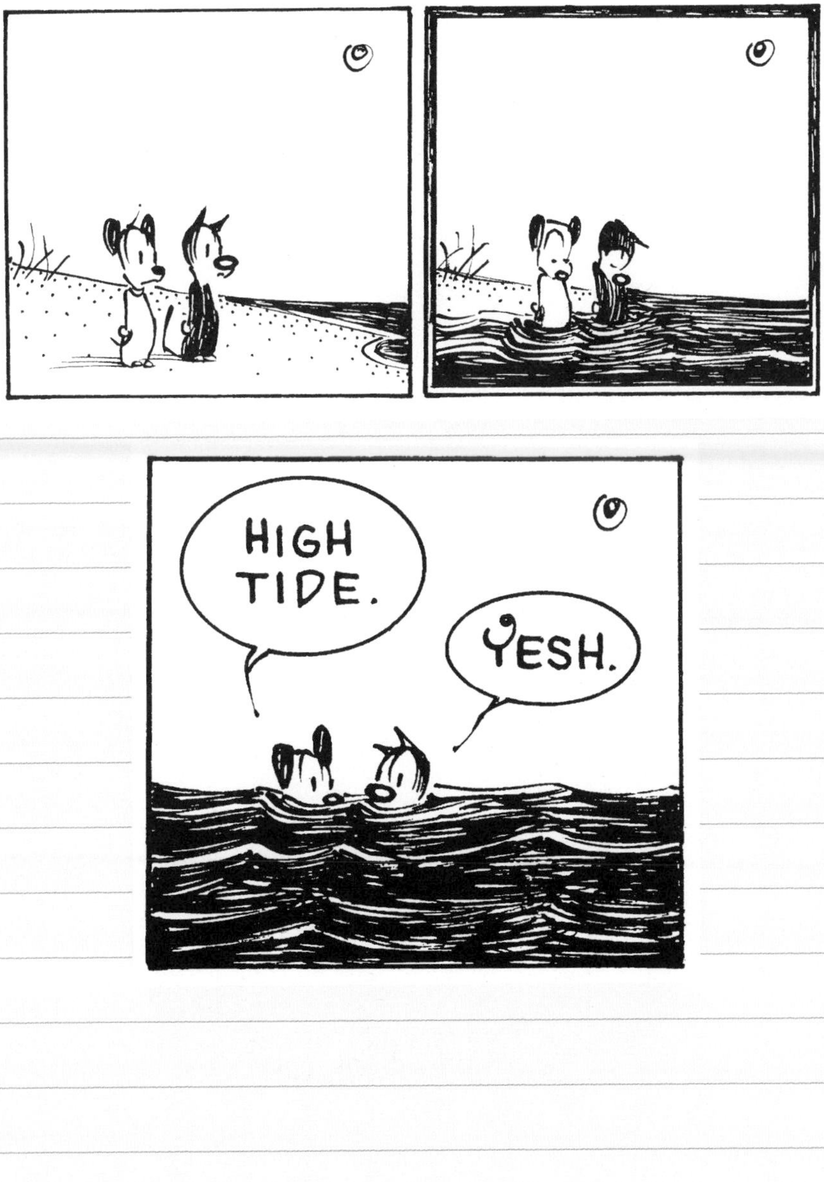
HIGH TIDE.
YESH.

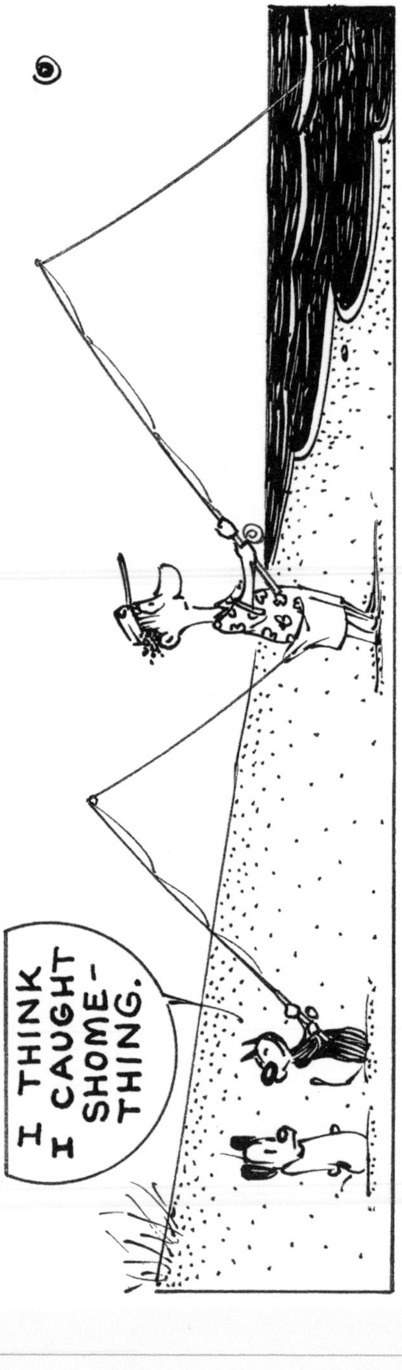
I THINK I CAUGHT SHOME-THING.

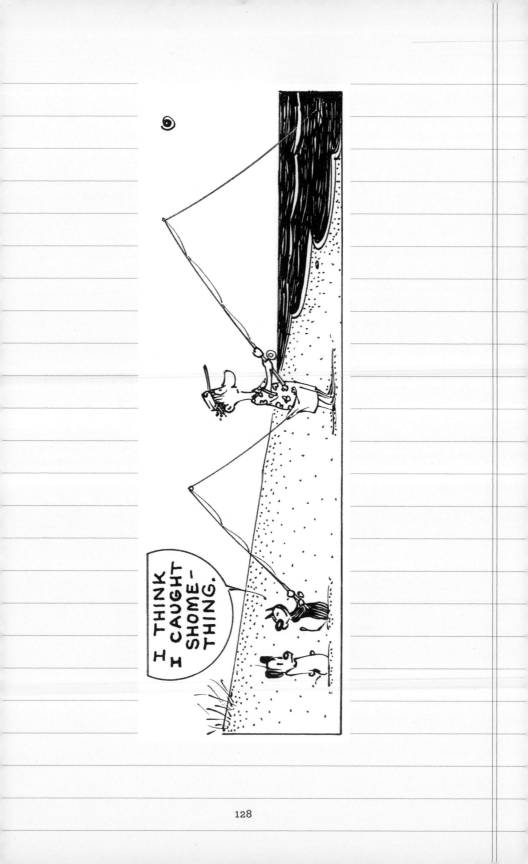

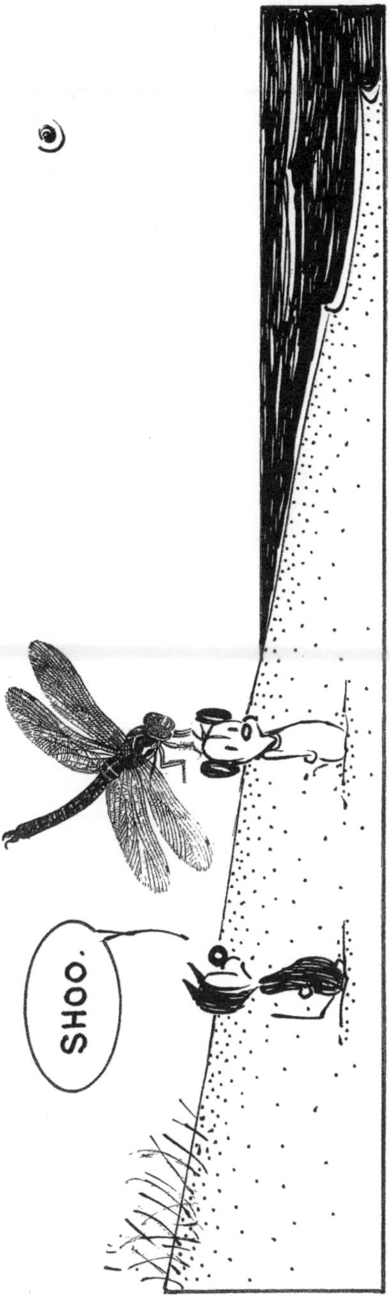
SHOO.

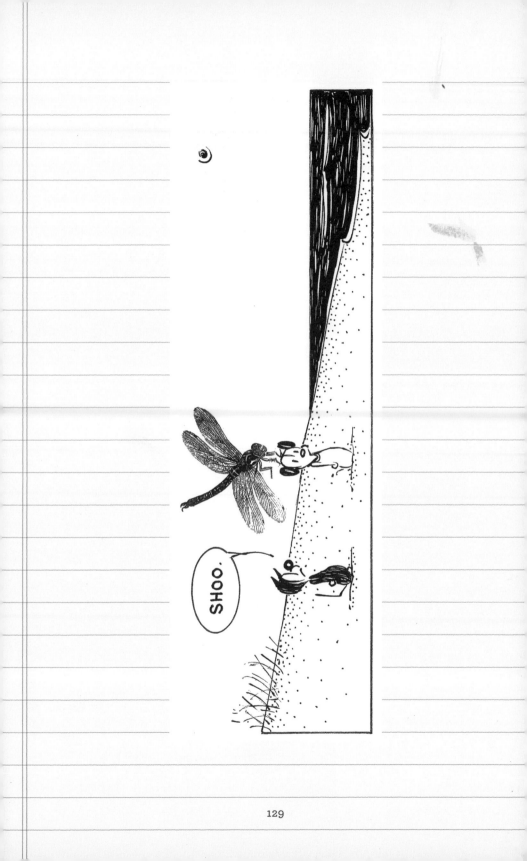

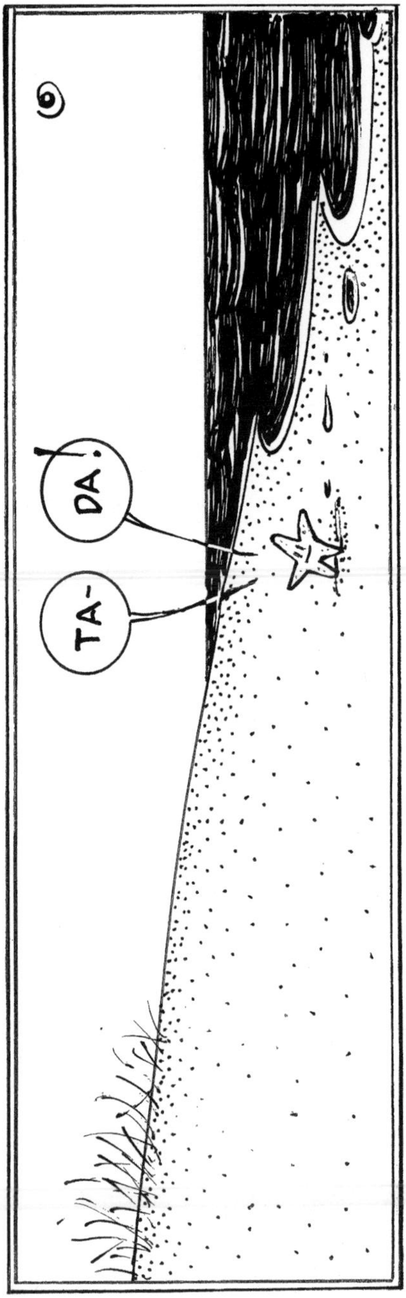
TA-
DA!

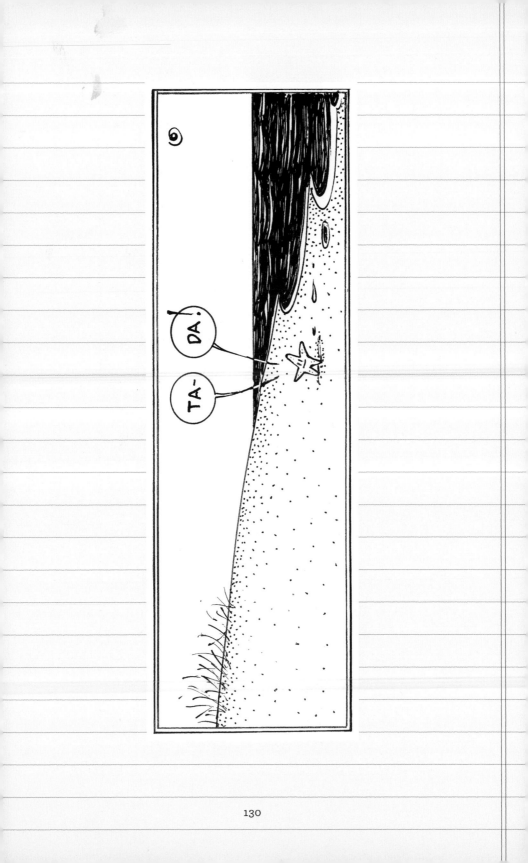

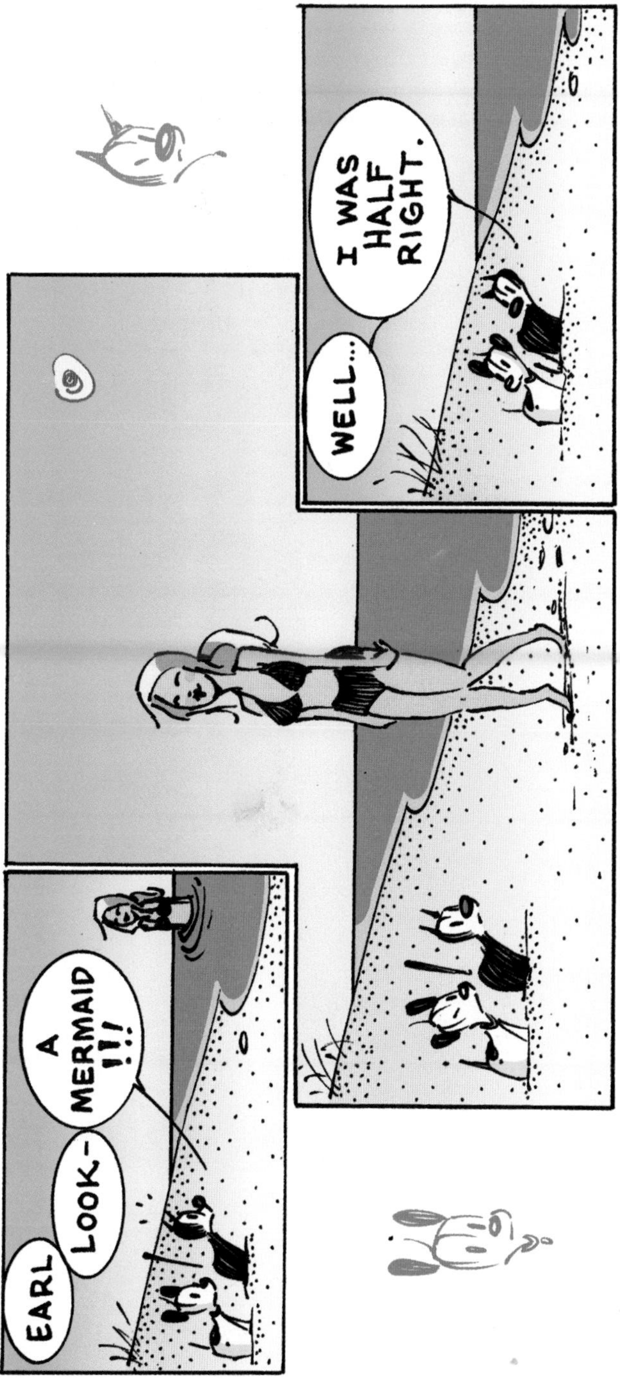
EARL
LOOK-
A MERMAID !!!
WELL...
I WAS HALF RIGHT.

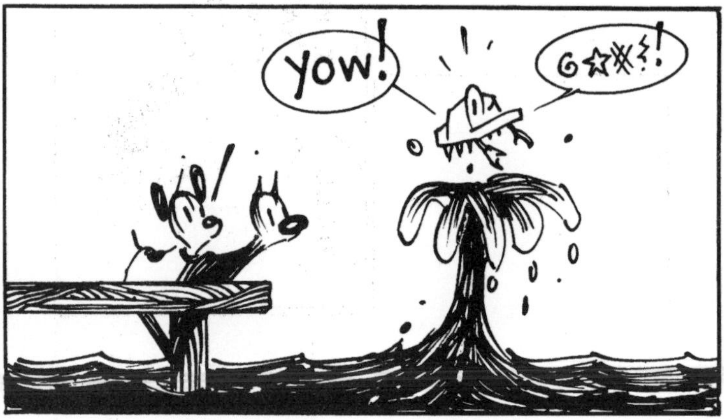
YOW!

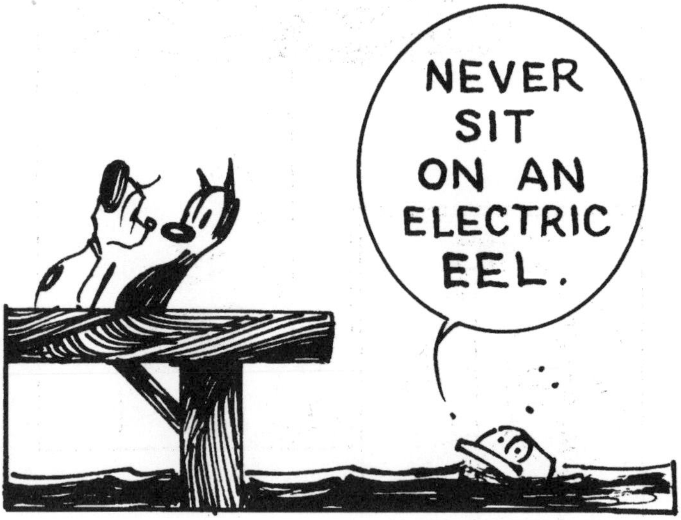
NEVER SIT ON AN ELECTRIC EEL.

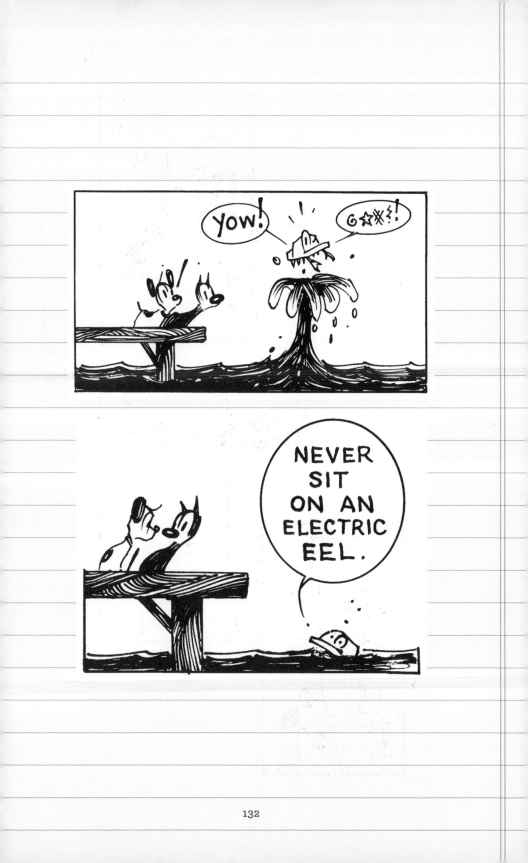

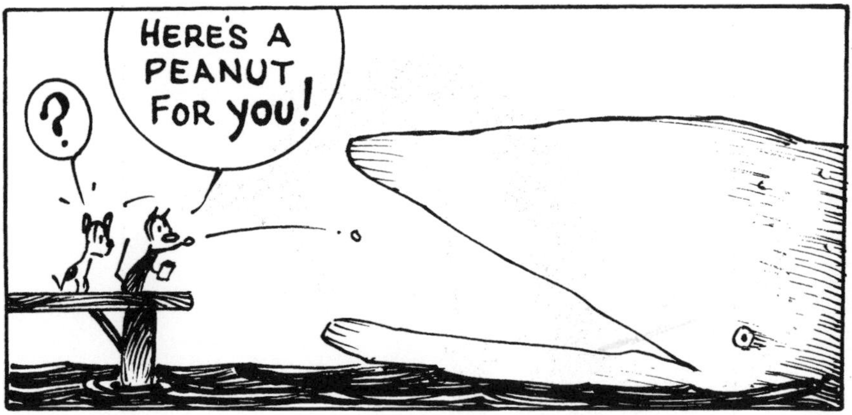
?
HERE'S A PEANUT FOR YOU!

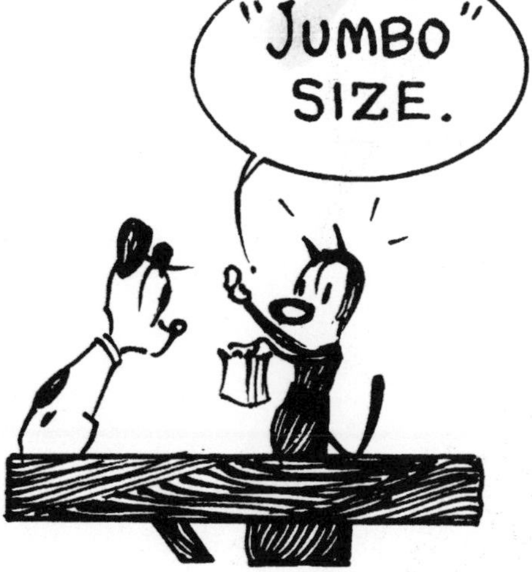
"JUMBO" SIZE.

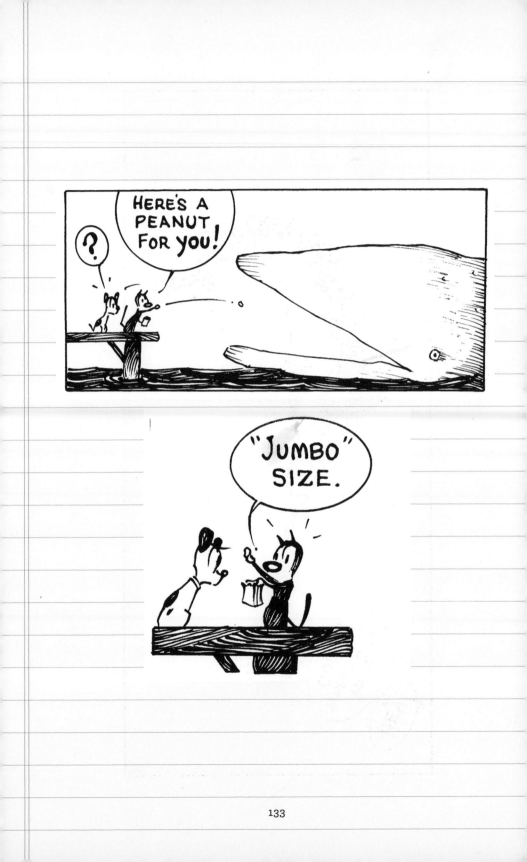

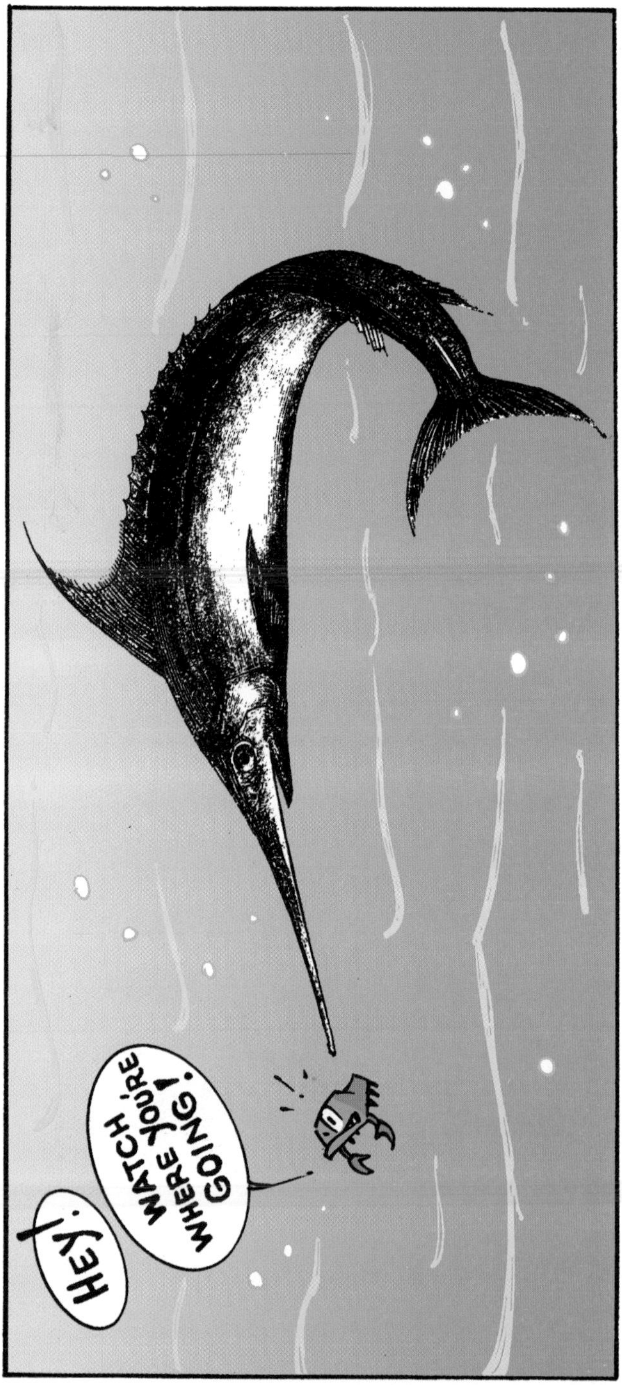
HEY!
WATCH WHERE YOU'RE GOING!

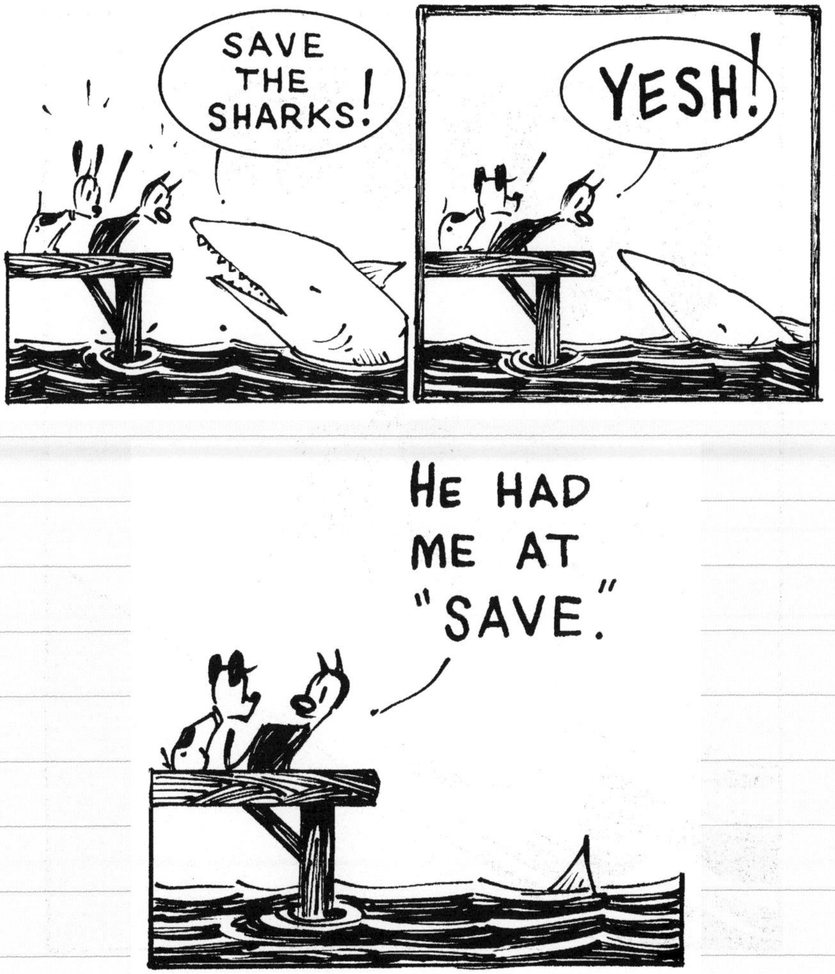
SAVE THE SHARKS!
YESH!
HE HAD ME AT "SAVE."

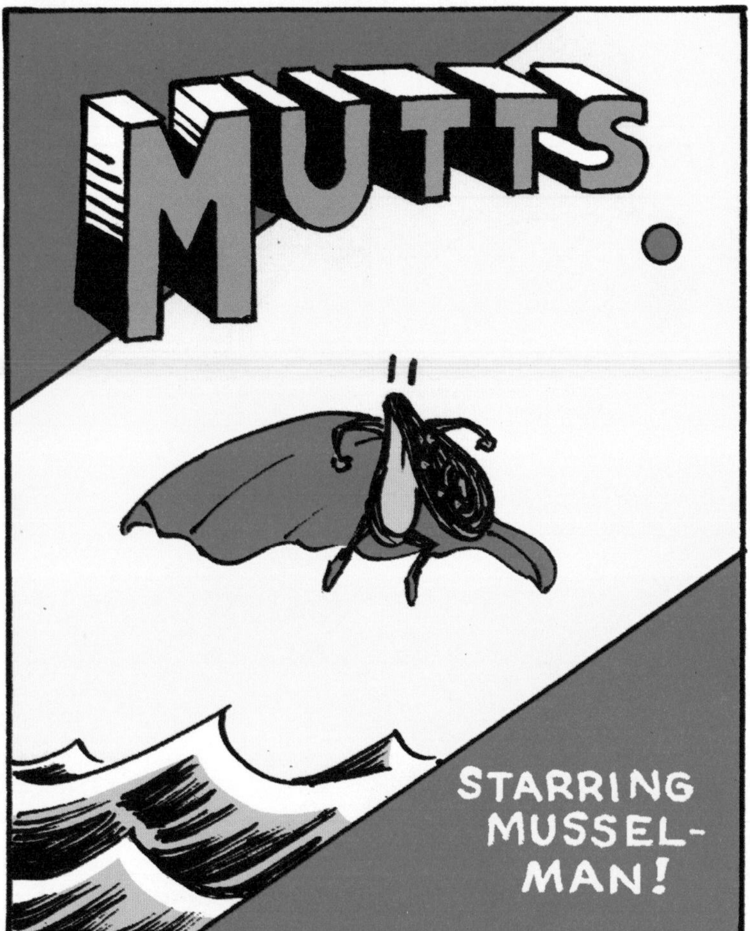
MUTTS.
STARRING
MUSSEL-
MAN!

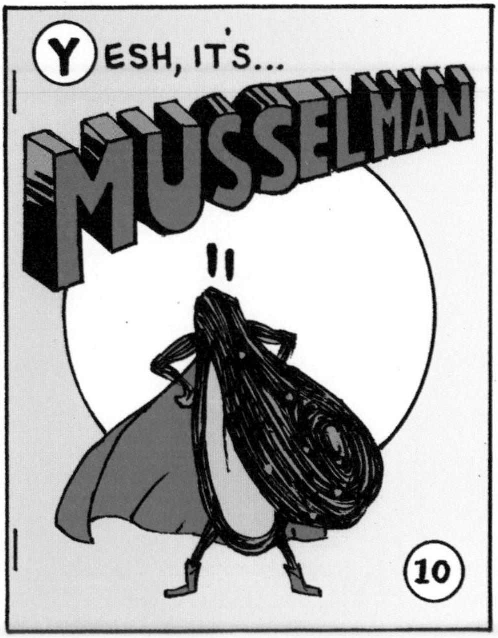
YESH, IT'S...
MUSSELMAN
10

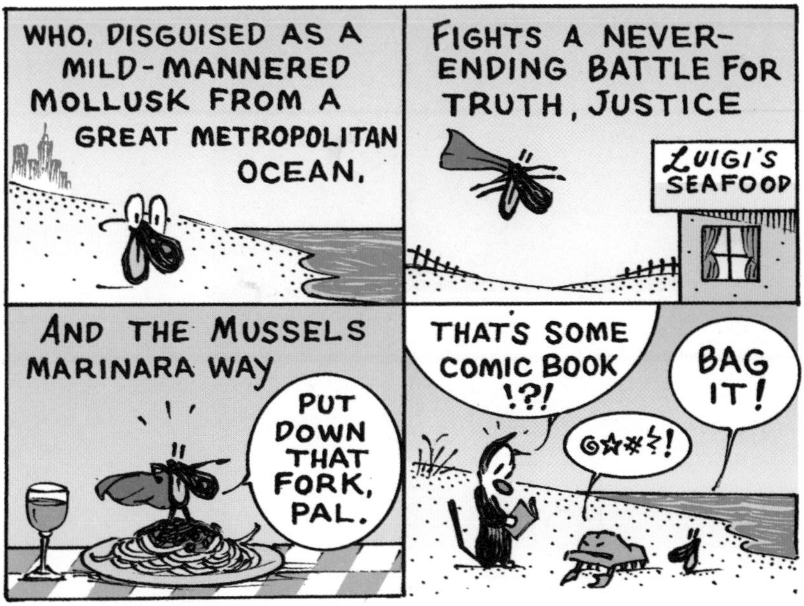
WHO, DISGUISED AS A MILD-MANNERED MOLLUSK FROM A GREAT METROPOLITAN OCEAN,
FIGHTS A NEVER-ENDING BATTLE FOR TRUTH, JUSTICE
LUIGI'S SEAFOOD
AND THE MUSSELS MARINARA WAY
PUT DOWN THAT FORK, PAL.
THAT'S SOME COMIC BOOK !?!
@☆#ϟ!
BAG IT!

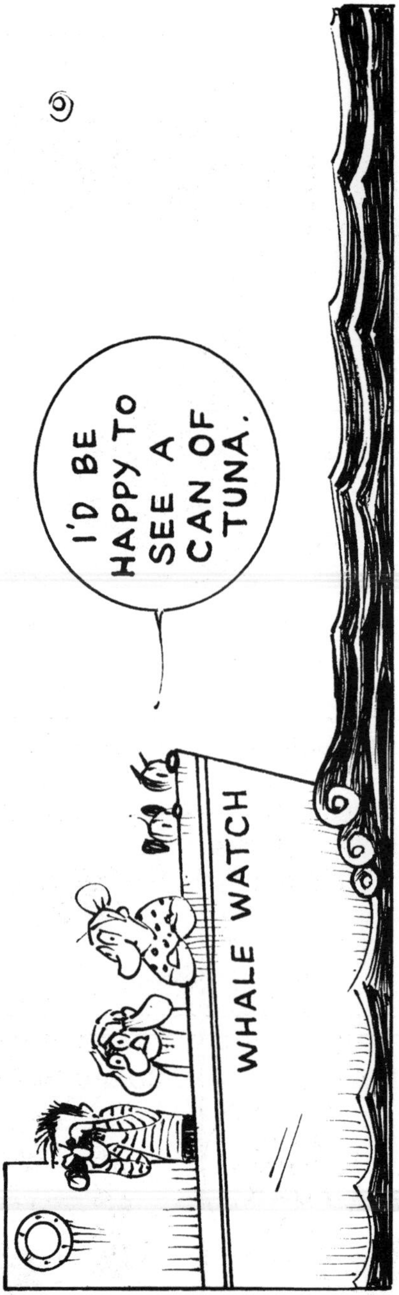
WHALE WATCH
I'D BE HAPPY TO SEE A CAN OF TUNA.

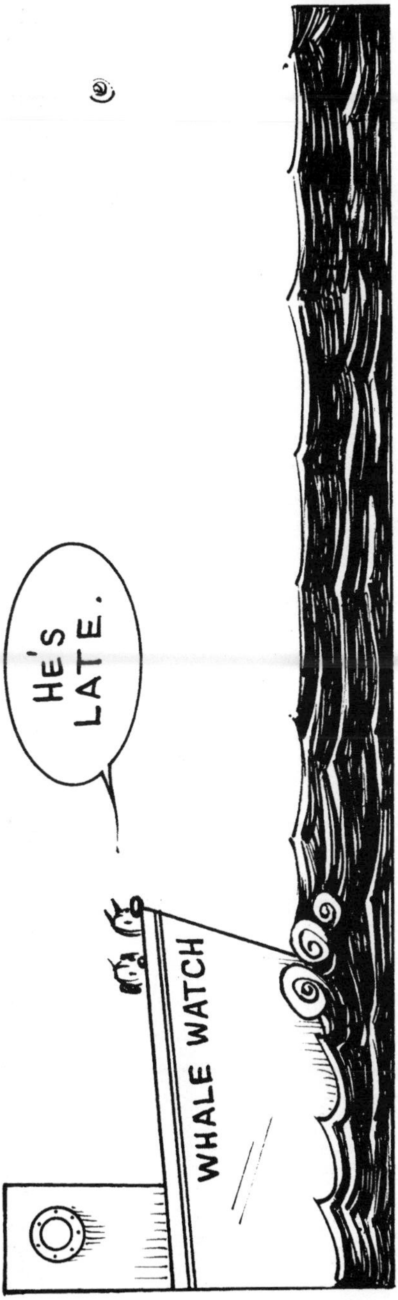
HE'S LATE.
WHALE WATCH

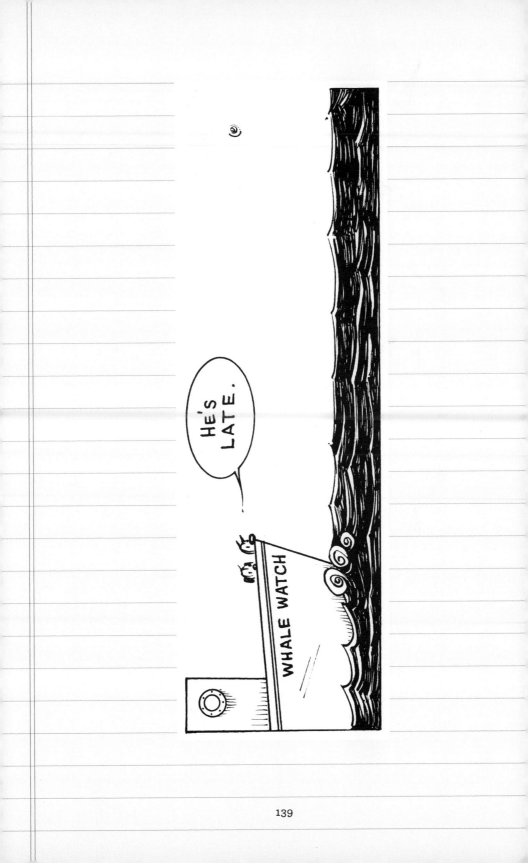

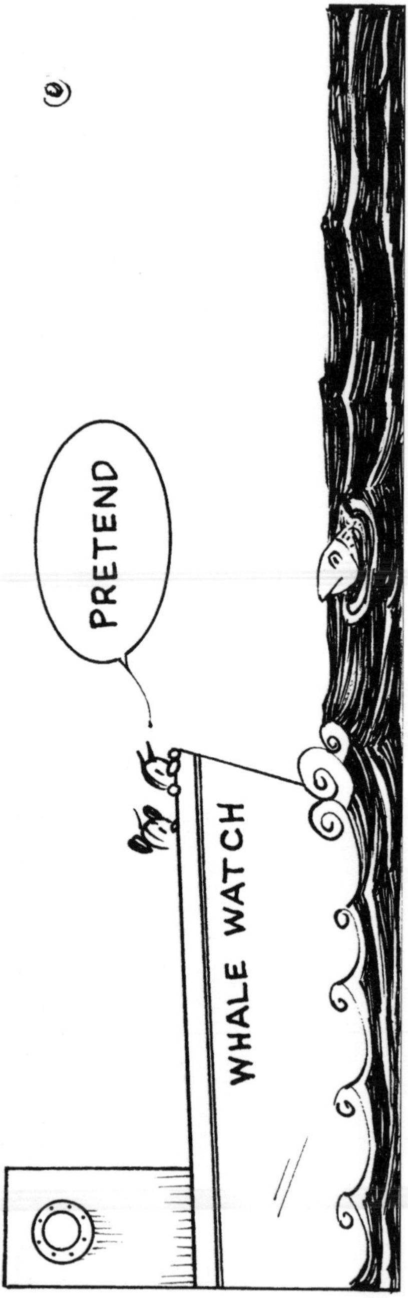
PRETEND
WHALE WATCH

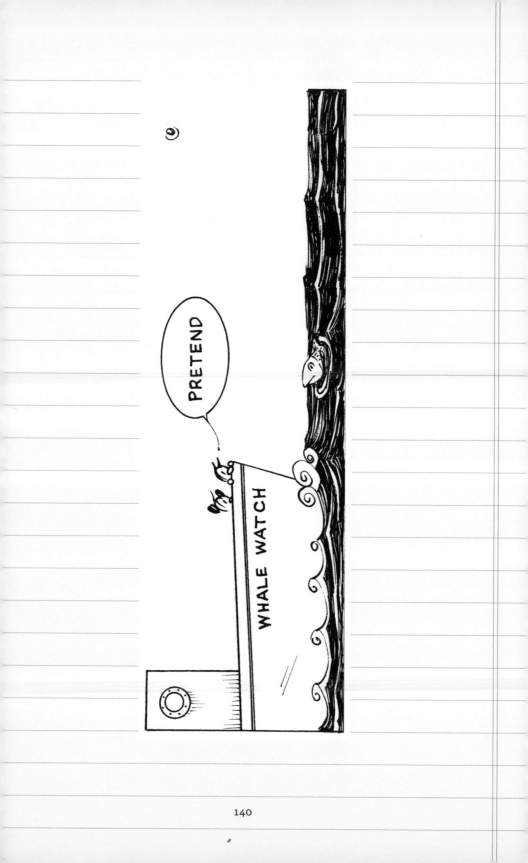

PINOCCHIO!!!!
WHALE WATCH

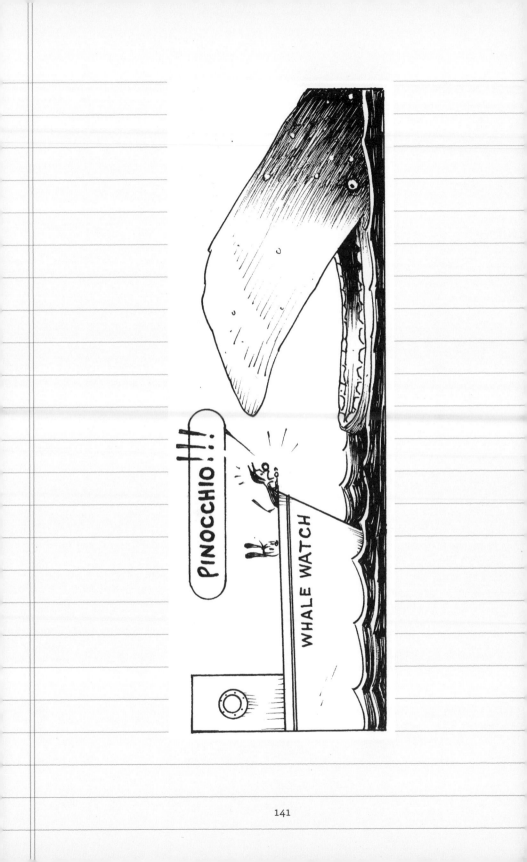

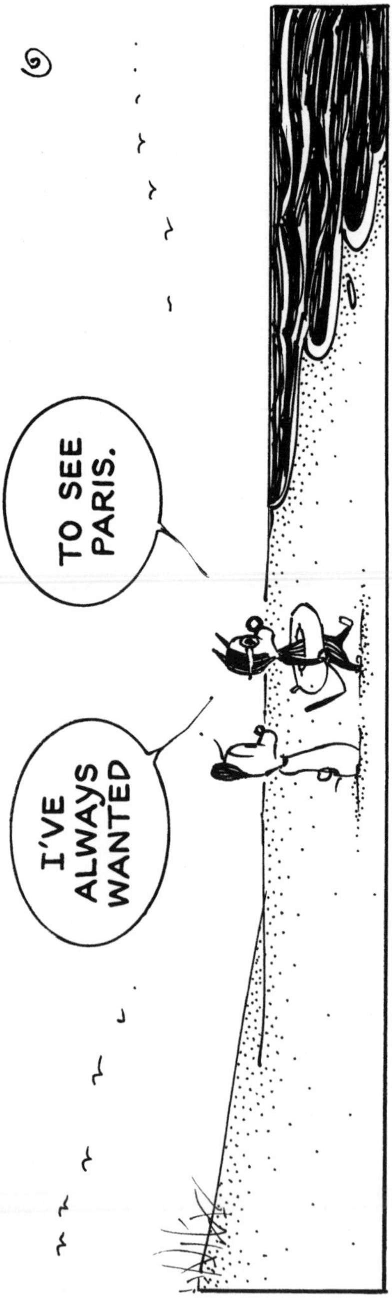

I'VE ALWAYS WANTED
TO SEE PARIS.

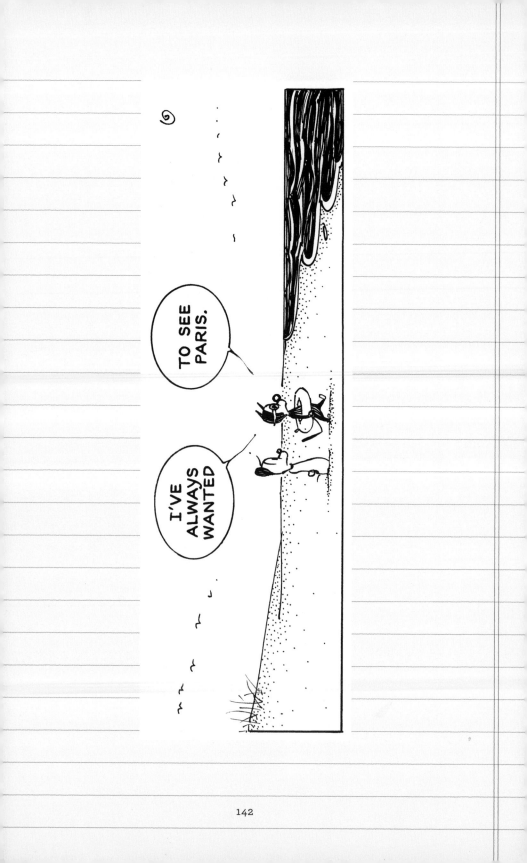

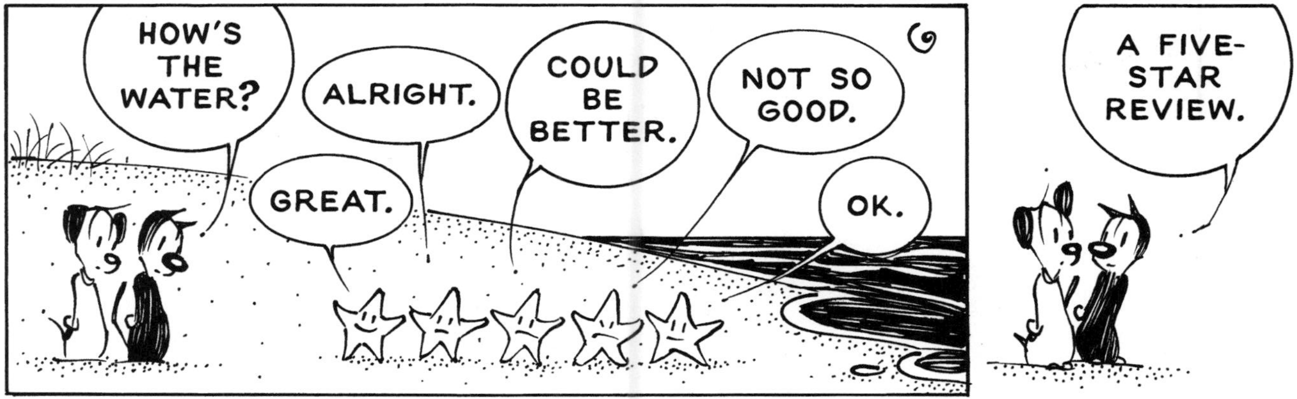
HOW'S THE WATER?
GREAT.
ALRIGHT.
COULD BE BETTER.
NOT SO GOOD.
OK.
A FIVE-STAR REVIEW.

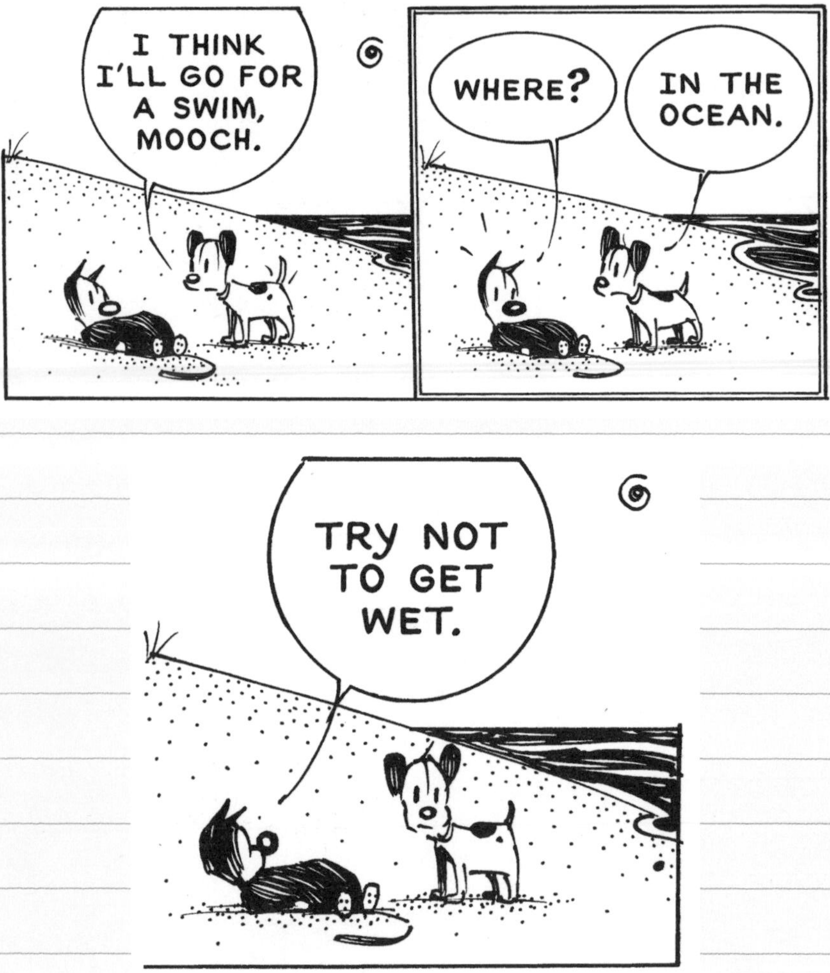
I THINK I'LL GO FOR A SWIM, MOOCH.
WHERE?
IN THE OCEAN.
TRY NOT TO GET WET.

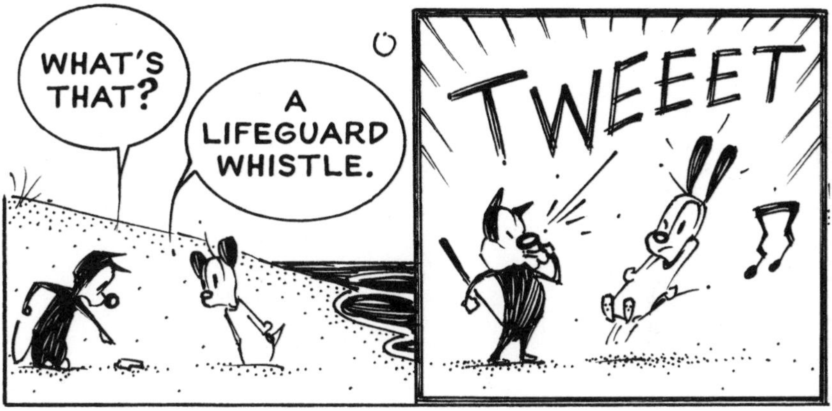
WHAT'S THAT?
A LIFEGUARD WHISTLE.
TWEEET

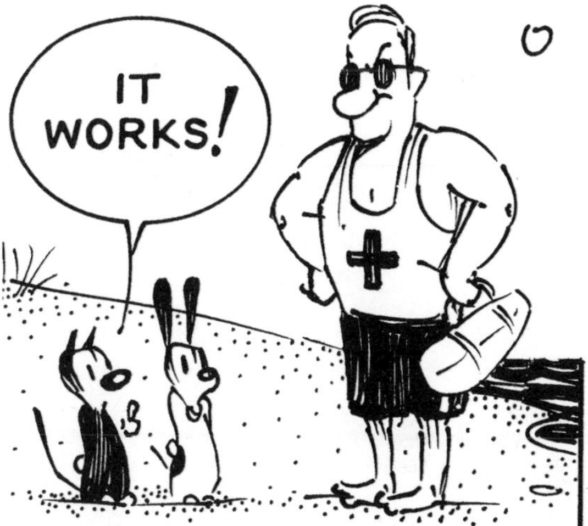
IT WORKS!

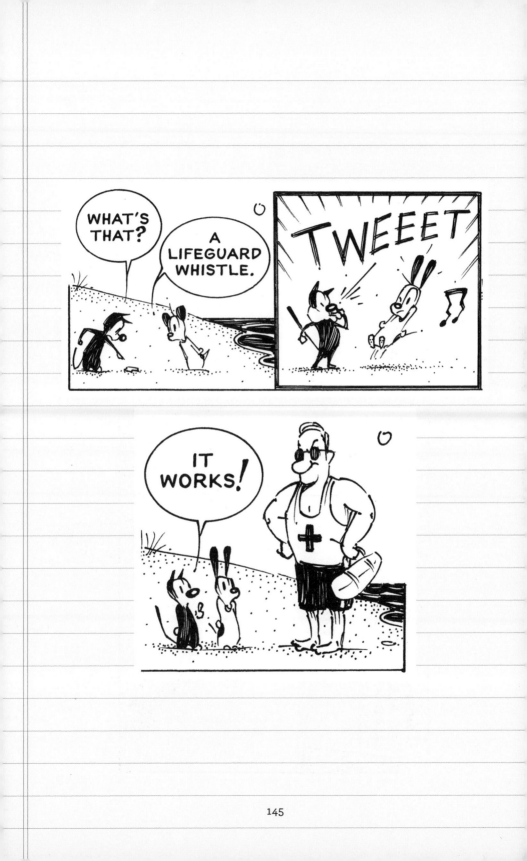

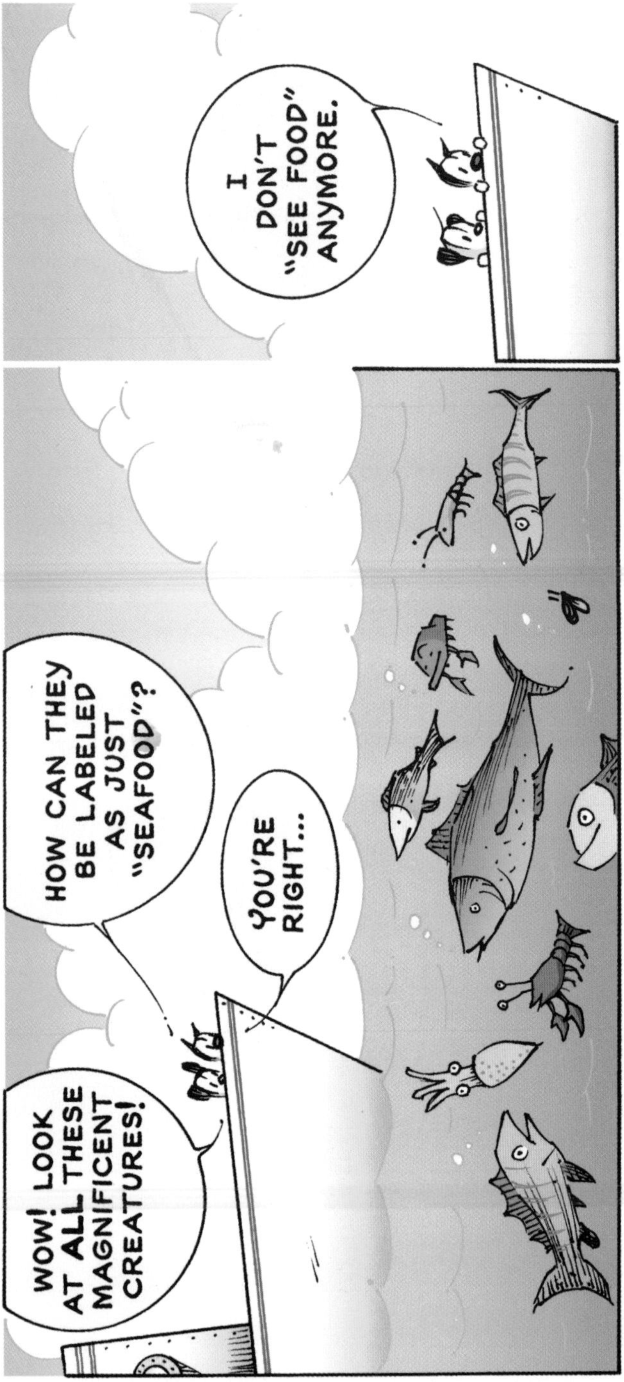
WOW! LOOK AT ALL THESE MAGNIFICENT CREATURES!
HOW CAN THEY BE LABELED AS JUST "SEAFOOD"?
YOU'RE RIGHT...
I DON'T "SEE FOOD" ANYMORE.

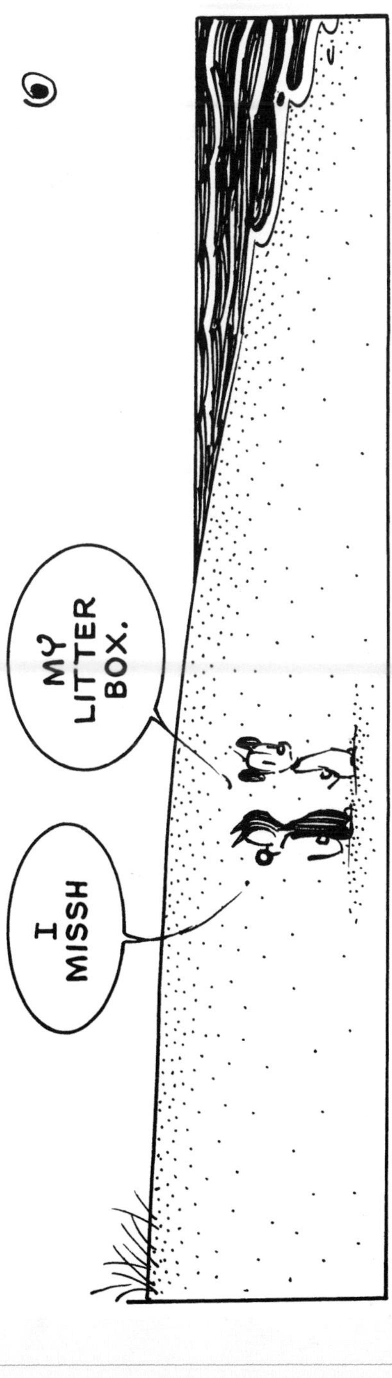
I MISSH
MY LITTER BOX.

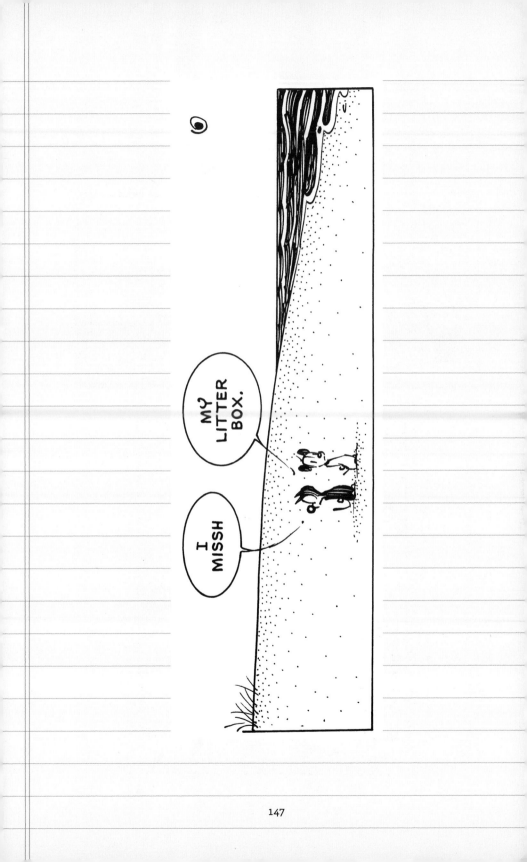

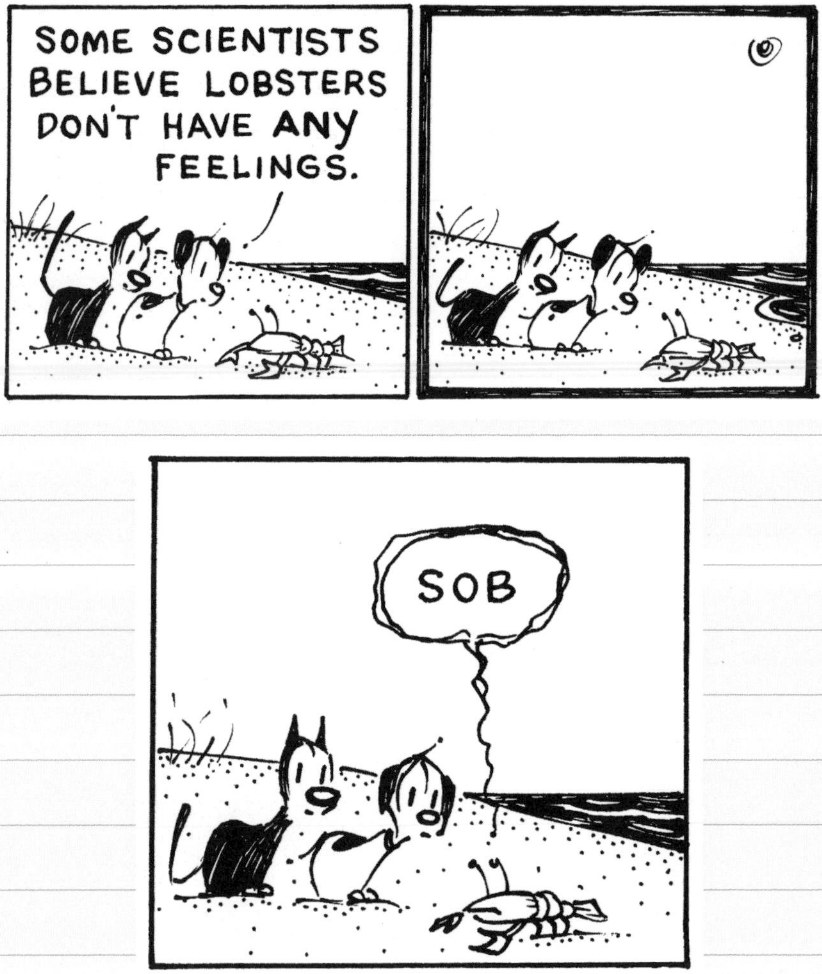
SOME SCIENTISTS BELIEVE LOBSTERS DON'T HAVE ANY FEELINGS.
SOB

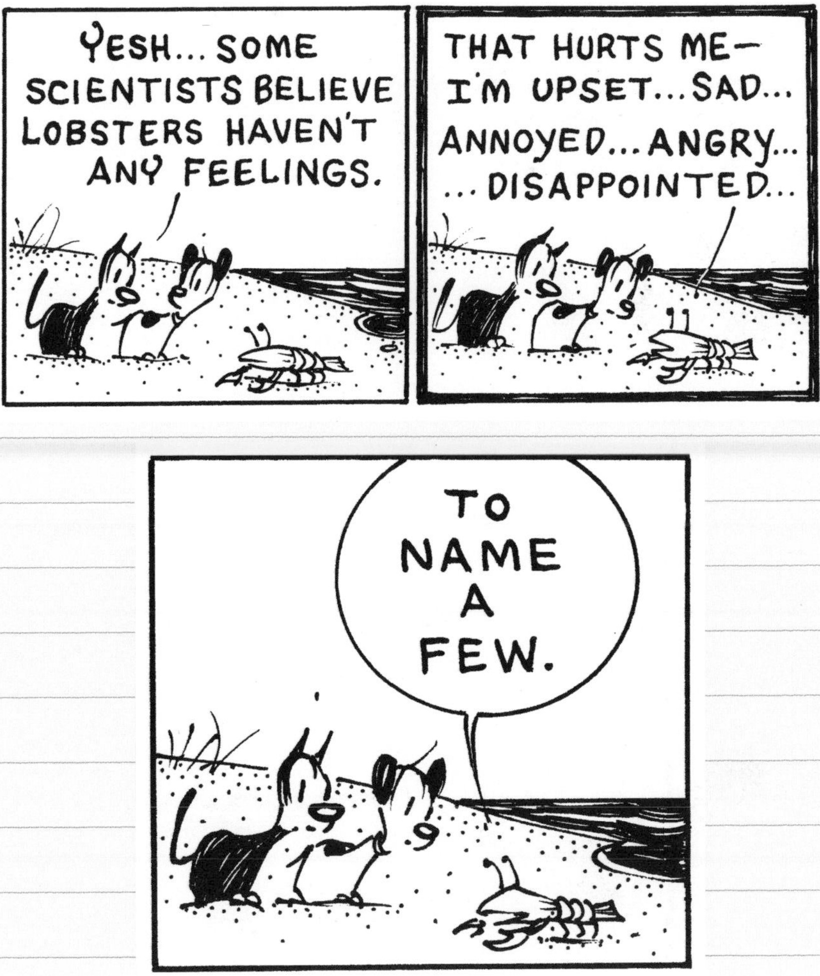
YESH... SOME SCIENTISTS BELIEVE LOBSTERS HAVEN'T ANY FEELINGS.
THAT HURTS ME— I'M UPSET... SAD... ANNOYED... ANGRY... ... DISAPPOINTED...
TO NAME A FEW.

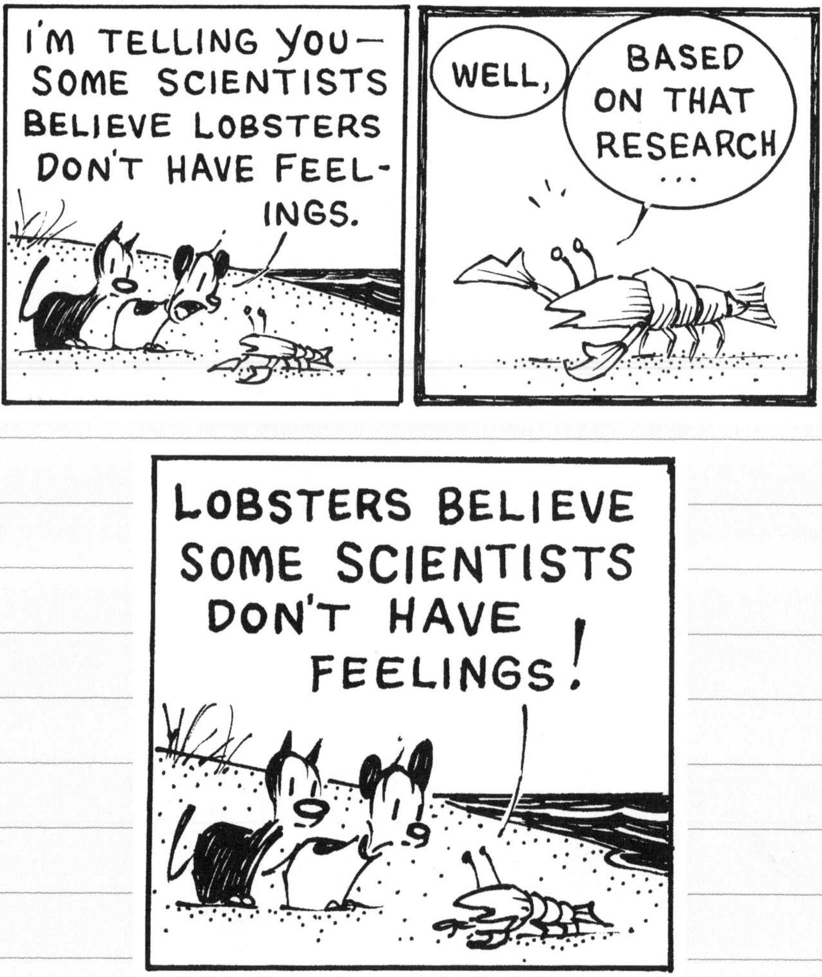
I'M TELLING YOU—SOME SCIENTISTS BELIEVE LOBSTERS DON'T HAVE FEEL-INGS.
WELL,
BASED ON THAT RESEARCH...
LOBSTERS BELIEVE SOME SCIENTISTS DON'T HAVE FEELINGS!

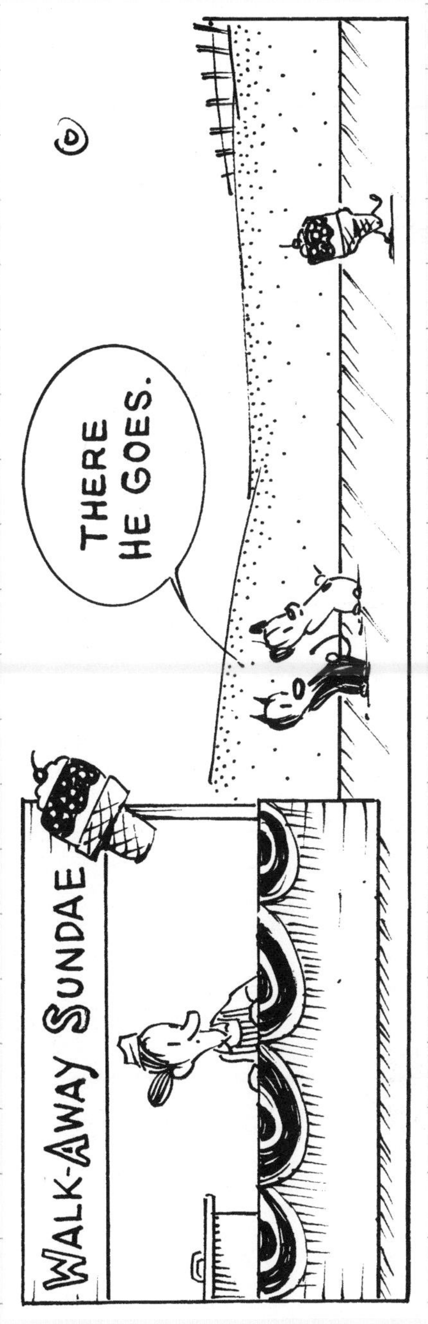
WALK-AWAY SUNDAE
THERE HE GOES.

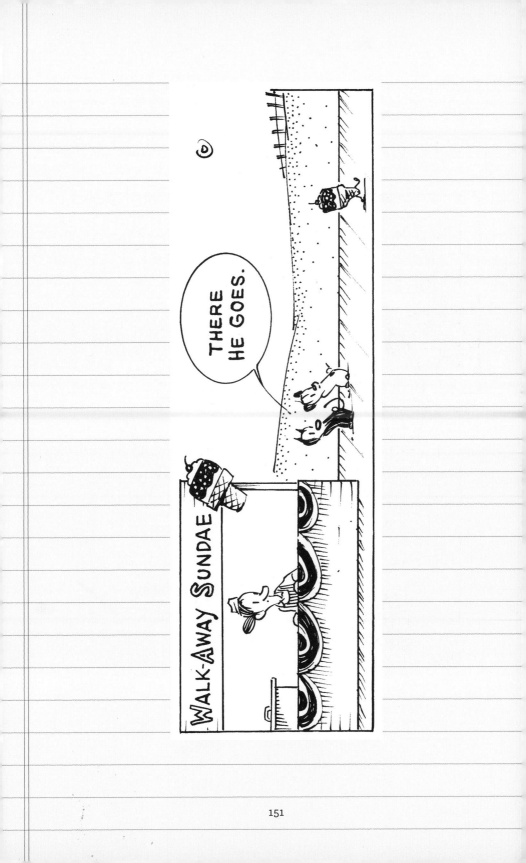

PATRICK
McDONNELL'S
MUTTS
TALES OF THE
SEA

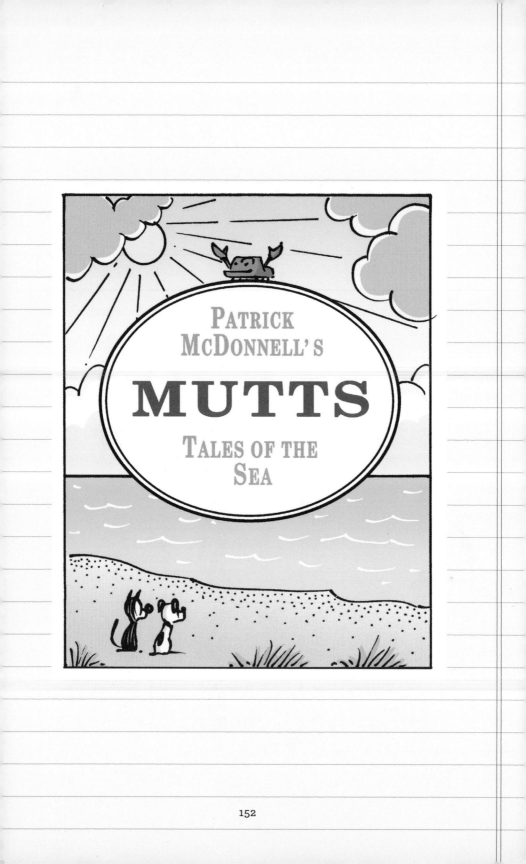

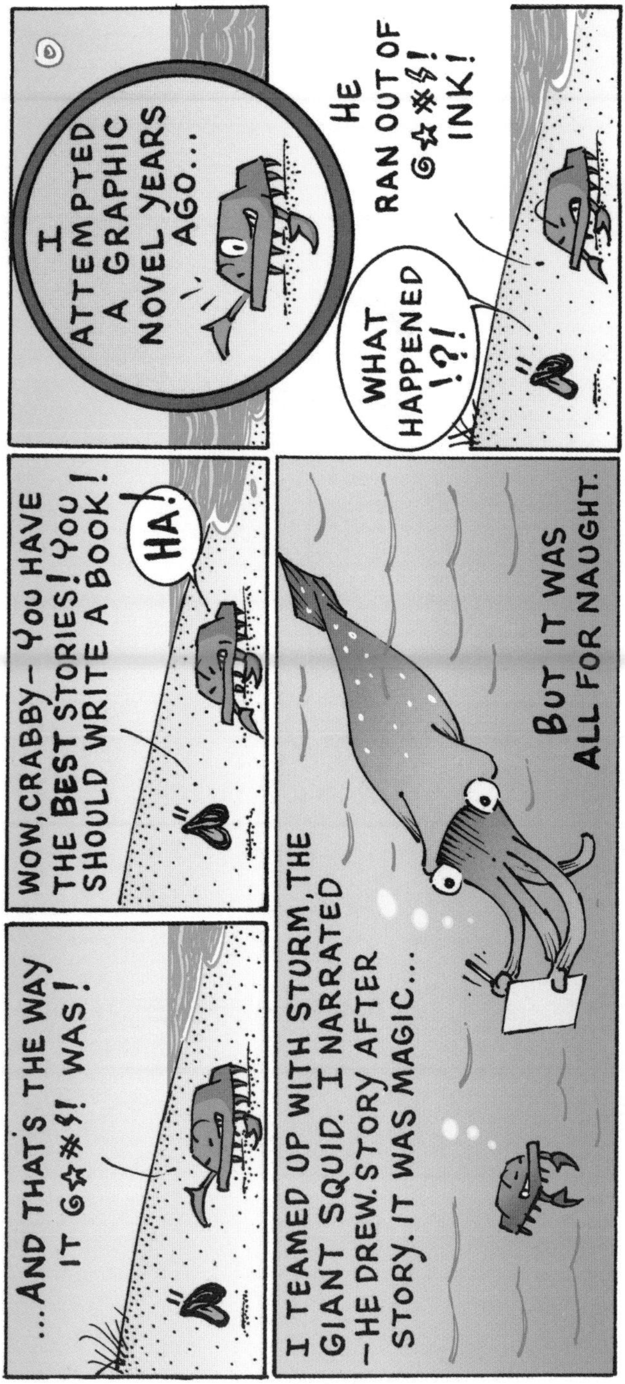
...AND THAT'S THE WAY IT G☆#$! WAS!
WOW, CRABBY— YOU HAVE THE BEST STORIES! YOU SHOULD WRITE A BOOK!
HA!
I ATTEMPTED A GRAPHIC NOVEL YEARS AGO...
I TEAMED UP WITH STURM, THE GIANT SQUID. I NARRATED —HE DREW. STORY AFTER STORY. IT WAS MAGIC...
BUT IT WAS ALL FOR NAUGHT.
WHAT HAPPENED !?!
HE RAN OUT OF G☆*$! INK!

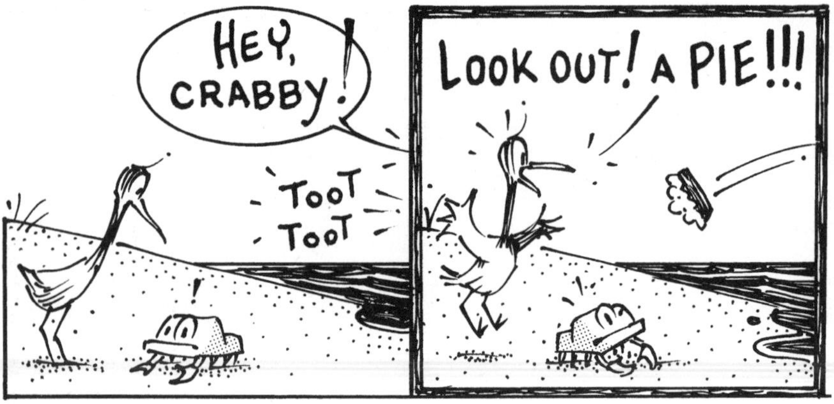
HEY, CRABBY!
TOOT TOOT
LOOK OUT! A PIE!!!

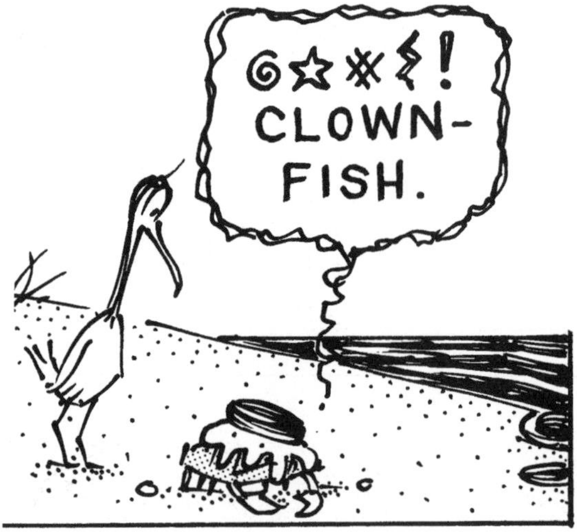
CLOWN-FISH.

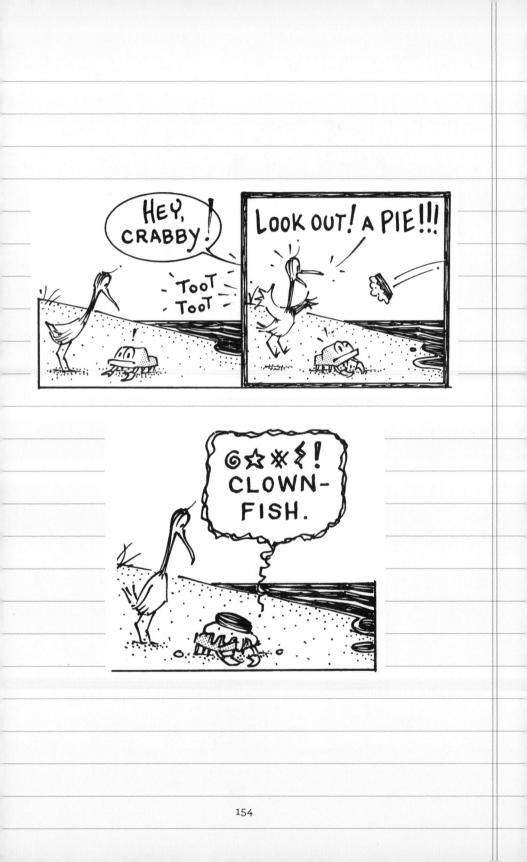

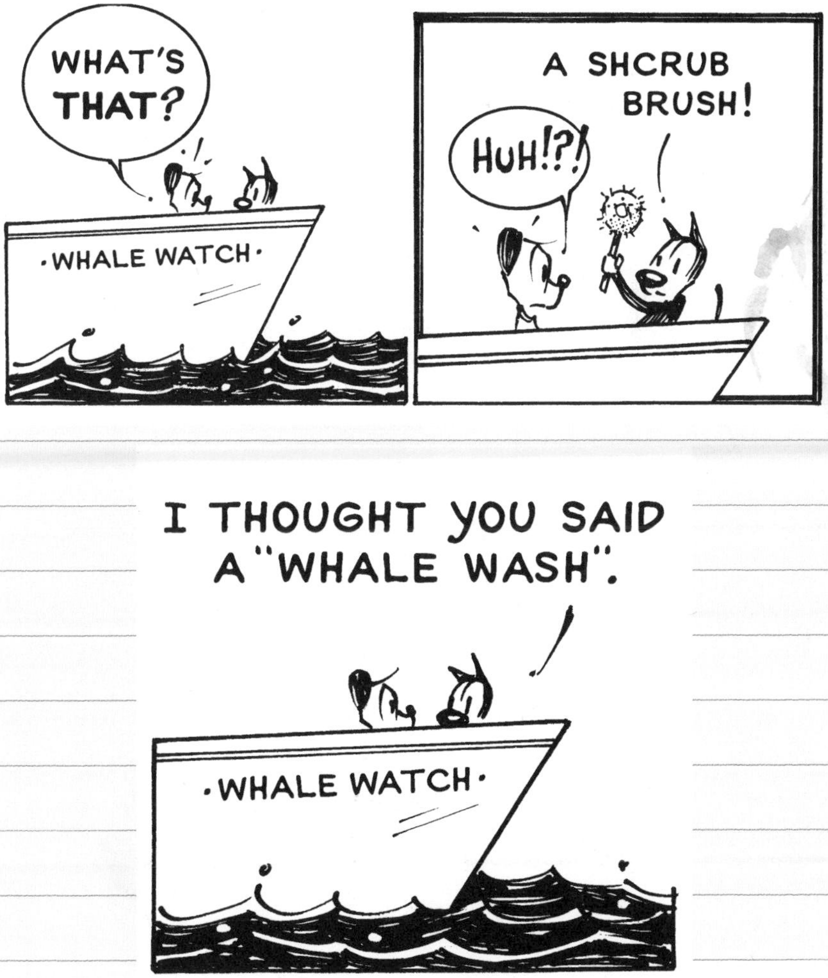
WHAT'S THAT?
•WHALE WATCH•
A SHCRUB BRUSH!
HUH!?!
I THOUGHT YOU SAID A "WHALE WASH".
•WHALE WATCH•

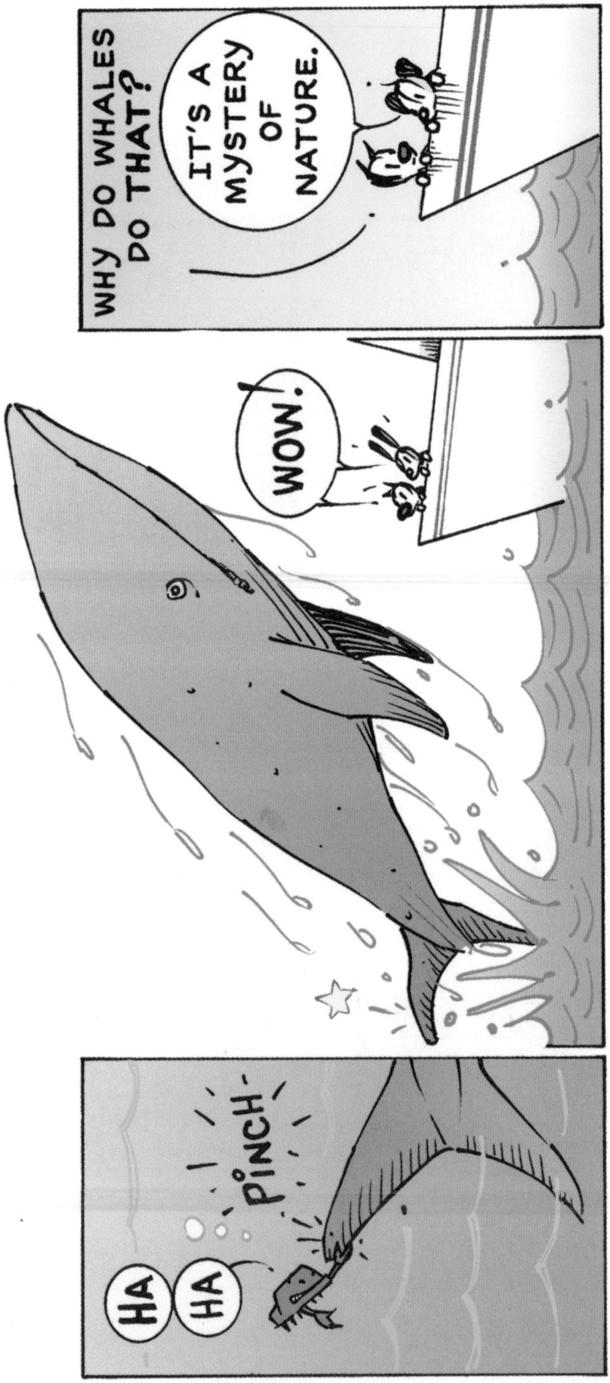
HA
HA
PINCH
WOW!
WHY DO WHALES DO THAT?
IT'S A MYSTERY OF NATURE.

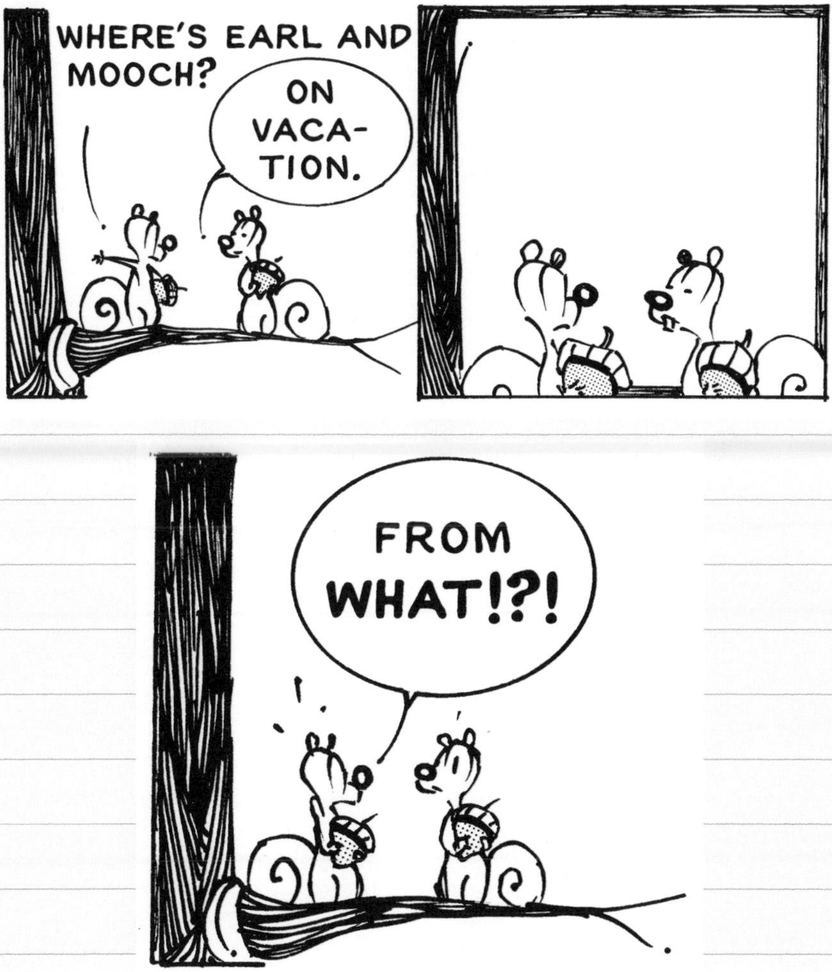
WHERE'S EARL AND MOOCH?
ON VACA-TION.
FROM WHAT!?!

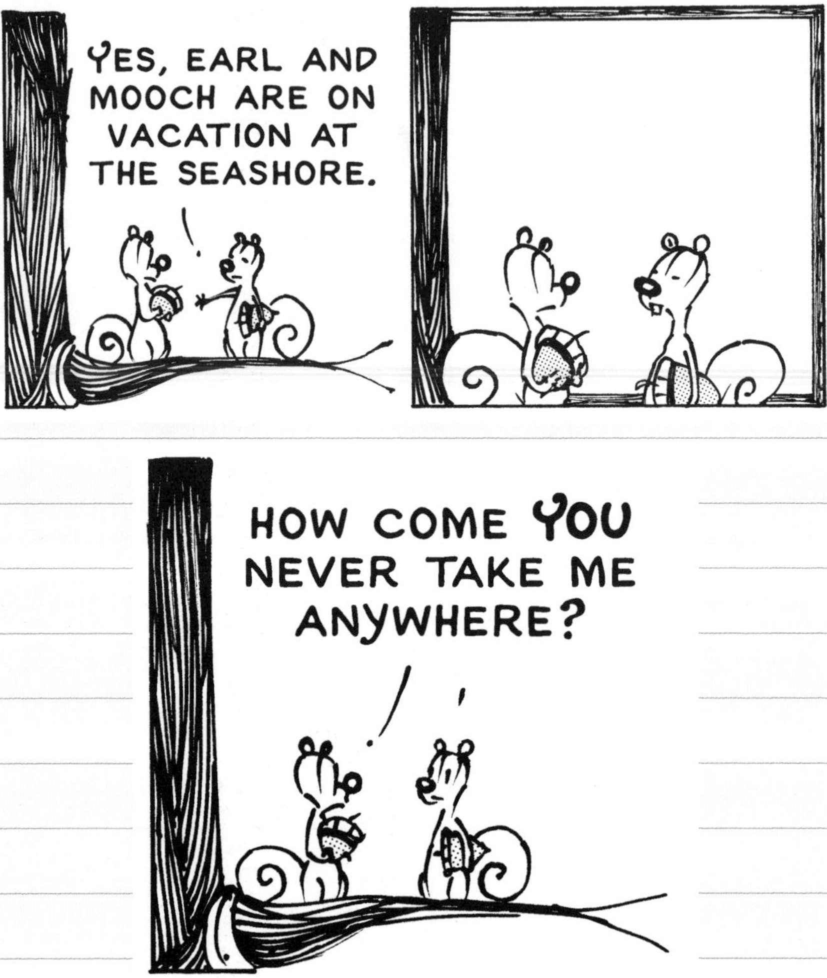
YES, EARL AND MOOCH ARE ON VACATION AT THE SEASHORE.
HOW COME YOU NEVER TAKE ME ANYWHERE?

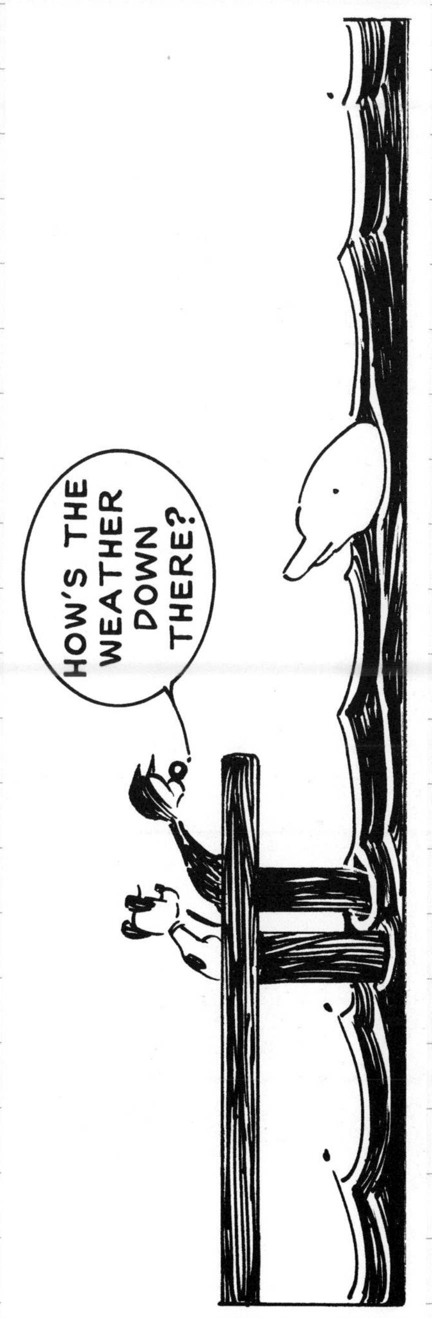
HOW'S THE WEATHER DOWN THERE?

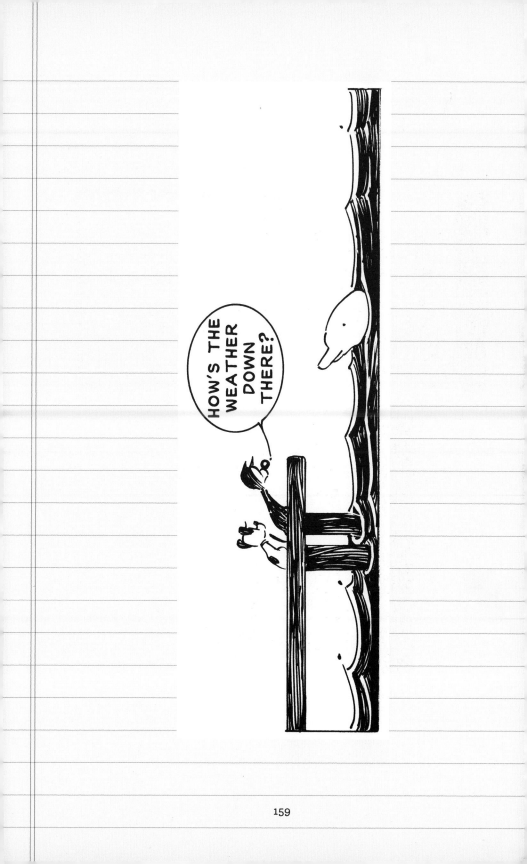

SNOW CONES
I'VE ALWAYS WONDERED WHAT THEY DID WITH THAT SHTUFF AFTER THEY SHOVELED IT.

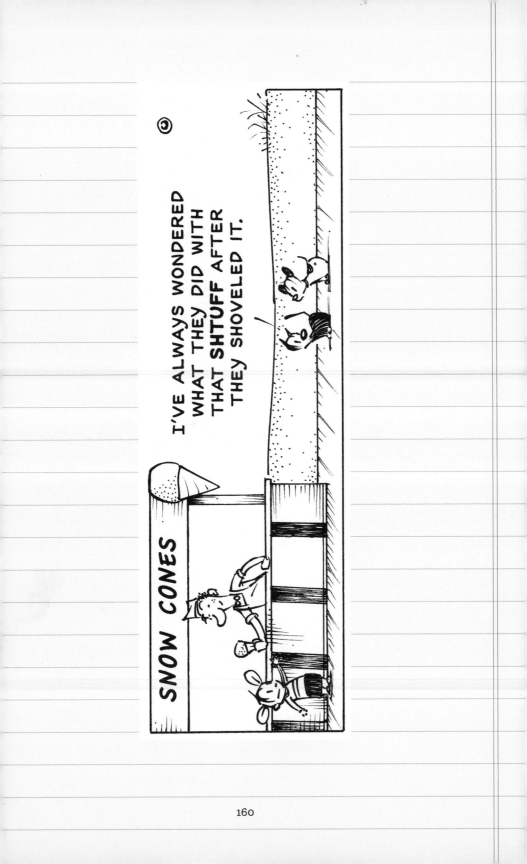

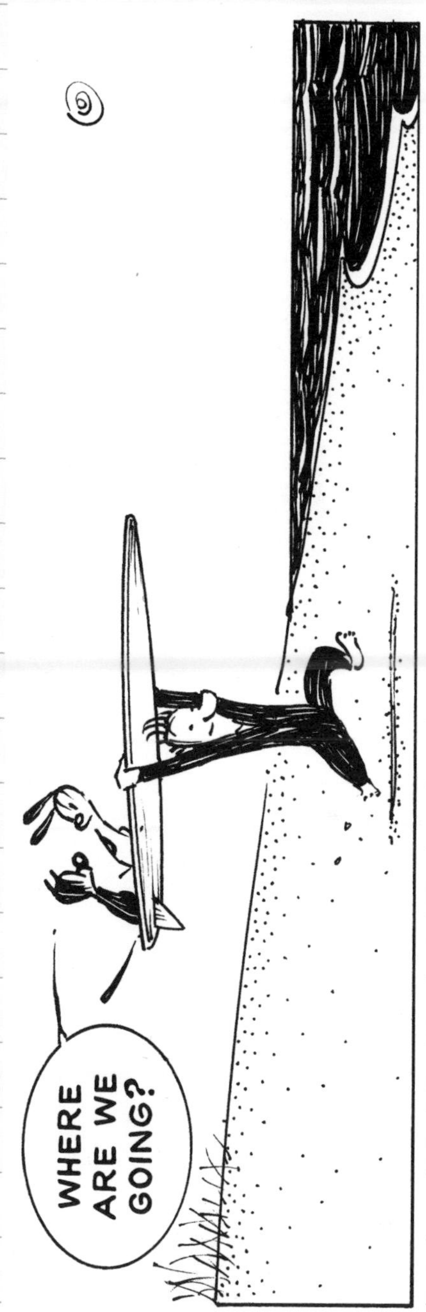
WHERE ARE WE GOING?

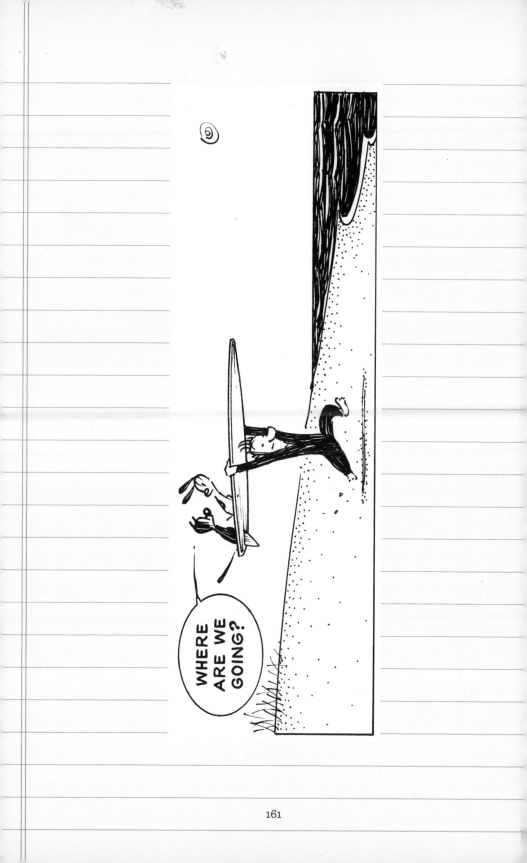

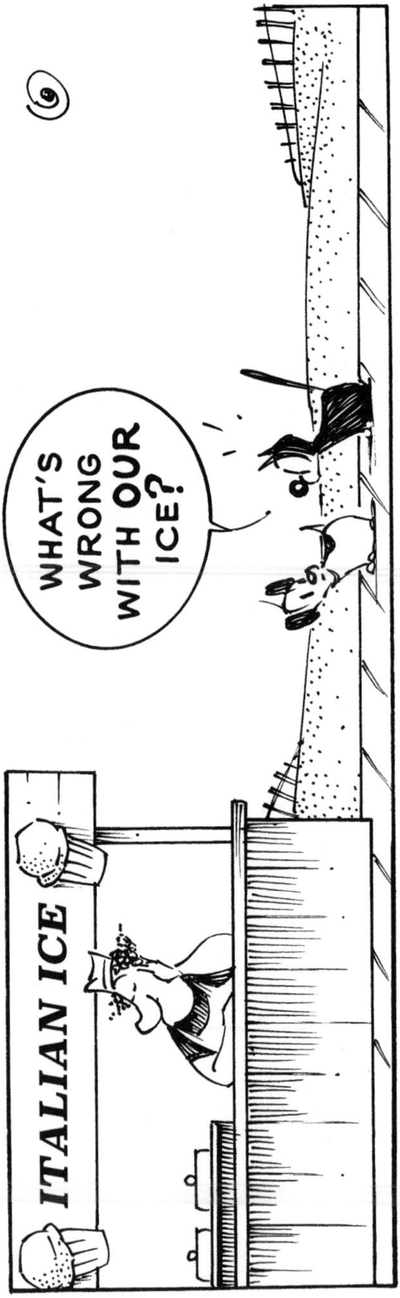
ITALIAN ICE
WHAT'S WRONG WITH OUR ICE?

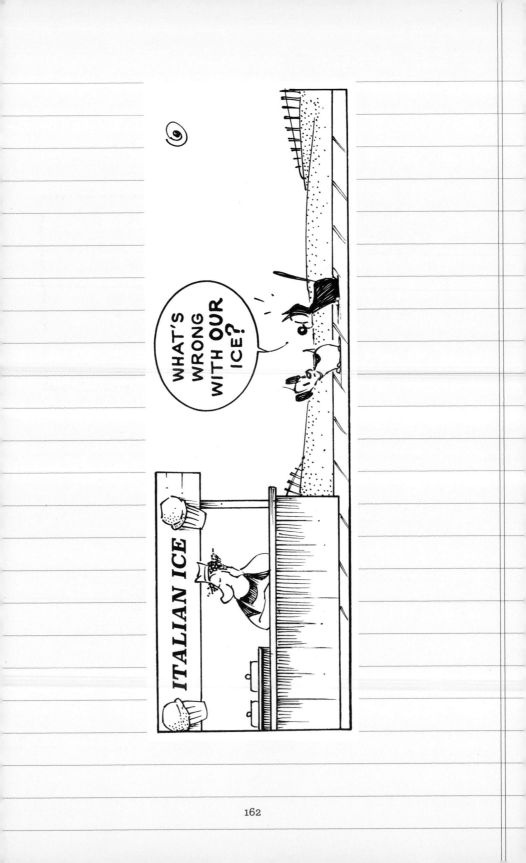

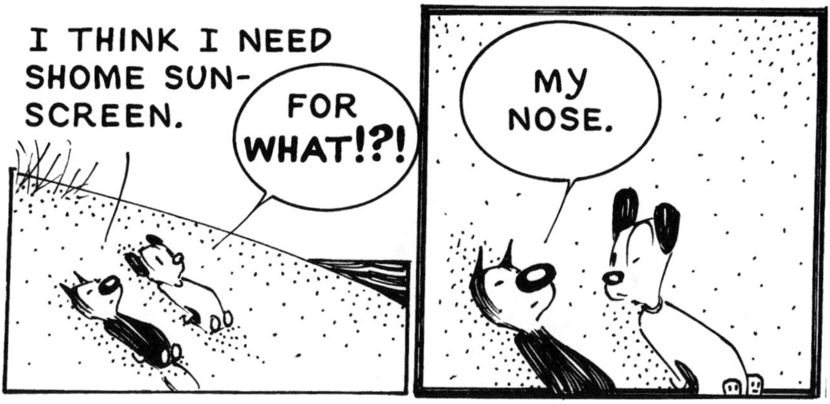
I THINK I NEED SHOME SUN-SCREEN.
FOR WHAT!?!
MY NOSE.

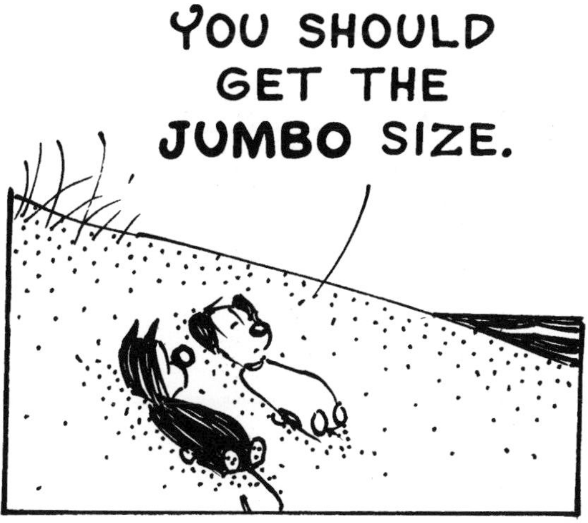
YOU SHOULD GET THE JUMBO SIZE.

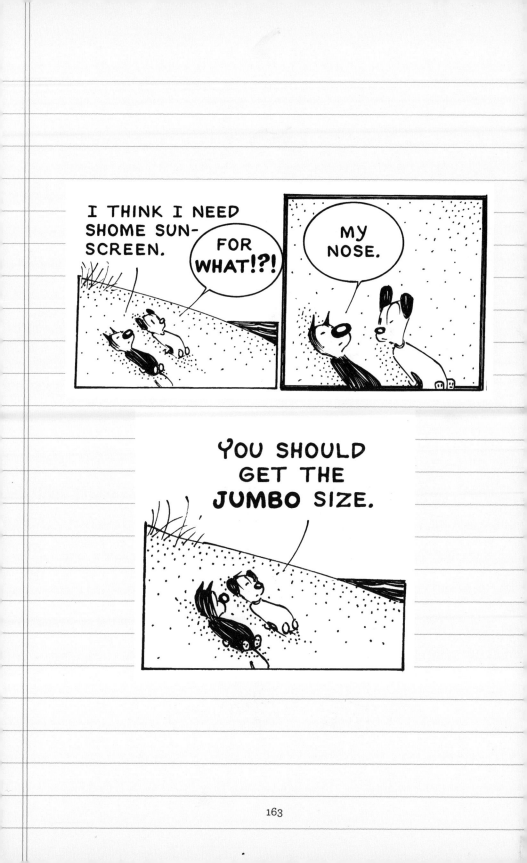

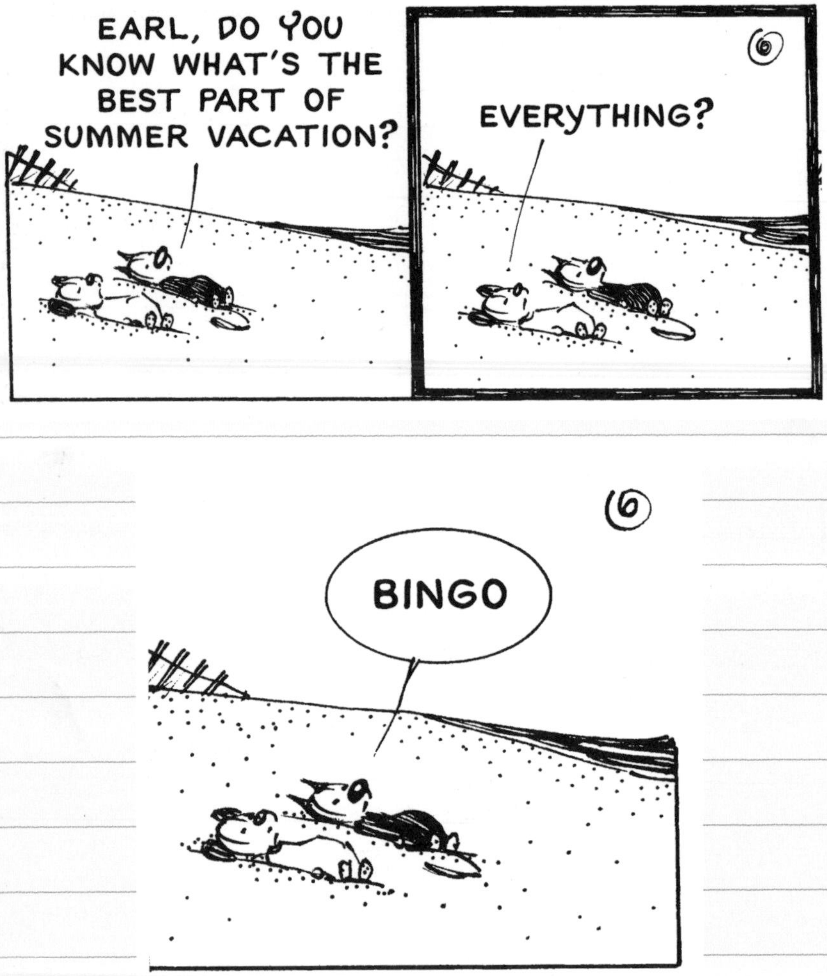
EARL, DO YOU KNOW WHAT'S THE BEST PART OF SUMMER VACATION?
EVERYTHING?
BINGO

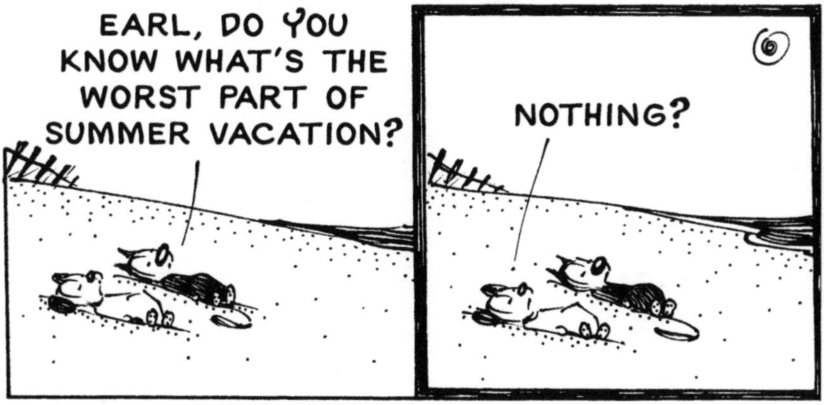
EARL, DO YOU KNOW WHAT'S THE WORST PART OF SUMMER VACATION?
NOTHING?

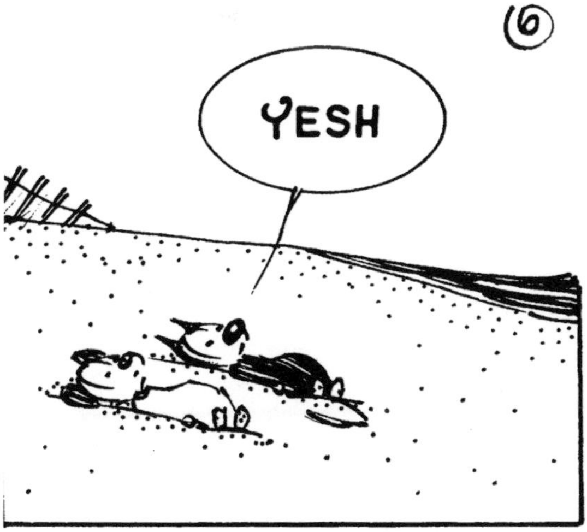
YESH

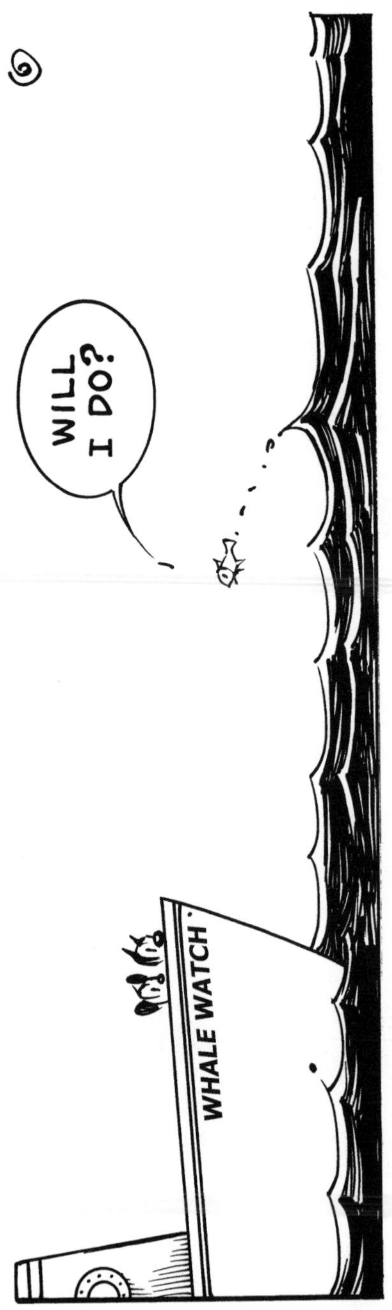
WILL I DO?
WHALE WATCH

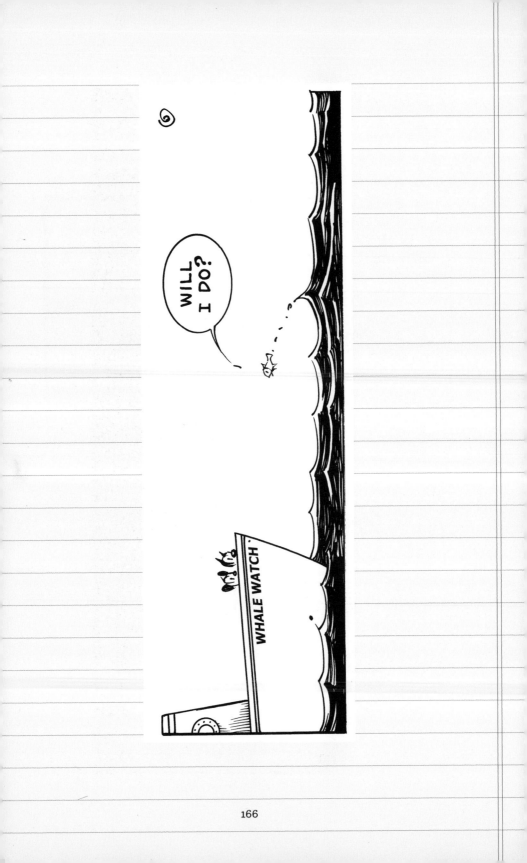

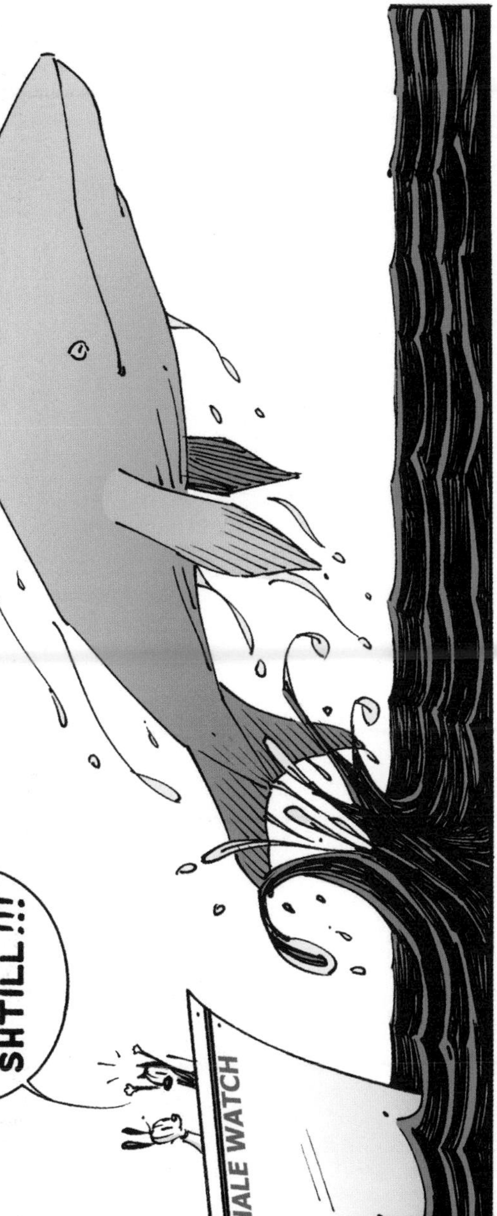
AUGH!
HE WON'T SHTAY SHTILL!!!
WHALE WATCH

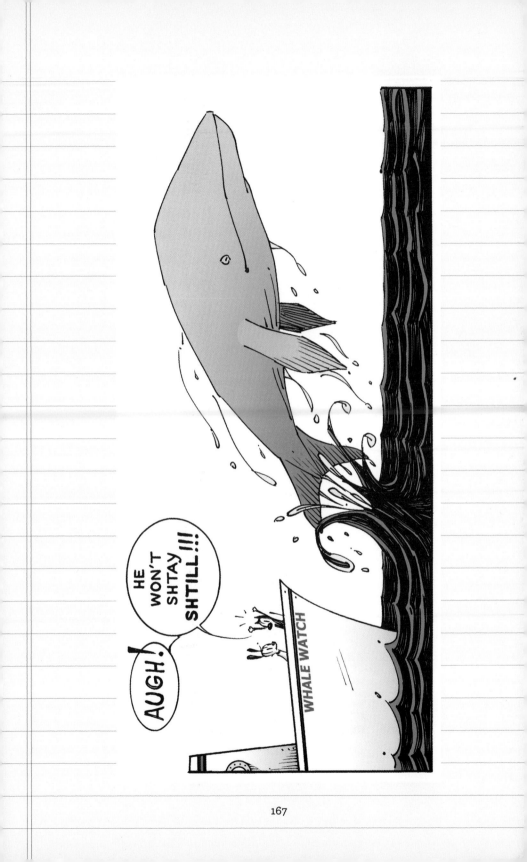

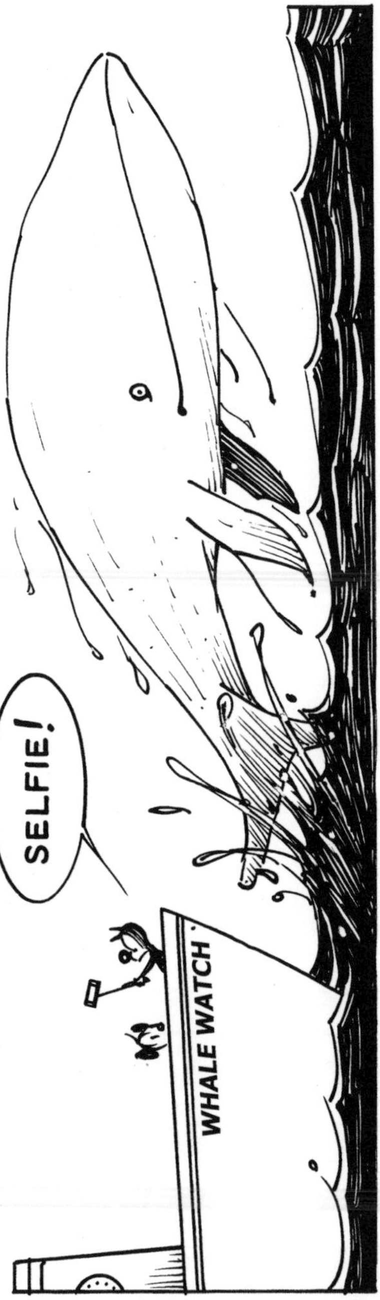
SELFIE!
WHALE WATCH

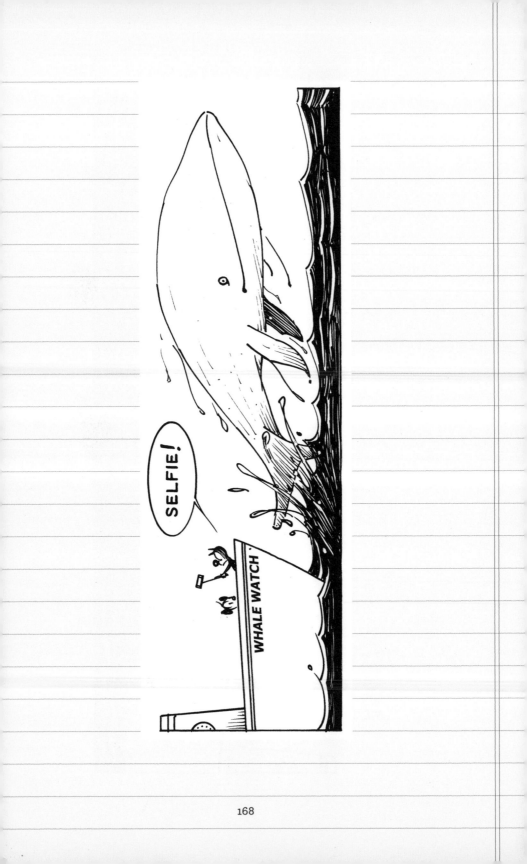

S'LONG
SUMMER

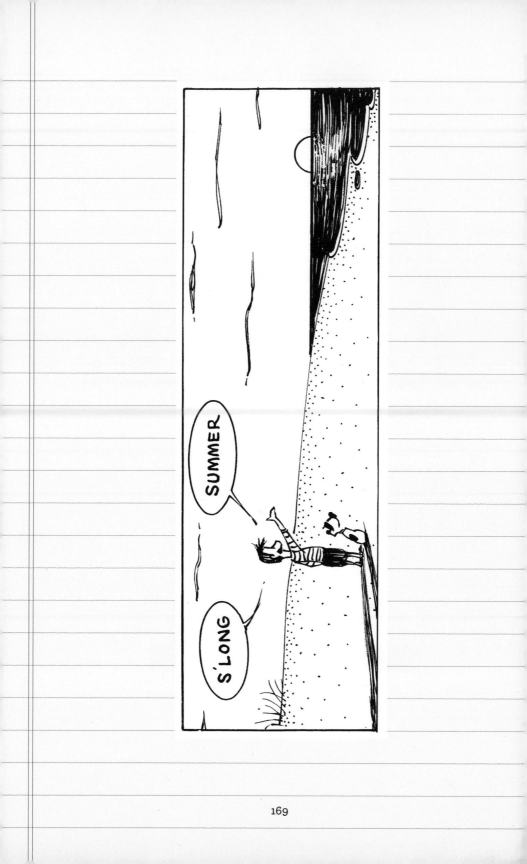

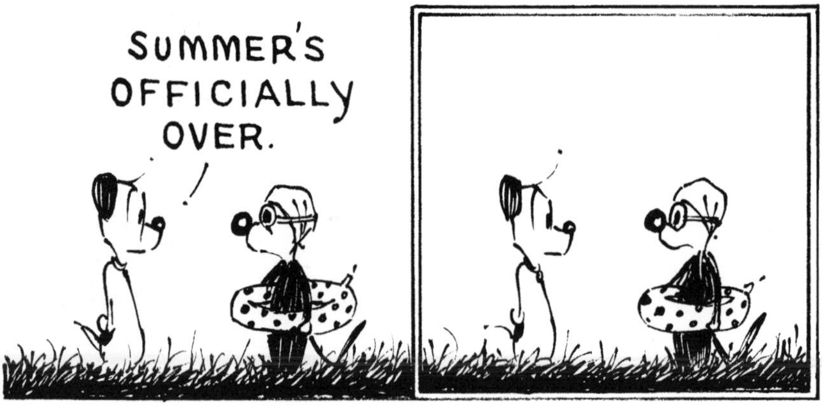
SUMMER'S OFFICIALLY OVER.

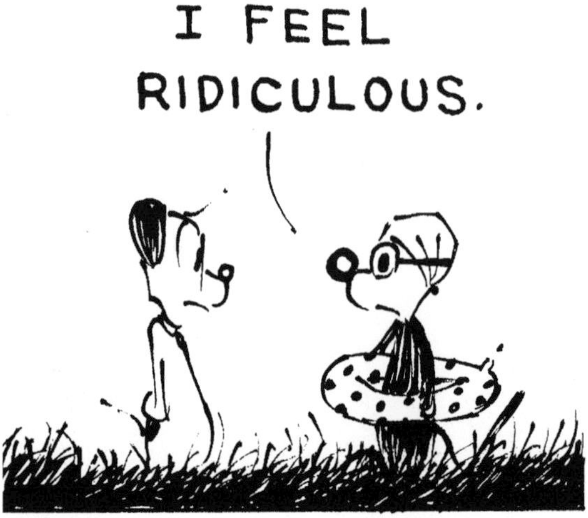
I FEEL RIDICULOUS.

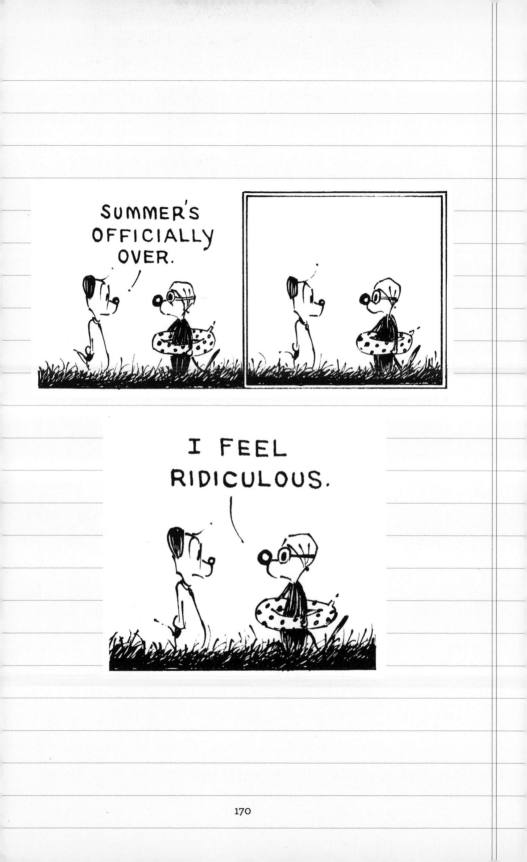

MORE TO EXPLORE! Learn interesting facts about marine animals!

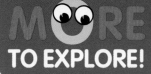

Do dolphins tell knock-knock jokes?
Probably not, but dolphins do communicate with each other by squawking, whistling, clicking, and squeaking. They also relay messages through body language, such as blowing bubbles and touching fins.

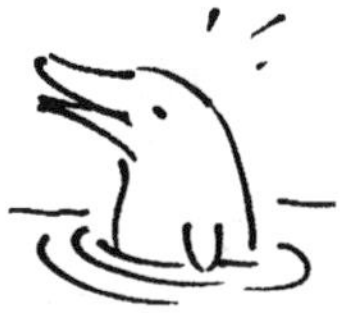

What color is squid ink?
Cephalopods (the family of mollusks including squids and octopuses) can expel a cloud of dark ink to help them escape from predators. Octopus ink is black, squid ink is blue black, and cuttlefish ink is brown.

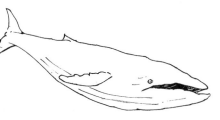

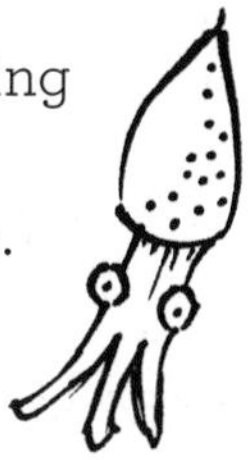

How big are blue whales?
Blue whales weigh almost 200 tons. At 100 feet long, they are the largest animals ever to have lived on earth—even bigger than the dinosaurs.

Do sea gulls drink fresh water or seawater?
Both. Seagulls have a special pair of glands above their eyes that help flush out the salt from their bodies.

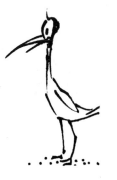

Are mussels strong?
Very! Mussels are able to cling to ocean rocks even while being battered by waves. Scientists have studied mussels' byssal threads (the ropelike structures they use to cling to rocks) in order to develop new materials for surgery and other engineering purposes.

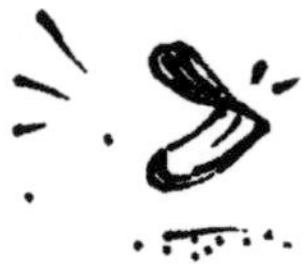

What are the biggest and smallest kinds of crabs?
Of the 4,500 species of crabs, the smallest is the pea crab (¼ to ½ inch long), and the largest is the Japanese spider crab (up to 12 feet long).

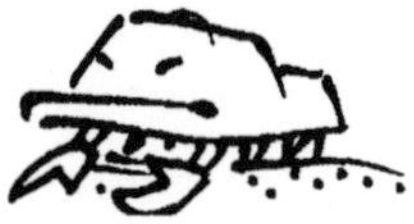

Do lobsters show affection for each other?
It's hard to say for sure what exactly lobsters are feeling, but lobsters have been observed walking together and holding claws on some occasions. Usually this is an older lobster leading a younger one.

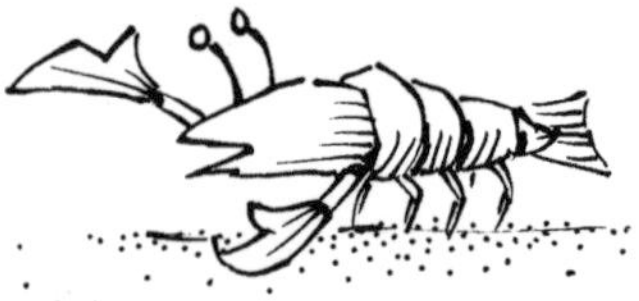

Is a starfish a fish?
No. Starfish do not have gills, scales, fins, or a brain. They are more closely related to sand dollars, sea cucumbers, sea urchins, and other marine animals known as echinoderms.

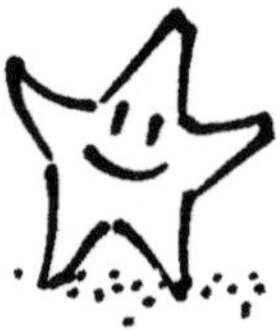

What color are jellyfish?
Jellyfish are often clear, but they can also be bright colors of pink, yellow, blue, and purple. Some jellyfish are bioluminescent, which means they produce their own light and are able to glow in the dark.

How can I help keep the oceans and beaches clean?

There are many easy things you can help with beach and ocean cleanup. For example:

- Avoid plastic drinking straws, bottled water, and other plastic packaging. Instead, pack snacks in reusable containers, bags, cups, and tableware.

- If you see trash, help out by throwing it away! You can also volunteer for beach and ocean cleanup days sponsored by local parks, organizations, or wildlife programs.

- Support organizations dedicated to marine conservation, natural preservation, and wildlife education.

- Learn more about the ocean and marine life, and share what you know with your family and friends!

Mutts is distributed internationally by King Features Syndicate, Inc. For information, write to King Features Syndicate, Inc., 300 West Fifty-Seventh Street, New York, New York 10019, or visit www.KingFeatures.com.

Andrews McMeel Publishing
a division of Andrews McMeel Universal
1130 Walnut Street, Kansas City, Missouri 64106

19 20 21 22 23 SDB 10 9 8 7 6 5 4 3 2 1

ISBN: 978-1-4494-9523-7

Library of Congress Control Number: 2018945949

Printed on recycled paper.

Mutts can be found on the Internet at www.mutts.com.

Cover design by Jeff Schulz

Made by:
Shenzhen Donnelley Printing Company Ltd.
Address and location of manufacturer:
No. 47, Wuhe Nan Road, Bantian Ind. Zone,
Shenzhen China, 518129
1st Printing — 1/14/19

Look for these books!

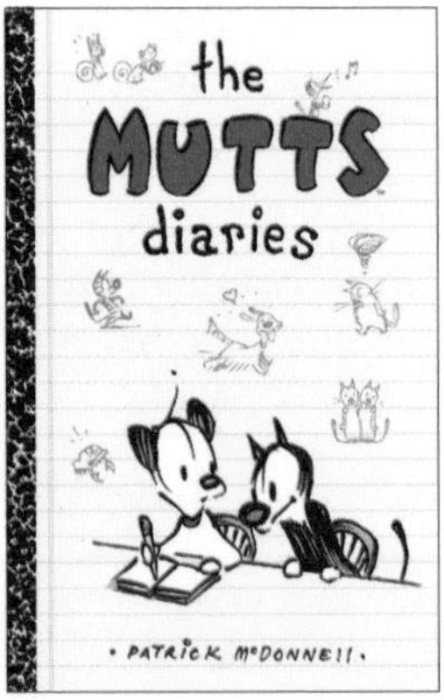
the
MUTTS
diaries
PATRICK McDONNELL

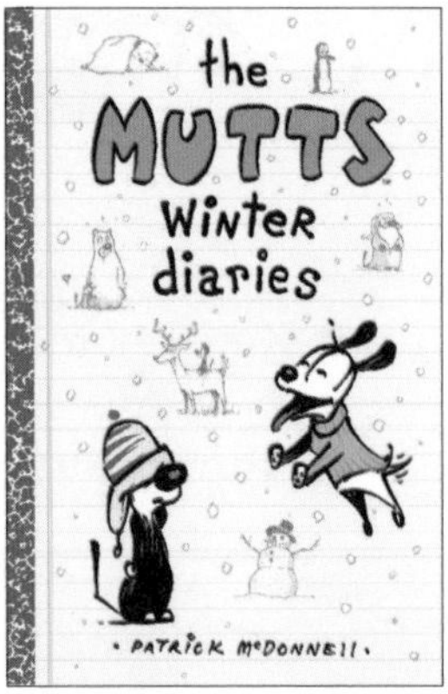
the
MUTTS
Winter
diaries
PATRICK McDONNELL

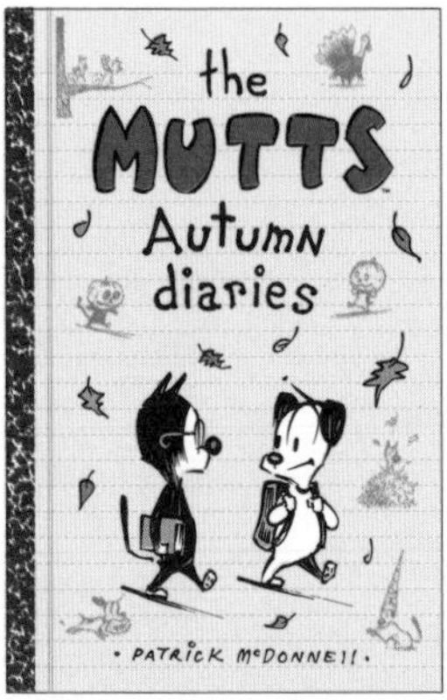
the
MUTTS
Autumn
diaries
PATRICK McDONNELL

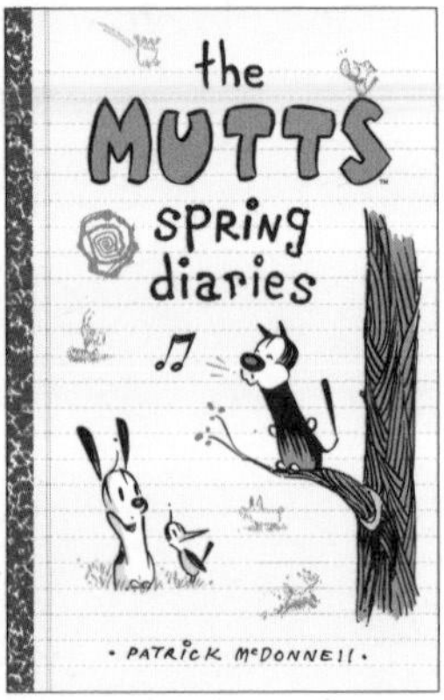
the
MUTTS
spring
diaries
PATRICK McDONNELL

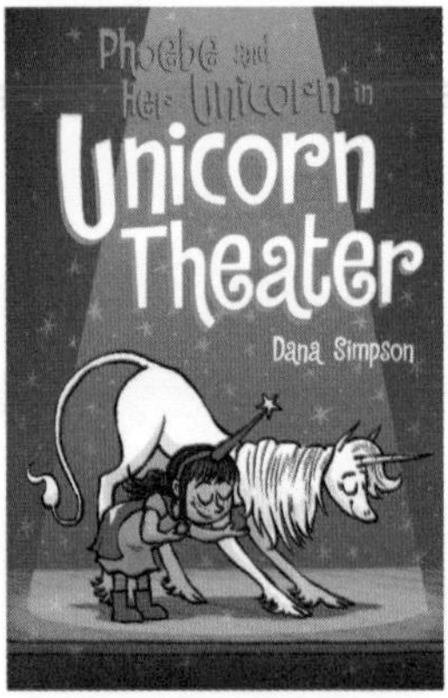
Phoebe and Her Unicorn in
Unicorn Theater
Dana Simpson

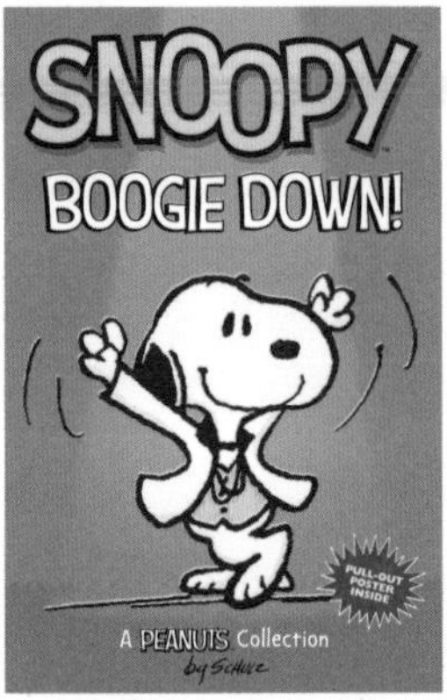
SNOOPY
BOOGIE DOWN!
A PEANUTS Collection
by Schulz

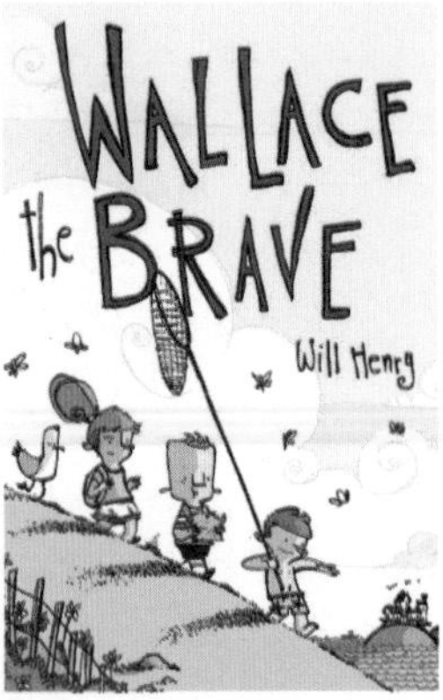
WALLACE the BRAVE
Will Henry

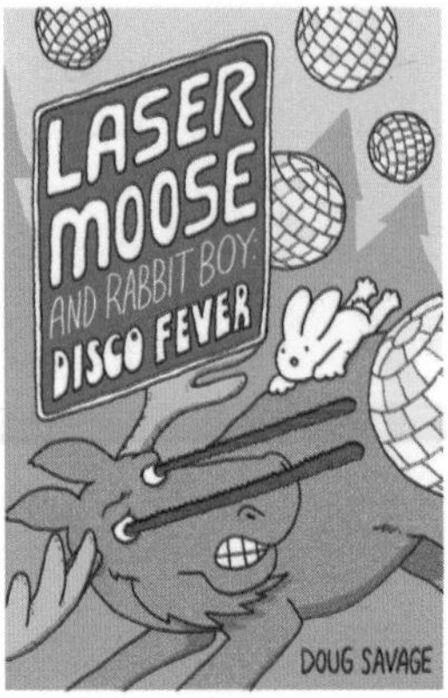
LASER MOOSE AND RABBIT BOY
DISCO FEVER
DOUG SAVAGE

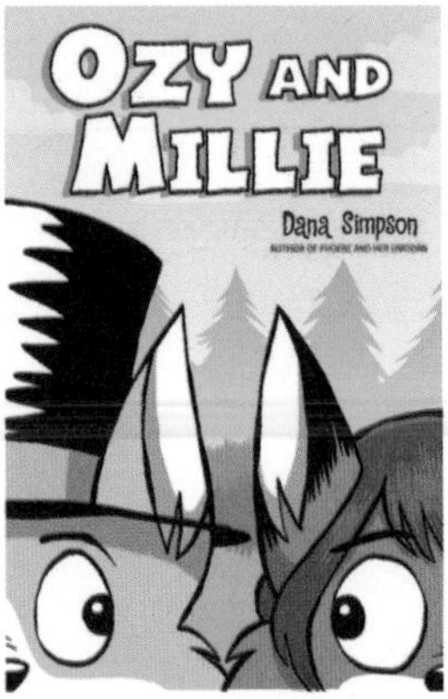
OZY AND MILLIE
Dana Simpson